Dust Storm

MAGGIE GATES

ISBN: 9798877442320

Cover Design by Melissa Doughty - Mel D. Designs

To my brothers-in-law, for talking about stitching up a cow's prolapsed uterus over dinner as if that's completely normal. (It's not.)

Dust Storm

CONTENT WARNINGS

While my books are generally upbeat and uplifting, each story can delve into heavy topics. This book is intended for mature audiences and contains explicit language and sexual content. I encourage you to read the content warnings made available at www.maggiegates.com/content-warnings

Treat yourself with care.

With Love,
Maggie Gates

PROLOGUE

CASSANDRA

Camera flashes blinded me as I stumbled behind the red-carpet backdrop.

Shouts rose from the press line. "Miss Parker, do you have a comment on the allegations made by Lillian Monroe?"

The spike of my stiletto snagged a duct-taped cord, and I jolted forward.

Someone jumped the barricade and shoved a camera in my face. "Is it true that you paid off a judge?"

I gripped my clutch like the last life preserver on a sinking ship.

"Miss Parker! Look right here!"

Another flash.

And another.

And another.

A catering van parked in an alleyway caught my attention. I hurried toward it, but kept my pace under a run.

Paparazzi had a prey drive. If I ran, they would chase me down and eat me alive.

I slipped behind the van and fumbled through my clutch for my phone. Servers and cooks gave me odd looks as they shuffled through crates of prep work.

Just ignore the blonde in a designer dress, hiding behind cases of champagne.

I thumbed through my messages, looking for one from Tripp.

Nothing.

I peeked around the edge of the open van door as I tapped the call button and waited for it to connect.

You've reached Tripp Meyers. Please leave a message at the beep.

I swore under my breath and stuffed my phone back in my clutch. My chest pulled tight like a rubber band about to snap.

The car was there, but it was Lillian's. There was no way I'd be able to take it.

Tripp was, presumably, doing damage control.

Which meant I was on my own.

With a breath, I tied the sash of my long coat tight to hide my dress.

The Carrington Group headquarters were ten blocks from here, which meant I had to keep my head down and not draw attention to myself.

That would be difficult, considering my face had been plastered on every screen nationwide as a backstabbing actress looked me in the eye while she flushed my career down the toilet.

Ten blocks in sky-high stilettos that were already

shredding my feet. *Fantastic*. If I kept my head down, I would be able to hide the tears I wasn't supposed to cry.

I'd get in the building, hunker down away from prying eyes, and make a plan.

I just needed a minute to think.

The pit of vipers turned to a mob, fueled by the click of camera shutters. I peered in the side mirror of the catering van, watching as my fiancé escorted my former client and new enemy out of the historic theater.

For a split second, the vultures were distracted.

And I ran.

1

CHRISTIAN

"Come on squirrels—get a move on!" I hollered up the stairs.

"Dad!" one squirrel said with a giggle. "We're *girls,* not squirrels!"

The hand-held radio sitting by the coffee pot crackled as my youngest brother, CJ, gave a report on the herd movement.

The nine thousand head of cattle that sprawled across the Griffith Brothers Ranch kept us on our toes, but what kept me busiest were the two tornadoes who were supposed to be getting ready for school.

When I didn't hear them moving upstairs, I set the spatula down and craned around the corner. "Bree! Gracie! Finish getting dressed, brush your hair, and brush your teeth!"

"I want braids!" Bree called as she thundered down the stairs with the stomp force of a linebacker.

"Me too!" Gracie echoed from their bathroom.

"No! I called braids. Do something else," Bree snapped.

"Hey! No fighting this early in the morning," I bellowed loud enough for them to hear me around the corner.

"But I called braids first!" Bree huffed as she stormed into the kitchen and grabbed a pancake off of the pile I was busy making.

I rinsed my hands off and did a quick towel dry. "You can both have braids."

"But she's copying me."

At thirteen, all Bree wanted was for eleven-year-old Gracie to stop following her around like a wide-eyed puppy.

It made me chuckle at the years Gretchen and I thought having two toddlers was bad. Now, I had two middle schoolers all on my own.

"Then I'll give you different braids," I said as I turned back to the stove and finished cooking the batch of pancakes. "Get the box."

Bree heaved the giant tackle box I used to organize all their hair accessories on top of the kitchen table and plopped down in a chair. I slid a plate of bacon and eggs in front of her to go with the pilfered pancake she'd stolen from the counter. She chowed down while I pawed through the little compartments full of elastics, hair clips, combs, brushes, and a million other things the girls insisted on.

"What kind of braids today?" I asked in a yawn as I ran a brush through her dirty blonde hair, catching the few tangles she had missed.

"Fishtails," she said around a mouthful of scrambled eggs.

"Tight or loose?"

"Loose. The puffy kind. With clips."

Life wasn't easy. There was running the ranch. There was fatherhood. There was finding time for myself, which usually fell by the wayside.

Doing it on my own sucked, but I never wanted my girls to feel like they were a burden. I wasn't great at everything. The way I'd stammered through the period talk with Bree a few months ago was proof of that.

But I tried.

Dammit, I tried hard.

Bree sat stock-still as I sectioned her hair and started weaving flat strands, one on top of the other.

Braids were easy. It was that fucking curling iron that was the death of me.

The burns on my fingers were proof of that.

By the time she finished her plate, I was tugging the neat fishtail braids so they were loose and puffy.

Apparently, tight braids weren't cool anymore.

"My turn!" Gracie said as she elbowed her way to the tackle box. "I want—"

"*Not* fishtail braids," Bree clipped.

I stifled an eye roll.

All I wanted was one morning where they weren't at each other's throats about who got what. Was that too much to ask?

I should have already been at work.

"I want a halo braid."

That seemed to appease Bree.

Gracie made a taco out of her pancake, filling it with

eggs and a crumble of bacon before meeting me on the couch. She laid on her side and rested her head on my leg while I braided her hair into a crown.

As I was pinning the tail under the braid with a bobby pin, Bree called out, "Grandma's here!"

Gracie shot off the couch like a rocket.

"Lunches are in the fridge," I said as I cleared the couch of hair paraphernalia.

They shouldered their backpacks and stomped their shoes on. The fridge door slammed as they grabbed their respective lunchboxes.

No matter how much they begged to buy lunch at school, a homemade lunch meant I cared. It meant I put in the time and effort. *Right?*

Maybe I should just let them get lunch at school.

I ran a hand down the side of my beard as I watched them load up like pack mules.

My mom sat in her idling minivan as the girls bolted into the back and buckled up.

"Thanks," I said to Mom as I craned through the passenger window.

I tried to be all things for all people. Especially *my* people. And my daughters were my people.

After Gretchen passed, I grieved. I took a minimal amount of time to be selfish. And then I picked myself up and had to be dad *and* mom for my girls.

Unfortunately, there weren't enough hours in the day. So, I finally broke down and accepted help for things like school drop off and pick up.

"Anytime," she said over a sip of coffee from her thermos. "Don't forget about that consultant coming in today."

I scoffed over the symphony of buckling seatbelts. "Pretty sure I said that was a *you* problem. I'm not the one who hired her."

Mom snickered. "I'm not either. Becks is the one who recommended her, and you know better than to act ugly to your sister-in-law."

I chuckled, thinking about the sharp-tongued war correspondent my older brother fell in love with while he was deployed.

Yeah, I knew better than to mess with Becks.

"Your dad thinks it's a good idea. I think it's a good idea. Be on your best behavior and I'll leave you be until dinner."

I shuffled down to the open side door, leaning in to drop kisses on Bree and Gracie's foreheads. "Have a good day. Love you."

"Love you, Daddy," they said in chorus.

I rolled the door closed and watched as the van lumbered down the dirt path toward the service road that would take them into town.

I glanced at my watch. Not even 7:15 yet.

I jogged back up the porch steps and headed inside, snagging a pancake for myself on the way. I trapped it between my teeth as I stole Gracie's purple hairbrush and used it to untangle my hair. I worked the knots out of the ends that hung past my shoulders before tying it into a bun.

"Boss, you there?"

I picked up the radio. "Go ahead."

CJ's voice crackled on the line. "Fence is down on the west border."

"You need me out there?"

"Nah," he said. "Just letting you know."

"I'll be in the office most of the day taking care of vax records. Holler if you need something."

"10-4."

Sadie came wandering in, her brindled tail thumping with excitement as she looked up at me.

"Sorry, girl. No cows for you today. Gotta do paperwork."

She huffed, loping to the door as I slid on my boots and clipped the radio to my belt.

I emptied the coffee pot into a travel mug and jogged down the steps, not bothering to lock up.

There was a benefit to living on the ranch that had been in my family for generations. I could leave the door unlocked for the girls when they got home from school. I could leave my keys in my truck. And, while there was a limit to how far I'd let them go on their own, Bree and Gracie had plenty of space to run free.

My brother, Nate, had found peace in a warzone. But me?

I stepped out and surveyed the land as the February sun peeked over the horizon.

This was my kingdom.

My kingdom could go to hell.

I pinched the bridge of my nose to ward off a migraine, and wondered which Griffith was to blame for saddling me with a legacy of cattle ranching.

Fuckin' animals trying to kill themselves.

The AC window unit sputtered as a steady drip

thwopped into the bucket beneath it. At least it kept the condensation from pooling on the floor.

I'd gone through the vaccine records with a fine-toothed comb to make sure nothing was out of place. Bills had been paid. A sticky note with a hydraulic oil pressure switch I needed to get was in the trash after the order had been placed. I was waiting on a call from the livestock vet we kept on retainer, but waiting for that call was like watching paint dry. She was a busy woman.

Honestly, I missed doing what CJ did every day. I missed the camaraderie of working the land with the rest of the crew. I missed saddling up before daybreak and not returning to the stables until after sunset.

From the looks of things, Sadie missed it too.

But taking over for my dad on the management side gave him a chance to retire, and gave me a more stable schedule so I could prioritize the girls. CJ had stepped up to fill my old role and thrived in it.

It was great for everyone else.

I glanced at the clock. The girls were at dance class, and if the vet hadn't called by now ...

I pushed out of the rolling desk chair that was decades past its prime, and whistled for Sadie as I grabbed my hat and dropped it on my head.

"C'mon, girl."

She trotted along obediently toward the barn.

Libby, the thoroughbred American quarter horse I had been riding since I was in my twenties, let out a blustering huff as I tacked her up.

Sadie looked antsy, prancing around the barn as I mounted Libby and gripped the reins, guiding her out of the barn.

Libby let loose when we rounded the corner and headed away from the barn and outbuildings. She grunted, hooves thundering into the dirt.

When the conglomerate of structures turned to a speck in the distance, the stress began to loosen and melt away. Clean air and sunshine surrounded me. Sadie, the ranch's retired cattle dog, bolted like a bullet from a gun.

Maybe we were all a little stir crazy.

I used the spur-of-the-moment ride to survey the near side of the property to make sure nothing was out of place.

After a few miles, Sadie looked like she was tuckered out. I tugged on the reins and slowed Libby to a canter as we rounded the corner to Nate's house.

No one was home.

Huh. That was weird. Nate and Becks had a pipe burst yesterday and were in the process of fixing the sopping mess. Becks was on maternity leave from her job as an international news correspondent. She should have been there.

Apart from my momma, I hadn't seen any vehicles leaving the property today through the cameras.

Shit.

Libby must've sensed my urgency as I nudged her into a gallop again. The dog peeled off and trotted down the path to my place, but I headed for the front gate.

Becks sat on the porch of my parents' house, her hands over her baby bump as she watched dust plume from the tires of a sedan as it peeled down the drive.

Her red hair was tied up in a bun on top of her head, and a glass of tea was in hand. As far as sisters-in-law went, I'd take her. She was a far cry from Nate's first wife, Vanessa.

As much as I hated seeing him torn up about it in the moment, none of us were surprised when they divorced. What surprised the hell out of us was seeing him on TV, rescuing a reporter out of rubble while he was deployed.

But it worked out well for them. Now, Bree and Gracie were over the moon to be getting a cousin.

I slowed Libby a safe distance from the house, giving myself a chance to watch as the sedan stopped. The doors opened and a man hopped out from the driver's side.

The guy wrinkled his nose, sneering at the scenery.

Great.

Becks hooked us up with some uptight city slicker. This was gonna go over like a fart in church.

Libby let out a displeased grunt.

Then the other door opened.

Blonde hair danced on the wind like rays of gold. The woman straightened and turned, studying her surroundings through the privacy of an oversized pair of sunglasses.

Libby eased forward, letting me steal a look at her from behind.

She had a pair of fuck-me legs and an ass to match.

Her fingers flexed as she grabbed the door and slammed it shut. The sun caught something shiny on her hand.

A goddamn engagement ring.

2

CASSANDRA

Exiled. A smoke trail lingered in my wake as I fled Manhattan like an outlaw on the run. 1,700 miles sat between me and the life I had worked tirelessly to curate.

We need time for things to cool down.

The situation is too volatile.

We'll bring you back once a new headline has everyone's attention.

I hated Texas already. The air was so fresh it was nauseating. The breeze was giving me a headache.

Tripp cut his eyes at me as he guided the rental car down the poorly paved service road. "I don't think a media blackout includes checking the headlines."

"I need to see how they're spinning it."

With a snap of his wrist, Tripp confiscated my phone. "Lillian isn't your problem anymore."

"She's still a problem."

"Well, she's my problem now," he stated with an odd mix of dismissiveness and finality.

That was the problem with being engaged to a colleague. Well... Technically, Tripp was my boss.

But that was just semantics.

I looked down at the diamond glinting on my finger, willing it to become a wishing star.

I would have wished for a time machine to take me back to the beginning of the week to when I had a job. When I was respected. When I wasn't being banished to the Lone Star state by my boss turned fiancé.

I settled back in my seat, closed my eyes, and counted to three. "I'm not sure why you think it's a good idea to hide me away on some ranch. And stop trying to convince me it's a business development project. We both know I'm being put in timeout."

Tripp reached for my hand, but I snatched it away. I wasn't feeling particularly affectionate at the moment.

Swallow a demotion and take the project Rebecca Davis—now Rebecca Griffith—offered, or start looking for other employment.

Tripp called it "crisis management." I called it an ultimatum.

"It's for your own good. One-hundred percent of people read the headline, fifty-percent read the body, and no one reads the retraction. Lying low and giving everyone time to forget what happened is preferable to demanding retractions and rebranding," he said, putting a palatable spin on the situation.

It was complete horseshit.

And I was about to be inundated with a Biblical amount of horseshit. And bullshit.

"I'm not chicken shit. I can fix this."

"Just because you can fix it, doesn't mean you should

be the one to fix it." He took a left onto a dirt road. "I have to think about the firm. And if you cared about me and your job, you'd be thinking about what is best for the firm, too. Do you want to be right or win?"

"I can't win if I'm in the penalty box."

Tripp scoffed. "A business development project is hardly the penalty box, Cassandra."

"You're sending me to Texas."

"Which is one of the largest state economies in the country."

"On a cattle ranch," I hissed, then cut my eyes to the Manolos on my feet. They weren't made for dirt. *Neither was I.*

I should have been sitting in my office preparing press releases to quell the rumors around Lillian Monroe's very public meltdown. I should have been fielding calls and scheduling meetings to spin the story and drum up some public goodwill.

Instead, Lillian was sunning herself on a yacht in Spain, and I was heading for bullshit.

Tripp's face was unbothered. "I know it's not optimum, but this is best for everyone."

Great. Now he was using his publicist voice on me.

I stared out the window as grassy plains rolled by. "What about us? How is this the best thing for us? What about our wedding?" My throat grew tight, but I effectively choked it down and put on my game face. "When do I get to come back?"

Tripp flashed a placating smile. He had tuned out of the conversation the moment it started. "Once things cool down, we'll talk about setting a date. The optics are—"

"More important than our comfort."

I knew the saying well. It was Tripp's party line whenever he put the firm or one of his clients ahead of our relationship.

Shove it down. Fake a smile. Don't flinch. Don't let them see you crack.

I wondered why I had a ring in the first place. Was that just optics too?

On many occasions, he told onboarding publicists to get a fake engagement ring to wear. It kept the tabloids from speculating if our PR experts were dating the clients they represented.

I twisted the ring on my finger.

No ... it wasn't fake.

He had proposed to me. We had an engagement party. We had...

No date.

No dress.

No bridesmaids or groomsmen.

We had nothing.

"Game face," he chided as a farmhouse came into view.

Dust rolled in the distance. I slid my sunglasses on and took in my new prison.

Tripp put the car in park and handed my phone over.

No service. Not a single bar. I had truly been exiled.

Without a word, Tripp hopped out.

Might as well not put off the inevitable. *Game face.*

My stiletto sunk into the dirt as I eased out of the car, and I shifted my weight to my toes. At least February in Texas was better than February in New York.

A shadow loomed to the right.

Holy shit. With the sun to his back, all I saw was the silhouette.

But damn. What a silhouette.

The horse was a little terrifying. Were all horses that much bigger in person? I'd always imagined horses being more approachable.

That thing was a tank.

The horse shifted, letting rays of sunlight illuminate the man's face.

The brim of his cowboy hat still shadowed most of his features, but I could make out a thick beard along his jaw and long hair tied in a knot at the base of his neck.

The rider braced his heavy boots in the stirrups. My gaze ran up those long, thick thighs to find his wide hands resting casually on the saddle. His chest was wide, gently curving down into a soft belly. A plaid button-up was tucked into his belt, accentuating his rounded abdomen. It was proper and rugged all at once.

Not wanting to be caught staring, I averted my eyes and slammed the door. My calves sang as I tiptoed around the hood.

"You made it." Rebecca Griffith lumbered down the porch steps, resting a hand on top of her baby bump.

It had, admittedly, been a while since we had seen each other. She left New York for greener pastures, and I kept climbing the ladder until the day I took a metaphorical stiletto to the face and tumbled down to rock bottom.

"Look at you," I said, slapping on a smile.

Becks groaned. "Don't remind me. I feel like I'm going to explode. And a pipe burst at our house so we're staying with Nathan's parents. I started sleeping on the couch because I hate going up the stairs to bed." She laughed.

"Sorry. That was too much information. How was the flight?"

Tripp opened his mouth—probably to complain about how packed the plane was—but I cut him off.

"Just fine. Thanks."

An older man joined Becks. He was a spitting image of the cowboy, just a little more cleaned up.

What had once likely been a salt and pepper beard was now completely salt. He wore a flannel tucked into his blue jeans, and a pair of boots that had seen better days.

"Ma'am," he said as he lifted his cowboy hat by the crown and extended a hand. "Pleasure to have you with us." His eyes cut to Tripp. "And who's this fella' you brought? Your chauffeur?"

Tripp sneered. "Tripp Meyers. VP of publicity for the Carrington Group."

The older gentleman studied him with an unflappable poker face. "Your—uh—group. They always send a VP as a chaperone?"

Gravel and dirt crunched behind me. Darkness hovered over us like a storm cloud.

"Doesn't inspire much confidence if she needs a babysitter." The bass rattling behind me shook my bones.

"Tripp is my fiancé," I clarified to everyone, taking control of the narrative. Although I was less than thrilled to be here, doing my penance was the fastest way to get my life back on track.

Someone snorted, and I wasn't sure if it came from the cowboy or the horse.

I put on a boardroom face and laid my hand on

Tripp's arm. "He had the time in his schedule to see me off before he heads to Europe."

The shadow behind me was silent. The old man softened. Becks looked like she wanted to throw up.

And honestly? So did I. But I didn't have time for unexpected vomit today.

"Well," the old man said. "Pleasure to meet you both. I'm Silas Griffith." He pointed a finger at the looming presence behind me. "I'm that one's daddy, and a soon-to-be grandaddy—again—to this one." He pointed to Becks's belly.

Tripp's eye twitched with annoyance. "Can we skip the hillbilly pleasantries?" he sneered through gritted teeth with practiced discretion.

"Mr. Griffith, I'd like to meet with you as soon as possible to discuss the current financial state of the ranch, and the deliverables you're envisioning at the end of my contract."

His mustache twitched with amusement as he lifted a weathered finger and pointed behind me. "Then you'll have to talk to *that* Mr. Griffith."

I turned and nearly ran into a wall.

The cowboy had hopped off his horse. He crossed thick arms over his barrel chest. His boots were wide-set, as if he was bracing for impact. "Pretty sure I said I was fine with her being here as long as she wasn't my problem."

That was quite the welcome. Apparently, southern hospitality wasn't all it was cracked up to be.

Silas laughed. "Son, when you took over for me, everything became your problem. Congratulations. I'm gonna go take a nap."

"I have work to do," he argued.

But Silas was already back up the porch steps. "Jackson should have the cabin ready for her. Momma told him to get it cleaned up. See you all at dinner."

Becks—my fellow Manhattan expat—groaned as she turned back to the house. "Sorry. Gotta pee. Don't get pregnant. It's awful."

"But—" My voice cracked as Becks scrambled into the house as fast as she could.

Tripp checked his watch. I didn't know why he looked so antsy. His flight didn't leave until tomorrow.

Hot breath blasted against my skin.

Was the other Mr. Griffith breathing down my neck already? That wasn't how this was going to go.

I turned to tell him to back the hell off when hairy lips brushed my shoulder. I shrieked, nearly jumping out of my skin.

A flash of white caught me by surprise as the cowboy —Silas's son—grinned. "She won't bite."

But did he?

"That horse is the size of a tractor-trailer. I was more concerned with getting trampled."

Offended by my assessment, the animal stomped a hoof into the ground.

I looked over my shoulder and found Tripp wandering around the car aimlessly as he searched for a single bar of cell phone service.

I didn't have the patience or desire to deal with him at the moment.

"Cassandra Parker," I said, finally making the introduction so we could stop standing here and spinning our wheels.

He didn't offer a handshake. Rather, he kept those wide arms crossed for a long moment before mimicking his dad and lifting his cowboy hat by the top. "Christian Griffith."

His eyes raised to track something behind me, so I turned to follow his gaze.

Tripp had wandered off, chasing the ever-elusive connection to the rest of the world as he repeatedly tried to talk to whoever was on the other end of the call. His endless string of "Hello? Hello? Can you hear me now?" was grating.

"Does your boy toy need to be put on a leash?" Christian asked.

Some days I felt like he needed a muzzle.

"He'll be fine."

Tripp, not paying any attention to his surroundings, walked straight into the back of a pickup truck, slamming his knee into the trailer hitch.

"Motherfucker!"

He doubled over, grabbing his leg as he checked the screen of his phone to see if the person on the other end heard him. He stumbled backward until the heel of his loafer let out a horrifying squelch.

Tripp froze. Slowly, he looked down at what he had just landed in.

Christian had moved to stand shoulder-to-shoulder with me. An amused smirk curled up beneath his beard.

"Why is there mud?" Tripp huffed as he pulled his foot out of the pile with a disgusting squish.

Christian chuckled. "Hate to break it to you, but that's not mud."

The stench hit me immediately and, from the looks of things, Tripp realized it too.

"Shit," he said with disgust.

"There you go, buddy. Now you got it right," Christian said in the most placating tone possible.

Tripp took a step back to try and wipe the bulk of the manure on the grass, but slipped.

I clasped my hands over my mouth in horror as he pivoted to avoid the hitch again, and landed back in the pile of manure.

"Look at that," Christian mused with a flat expression. "You live up to your name."

Without another word about Tripp, he turned and hopped back into the saddle. "Cabin's this way."

3

CHRISTIAN

Libby was peeved as I rode out past my house to the cluster of cabins that had been sitting unused for the better part of a decade.

I couldn't blame her. I was annoyed too.

I tipped my chin down to peer over my shoulder. Cassandra drove the rental car behind me while Tripp—still shouting into his phone as if a cell tower would magically appear—trudged along beside her, covered in shit.

I didn't blame her for not wanting to be trapped in a car with the human cow patty, but he seemed like the kind of guy who could afford the incidental charge for fucking up the rental. It sure beat the mile walk out to the cabins. He was red as a cherry and seething in anger.

Tripp.

What kind of fucking name was that? Was it short for something?

Trippworth?

Trippington?

Tripped-over-his-ego?

Libby let out a displeased grunt as I hopped down. I used a manger knot to tie her to the post in front of the cabins for the few minutes it would take me to show Cassandra around inside.

Then I could get back to the never-ending to-do list that seemed to get longer and longer each day.

When I finished here, I'd get Libby squared away and head back to that fucking desk for another hour before I went to the house to oversee the girls doing their homework.

Then it'd be time for showers all around and bedtime before we did it all again tomorrow.

Thank God for aftercare at school, extracurriculars, and my mom being a taxi service.

There just weren't enough hours in the day.

Cassandra pulled up in front of the cabins and hopped out. I could feel the displeasure radiating off her body.

Before we built the new bunkhouse right after Gracie was born, the ranch hands lived in the cabins.

That had been...

Shit. Gracie was eleven.

How was the *new* bunkhouse a decade old?

"Home sweet home," I said as I turned to face Cassandra.

I couldn't get a good look at what was going on in her head behind those big sunglasses, but her face was passive.

Twenty feet away, Tripp had stopped to shout at someone through his phone, as if they'd hear him yelling halfway around the world.

Lord knows they weren't hearing him through the call.

Cassandra had popped the trunk and was heaving a suitcase the size of a small bedroom out of the back. She didn't even teeter on those ice picks she was walking around on.

I cut my eyes to the jackass who didn't care enough to give her a hand. "He's not gonna help you?"

She didn't even give her fiancé a quick glance. "He's busy."

"I'll get it, Cass," I grunted as I stepped up to help.

Her head snapped so hard I was surprised she didn't give herself whiplash. "It's *Cassandra.*"

I chuckled as I unloaded the rest of her five suitcases. "Alright, Princess."

Her lips twitched in a thin line.

I tipped my chin toward the cabin. "Go on in. Should be unlocked."

"I can get my bags," she insisted.

I stepped closer. "Just because you can, doesn't mean you should have to." I tipped my head toward the door. "Inside. I have shit to do."

Cassandra relented and strutted toward the cabin. If I was a betting man, I'd say that a cabin with electricity and water was her version of "roughing it."

But I didn't say that out loud.

I hung back a second longer and indulged myself in another look at that ass. Cassandra's fancy white pants were out of place on a cattle ranch, but I wasn't complaining.

I let myself appreciate the way they made her legs look a mile long. If the shit stain who put a ring on her finger wouldn't appreciate the way she looked, why shouldn't I?

I snapped out of it when I smelled Tripp getting closer.

It took Cassandra a few tries of wiggling the doorknob before she got the door open.

"The light switch is on the wall to the right," I said as I pack-muled her luggage toward the cabin.

She reached inside, feeling around on the wall until she found the switch. Her head of blonde hair had barely slipped inside when I heard the scream.

I dropped her suitcases and shoved my way inside, while Tripp bolted behind the car.

I huffed when I saw what gave Cassandra a conniption. "Goddamn it, Mickey."

Gracie's pet was lying on a couch that had seen better days.

He let out a moo, and Cassandra screamed again.

"Why is there a cow in the cabin?!"

"His name is Mickey. He's real sweet."

"There's a cow in my house!"

"Pet cow."

Slowly, I unloaded my arms and picked up her fallen sunglasses.

Shit.

I froze on one knee as I looked up at her. She had the prettiest eyes—slate gray and sparkling.

Cassandra stammered as she ran a hand through her thick blonde hair. "And why are there—" she blinked in disbelief "—are those pool noodles on his horns?"

"He's clumsy. It keeps him from breaking shit on the property."

"Oh my god," she muttered.

"Out, Mickey," I barked.

"How did he get in?" she asked as her well-bred façade began to unravel.

I trudged through the dust-covered cabin and poked my head into the kitchen. The back door was open.

Actually, it was lying on the ground outside.

The upside was that it let in a nice breeze, which was necessary considering it was clear Jackson hadn't been in here to get the place ready.

Dust-covered sheets laid over the kitchen table and chairs.

The refrigerator was silent.

Bird's nests and cobwebs filled the space between the top of the cabinets and the ceiling.

I scrubbed my palms down my face. I didn't have time for this shit.

Mom was with the girls. Dad was napping, because fuck him. Now was not the time for character building, "you're on your own" sentiments.

Bringing in a business consultant to give unwanted opinions on how to expand and shore up our interests wasn't my decision.

Ergo, not my problem.

Maybe I could dump her on Becks for a couple days.

With that decided, I went to deal with the bovine on my furniture.

"It was supposed to be cleaned up for you," I said as I swatted Mickey off the couch.

He lumbered off of it and sauntered to the door with more sass than both of my daughters combined.

Cassandra stepped aside to give him a wide berth.

Her ass bumped into a decaying bookshelf, and something hissed.

Her scream pierced my eardrums.

"Don't get your panties in a twist." After a second, I spotted the snake curled up in a nook. "Just a rat snake," I said as I pulled a pair of gloves out of my back pocket. "It's not venomous."

Cassandra clapped her hands over her mouth. "You're going to pick it up?!"

I shrugged. "Yeah. I'm just gonna move it outside so it doesn't bother you."

Her eyes widened. "You're joking."

I managed to pick the snake up with one hand on the tail and the other mid-body. "He won't hurt you, and he'll keep the mice away."

Her face went hard as stone.

I made a move for the door, but she put out a warning hand to stop me. "Don't come near me with that thing."

Spooked by her shrill voice, the snake decided to latch on and try to take a chunk out of my arm.

"Oh my god!" She clapped her hands over her mouth. "It bit you!"

I pinched its head and pried it off of my skin. *Little thing hurt like a bitch.*

"Kill it!" she shrieked.

I just shook my head, stifling a chuckle. "I'm not gonna kill it. Can't blame a snake for acting like a snake."

"That's it. I'm done. I quit." And with that, she stomped out the door.

I followed her and released the snake into a bush.

Tires crunched over the smattering of pebbles that made the dirt drive a little less dirt-like.

"Where are you going?!" Cassandra shouted.

Tripp, sitting behind the wheel in shit-covered pants, barely lifted a hand to wave. "Back to the airport. I caught an earlier flight. Gotta work."

Her face turned beet red. "Tripp!"

"I'll check in next week," he called as he rolled up the window.

"*Tripp*!" The pitch and rasp of her scream probably tore her vocal cords.

I had a backhoe that could dig a Tripp-sized hole in the blink of an eye, and I was more than tempted to use it.

What a dick.

I sided up to Cassandra as I pulled my gloves off and shoved them back in my pocket. "Did he really just leave you like that?"

Her ring finger twitched, but her face didn't flinch. I knew that face. A woman on the verge of eruption.

Bree was starting to practice that look, and it scared the shit out of me.

I pointed to the ground. "If it makes you feel any better, he stepped in a fire ant colony before he hopped back in the car. That's some long-term karma. They'll be up his britches and in his drawers before he makes it to the front gate." I pulled the radio off my hip, changed the channel, and lifted it to my mouth. "Becks?"

No answer.

I pressed the button again. "Becks, you there?"

Still nothing.

Why was everything my problem?

I looked down at those fuck-me heels she was in. I couldn't rightly make her walk back in them.

"I'll come back for your bags," I said as I untied Libby and led her over.

Cassandra squeaked and stumbled backward.

"This is Liberty. We call her Libby."

"Let me guess," Cassandra said, using sarcasm as her first line of defense. "She's sweet like the cow who should be charged with breaking and entering, and the snake who should get the death penalty for assault."

Her sass was fun.

I cracked a grin. "Trust me, Libby's a sweetheart. She doesn't spook easily."

Cassandra didn't look convinced.

I stood behind her and reached in my pocket. "Hold out your hand."

She tried to take another step back to escape, but bumped into my chest. I picked up her wrist, turned her palm up, and dropped a peppermint into her hand.

"Give Libby some sugar, and she'll love you unconditionally."

Cassandra didn't move. She was stiff as a board, so I did what I had done with the girls when they had to get acquainted with the animals as babies. I cradled the back of her hand in my palm and lifted the peppermint to Libby. The horse didn't hesitate to go for it.

Cassandra flinched, letting out a petrified shriek as Libby's mouth touched her fingers.

"You've gotta stop screaming," I murmured into her ear. I put my hand on her hip to keep her steady as Libby nibbled away at the candy, then backed away.

"See? That wasn't so bad."

Cassandra spun on me. "You're fucked in the head if you think I'll get up on that thing."

"Take your shoes off."

"Absolutely not," she clipped.

"That's fine," I said as I positioned Libby so Cassandra could get up using the stirrups. "Keep 'em on then. Up you go."

Cassandra protested the entire way up. Finally, I got her situated on the saddle.

"Sorry. Tight fit," I said as I settled on Libby's back, behind the lip of the saddle. "Riding double sucks."

What didn't suck was my view of her hips and thighs. *Damn. That ass.*

I looked up at the sky and prayed for my dick to calm down.

It had been a while since I'd gotten any action.

Okay, it had been a long while.

The moment Libby took a step, Cassandra flopped forward and nearly fell off.

"Keep your back straight," I said as I bracketed her between my arms and took the reins.

"You'd better be taking me straight back to the airport on this thing."

Her walls were crumbling and it tugged at something inside of me. "How about I take you to a spot with cell service and the internet?"

CASSANDRA WAS PACING my living room when I carried her bags inside. After putting Libby back in her stall, I drove my truck down the cabin to get her luggage and bring it up to my house.

Her posture was tight as she paused and stared at the wall while listening to whoever was on the other end.

Dirt streaked the white pantsuit she was in. Her hair was slightly mussed and disheveled from running her hands through it.

She pinched the bridge of her nose as she stared at a spot on the rug where Gracie had spilled a cup of juice a few years ago. I had tried and tried, but the stain never came out.

The floorboard creaked under my boot, and Cassandra whipped around. From the look on her face, it was clear as day that the conversation wasn't going in her favor. Her brows were furrowed and her lips were pursed. She tapped the pointed toe of her high heel on the carpet and returned her eyes to the other side of the room.

Every time her gaze hit me, it was sharp, quick, and decisive. She made fast judgments about who people were and what they would mean to her faster than I could rope a calf.

I emptied my arms and headed to the kitchen while she finished her phone call with clipped, staccato acknowledgements.

"Doesn't sound too good," I said when she ended the call with a soft growl of frustration.

"You could say that," Cassandra said as she kept her back to me.

I checked the time. The girls would be home from dance any minute, and we'd head up to the ranch house for one of the bi-weekly dinners my mom insisted we join her for.

I knew it was her way of giving me a break. I should

have refused, but truthfully, it was nice not having to cook twice a week.

"Doubt you'll get a flight out at this hour. You'll have a better chance tomorrow."

Cassandra let out a slow breath, then turned on me. "I have a job to do," she said as if she hadn't been fighting back tears at the cabin. "I'll be meeting with Silas tomorrow to discuss the possible avenues he would like me to explore to generate new revenue streams for the ranch. I'll need an office with internet and—ideally—cell service. But at the least, a landline."

I looked around the living room, giving it a quick study. A pile of laundry sat on the couch. Photo frames and a stack of opened bills covered the roll-top desk. Shoes were in a chaotic pile by the door. Unless she wanted to share my office, which was—well—*mine,* this was it.

"What?" she hedged.

Resigned to the fact that life was just going to keep fucking with me until the day I died, I shrugged. "You're looking at it."

Cassandra raised an eyebrow. "Excuse me?"

"Welcome to your new office."

4

CASSANDRA

He was joking.

He had to be.

This whole day was a nightmare. At any moment, I would wake up in my bed in Manhattan.

Why wasn't I waking up?

"I'm sorry the cabin wasn't ready," Christian said as he moved about the house. "Trust me, Jackson's gonna get his ass chewed out for it."

I stifled the urge to drop my head into my hands. *That wouldn't be very good for the optics.*

Fuck Tripp.

My engagement ring burned my finger. I wanted to take it off and leave it for that fucking cow to shit on.

I had cried when Tripp proposed. Actually *cried.* Now here we were, two years later.

He left me here without an "I love you" as he disappeared for work ... again.

Christian paused in the kitchen when he saw me staring at my ring. *Dammit.*

"You alright, Princess?"

I swallowed. "Fine."

He arched an eyebrow. "That look on your face wouldn't have anything to do with that bag of ass who sped off and left you here, now would it?"

"This is my assignment. Him leaving just means I can get to work without the pleasantries. I don't need him here to do my job." Somehow it was one hundred percent true, but also a complete lie.

"Good. I hate him."

I was a straight shooter, but I was surprised at his bluntness.

The front door burst open and two small humans barreled through in a cacophony of voices. Bags were thrown about, shoes were kicked off, and casual shouts of, "Hi, daddy," rang out.

I stood amidst the flurry of activity, half surprised and half horrified.

Christian's attention immediately left me. "There are my squirrels," he said as he doled out hugs. "How was school?"

"It was fine," the older one said. "Grandma already checked my homework. Can I have a snack?"

"No. Grandma's making dinner," he said without skipping a beat. "Change clothes and wash up. How was dance class?"

It was strange, standing in the middle of an unfamiliar house, watching someone else's life play out.

Christian was a dad.

I didn't know why I was surprised. He seemed like the type.

That was when I realized there was a fourth person in

the family photos on the walls. A woman—blonde and smiling—holding a toddler and a baby.

At some point, the photos turned to just Christian and the two girls.

"Gracie—how was your day?" Christian asked.

"Fine," the smaller one said.

"Tell me about it. What'd you do in school?"

"I can't remember," she said nonchalantly.

He raised an eyebrow. "You were there for seven hours and you can't remember anything you did?"

She shrugged again.

"Tell me with your words, not your shoulders," he said calmly as he opened a backpack and started thumbing through a folder.

"I hate Macy. She's the worst."

The sharp look that shot out of Christian's eyes surprised even me, but his tone was gentle. "We don't say that we hate people."

"Yeah, but she's—"

He lifted an eyebrow, and the girl clammed up.

"Who are you?" The older one had reappeared and was staring at me with curiosity.

The other one—Gracie—spun, realizing a stranger was standing in her living room. "Whoa. You're, like, really pretty."

I lifted my chin. "Thank you."

Christian tucked Gracie under his arm. "This is Ms. Parker. Grandpa hired her to work here."

Ah, the distancing language of someone trying to avoid taking responsibility.

"Cass," he said, addressing me. "These are my daughters, Bree and Gracie."

"It's Cass*andra*," I said, correcting him yet again as I offered a handshake to the older one.

She stared at me like I was insane, then gave me a sideways high-five. "Nice to meet you."

"You don't look like a ranch hand," Gracie said.

Christian groaned. "That's because she's not. Go change out of your dance clothes and put something on to go up to Grandma's."

The room cleared out at the prospect of dinner.

When it was just the two of us again, I crossed my arms. "You teach your kids not to say they hate people?"

He tipped his chin up. "That's right."

"You said you hated my fiancé."

He shrugged. "Yeah, well, I can interact politely with people I don't like. Once you're grown, it shouldn't be hard to compartmentalize being mature even if you have the desire to watch a human turd return to his roots and wade in a pool of shit. Be polite and let karma handle things. It can be a real bitch."

I crooked a finger, drawing him closer. "So can I."

His beard split, and he flashed a grin. "You want me to think that, don't you?"

The truck ride back to the ranch house was significantly better than the horseback ride to Christian's house.

I sat in the front while the girls giggled in the backseat. I still had no idea what I was going to do about my current living situation. That cabin was *not* habitable.

I also wasn't about to have a prolonged sleepover in a house that included children.

Maybe Becks could do me a solid ... again ... and let me crash with her and her husband.

Then again, she was pregnant. Pregnant people grossed me out.

The truck stopped and the girls barreled out of the back.

"Ah—what do you think you're doing? Get back inside," Christian said.

I watched the situation unfold as Bree and Gracie climbed back into the truck, even though dinner waited for us inside.

Christian closed the door, waited until they settled, then opened the door again.

They climbed out exactly how they had the first time and immediately ran inside. I reached for my door handle, but he beat me to it.

"Rule number one. You ride in my truck; you let me open the door."

I raised an eyebrow. "Is that what that was about?"

He nodded. "One day they're gonna be old enough to go on dates. That means I have to teach them about acceptable treatment. I don't know how you were raised, but my parents taught me to open doors for ladies. That's what my daughters will expect."

I slid out. The heels of my Manolos sunk into the dirt. "And here I was, thinking you'd be the 'wait on the porch with a shotgun' type. Or just lock them in their rooms until they're forty."

He chuckled as he slammed the door shut. "Don't tempt me."

I smoothed down the wrinkles and wished I could erase the dust smudges that streaked my favorite white power suit. It was low-cut and lethal.

I loved it.

I had been in these clothes for the better part of eighteen hours and desperately wanted to change, or at least put on fresh underwear.

I smelled like airports, horse shit, and spite.

Christian put his hand on my back as we made our way up the stairs, but I sidestepped his touch and caught a raised eyebrow in the process.

"I could run a marathon in these shoes. Stairs are nothing."

But Christian didn't argue. He merely faced forward. "Jackass did a real number on you," he muttered into that beard of his.

I had never been into beards. I liked seeing the chiseled jawline of a man. But the way Christian ran his hand down the side of his beard stirred something dormant inside of me.

His was smooth and neat; trimmed an inch beneath his jawline. As he ducked inside the front door of the ranch house, he removed his cowboy hat, giving me another peek at the man bun that held loosely tied brown hair.

How long was his hair?

I settled into the role of an observer as I followed Christian through the house. Something stew-like smelled incredible.

The sound of giggling girls echoed upward into the tall-pitched ceiling. Christian hung his hat on a hat rack, careful not to knock the other ones down.

"Hey," Becks said from a recliner in the open living room. She looked miserably happy.

I never understood the baby thing. Why would a

woman voluntarily put herself through nine months of hell and eighteen years of parental prison?

I knew, without a shadow of a doubt, that I was not a baby person. Or a kid person. Or a teenager person. Or a young adult person.

I mostly tolerated the twenty-six and up population.

"Did you get settled in?" she asked, taking a bite from a bowl of mashed potatoes that rested on top of her enormous baby bump.

I brushed my hair over my shoulder and lifted my chin. "Not exactly."

"Whoever sees Jackson next, tell him I need to have a conversation with him," Christian said, cool as a cucumber.

The room froze.

Becks's mouth dropped open. "Holy crap."

"What?"

When Christian turned his back and delved into a conversation with someone who looked almost exactly like him, Becks spoke quietly. "I've never seen him that angry before."

"That's angry?"

Becks smirked and shoveled in a spoonful of potatoes. "Oh yeah. Chris is as even-tempered as they come. I've never heard him so much as raise his voice." She pointed across the room at him. "*That's* fury."

Once, I had thrown a crystal vase across my office because I was pissed off at a client.

At least I didn't throw it at the client.

Such was the life of a publicist.

Well ... an ex-publicist.

"It makes me wonder how he gets out all his stress," Becks whispered.

But she didn't elaborate. Christian and his look-alike headed for us.

From the back, they were the same height and build, but from the front, the differences were easy to spot.

Christian had a brown man bun, beard, and heavy dad bod with a curved belly. The other guy was more of a dirty blond with hair buzzed short in a military cut. His face was mostly clean-shaven, except for a light layer of sandy stubble. He was built like G.I. Joe.

"Cass, this is my brother, Nate," Christian said.

"Cass*andra*," I clipped under my breath.

Christian just smirked.

"That Griffith brother belongs to me," Becks said, pointing the potato spoon at Christian's brother.

Nate extended his hand. "Nice to meet you. Becks has told me a lot about you."

He didn't strike me as the cowboy type. His posture and presence screamed *military.*

"Well done," I said out of the corner of my mouth when Christian's girls tackled Nate.

Becks grinned and gently smoothed a hand over her bump as it moved like an alien was inside of her.

Oh God. My stomach roiled. *That was so fucking gross.*

"Are you okay, Miss Cassandra?" Gracie said, leaping off her uncle like a monkey swinging from a tree. "You look like Bree when she's about to throw up."

I took a steadying breath and put on a smile. "I'm fine."

"Daddy says that when women say they're fine that it's a lie, so we're not supposed to say we're fine."

Becks snorted.

I braced my hands on my knees and bent to be just above her level. "Did your daddy also tell you it's not nice to demand a different answer when someone has already given you one?"

Gracie didn't flinch. "No, but my therapist says that it's better to say how we feel so we can deal with it and move on rather than letting it soup."

"Rather than letting it *stew*," Bree corrected from across the room.

Gracie shrugged and skipped away, blissfully unbothered. "I like soup better. Chicken noodle is my favorite."

What kind of father encouraged his kids to go to therapy like an emotionally available, self-aware parent? Didn't Christian know he was supposed to ignore all expressions of personal feelings like the rest of the dads out there? Or at least like mine had.

"You must be Ms. Parker," an older woman said from behind me.

I turned just fast enough to catch a glimpse of silver hair before arms wrapped around me.

My back went ramrod straight.

Therapy and hugs. This family was so fucking weird.

"I would've been here to greet you when you got in, but I was taking the girls to dance class. How was your trip, honey?"

"Just fi—" And because I knew that child would correct me if I said "fine," I said, "It went smoothly."

She beamed. "Oh, that's just great to hear."

"Hey, Momma," Christian said with an incredible tenderness in his graveled voice. "Thanks for getting the girls."

Her eyes crinkled at the corners as she smiled. "Anytime. It gave me an excuse to go into town."

"Cass, this is my mom," Christian said with his burly arm still around her shoulders.

I nodded. "Pleasure to meet you, Mrs. Griffith."

"Please, call me Claire. Or Momma. Everyone does."

"Claire," I said decisively.

Calling someone who was not your mother "mom" was bizarre.

Claire looked around. "Where's CJ?"

"I'm here," a slightly younger-looking version of Nate said as he strolled in. He was positively filthy.

Like Christian had done, the man hung his hat on the hook and kissed his mom on the cheek.

She raised her eyebrows. "Who raised you to walk into this house when you're that filthy?"

He smirked. "The same woman who taught me to never be late for dinner."

Claire rolled her eyes. "Go wash up."

"That's Carson," Christian said. "He's the youngest. He's the ranch's cow boss. Oversees the ranch hands."

I didn't want to be a part of this family reunion. If this was the only place to eat, I would take my dinner to-go and get to work. The sooner I got the job done, the sooner I could get back to my life and away from whatever this nightmare was.

5

CHRISTIAN

I studied Cassandra from across the table as she was peppered with questions. Her posture was proper, her lips were pursed as she chewed, and she answered with as little information as possible.

Bree and Gracie looked at her like she was a movie star, asking for every detail about her life in New York.

Guilt boiled up inside of me over the fact that I rarely took the girls outside our little town, much less Texas.

New York probably seemed like somewhere that only existed in the movies.

Becks was chipper as she reminisced over her days as a Manhattanite.

It was weird to think that my brother shared some of that history with her.

Up until her third trimester, Becks had continued to be *Rebecca Davis*, foreign affairs correspondent. Nate traveled with her as her security detail after retiring from the military. Hearing her tell the girls about her days as the lead evening news anchor was wild. It was all taxi cabs, makeup artists, and high heels.

I saw the stars in Bree's eyes.

Or maybe that was just the reflection of the diamond sitting on Cassandra's finger.

CJ's brow furrowed as he stabbed his pot roast. "So, Cassandra, how do you know Becks again?"

She paused and took a sip of water, composing herself. "We work for the same media conglomerate."

"The network's parent company also owns the PR company she works for," Becks said.

A ruby-lipped smile curved at the corner of Cassandra's mouth. "I have no desire to be in front of the camera. Just the puppeteer behind it."

CJ's eyes cut to our dad. "And why does the ranch need a publicist?" He washed down his bite with a sip of tea. "We raise cattle. Not like we're the Kennedys with some Camelot shit or skeletons in the closet."

"Language, Carson James," Mom chided.

One would think that four boys raised on a generational cattle ranch would grow up to be carbon copies of each other, but we couldn't have been more different if we tried.

Nathan was the stereotypical oldest child. He was a natural-born leader. A protector. None of us were surprised when he made it into West Point with visions of a career in the Army. He was driven and determined. It served him well during his twenty years in the military.

Then there was me.

Too sensitive for his own good. Chris needs to toughen up. Comments like that had always been written on my report cards as a child.

The ranch had always been my safe place. It was a haven. I loved the quiet. I treasured the lack of people for miles and miles.

I liked to think that I stayed soft, but life had toughened me up. With Nate doing back-to-back tours overseas, I married my high school sweetheart, had Bree and Gracie, and worked sun-up to sundown to learn everything I needed to know from my old man.

Then I lost Gretchen.

My world ended the day a cop pulled down the long dirt drive, stirring up a dust storm with his tires.

Gretchen had been on her way home from the grocery store. It was her weekly solo trip into town; leaving three-year-old Bree and one-year-old Gracie with my mom so she could have a few hours of peace to run errands.

Hit by a drunk driver.

Gone in seconds.

And just like that, I became a single father. A widower.

The place I had always looked at as my haven had become my altar.

I prayed for weeks, pleading for whatever higher power was out there to bring her back.

I had seen the mangled station wagon.

I had held her lifeless hand when the cop took me to her body.

Then I went home to my baby girls, who looked to me for answers. For strength. For stability.

And I had to swallow it all down for them.

Ray, the next youngest of the Griffith boys, had just started out on the rodeo circuit when it happened. He stepped into the role of the fun uncle, helping with Bree and Gracie while I dealt with funeral arrangements and stole brief moments to grieve.

When he wasn't traveling on the circuit, his home base was in Colorado. I missed him like hell and always looked forward to the rodeo coming to town.

Mom always set a place at the table for him, even if she knew damn well that he wouldn't be here. Today, Cassandra was sitting in Ray's seat.

Carson James—the youngest and only one of us who got in trouble enough to be regularly called by his first *and* middle names—had only been seventeen when Gretchen passed. It seemed like a far cry from the twenty-seven-year-old man who was sitting across from me now.

I didn't know how my parents did it. Four unruly boys had turned into slightly less feral men.

I had my hands full with just two. I couldn't imagine doubling that.

"I'm just saying," CJ cut in again. "We're finally out of the red. Shouldn't we be upgrading the equipment or something? Not spending money on labor?" He cut his eyes to Cassandra. "No offense."

"None taken," she said without a care as she discreetly studied the table, taking in every breath and micro-expression.

Becks set her fork down and groaned, closing her eyes.

Nate nearly jumped out of his skin. "What's wrong?"

"Nothing," she choked out, waving him off. "Don't worry about it."

"Don't tell me not to worry about it, Red," Nate growled.

"Braxon-Hicks?" I guessed.

Becks nodded. "They suck."

I gave her a sympathetic nod. "I remember Gretchen hating them. Gracie gave her a time of it."

Becks pursed her lips, fighting against making a sound as she worked through another practice contraction.

"That's it." Nate wiped his mouth and tossed his napkin down. "We're going to the hospital."

Becks rolled her eyes and turned to Cassandra. "He threatens to take me to the hospital at least four times a day."

Nate pinched the bridge of his nose. "Because you're high risk."

"Because I'm forty," Becks countered. "Everything else is normal. I'm not going to explode. Now, will you calm down?"

Bree, Gracie, and my mom giggled. Nate looked like he was strangling his glass.

Cassandra was unfazed.

I was starting to think that unimpressed face of hers was really a cool façade. I saw the wheels turning in her head.

She was sharp and assessing, taking a wait-and-see approach as she studied the family dynamics.

"Do you know any celebrities?" Bree asked through a mouthful of potatoes and carrots.

"Table manners. You're not a wild animal," I reminded her.

Bree swallowed her bite. "Do you know any celebrities?"

Cassandra dabbed her lips, leaving a crimson print on the napkin.

Shit. I discreetly adjusted my dick under the table.

"Yes," she said.

Bree's jaw hit the table. "Who?" she whispered reverently.

Cassandra didn't flinch. "I sign strict non-disclosure agreements with all my clients."

"What does that mean?" Gracie asked.

"It means they could kill someone and I wouldn't say a peep. So, no, I don't name-drop."

Gracie's eyes turn to saucers. "Did someone here kill someone? Is that why you're here?"

Becks laughed. Nate chuckled. CJ spat his tea out. I dropped my head into my hands. "No one killed anybody, Grace."

"Then I don't get it. What's Miss Cass gonna do on the ranch? I don't think you can herd cattle in heels."

"My name is Cass*andra*."

My hackles raised at the tone she took with my girl. She could talk to me that way, but not my daughters.

Gracie was seemingly unbothered by it, though. "But what does a publicist do?"

"I'm a publicist for people," Cassandra said as she gingerly pushed her plate away. "I control their image, branding, and message so their public-facing persona is consumed by the masses in the right fashion. For businesses it's similar. I act as a consultant, creating and implementing new strategies to open up additional revenue streams and widen their reach beyond their original concept, ingratiating the company to their local market. I control their branding, message, and narrative throughout the changes to maximize the efficacy of the projects and return on investment."

The corporate fruit salad she spoke fluently was going to give me a migraine.

Bree blinked at Cassandra like she was staring at an angel and couldn't believe her eyes.

Gracie reached for another dinner roll. "That's cool. I want to be a marine biologist when I grow up."

Nate frowned. "What new income streams are we talking about?"

Nathan didn't work for the ranch, but he and Becks had a house on the property like the rest of us, which meant he had the same vested interest.

Cassandra folded her hands neatly. "I have a few thoughts, but I'll be able to present my findings and recommendations for what's possible after a full assessment of the property, finances, and the surrounding area."

CJ grunted in displeasure.

I didn't blame him.

There were few things I hated more than outsiders sticking their noses in our business.

In *my* business.

"How long do you think you'll be with us?" Mom asked.

"At this moment, I don't have a firm timeline. Depending on the scope of what you're wanting to do, it could be a few weeks to a few months."

Months.

Shit.

What was I going to do with her for a *few months*?

My dick twitched again.

What was *I* going to do for a few months?

And changes? *Geez, I couldn't think of anything worse.*

The ranch was finally doing well again. We'd made it through a drought that gutted our finances. There were lean years, and then there were years that were barebones.

We'd finally dug ourselves out of it.

We didn't need this. Didn't need *her*.

Cassandra cleared her throat. "I do need to know about my living accommodations." She put on a placid smile. "The... *cabin* I was shown is unacceptable."

"Yeah," I agreed, running a hand over my beard.

Becks frowned. "I'd offer our place, but we're not even sleeping there because of the water damage."

"Bunkhouse is full," CJ said around a mouthful of food. He cut his eyes at Cassandra, stealing a glance before quickly looking away. "Not that I'd recommend sleeping there anyway."

"She can stay in my room!" Gracie squeaked.

I had just opened my mouth to say "no" when Cassandra beat me to it.

"Absolutely not," she said with a patronizing laugh.

"Chris, you've got that spare room, don't you?" Mom asked.

When I saw the state of the cabin, I knew that's what the situation would probably come down to. But just because I was resigned to it didn't mean I liked it.

I sighed. "You got some spare sheets I can borrow? I haven't had a chance to catch up on laundry."

Cassandra's steel eyes darted around the table.

"Of course," Mom said with a smile.

I withheld an eye roll.

I had snapped at Bree for rolling her eyes at me yesterday, and if she caught me doing it, she'd never let me forget it.

"Wait—what?" Cassandra stammered.

I wiped my mouth and tossed my napkin onto my cleaned plate. "I have a spare bedroom."

She cut her eyes to Becks. "I'll just go back and get a hotel room in the town I came through."

Becks gave her a pitiful smile. "Trust me, you don't want to do that. Not unless you want bedbugs. There are no good places to stay around here."

Cassandra's perfectly arched eyebrow twitched. She closed her eyes and inhaled slowly. On the overdramatic exhale she said, "Fine. Given that I've been awake in this nightmare for longer than I'd like, I'll stay there tonight and find more appropriate accommodations tomorrow."

"Good luck," Dad said with a chuckle. "The only better accommodations you'll find will be if you sleep in the stable like the baby Jesus. The barn cats do a good job at keeping the mice away."

Cassandra groaned.

"THIS IS GONNA BE the best night *ever*," Gracie squealed as she bounced in the backseat.

I cut my eyes to the left, watching Cassandra as my parents' house faded behind us.

"Can we stay up and watch a movie with Miss Cassandra?" Bree asked.

"No," Cassandra and I said together.

I tacked on an, "it's a school night," for good measure.

The girls groaned like I had just told them they were going to the dentist.

I pulled up to the house and cut the engine.

Usually, I would have opened their doors and told the girls to go on inside while I checked something inexplicable outside.

That was just code for me needing a few minutes alone to breathe before I oversaw their bedtime routine.

The girls were older now and generally autonomous, which helped.

Still, there was always an argument.

Always a complaint.

Always one of them "forgetting" that brushing their teeth was a prerequisite to going to sleep that had been done since before they could remember.

Always something that needed to be done for school that hadn't been mentioned. I had a stockpile of art supplies and presentation necessities like poster boards for the semi-regular occurrence of "it being a last-minute assignment."

But I couldn't steal those coveted three minutes tonight.

"Get inside and get ready for bed," I told the girls as I popped their doors open.

I saw Cassandra getting antsy, but she didn't reach for the door handle. I opened it for her. "You too, Princess. We're early risers."

She sat stock still; her back straight and eyes closed. "I need a minute."

Her words were emotionless.

My eyebrows lifted, but I didn't argue with her. "Come on in when you're ready, then."

I stood at the sink washing lunchbox containers when the front door finally opened. Cassandra strutted in. The steady rhythm of her stilettos on my hardwood floor was a beacon for the girls.

They bounded out of the bathroom and down the stairs in their pajamas, nearly knocking each other over.

At the giggling chaos, Sadie popped up from her favorite spot on the couch and darted into the kitchen.

"Miss Cassandra, are you actually engaged?" Bree shouted as she beelined for her.

"When are you getting married?" Gracie chimed in.

The fur missile bolted, herding Bree and Gracie into a cluster. Cassandra was caught in the middle of the child and canine tornado. She put her hands up to protect her face.

I whistled, calling off the dog and the girls. They settled instantly.

"Bedtime," I said as I cut the water off. "I'll be up in a minute."

"But we wanna hang out with Miss Cass," Gracie whined.

"Cassandra," she corrected as she massaged her temples.

"Can we see your wedding dress?" Bree begged with clasped hands and puppy eyes.

"I don't have a wedding dress," Cassandra said.

The girls froze, but not for long.

"Why don't you have a wedding dress?" Gracie asked with shock and horror.

Cassandra hadn't opened her eyes yet. "I will tell you if you promise to stay at least two feet away from me at all times."

"Hey—" I said in a warning tone.

She plastered on a smile. "I like my personal bubble."

The girls backed up.

"Better," Cassandra said as she lowered her hands.

Sadie's furry ass was still planted on the floor beside her high heel.

Cassandra raised an eyebrow and glowered at the dog. "You too, fur ball."

To my surprise, Sadie wandered back to the couch.

Cass laced her fingers together and turned her attention back to the girls. "I don't have a wedding dress yet because I don't have a wedding date yet. Why would I wear a summer dress for a winter wedding or lace and sleeves in the middle of July?"

"Why don't you have a wedding date yet?" Bree prodded.

"My, my, aren't you inquisitive?" Cassandra retorted. She bent down, bracing her hands on her knees to get on their level. "I don't have a wedding date because I'm busy building my empire, not adding clout to his last name. Be your own happily ever after and you don't need a prince to save you."

"You're so cool," Bree whispered in sheer reverence.

Now I was the one rubbing my temples.

6

CASSANDRA

"Girls. Bed," Christian growled. "I'll be up in a minute."

"But, *Dad*," Gracie whined.

God, that sound made me want to stuff my head into a paper shredder.

The space behind my eyes throbbed as a migraine made its debut.

Christian cut her a look so severe that it startled even me. But his voice was gentle and steady. "No arguing."

Bree huffed. "But we—"

She clammed up with a raise of her dad's eyebrow.

"I'll come up and turn off the lights in a minute. Go on."

The Bobbsey Twins turned and loped up the stairs without another word.

Christian had dropped his hat on the hook by the door when he walked in, leaving his disheveled bun uncovered. I didn't move, opting to stand and watch as he dug his hands into his thick hair.

He tugged on the elastic holding the bun together, letting light brown hair spill past his shoulders. One hand delved deep into the locks as he let out a breath, assessed the situation, assessed me, and formed a plan in his mind.

"Just—uh—make yourself at home. I gotta make sure they're good to go for the morning, then I'll get your room set up."

"Take your time," I said with as much neutrality in my voice as I could muster while Christian climbed the stairs.

The optics are more important than our comfort. I could hear Tripp's haughty voice in my head, and I hated it.

I found my cell and opened it up, hoping for some small connection to the outside world.

I had two measly bars at Christian's house, which was enough for texts and grainy calls to come through. A few voicemails peppered the screen.

But nothing from Tripp.

No *I'm sorry* text. No voicemail explaining why the hell he had abandoned me.

Three years ago, I had been dreamy-eyed at the prospect of marrying him. His proposal had been planned by the best wedding planner in the industry.

He wanted to do it right.

He wanted to give me the fairytale moment.

He didn't have time to come up with something on his own.

He loved me, but planning how he would ask me to marry him wasn't in his wheelhouse, so he outsourced.

I hated the ring. It was hideously gaudy, but it was the right size karat to make a statement without being the headline. It was the right cut. The clarity was unmatched. It checked all the boxes for the perfect optics.

Three years ago, we had talked about dates and venues.

But something always came up to push it back until we stopped talking about it altogether.

And when I brought it up, he'd blame the delays on work.

Once, he offered a quick courthouse wedding just because he thought I would say no.

I said yes.

He didn't show up.

Of course, Tripp blamed it on work.

His meeting ran late.

His client was inconsolable and he couldn't slip away.

I should be more committed like he was.

I should be putting my clients ahead of my personal life.

Twisting the ring on my finger, I wondered what I was doing with it on my hand in the first place.

Voices carried down from the upstairs bedrooms.

"Can you do my hair like Miss Cassandra's tomorrow?"

That sounded like the older one.

Christian gave a well-worn sigh. "Your hair isn't long enough for big curls like that."

"I know," she pressed. "But can you try?"

"I don't know how to do it," he said.

I caught a glimpse of myself in the slick microwave door. My voluminous Marilyn Monroe bangs had fallen after a day of travel and ranch-induced trauma, but the length of my tresses still sported a nice bounce.

"You know the rule," Christian said. "I need at least

five days to learn a new hairstyle before you can wear it to school."

"Do you think Miss Cassandra could do my hair?" Bree pleaded.

"Absolutely not," I muttered under my breath as I studied the dog lounging on the couch.

"No," Christian said. His voice turned to mumbles as he moved around upstairs. He was probably kissing their foreheads and giving out heartfelt "I love yous."

How freaking nice.

Lights turned off upstairs and I looked at the time. It was barely eight in the evening. Usually I would have been getting ready to wrap up my workday. Maybe I'd be slipping out to a dinner reservation before going home to manage the lives of the rich and famous from my couch. *With wine because Lillian Monroe was a ladder-climbing lizard woman.*

Maybe my current headache was really the detox after being released from her orbit.

I had started my career with the Carrington Group at the bottom in strategic business development consulting before landing my dream job in public relations.

Being a publicist was my dream. Or so I thought.

I wanted the private jet lifestyle, the Michelin-starred restaurants, the camera flashes and shouts for attention, all while being the master puppeteer.

I wanted to be the wizard behind the curtain.

But one empty-headed starlet decided to rip the curtain down, strangle me with it, light the fabric on fire, then throw me off a cliff.

Now I was in cowboy hell.

Heavy boots thundered down the stairs, and Christian appeared. He grabbed the stack of linens he had carted in from his mom's house and disappeared into the spare room.

"Question," I said, moving to linger in the doorway as I watched him put sheets on the queen-sized mattress.

Christian looked up, deep brown eyes boring into mine for a brief moment before returning to the task at hand. "What's that?"

"Where's the woman in the photos?"

"What do you mean?"

"Is she going to come in here and slit my throat because I'm sleeping in your house?"

He didn't laugh, but he didn't look angry either. "She died when the girls were little," he said calmly as he shimmied a pillow into a fresh case.

Christian's tone wasn't begging for pity. He had simply stated a fact, so I responded in turn.

"Well, then I'm sorry to hear that."

He unfurled a large quilt and neatly draped it over the made bed. It was all so ... *quaint*.

"There's a full bath down the hall. It's next to my room. Holler if you need anything. The girls have a bathroom upstairs so they shouldn't bother you. Help yourself to whatever you can find in the kitchen."

I pinned myself to the door frame as he lugged my suitcases in from the living room.

After a quick look to make sure there wasn't anything that still needed to be done, he wiped his hands on his jeans and paused in the door.

It was a tight fit with the two of us face-to-face.

Christian's stomach brushed mine as he stared down at me intently. A small groove formed between his eyebrows. A low growl of frustration reverberated in his chest.

"What am I gonna do with you?"

His gruff timbre sent shivers racing down my spine. The breath snaking off his beard was intoxicating.

Christian Griffith was *not* my type. Besides, I was taken.

Kind of.

But my body didn't give a damn about logic. My skin prickled like I had touched a live wire.

He looked safe. His arms looked comforting. And after the day I'd had, it took every ounce of my professionalism not to lean into them for support.

I lifted my chin. "I'm here to do a job.

"Yeah," he said with one last heated look as he stepped out of the doorway and headed for the kitchen. "That's what I'm afraid of."

I WOKE to the sound of children. It was awful.

Their shrill morning shrieks of "I can't find my other shoe!" and "I don't want pancakes for breakfast!" immediately gave me a headache.

Need caffeine.

I rolled over and buried my head under the pillow to try and block out the cacophony of prepubescent chatter.

It wasn't even light outside yet.

The pillow and bedding were clean, but smelled a

little musty—like they had been sitting in a closet for an unusually long time.

I stretched, flexing and curling my toes beneath the heavy quilt.

Christian had only been in here for a few minutes while he made the bed last night, but his cologne lingered in the most delicious way.

Was it actually cologne, or was it just him?

I breathed in the masculine scent, letting it wrap around me like a hug, and drifted back to sleep.

"Rise and shine." Christian's deep bass floated in as the door creaked open.

Politely, fuck him.

No. On second thought, not politely.

Fuck him.

I lifted the corner of the pillow and glared at the clock. "I'm available between the hours of nine and five. Outside that, you'll need to send me an email that will be answered during the following business day."

Christian's chuckle was dark. "Not how it works around here, Princess."

The slide of ceramic on wood caught my attention. I cautiously peered through sleep-laden eyes and spotted the mug of coffee he had left on the nightstand.

"Nice pajamas," he clipped as he turned away from the door.

A breeze danced over my bare shoulder where the strap of my satin camisole kissed my skin.

But the breeze didn't stop there.

Crap.

I tugged the quilt up, covering the side of my boob that had spilled out of my top.

"I'm leaving in ten," he hollered across the house.

"My workday starts at nine," I reminded him.

Christian let out a sharp whistle. "Sadie. Bring 'em."

The click-click of dog paws on hardwood floors was instantaneous. Sadie—the annoying Aussie wiggle butt—scrambled up the stairs. Muffled thumps echoed all over the second floor as she scrambled from room to room like a fur tornado.

I was fairly sure she had tumbled head over tail down the staircase, then quickly realized the sound was from how fast her paws carried her back down the steps.

The incessant barking was worse than the children.

Earplugs were at the top of my to-do list this morning. I'd get up, beg Becks to let me use her vehicle to go back to civilization, grab a proper latte somewhere in town, make my phone calls and send my emails, and find somewhere to stay that had significantly less wildlife. And that included the children.

The barking grew closer.

And closer.

And closer.

I wrapped the pillow around my head and briefly contemplated smothering myself.

The headache grew. It was half-exhaustion and half-anger.

I hadn't slept well. It was too quiet here. Too dark outside.

I needed the lights and noise of the city to drown out my thoughts so I could get some sleep.

Children stomped down the stairs and out the door, screaming, "Grandma!"

Finally, the house was quiet.

Paws clattered on the floor in a drumroll. I peeked out of the pillow just in time to see a ball of fur leaping onto the bed.

Sadie barked repeatedly as she attempted to trample me to death.

"Out!" I shouted as I curled into the fetal position to protect my vital organs.

"Leave! Down! Back!"

I tried every command in the book to get her to stand down. I screeched in horror, blocking my face as she lunged for my head over and over again.

Ten minutes later, I was storming out the front door of Christian's godforsaken house, only to find him—arms crossed and smirking—as he leaned against the door of his truck.

"First of all," I bellowed, stabbing a finger in his direction. "Fuck you."

Sadie nipped at my ankles, and I jumped away.

Christian looked so damn pleased with himself as he took me in. My unwashed, day-old curls had been slicked back into a tight bun that accentuated my cheekbones. The linen blouse I usually would have taken the time to steam was mussed. I tucked it into wheat-colored trousers that tied in a bow at my waist and hid the rest of it beneath a white blazer.

With the yapping, I had to rush through my makeup routine, and made do with some concealer for the bags under my eyes, a coat of mascara, and a plum-colored lip.

My phone was in one hand, and my Mary Poppins bag was slung over my shoulder. "Happy?" I shouted over the barking. "Will you call off your canine alarm clock now?"

Christian grinned from ear to ear. "Down."

I glared at Sadie as she immediately turned into a rug. "Seriously? I said that at least thirty times!"

"You're not me," Christian said as he rounded the truck and opened my door. "Let's go. We're late."

7

CHRISTIAN

Cassandra looked so fucking pissed. It was cute.

She threw that oversized bag into the floorboard and grappled at the seat as she stepped up onto the running board.

The bottom of her high heel slid off the edge. I caught her hips as she teetered backward.

"Those are the shoes you're gonna wear all day?" I asked as I gently pushed her into the cab.

Her eyes dropped to her feet, then lifted back to me. "I wear these every day. I'll be fine."

Sadie hopped into the bed of the truck to hitch a ride. I slid behind the wheel and pulled away from the house.

"I need to go into town," Cassandra said without hesitation as she reached into the depths of her bag and pulled out a sleek, leather notebook. Lists upon lists filled the pages.

"Not on the schedule for today."

She arched an eyebrow. "I wasn't asking for your permission."

"Fine then," I said as I pulled up in front of the warehouse office. "Hope you like walking in those heels. I'll see you in a couple days."

I hopped out, popped her door open, and left her to stew. If she wanted to sit there and pout, she could sit there and pout.

If she wanted to attempt grand theft auto and take my truck, she could try. But Cassandra didn't strike me as the type who knew how to drive stick shift. She'd stall out before she got to the property gate.

I had just flipped the lights on when she came storming in. "What is your deal, Griffith?"

"My deal?"

She pinched the bridge of her nose. "I'm being held hostage here."

I lifted an eyebrow. "You're supposed to be working a job."

"Which I can't do unless I have some connection to the outside world."

I pointed to the chunky desktop computer that took up most of the space on the desk. "What do you think that is?"

"A relic that belongs in a museum."

"Beggars can't be choosers."

"I'm not begging!" she shouted. One arm darted out and pointed to the corner. "Why is the cow in here?"

Mickey was resting peacefully on top of Sadie's dog bed. The edge was the only thing that peeked out from under his mass.

I shrugged. "He goes where he wants."

Cassandra dropped her bag on my desk, sending a stack of paperwork for the Texas Animal Health

Commission onto the cement floor. "Why doesn't anything bother you? There's a flipping cow in your office!"

I pursed my lips, thankful that my beard hid my smile. It'd probably piss her off. "It's a cattle ranch."

"They should be outside! Far, far away," she argued. "You do know the difference between people and animals, right? You eat animals."

I choked on a laugh. "You can eat people, too. Particularly women. Or did your fiancé not do that for you, Princess?"

Her face turned bright red and she gaped at me. "What do you think gives you the right to—"

I held up a finger. "One thing you should know about me. I don't have time for bullshit. I will tell you exactly what's on my mind. If you have a problem with that, then you're just going to have to get over it."

Thick lashes lowered and lifted as she looked me up and down. "That makes two of us."

The steel toes of my boots bumped the pointed triangle of her heels. "I've gotta make some calls before we head out. You've got fifteen minutes to get your shit in order."

Fourteen minutes and fifty-six seconds later, we were heading out of the office. "Think you can ride today?" I asked as I secured my radio to my belt and patted down my pockets, double checking that I had gloves, a knife, the cattle tag and applicator, and a multi-tool.

"Ride in an air-conditioned truck? Yes, I suppose that'll do."

I shook my head. "No, ma'am. Your options today are a horse or an ATV."

Her jaw flexed and I could almost make out the chalky sound of her teeth grinding together. "The ATV, I suppose."

"You'll get dirtier riding that than if you ride a horse."

She chose the ATV anyway.

Not that I was surprised, but it did make for an interesting fit. I loaded up the two-seat Outlander and double-checked the fuel.

"You know," I hollered as we ripped over the terrain. "One of these days, you're gonna have to start dressing for the ranch."

"I dress for myself," she shouted from behind me.

"Yeah, I can see that. Your dry-cleaning bill is gonna be high."

Low brush was eaten up by the tires as we crossed the plains. CJ and the ranch hands had been working to move the herd to the west pastures so the southern pastures could recover.

Cassandra's arms were wrapped tight around me, squishing into my stomach as we bumped and bobbed over rocks and divots.

Horses would've been so much easier, but I didn't have the time to spare to argue with her about it.

The ground smoothed out, but instead of loosening her hold on me, I felt her head press against my back.

I stole a look over my shoulder and caught her with her cheek resting against my spine.

I let go of one handle and gave the hand holding onto my middle a reassuring squeeze.

As much as I wanted to bitch and moan about her being here, I knew my old man was right. We needed to shore things up. I just didn't have time to do it.

Cassandra was having a shitty time, and it was about to get a lot harder.

Cattle dotted the horizon. The herd's movement froze at the sound of the engine.

I reached back and patted Cassandra's knee to get her attention. She straightened, loosening her grip as I slowed and swung left to circle the herd.

"What are we doing out here?" Cassandra shouted when I cut the engine.

"I can hear you," I said with a chuckle.

She rubbed her ear. "Yeah, well I can't hear you."

"A calf was born last night."

She looked around. "Out here? Should that be done in a barn or something?"

"Sometimes," I said. "If we know the momma's distressed. But letting calves be born in the pasture with limited intervention allows them to behave naturally. I had two guys out here making sure everything went alright."

Her eyes widened slightly. "All night?"

"This isn't a nine-to-five, Cass." I slid off the seat and offered a hand to help her down.

Cassandra ignored my polite hand, and opted to wobble off the seat like a newborn giraffe.

Now it wasn't just cattle staring at us.

"Morning," CJ said as he walked across the grass. He gripped the crown of his hat and lifted it toward Cassandra. "Ma'am."

"At least he didn't say *good* morning, because we all know it's not," Cassandra muttered.

"How'd it go?" I asked, shouldering the supply bag and following him to a shrouded area where the mother had sought coverage to give birth. I glanced over my shoulder to make sure Cassandra was following. "C'mon, Ms. Parker."

She picked up her pace.

"Nothing abnormal. Calf was born around three this morning. Momma licked him clean and let him nurse."

"Afterbirth?" I asked as we trudged along.

"Expelled the placenta about two hours later and then ate it," Carson said.

Cassandra dry heaved.

Sure enough, there was a newborn standing beneath the white and reddish-brown cow, latched to the udder. The momma was seemingly unbothered by me approaching, but I could sense her eyes on me.

Cassandra watched while I made quick work of tagging the calf's ear and administering a round of vaccines to keep it and the herd healthy.

Cassandra stayed close while I checked in with the men on horseback. I studied the herd, looking for anything abnormal, and checked over the pasture.

I sent a handful of them on errands—fixing fences and repairing the storage buildings.

Everyone eyed Cassandra with distrust. Even the cows.

I didn't exactly blame them.

"Nothing like being acutely aware of everyone talking about you in front of your back," Cassandra said when I told her to get back onto the ATV.

"Don't worry about it."

"It's hard not to."

"They're pissed I brought the ATV out here."

"Why?"

"The engine makes the herd antsy. Horses are safer for cowboys. If a cow decides to charge, it's easier to get out of the way. We try to keep things low-stress when we're working cattle. It's a lot like life. We put gentle pressure on them, and guide them rather than forcing them to go where we want them to go. I've learned my best parenting tactics from animals."

She blinked, unimpressed. "Yeah, this isn't 1812. If you could stop speaking in spooky cowboy proverbs, that would be great."

I kept my eyes on hers, rather than looking down the deep "V" of her blouse like I wanted to. "Get on the seat, Cass."

She rolled her eyes and plopped down. "It's Cassandra."

I deposited her back at the office, leaving her to the near dial-up internet while I puttered around the shop, fixing machinery and making sure the vehicles were in good working order.

Cassandra deemed the one o'clock hour a working lunch and demanded a look at the books to see the kind of budget she had.

I was fine with it as long as it kept her from complaining for ten minutes.

The woman stuck out like a sore thumb, but part of me—a deeply repressed part of me—really fucking liked it.

I got Bree and Gracie settled at the house when they got home from school, then took care of my evening chores before swinging by the cabin to see what work needed to be done to get it habitable.

Everything. Everything needed to be done.

The pipes were cast-iron and corroded. I was fairly certain if I turned on more than one switch, I'd spark an electrical fire. More critters lived inside than outside.

I could get one of the more reliable boys to get in there and fix it up over the next few weeks. But for now, it was uninhabitable.

Fuck.

"She's got a nice rack."

The comment from good-for-nothing Jackson ate at me as I scrubbed grease from my hands under the spigot.

He was already at the top of my shit list for dicking around when he should have been working on the cabin. If he ran his mouth anymore, he was about to be unemployed.

Someone else laughed. "I bet that pretty face hides her crazy."

"Did you see the rock on her finger? Bet she's got some poor guy by the balls."

"A nice piece of ass isn't worth her bitch face," Jackson said.

I cut the water off and rounded the corner. "What was that?"

The cluster of cowboys froze around the turnout.

I had heard the whispers all damn day. I knew Cassandra had too. Maybe that's why she had holed up in my office, taking over my desk and color coding shit.

I raised my eyebrows. "Well. Speak up if you've got somethin' to say."

Jackson shifted his eyes left and right, waiting for someone else to be the sacrificial lamb.

"You look like you've got something on your mind," I said as I rested my hands on my hips. "Wanna share with the class?"

"Doesn't make sense, is all," he sneered.

I beckoned him closer with a crook of my finger. "What's that now?"

Jackson was out of grade school, but he acted like a twelve-year-old. CJ swore up and down that he was a good kid—that he just needed some guidance.

That made him CJ's problem.

But since Cassandra was my problem, I wasn't going to let this slide.

He scuffed the toe of his boot into the dirt. "Just don't make sense that we can't get raises, but you're spending big bucks bringing in that snooty bitch to fuck around the ranch."

A wry laugh escaped my mouth as I crowded him up against the pipe fencing that kept the horses contained. "I don't remember asking for your opinion or seeing any work from you that's worth a raise." I fisted the front of his plaid-checked shirt instead of clocking him across the jaw. "Now. I have another question for you."

His top lip pulled up in a sneer. Jackson had the body of a string bean with a linebacker attitude. But he didn't make a peep.

"Is that how you talk about my daughters?"

Jackson's nostrils flared. "No."

"What was that?" I clipped.

"No, *sir*."

I tightened my grip on his shirt. "Is that how you talk about my momma?"

He gritted his teeth. "No, sir."

I let go of his shirt, letting him fall backward against the fence. "Then that sure as hell isn't how you talk about Miss Parker."

"She ain't a Griffith," he spat.

I pointed a finger at him. "Neither are you, son. You'd better remember that." I eyed the cluster of ranch hands as I pointed toward the office. "She carries the weight of *my* name. She's a Griffith to you."

They nodded in agreement.

I turned back to Jackson. "If you so much as look at her wrong and she wants you gone, you're gone. Have I made myself clear?"

8

CASSANDRA

My hand was sweaty around the doorknob as I peeked through the crack, watching Christian from a distance.

Something had gone down around the enclosure where the ranch hands had turned out the horses.

I'd never seen him like this. So rough and brusque.

I almost turned to go back to the desk, then Christian said my name. *Miss Parker.*

He didn't call me Cass.

Truthfully, I didn't mind it coming from him.

Growing up, I was Cassie to my friends and family. But I let go of shortening it after the millionth lecture where Tripp hounded me about using my full name.

Cassandra is much more professional. You want to be taken seriously, don't you?

So I became Cassandra.

My attention was glued on Christian as he spat fire and brimstone at some kid who had been running his mouth within earshot of me for most of the day.

It's not like I hadn't heard it all before.

"She carries the weight of my name. She's a Griffith to you."

I froze, paralyzed with shock.

I hadn't heard a man talk about me like *that* before.

CRICKETS SERENADED me as I checked the time ... again.

I had skipped the picture-perfect family sitcom dinner Christian had invited me to partake in, and waited out the dinner hour in the privacy of the office.

To my dismay, Mickey slept soundly in the corner.

I pored over stacks and stacks of financial statements, building a reasonable working budget for my pet projects while eyeing my phone every few minutes.

I had finally gotten Tripp to respond to a message I sent to his work email, where he said he would give me a call at five. It would be the end of my work day and midnight for him.

But my phone never lit up.

Tripp never called.

I just needed ... something. Reassurance maybe?

This was outside my wheelhouse. I had been stripped of my regular responsibilities and Tripp had shouldered them in the aftermath.

It made sense, I guess. He was my boss.

Lillian's people probably wanted someone more senior from the firm to clean up the situation.

Although it was her fault. Not mine.

I shut down the computer and gathered my things. It

was just after eight, which meant Christian's kids would hopefully be in bed.

Tripp had just gotten busy. That had to be it.

My phone rang, and I dropped the files in my hands as I lunged for it.

"Hello?"

Static crackled as I caught my breath.

"Sorry for calling so late," Tripp said over the laughter in the background. "Dinner really got away from us, but you know how things are over here. I don't think we started eating until 10:30."

"Right. Yeah," I said as I loosened my bun and ran my fingers through my hair. "How are you? How are things in Spain?"

Selfishly, I wanted him to ask how I was doing, but it was easier to let Tripp talk about himself first.

He laughed. "You would have loved it over here. Bummer you couldn't do the trip."

Bummer? It was a bummer that I had my career ripped away from me? It was a bummer that I was exiled to motherfucking Texas? It was a bummer that my fiancé was representing my client while my name was being dragged through the mud? It was a bummer that I had been put on ice and wasn't supposed to defend myself?

I choked down the cocktail of rage and humiliation that hung in my throat. "I miss you."

Or at least I thought I did.

I was supposed to miss him. To miss my life. To miss the bells and whistles that I was supposed to love.

I was stressed, uncertain, and insecure. I wasn't reacting to anything well because of it. *Especially Christian's kindness.*

But in the last twenty-four hours I had done something that I hadn't done in a long time.

I breathed.

"What was that?" Tripp asked.

It wasn't that he couldn't hear me. He just wasn't listening.

"I said I miss you."

"Oh. Yeah. I miss you too."

My fingernails bit into my palm, leaving shallow crescents in my skin. "You seem distracted."

"Yeah, uh—well—dinner's wrapping up. The wine over here is great."

By my guess, Christian would sic his dog on me at the ass crack of dawn again, so I wrapped it up. "When can we talk about this?"

"About what? The gig in Texas? I thought I told you to report to Mike?"

Whereas Tripp was the head of public relations for individual clients, Mike McDaniels was his business development counterpart.

"About *us*," I clarified.

"Now's not a good time. We need to let things cool down before—"

"I'm not talking about the wedding, Tripp! I said we need to talk about *us*."

"Look, I gotta go." He let out a laugh. "Lillian is a handful and she's had a bottle of wine."

The call ended without a goodbye.

Mickey huffed in the background as I stared at the dark phone screen and wondered where it all went wrong.

Christian found me on his porch, sitting in a rocking chair with a cereal bowl on my lap.

Moths flitted around, dancing high in the porch light. Shadows were cast at my feet.

"I'd have to ask Becks about normal New York City dinners, but I don't think that's a proper meal, Princess."

I didn't look up from my bowl of ice cream. "You told me I could help myself to whatever I could find in the kitchen."

The rocking chair beside mine creaked as he lowered himself into it. "Yeah, to the pantry or the fridge or whatever leftovers were in there." He leaned over the rocking chair arm and studied my bowl. "Really? Mint chocolate chip and... whiskey?"

I swirled my spoon around the spiked float I had fixed myself when I snuck back from the office. "Don't knock it 'til you try it," I said as I shoveled in a spoonful.

Christian disappeared without a word.

What was it about men and their propensity to walk away unexpectedly?

I was one silent exit away from losing my shit.

Utensils clanked and clattered inside as I stared at the melting mound of mint ice cream swirling into warm brown whiskey. Was this was rock bottom?

I took a big scoop and let the burn of liquor be cooled by the sweetness of peppermint.

"I'll trade you."

I looked up and found Christian standing in front of me with a matching bowl full of chili. It was topped with a wedge of cornbread dripping in butter.

"You missed dinner," he said as he took the ice cream from me and replaced it with the chili bowl that was warm from the microwave.

"I was working," I lied.

Christian took a testing bite of my ice cream concoction and grimaced. "That's repulsive."

"It's an acquired taste," I retorted without much enthusiasm as I poked at the chili.

The wooden slats of the porch creaked as Christian gently rocked back and forth.

I watched him out of the corner of my eye. He rested comfortably; knees wide and boots flat, leaning back in the chair. His hair was still in a bun, but it was loose after a long day. Tendrils spilled out across his shoulders.

It was unnerving to be around someone so relaxed.

Tripp was always running around, so I was too.

"Shouldn't you be asleep?" I asked as I took a meager nibble. The buttery sweetness of the cornbread, the earthy warmth of cumin, and the acidity of the tomatoes blended perfectly.

"I don't sleep until everyone in my house is settled."

"You don't have to wait up for me. I'm capable of going to bed and getting myself to your office in the morning."

Christian tilted his head and looked at me. "I didn't say asleep. I said settled."

"And you don't think I'm settled?" I asked before shoveling in a bite. I didn't realize how hungry I had gotten.

"Are you?"

If this was the "gentle pressure" he talked about using on cattle and children, I could admit that it was effective.

"I finally talked to Tripp," I admitted.

A dissatisfied growl simmered in his chest. "And how is the world's most pretentious asshole?"

I gritted my teeth. "Living it up in Spain with my cli—my *former* client."

He lifted a finger off the arm of the chair and pointed at my ring. "When's the big day?"

Suddenly, I wasn't quite so hungry. "Your guess is as good as mine," I said as I set the bowl on my lap.

"You done?" he asked, picking up the ice cream and reaching for the chili.

"Yeah."

Christian took both bowls inside and came back with a pair of socks and cowboy boots. "What size do you wear?"

"Sevens."

"These are sixes. Put 'em on."

"Excuse me?"

"Put the boots on. We're going on a ride."

I studied them, taking in the scuffed-up leather. "Please tell me you are not asking me to put on your dead wife's shoes. That's just weird."

I half-expected him to get offended, but Christian cracked a smile. "They belonged to Becks. She got 'em, but they were too small so she gave them to Bree to grow into."

Oddly curious, I took the socks and toed off my high heels. Blisters had broken my skin in angry red circles.

"Cass..." Christian said in a scolding voice as he knelt in front of me. "You told me you could handle yourself in those shoes." He pointed to the heels.

"I can."

Calloused fingers gingerly cradled the sole of my foot as he took another look. "Your feet say otherwise."

"I'm fine. Walking in pastures, dirt, and gravel is a little different than sidewalks and offices. I'll deal with it."

"I'll take you into town tomorrow. You can get a pair of boots while I pick up supplies."

I wasn't arguing with that. I wanted to get back to civilization—even if it meant settling for small-town USA.

The cotton sock abraded my blisters. I hissed as I slid it on.

Christian looked up with concern in his eyes. "You okay?"

The bite of discomfort was welcomed. It kept me from crying about the million other things weighing on me.

I could be angry about a few blisters, especially if it distracted me from Tripp.

Christian waited patiently as I squeezed my feet into the boots. My trousers and blazer didn't exactly scream "cowgirl chic," but it was dark, and the ranch was asleep.

I followed Christian to the stables and waited while he saddled Libby.

My body was present with him, but my mind was a thousand miles away.

"You ready?"

Suddenly I was acutely aware of the fact that he expected me to ride that thing again.

"On second thought, I'm just going to go to bed," I said, turning for the barn entrance.

Christian caught my hand. "Come on, Princess." He nudged me toward the massive chestnut-colored horse. "Up you go."

"Christian, I—"

"Left foot in the stirrup. I'll give you a boost if you need it."

"I really don't—"

Apparently, his boost was more of a lift than a hand. My boot barely touched the stirrup before my ass was on the front part of the double-seated saddle. Libby shuffled, getting used to my weight, but it scared me to death.

I shrieked, grabbing at whatever I could to keep from falling to my death.

Then Christian was stepping up, slinging his leg around, and sliding into the seat behind me. "Calm down. There's no need to shout."

"Easy for you to say! I almost fell off!"

"You didn't almost fall off," he said without a care in the world. "I won't let you fall." The brim of his hat bumped against the back of my head as he leaned forward. "I'm gonna touch you. Are you okay with that?"

"Only if you help me get down."

"If you're gonna be out here, you need to learn. At this hour, no one will be watching you."

"I have absolutely zero reason to be on top of a horse."

But Christian ignored my protests. His hands slid down my waist. "Square up your hips," he said, giving my thighs a squeeze.

Carefully, I shifted, sitting firmly in the middle of the saddle as I ignored those damn butterflies.

A ridge of leather separated him from my ass. At least he had fitted Libby with a saddle meant for two. I didn't know if I could handle his body wrapping around mine.

His gentle rumble sent shivers up my back. "Take the reins."

I didn't realize I had a vise grip on the front of the saddle. Libby shifted between her feet again. I squeaked, white knuckling the front of the saddle.

Christian's hands on my hips steadied me. "That's just her way of saying she's ready to go."

"Yeah—well—I'm not."

"Have you been around horses before?"

"Do the horses in Central Park count?"

"No." He took my hand in his and leaned forward. Christian's abdomen was warm against my back as he pressed my palm against Libby's shoulder. "Give her some love. She'll love you back."

"I thought I already had her undying love after she nearly ate my hand off when she was going for the peppermint?"

Christian chuckled. "You do."

His palm stayed pressed against mine as I gingerly stroked her short hair.

"You ready?" he asked as the fibers of his beard tickled my neck.

I looked over my shoulder. "Do I have a choice?"

"No."

"I suppose if I get thrown off this beast, I'll get a nice nap in a vegetative state. Let's go."

Christian let out a loud laugh, startling Libby and me. "Take the reins."

Apparently, I did it wrong because he delicately changed the way I gripped the leather.

"Squeeze her with your legs," he said as he let go of my hands and sat back.

I pinched my lips between my teeth as I tried to hide my terror.

Apparently, I didn't do a good job of hiding it because Christian put his hands back on my hips and offered a reassuring, "I've got you," as Libby slowly took off into the grass.

And I believed him.

"Keep your back straight.

"It is straight," I argued.

Christian snickered. "You're hunched over so far that Libby's head is higher than yours." Strong hands pressed against my stomach. "Posture like a princess, hips like a whore."

"Excuse me?"

"Keep your back nice and straight. Sit tall in the saddle, but keep your hips loose so you can move. Kinda like riding a motorcycle."

"Do I strike you as a woman who rides a motorcycle?"

"You strike me as the kind of woman who is full of surprises."

A caustic laugh slipped out of my mouth. "I'm not. What you see is what you get."

"Ahhh—I don't know about that." He paused to correct my grip on the reins. "No one's that simple."

"Are you really supposed to be dissecting someone while you have them hostage on top of a horse?"

"You uncomfortable, Princess?"

"With the horse, yes. With the inquisition, also yes."

But with him? I wasn't uncomfortable. It was the most at peace I had felt in a long time.

His breath was warm against my temple as he said, "Gently pull the rein on the left side so she'll make the turn onto the trail up here."

I pulled back until there was tension on the leather

strap. Libby dipped her head and—to my surprise—headed to the dirt trail that split to the left.

"Let up when she does what you want and give her a rub."

With a little more confidence, I leaned forward and smoothed my hand down her mane.

Libby, pleased with the attention, picked up her pace, jolting me in the saddle.

"Christian!"

"You're alright," he said as he settled his hands back on my hips. "I'm not gonna let you fall."

"I bet you say that to all the women you take on midnight rides."

"It's hardly midnight. It's just after nine."

"That's midnight for you, cowboy," I sassed.

"You're not wrong," he said with a laugh. "I haven't been up this late in a while."

I peered over my shoulder and caught him looking down at me. "Are you sure you're qualified to be giving riding lessons?"

He hit me with a quick flash of his smile. "I taught both my girls how to ride before they could go up and down the stairs by themselves."

"Really," I mused. "You taught your girls the phrase 'posture like a princess, hips like a whore?'"

Christian's laugh was dark. "That was the saying I was taught with. My girls got the G-rated version." His hands pressed against my waist, and I could feel the rhythm of my hips matching Libby's strides. "Hips like a hula hoop."

9

CHRISTIAN

"How properly parental of you," Cassandra said with a light laugh.

I snickered. "Sometimes it's hard to turn off. I'll either be swearing in front of the girls or I'll be telling the guys I gotta go potty."

Her hair slid to the side as she laughed.

She sounded so fucking pretty when she did that.

Cassandra and I settled into a comfortable silence as she slowly slipped into a cautiously trusting relationship with Libby.

"Relax," I reminded her. "You're tense."

"Sorry," she mumbled as she fixed her posture. But the tension never left her shoulders.

"You got something on your mind?"

"No," she clipped.

I didn't believe her. "Come on, Cass. Don't bullshit me like that."

"Nothing you need to worry about. I'm here to work for you, not the other way around. Remember?"

Evasive. Okay.

"The door's open if you wanna talk."

I could hear her grinding her teeth down to nubs, but I waited.

And waited.

And waited some more.

The stress never left her. Those elegant fingers were rigid around the reins.

"You're doing well. Give her a little tap with your feet if you want her to go faster."

Cassandra didn't say anything.

It wasn't the horse I was worried about. Libby knew this path well.

"Next time we go out on the property, I'll put you on Dottie. She's a big softie. You'll be able to handle her on your own. She doesn't spook easy."

"So, is this little trail ride because everyone has an opinion about you carting me around on the ATV? Or about me being here in general?"

"No. I just figured you might want to do something to clear your head. Sometimes when I can't sleep I'll take Libby out and find a pasture to look at the stars."

"I hadn't even gone to bed yet."

"You know what I mean, Cass."

She stiffened, but didn't correct me like she had every other time.

"Something's off with Tripp," she admitted.

She was trying so hard to spoon-feed me the palatable, sugar-laced version of her shitty relationship. She was probably justifying it in her mind, too.

"You mean it's not normal for a man to dump his

fiancé in an unfamiliar situation and bolt?" I asked with an air of amusement.

She huffed and whispered, "Fuck him."

"Take us right when you hit the fork in the trail. It leads back to the house."

"He used to at least act like he was invested in our relationship," she blurted out in frustration.

I itched to wrap my arms around her, but I didn't. "How long have you been with him?"

"Six years," she admitted. "Dated for three years before he proposed. I will have been engaged to him for four years in a few months."

"Be straight with me."

"I am."

I scoffed. "He proposed to you *three* years ago?"

Her shoulders dropped. "He said he wasn't in a rush to get the wedding over with."

"Do you live with him?"

"No," she said quickly. "I like my space and so does he."

I worked my hand over my beard. "So. You don't live with him. You have no plans to get married. And he's allergic to commitment?"

"Well, when you put it that way—"

"He gave you a ring as payment for sex."

She wasn't fazed by my candor. "That would be true if we were having sex."

"You waiting for the big day or something?"

Cassandra peered over her shoulder, hitting me with those steel gray eyes. "Is this an appropriate conversation to have with your employee?"

"You're also sleeping in my house and my kids think you're a Barbie doll come to life."

"Fair." She sighed. "No, I'm not waiting or anything. We used to have sex. We just stopped when things got busy. And then..."

"And then what?"

"Then they stayed busy. Or at least he keeps making it out to be that way."

Cassandra didn't seem to be bothered by me speaking my mind, so I didn't hold back. "He's getting it from somewhere else."

That motherfucker would have to be out of his mind to be celibate when he had a woman like Cassandra, who found some slightly redeeming quality in him.

She stared down at the reins, her gaze never leaving Libby's rust-colored coat.

Libby led herself back into the barn and self-parked beside her stall. I dismounted and took Cassandra's hands, coaching her through getting down. She fell at me rather than hopping down.

It was slightly less graceful than a bird kicking its baby out of a nest.

I caught her as she collided into my chest. "Yeah," I grunted. "We'll work on that."

Instead of making her untack Libby the way Bree and Gracie were always supposed to, I talked her through each step as I did it while she stroked Libby's nose.

"Thanks for the ride," she said as we headed back to the house.

I shoved my hands in my pockets to keep from reaching for her hand. Having her against my body while we were riding felt so natural. The loss of it stung.

"Yeah?" I lifted a curious eyebrow. "You liked it?"

"I didn't say I liked it. I said thank you," she clarified.

But I caught her smiling.

I stopped on the porch and grabbed her discarded high heels. "That's alright, Princess. Keep it to yourself, but I know Libby will win you over eventually."

Cassandra paused in the doorway, leaving us chest-to-chest again. Her eyes were heavy as she studied my mouth. "I doubt it."

"Challenge accepted."

Electricity sizzled between us, sparking and crackling, but neither of us made a move.

Something heavy thumped on the far side of the porch. Cassandra's eyes finally lifted from mine, then rolled.

I looked over my shoulder and found Gracie's pet lumbering up the steps. Someone had put a fresh set of pool noodles on his horns.

"Get out of here, Mickey," she hollered.

I smirked as I threw my arm around her shoulders and steered her inside.

Cassandra would do just fine here. She just didn't know it yet.

"I'M NOT A BREAKFAST PERSON," Cassandra said as she emerged from the guest room.

Of course she wasn't. I kept the thought to myself as I shoveled eggs and sausage onto Bree and Gracie's plates and tried to coax them into eating.

Cassandra didn't float past me. She didn't even strut.

She stomped toward the coffee maker like an angry runway model.

Another day, another pair of heels.

I was starting to wonder how many pairs of shoes she'd brought.

I owned a grand total of three pairs of shoes. A pair of work boots, a pair of dress boots, and a pair of rarely used sneakers.

Cassandra had been here for three days and I had seen five different pairs of shoes.

"Whoa," Gracie said as a waffle hung halfway out of her mouth. She looked at Cassandra like Dolly Parton herself had just walked into the kitchen.

"Where'd you get that dress?" Bree whispered with reverence.

Cassandra didn't pay them any mind as she plucked a mug from the cabinet, inspected it, and deemed it worthy of holding her coffee. "Teddy Crenshaw. It's from his little atelier on Seventh Avenue. He's a designer who used to dress a client of mine and we hit it off."

"You know fashion designers?" Bree squealed, one word tumbling out on top of the next.

Cassandra grimaced like the sound of my daughter's voice was an ice pick to her eyeballs. "It is far too early for that much excitement."

With the girls distracted by breakfast, I grabbed the handle of the coffee pot and held her caffeine hostage.

I kept my voice just low enough for her to hear me. "I know you didn't have enough whiskey in your ice cream to give you a hangover, so this attitude you have with my girls? Cut it out."

Cassandra made eye contact with me as she

wrapped her hand around mine and yanked the coffee pot out from under the machine. "I don't have an attitude."

"My house. My rules. If I say your attitude sucks, then it sucks. Fix it."

She put on a patronizing smile. "I interact with humans. Adults are big humans and children are small humans. I treat them the same, and I speak to them all the same." Her eyebrow raised in a severe arch. "Would you like me to talk down to your small humans and treat them like they're less than an adult?"

"While you're at it, you can fix the attitude you're getting with me, too."

I didn't know why I was so crabby this morning. Even with the impromptu trail ride, I still got a reasonable amount of sleep.

"Side part with a braid down the front, please," Gracie said as she deposited her empty plate in the sink.

"Get the tackle box," I said, leaving Cassandra to the coffee.

"Can you plug the curling iron in?" Bree asked as she stabbed a piece of sausage.

I tackled Gracie's hair first. Even at eleven, she hated brushing it and always missed the tangles in the back. She tossed and turned every night, resulting in a tumbleweed of hair in the morning.

I doused it in detangler and went to work, keenly aware of Cassandra's eyes on me.

When Gracie's hair was tamed and her bangs were held back with a thin braid, I moved on to Bree.

She handed me the heat protectant spray. "Loose curls. Not the tight ones like you do for dance."

I bit back a huff of irritation. I had just mastered the dance ones that made the girls look like Shirley Temple.

Racking my brain, I tried to recall the video tutorial I had watched a few weeks ago during my lunch break.

Bree sat still while I fumbled my way through the soft curls she requested.

It was uncanny how much she looked like Gretchen. Gracie had the Griffith features since birth, but Bree had always looked like her mom.

I knew I was living on borrowed time. Bree was a teenager and Gracie wasn't far behind. Soon, they wouldn't want their dad to fix their hair in the morning.

Maybe that's why I put so much effort into learning how to do it.

I wanted them to need me.

I wanted to be enough.

"How's that?" I asked as I released the clamp on the curling iron, and let the last spiral cool in my hand. I gently combed through the curls to separate and loosen them, then gave her shoulders a squeeze.

Bree scrambled out of the kitchen chair and darted into the bathroom to get a peek in the mirror. "Perfect!"

I left her to douse her hair in hairspray. "You ready to go, Gracie?"

"Putting my shoes on."

"Bree?" I hollered.

"Getting my backpack!"

"Kitchen's closed. Meet me at the truck," I said before turning to Cassandra. "Get a move on, Princess. Can't be late for school."

"You said we were going into town," she bristled.

"We are." I grabbed a thermos from the cupboard and

filled it with the rest of the coffee. “After we take the girls to school.”

Cassandra’s unemotive face never wavered as we loaded up in the truck and headed into town.

Gracie’s mouth ran faster than the truck as she filled Cassandra in on the happenings of the middle school.

Cassandra volleyed back with minimal, barely interested acknowledgements until something piqued her interest.

“What did you say?” Cassandra asked.

Gracie was staring out the window. “What? The part about pajama day where we get to build a fort in the classroom and read books all day?”

I white knuckled the steering wheel as Cassandra shook her head and dismissed Gracie’s excitement.

She and I would be having a very blunt conversation once the little ears weren’t listening.

“No. The other thing about your science class,” Cassandra said.

“Oh.” Gracie’s giddiness faded. “When I said the teacher made me desk buddies with Dylan even though I don’t like Dylan.”

“Gracie,” I chided. “Choose nice words.”

“Why don’t you like this punk?” Cassandra pressed, still craning over the center console so they could be eye to eye.

“We don’t call children ‘punks,’” I hissed.

Cassandra cut her eyes at me. “I’m not a parent. I can say whatever I want about them. Sometimes you gotta call a punk a punk.”

Gracie huffed. “He bothers me during class. I *love*

science and he *hates* science so he just goofs around the whole time and distracts me."

"Did your teacher put you with him intentionally?"

I peered in the rearview mirror to get Gracie's reaction to Cassandra's interrogation, but she didn't seem bothered by it.

"Yeah. She says it's my job to get him to focus. And since I'm good at science, I should be able to help him."

"Absolutely the fuck not."

"*Miss Parker,*" I stated, slamming my palm on the top of the steering wheel to catch her attention. "You *cannot* swear around my girls."

"You swear in front of us all the time, Dad," Bree countered.

Just fucking great.

Cassandra snorted. "I don't think I'm contributing to the delinquency of a minor by saying the F-word, when she's probably seen cows doing the deed since she could walk."

"Sometimes," Gracie said without a care in the world. "But sometimes the cows are artificially incinerated."

"Inseminated," I corrected.

"Like I'm the one corrupting them," Cassandra muttered before putting her game face back on. "Talking about livestock insemination is *totally* normal."

I watched out of the corner of my eye as Cassandra put on a smug smile and let out a quiet breath.

"Listen to me," she began. "You are not responsible for anyone but yourself. Unless you're getting a paycheck to be a teacher or a babysitter—that punk, Dylan, isn't your concern. I don't care if he's running circles around the classroom with his clothes on fire. *He is not your prob-*

lem. If he wants to be a distraction, let him. If he makes a mess, let him sit in his own shit. It's the teacher's job to teach him. Not yours. You keep your eyes on the lesson. Put your blinders on and stay unbothered."

I ... couldn't argue with that.

Cassandra pointed a manicured nail at Gracie. "Are you on the payroll?"

"No, ma'am," Gracie said with more assertiveness than I had ever heard her muster.

"Is that kid your responsibility?" she pressed.

"No, ma'am!"

"If he wants to be a problem, what are you gonna do?" Cassandra snapped.

But it wasn't a question spawned out of irritation. She was a coach. A drill sergeant.

Gracie beamed. "Let him run around on fire."

Cassandra blinked at Gracie, stunned, before turning to sit back in her seat. "This family is so weird."

10

CHRISTIAN

"Have a good day," I said as the girls climbed out of the truck and onto the sidewalk.

Teachers and parents stared when they realized I had a woman in the front seat.

Rumors about my dating life circulated from time to time, but I kept to myself. It minimized the fuel for the wildfire of small-town gossip.

"Love you, Daddy," Bree said.

"Love you too, beautiful."

"I love you, Daddy," Gracie chirped as she shouldered her backpack.

"I love you, pretty girl."

Before I could get another word out, Gracie beamed at Cassandra. "Bye, Miss Cass. Have a day as pretty as you are!" And with that, she skipped down the sidewalk, laughing with her sister.

The carpool monitor shut the doors, and I pulled out of the line to head into town. Cassandra didn't say a word, but the corner of her lips twitched.

When my tires left the school property, she broke. "Let me guess. I'm about to get chewed out."

I caught a whiff of expensive perfume and wondered if it was a fragrance she chose for herself or if her dick-face fiancé had bought it for her.

"Go ahead," she said, closing her eyes as she relaxed on the headrest. "Let me have it."

"Why do you think I'd chew you out?" I asked as I shifted, resting my wrist on the top of the steering wheel.

She tapped a finger on her lip. "Where do I even begin? For corrupting your children. For talking to her like an adult. For—"

"Telling my girl how to advocate for herself?" I cut in.

Cassandra peered over at me.

A sad smile crept up without warning. "They're growing up. It's probably good that someone balances out my desire to keep them little forever. Once in a while, at least."

She pretended to gag, and it made me laugh under my breath.

"I don't know if you've noticed this about me," Cassandra said as she inspected her nails. "But I'm not a kid person."

"You're not much of an adult person either," I added. "Or an animal person."

"I'm not big into being needed. I like my space."

"That's funny coming from someone whose whole career is based on being needed."

"There's a difference between wanting to be needed and needing to be in control. I like being in control."

I bet Cassandra thought she liked control, until she finally let someone else take it.

I pulled into the small downtown district and parked along the sidewalk. "I'll be a few hours. I'm meeting a grain supplier, then I gotta run some errands and pick up supplies from the hardware store."

She eyed the line of quaint storefronts. "A few hours alone of shopping and—" she spotted the coffee shop with a blinking WiFi sign "*—high speed internet.*" Cassandra lunged for the door. "Sweet, sweet civilization. I missed you."

I managed to make it out and around to her door before she jumped out, but just barely. I grabbed the door handle and blocked her in.

"Please," she begged.

Huh. I liked that.

"What's the rule, Cass?"

She rolled her eyes.

I pressed in, wedging my knee between hers as she pivoted in the seat to climb down.

God, that perfume was so fucking pretty...

"Please," she groused.

"I open the doors."

"Let me out," she pleaded in a whisper. "I need society. I need to walk into a store. I need to see asphalt and cars. I need coffee that's made in an espresso machine."

"Cass."

She huffed and rolled her eyes, but turned and sat back in her seat.

I closed the door. With a dramatic flourish, I reopened it and offered my hand to help her down.

Her palm was soft as it slid into mine. Delicate fingers draped over my skin.

She stepped down and stopped when we were hip to hip. "Dramatic much?"

"Was it so hard to let me do that for you?"

Thick lashes lifted and her stormy eyes met mine. "Yes."

I smirked. "Deal with it, Princess."

Cassandra didn't move. Her tongue peeked out and wet her lip. I was captivated by the way her throat constricted as she swallowed.

The sparks were back, dancing off of us in sprays.

My hand brushed hers; fingers almost twining. The sharp edge of her ring caught me by surprise.

I moved back and took a breath, letting her step up onto the sidewalk.

That fucking diamond sparkled in the morning sun.

"You, uh—" I cleared my throat. "You have my number, right?"

She looked at me like I was daft. "We've spent nearly every waking moment together since I got here. When have I needed your number?"

I held my palm out and she relented, giving me her phone.

When I gave it back, she looked at the screen. "Really?" Her tone was flat and unamused.

I grinned. "What?"

She turned the screen around. "Daddy Griffith?"

"I figured since you're so opposed to children and people in general, that'll lessen the likelihood of you calling." I stepped off the sidewalk and shut the passenger door. "I put CJ's number, Nate's number, and the main house's landline in there too."

Cassandra looked down and scrolled through.

"Daddy Griffith... Cow Boss ... GI Joe... Prison." She slid it back into her oversized purse. "Very funny."

"See you in a few hours, Cass," I called as I walked around to the driver's side.

"It's Cassandra," she said, pivoting on those fuck-me heels to head toward the coffee shop.

I pressed my fist to my mouth to hide my smile. "Stay out of trouble, Princess."

Her ass had an extra swing in it as she strutted away.

I climbed in the truck and leaned back against the seat, closing my eyes.

I just needed a minute.

It usually took me two or three minutes of breathing to let the stress go, but after a mere thirty seconds, I was calm.

Cassandra's perfume lingered in the cab, dancing over my morning coffee and the ever-present smell of cattle and diesel. It was sweet and sultry. Womanly and strong.

I had risen with the sun since I was a child. Mornings were my favorite time of day. But now, all I wanted was to fall asleep to that scent.

I didn't have time for that, though. The day was wasting away while I sat and fantasized about a woman who wasn't mine.

Whispers floated through the bank lobby as I filled out deposit slips.

Muttered comments were made as I perused the boot store.

Chatter ran around the hardware store as I loaded up the bed of my truck with fencing.

Murmurs filled the diner as I sat with George Thompson, negotiating prices for the winter feed I was sourcing from his farm.

All those rumblings were about one person.

Her.

I gave Mr. Thompson a firm handshake and thanked him for driving out here from Maren.

Cassandra hadn't texted or called, so I assumed she was alive and headed to the gas station.

A familiar truck pulled through the Buc-ee's lot and parked in a space by the front doors.

I let out a sharp whistle as the numbers on the gas pump ticked higher and higher.

Nate's head whipped around as he jumped down and slammed the door shut. "Hey," he hollered as he crossed the parking lot.

I tipped my chin. "What'chu doing in town?"

Nate shoved his hands into the pockets of his jeans. "Becks had a craving."

"Should've called. I would've brought something back so you didn't have to drive all the way out here."

He shrugged. "Didn't know how long you'd be."

He was in a t-shirt today, which surprised me.

Nearly ten years ago, he had been injured during a tour in Iraq. Burn scars mottled his hand and arm. He didn't talk about it much, and usually wore sleeved shirts so it wouldn't upset our mom.

Guilt seared me like a brand.

When we got the call that he was being treated at the Army hospital in Germany, my world came crashing down. Gretchen passed not long after that.

Thank God for Ray.

The other middle Griffith brother was Uncle of the

Year to Bree and Gracie when I could barely function as their father.

I couldn't save Gretchen.

I couldn't keep Nate from getting injured by a suicide bomber.

It should have made me hold my girls closer. It should have made me grateful that Nate was okay.

But it only made me guilty.

"Had to take care of some business." I yanked the pump out of the gas tank and put it back on the cradle. "Brought Cassandra with me so she could pick up some stuff she needed."

Nate let a smile slip as he crossed one arm over the other. "How's she doing?"

I worked it over in my brain for a second. "She's tough. She'll be alright."

"Sounds like Becks when I met her on deployment."

I laughed. "Nah. It's not like that. We don't actively hate each other."

Her snippy remarks didn't bother me. Our banter—it wasn't fighting. *It felt like foreplay.*

"How are you doing with it?" he asked.

"Unaffected," I lied, leaning casually against the truck.

Nate howled. "Now you sound like me when I met Becks. So, bullshit."

I shook my head. "It's not like that. She's engaged."

"And I was still trying to convince Vanessa not to divorce me," he countered.

"It's not the same thing."

Nate's ex-wife was a cold-hearted bitch. Cassandra's fiancé was a sneaky little weasel.

Nate lowered his voice. "It's been ten years."

"And in those ten years I've gone to more therapy than you have." I raised my hands. "I'm good, man. I've dated, I've had flings. I'm not repressed and I'm not blind. Cass—I like her even though I think she's dead set on trying to make me hate her. And yeah. I think she's attractive. But I'm not crossing any lines with an engaged woman, or with my girls under the same roof."

He stepped back and nodded. "That's fair. I'm just making sure your head's on straight." Checking the time, he added, "I'd better run in and get Becks her brisket tacos."

We split, Nate heading inside and me jumping back in the truck. When I put my number in Cassandra's phone, I called myself so I'd have hers. I fired off a text.

CHRISTIAN

Heading back your way. Where are you at?

CASS

I decided that "Daddy Griffith" makes me think of your father, so I changed your contact to "Cowboy Daddy." I'm at the nail salon getting some work done while this lovely lady makes my feet look less ogre-like. Be done in half an hour.

CHRISTIAN

You seem like you're in a better mood.

CASS

A proper latte, retail therapy, and a mani-pedi will do that.

CHRISTIAN

See you soon, Princess.

Twenty-five minutes later, I pulled up to the nail salon. Instead of waiting it out in the truck, I moseyed inside and spotted her sitting tall in a throne.

While the nail artist finished her pedicure, I squared up with the receptionist.

"What's the damage, Margo?" Cassandra asked, appearing next to me at the front desk when she was done.

Margo, who was apparently Cassandra's new best friend, beamed. "Not a dime, honey. Mr. Griffith took care of it. Tip and all."

Her eyebrows lifted as she whipped around. "You did what?"

I didn't want to talk about it, so I reached for her shopping bags instead. "Let me carry those."

"I can—" she paused and huffed. "You're going to make a scene if I carry my bags and open the door, aren't you?"

I smirked. "Yes, ma'am." Looking over her head, I nodded toward the salon. "Have a good day, folks."

"You paid for me?" Cassandra asked abruptly when we hit the sidewalk.

I unlocked the truck and put her shopping bags in the back before opening her door. "Yeah."

She paused in front of me instead of climbing in. "Why?" It wasn't curiosity. It was blatant mistrust.

"Because I thought it'd make you happy," I said simply. "You've had a time of it out here, and if I can do something easy like that to make it better, I will."

Then, just because I knew *he* wouldn't give her a fucking compliment without it being backhanded as hell, I said, "Your nails look real pretty."

Blush painted her cheeks as she climbed into the truck and picked up the box that was waiting for her in the seat.

"What's this?" she asked as I slid behind the wheel.

"Boots."

She lifted an eyebrow as she shimmed open the box. "You wear a women's size seven?"

I chuckled. "They're for you."

"Why?"

"What's with you and all your why's?"

"Gifts come with strings," she said as she smoothed her fingers down the lacquered leather.

"Not mine." I pulled out of the space and headed toward the ranch. "I said that I did something easy to make it better for you. I never said I would take it easy on you." I stretched my arm across the back of her shoulders. "How was the nail salon? Up to your big city standards? You feel pampered?"

She smirked, a wicked look lifting her lips. "Oh, it wasn't pampering."

"No?"

She cracked her knuckles. "It was reconnaissance."

11

CASSANDRA

"I thought you were working from Chris's house," Becks said as she waddled into the warehouse office. She was drenched in sweat.

I looked up from the notebook I was plotting in like a mad woman. "Sometimes," I said as I shifted over to my laptop and added to the spreadsheet on the screen.

"The internet's faster over there," she said.

"Yes, however, there are children. I cannot work in the presence of mayhem."

Becks looked at the time. "Early dismissal day?"

"Something like that."

Becks's smile was easy as she lowered into a chair and tossed her hair over her shoulder. "They're not that bad. It's not like they're toddlers. Bree's a teenager and Gracie isn't far behind."

"Even worse," I said as my fingers flew over the keys. "I remember being a teenager. I was a hormonal psychopath." I saved the file and turned back to her.

"Why does it look like someone dumped a bucket of water on your head?"

She groaned. "I'm trying to make myself go into labor. I did a five-mile walk around the property."

"Why on earth would you want to do that?" I shuddered. "Granted, I'm not sure what possessed you to get pregnant in the first place."

Becks snorted. "My husband's big di—"

I lifted a hand and silenced her right then and there.

She laughed softly. "Time flies. Chris's girls were seven and four when I first met them. It's crazy to think that Nathan and I are older than Chris is, but his kids will be grown soon and we're just starting." She looked rather wistful as she laced her hands together on top of her stomach.

"You'll be exhausted," I said pragmatically.

"That's an understatement." She closed her eyes. "I'm hoping for an epidural just so I can take a nap before the baby's born. I haven't slept well in weeks."

"How's the water damage situation?" I said, recalling what she had said about a busted pipe flooding their house.

She sighed. "Nathan's working on it. Hopefully, I'll be back in my bed before we have another occupant. For what it's worth, I'm sorry our spare bedroom is out of commission. You probably would have preferred that over shacking up with Chris and the girls. But, by the time it's fixed, we'll have a newborn."

"We're *not* shacking up," I clarified as I searched my phone for an old contact who owed me a favor after I got their brand out of hot water.

"Right," Becks said dryly. "Because you're engaged to Tripp."

"You've never been one to hold back," I noted as I shuffled papers around. My train of thought had been derailed at the mere mention of his name. "Why start now?"

Becks cocked her head, ginger hair spilling down her shoulder. "Are you actually happy with him?"

"Of course." The lie was bold-faced, but my façade was all I had left. I was crumbling on the inside. "Why wouldn't I be?"

"Because he's abysmal to be around."

"He's just driven," I countered, though I didn't know why I was defending him. He had done nothing but throw me under the bus, then lock me away.

Out of sight, out of mind.

"Can I be mean for a second?" she blurted out.

I raised my eyebrows. "Is anything stopping you?"

"Not really, and the baby hormones overpower my filter." She looked rather fired up and I was more than a little curious.

"Then by all means..."

"Tripp is the worst. If I could hit him with a dump truck, I would."

I couldn't help the unladylike laugh that ripped out of my chest. "I wish you weren't pregnant. I need someone to get wine drunk with."

She smirked. "Chris would be a great drinking buddy."

Oh god no. The fireworks that sizzled between the two of us nearly scorched me when he picked me up from the nail salon. I didn't know what would happen if I let my guard down around him.

"Tripp is..." I tried to think of some redeeming quality that would help me come to his defense, but I fell short.

"Look," Becks said. "I get it. I loved the city. I love the grind. But maybe being out here isn't a bad thing. When I pulled away from it all, I found Nathan. But I found myself, too. Are you really happy or are you just acting happy because the sum of your personal and professional life says you're supposed to be?"

Was she right? Was I just holding on to him because it was what I was supposed to want?

Instead of admitting that the comment hit a little too close to home, I flipped my hair. "I'm successful. I'll take that over happiness any day."

"You work for success. You deserve happiness."

I pressed my lips together. "Look at you. Already armed with the cliché parent-isms."

The door swung open and Christian filled the frame. My blood sang at the mere sight of him.

Blue jeans that were pale and faded with age clung to his ass and thighs. They stretched and strained as he strode across the office. His boots thumped heavily against the cement floor.

"Becks," he said as a no-nonsense greeting.

I could respect that.

"How you feeling?" he asked.

And there he went with the feelings again. Absolutely unnecessary.

"Tired. Everything hurts. I think I broke a rib after being punched from the inside all night long." Becks huffed. "But I'll get out of your hair. I've got a nap calling my name."

Christian gave her a sympathetic smile. "Want me to drive you up to the house?"

"Nah." She eased out of the chair. "Thanks, but I'm trying to get this baby to drop."

He nodded as he walked behind me and braced his hands on the desk, trapping me between them as he reached for the desktop computer mouse. "Sit tight. I just have to print something off."

I stiffened as his chest pressed against the back of my head.

Becks pointed between Christian and me and wiggled her eyebrows as she mouthed, "Oh my god!"

I rolled my eyes as the printer spat out a sheet of paper. "Go take your nap."

She cackled as she wobbled out into the bright afternoon sun.

"Wanna tell me what that was about?" Christian asked.

"Not even a little bit."

He had printed his document, but still kept me caged between his arms.

His chest was right there. He smelled like the great outdoors and leather. His softness pressed against me again as he peered over my shoulder.

I closed my eyes and remembered the way it had felt to have him behind me on the horse. All warm and safe. If I was being honest, I daydreamed about what it would feel like for him to hug me.

Tripp wasn't a hugger. We had done it a few times, but

it was always awkward and stiff. He was a "kiss on the cheek when saying hello" kind of guy.

It would feel so good...

What if I just...

...Just for a minute.

"Plans coming along?" he asked, snapping me out of the day dream.

"What? Um—" I cleared my throat. "Yes. I should have a working concept by the end of the day."

He hummed deep in his throat as he thumbed through my notes. "That's a lot of numbers. I thought you just did branding and shit."

"Everything is money," I insisted. "And you'll be appreciative that I can operate within a budget."

He hummed something non-committal.

I slammed the notebook shut. "These are not ready for client eyes yet, but you can tell your father that I'll have a presentation ready at four if he'd like to hear it."

"I think you're forgetting who makes the decisions around here, Princess."

I looked over my shoulder, peering at one strong arm. "I think you're forgetting that I don't work for you. I work for your father."

"You work for the ranch, ergo you work for me. Trust me, my dad will just tell you to talk to me."

"Do you take all your employees on midnight horseback rides?" I countered.

He let go of the desk and took a few steps away, giving us both a little breathing room. "It wasn't midnight."

"The point still stands."

I watched as he licked his lips, trying to calm himself—

though he wasn't doing a very good job of it. I had started to learn his tells. From the outside, he was cool and collected, but I could tell Christian was on edge. A powerful energy ran through him. It was a living, breathing danger.

Becks's comment from my first night here floated through my memory. *It makes me wonder how he gets all his stress out.*

Suddenly, I was wondering too.

"I'll see you at four." Christian grabbed the paper and stormed out. Of course, that just meant he walked out all calm and casual, but there was an unmistakable tension between us.

FOUR O' clock came and went without a single appearance by Christian. The only visitor to the office was Mickey, who nearly broke a window had it not been for the pool noodle on his horn.

This place was so bizarre.

I reviewed the plan I had compiled one more time, alternating between making small tweaks to the language and checking the clock.

For some reason, not hearing from Tripp for days didn't eat at me the way Christian being an hour late did.

I stared at the pages, feeling stupid for getting excited to show him what I had come up with.

I never got giddy about work. Being Lillian Monroe's publicist was like being a chess coach for a Godzilla. I stood on the sidelines, whispering what moves to make while she stomped all over the board and terrorized civilians.

It was ninety percent frustration, which made the nine percent that ended in success complete elation.

Then there was the one percent that ended it all.

I didn't realize how much I missed business consulting. It ignited part of my brain that craved to be used for more than damage control, quippy responses, and official statements online.

Not that I didn't like doing that. It put my sass and sarcasm to good use. But I liked the big-picture stuff; the long-term projects.

I liked being the architect, not the firefighter.

The radio sitting in the cradle on Christian's desk chirped. "Cass."

Was I supposed to answer that? It sounded like Christian, but everyone on the ranch had access to all the channels, so conversations stayed short and business only.

He had given me a quick run-down on the radio system on my second day, but I had never needed to use one.

"Cass. You still in the office?"

I huffed and eased out of the chair as the static-filled message came across again.

What did I answer with? Hello? Cassandra Parker speaking? Yeah, I'm still here waiting for you?

I pressed the button and decided to answer it the way he always did. "Go ahead."

"I'm sorry I didn't make it back up there by four. I'm hung up on the northeast side working a problem with CJ."

Something inside me lurched. I almost asked if he was okay.

Then my mind went to the girls. They had gotten out of school early. Were they still at the house by themselves? Were they allowed to be alone that long?

Rule number one of public relations floated through my mind. *Don't give fuel to people holding matches.*

The ranch hands already hated me. Why would I make them think I cared?

"We can reschedule the meeting," I clipped, keeping it vague and professional for the other listening ears on the line.

"I'll be back tonight," he said.

The girls...

But before I could bring it up, his voice came over the line again. "Momma's got the girls up at her house, so you're on your own for dinner. You good with that?"

Mickey, the long-horned menace squeezed through the door and lumbered into the office.

"Only if I can cook the cow that's currently taking up residence at my desk."

A chorus of voices came on the line from different radios. "Get lost, Mickey," they said together.

Slowly, he backed his bovine ass up and retreated outside.

There was a pause. Was I supposed to say something? For someone who was used to being around the public eye, I didn't like the spotlight on me. I preferred to lurk in the shadows. Talking to Christian should have been all business, but it didn't feel like it.

Christian's voice was softer as it came across the line again. "See you tonight, Cass."

I gathered my things and piddled around Christian's

house, reheating a container of leftovers I found in the fridge.

I had just slipped out of the shower when the front door opened. Bree and Gracie's voices filled the house. The dog joined in, raising the volume to an ear-piercing decibel.

I listened from the solitude of the simple guest room. Christian's deep timbre calmed the chaos.

Muffled voices clouded together as they hung out for a few minutes before he sent them to bed and doled out goodnight kisses.

The bathroom door clicked and locked, and the shower squeaked on.

After failing to focus on a few chapters of a murder mystery I swiped from Christian's bookshelf, I took a chance and tiptoed out of the bedroom, heading for the porch.

I missed the amenities of big-city living, but maybe Becks was onto something when she talked about taking a break from it all.

I used to be afraid of slowing down. If I slowed, I'd have to confront the things I was running from.

If I sat in peace and quiet, I couldn't drown out my intuition with hustle and bustle.

Being kicked out of my beloved city and put on a strict social media blackout forced me to sit with myself.

I hated it.

Silently, I closed the guest room door behind me and rounded the corner as the bathroom door opened.

Christian stepped out with a towel wrapped low around his hips and tucked under his belly. Steam clouded around him as droplets of water clung to his arms and chest.

My heart rammed in my ribcage as I took in the bear of a man in front of me.

His hair hung in long, damp strands. His beard glimmered from the shower like it was covered in diamonds. I wasn't usually attracted to chest hair. *Or at least I didn't think I was. Tripp always waxed his.*

But Christian...

He was soft everywhere, but unmistakably strong. His bulk was sexy. Rugged, but still safe. I was drawn to him like a moth to a porch light. I ached to know what it was like to be in his arms. To feel the potent mix of comfort and attraction.

His eyes were soft as he looked at me with an uncanny warmth.

"Hey." The single syllable was gruff, but tender.

"Hi," I said on an exhale.

His solid frame shook as he shifted, holding the towel together with one heavy hand. Dark brown hair ran from his navel down to...

I wanted him to drop that towel.

The realization slammed into me, stealing the wind out of my sails.

What the hell was I doing?

"About today—"

"It's fine," I blurted out.

Christian shook his head, then said the sexiest thing I had ever heard. "It's not fine. I told you I'd be there, and I wasn't. So, I'm sorry."

I was so fucked.

12

CHRISTIAN

Cassandra looked at me, wide-eyed and blinking. She looked baffled.

I didn't know why, either.

But the way her lips parted with a soft exhale of shock made my dick wake up and press against the towel.

I hid it behind my hand as I stood there, dripping from the shower.

I cleared my throat. "I know it's after your working hours. But if you'll give me a second, I'll throw on some clothes and we can talk."

Cassandra stammered for a moment. "Right. Talk. Okay."

I hid my laugh until I made it back to my room. I liked seeing her flustered.

There were so many sides to Cassandra Parker. She was a consummate professional. A dedicated publicist. A savvy businesswoman.

But she was so much more than her job, and maybe that's where I had gotten it wrong when we first met.

She was fiercely protective. She didn't pick her battles; she fought every damn one.

Cassandra wasn't necessarily flexible, but she was willing to storm a castle, plop down on the throne, and stake her claim.

She didn't mind sticking out like a sore thumb. She was who she was, and I respected that.

Hell—I liked it.

A lot.

Not that I would do anything about it.

She was prickly when it came to kids. I understood that some people weren't "kid people," but I didn't put up with unwarranted attitudes aimed at my girls.

My mind wandered back to Cassandra's inquisition when she rode along with me to take the girls to school. I had bristled at the way she pressed Gracie for answers, but Gracie wasn't bothered by it.

In fact, she came back from school a whole new kid.

Parenting was fucking hard. Bree and Gracie had gone through the full spectrum of pain and grief when we lost Gretchen. I wanted to protect them as much as I could. I wanted to shield them from being hurt.

But Cassandra... Her little speech hadn't shielded Gracie. *It armed her*.

I finished throwing on a pair of sweatpants and a clean shirt, grabbed a couple beers from the fridge, and found Cassandra on the porch.

She had changed too, wearing cream colored yoga pants and a loose matching sweater that slumped off her shoulder.

Her skin peeked out, a warm ivory that looked smooth as silk.

God, I wanted to run my hands over it.

I lifted the beers, offering her one. "Sorry I don't have anything nicer. I drink the cheap stuff."

Her smile was seductive and dangerous as she took the bottle. "Then it's a good thing I don't usually drink beer and won't know the difference."

She had perched herself on one side of the porch swing, tucking her legs beneath her, so I took the other half.

"Everything get taken care of today?"

"Yeah," I grunted. "They were having trouble moving the herd and needed another body."

Cassandra hummed as she wrapped her lips around the mouth of the bottle and took a drink. "Gentle pressure, right?"

"That's right." I kept one foot planted on the porch, gently rocking us back and forth as the crickets sang. "You ready to show me what you've got in there?" I asked, using the bottom of my beer to tap the manila folder in her lap.

Freshly manicured nails slid between the pages and opened them up to a budget breakdown. She pilfered through the stack until she found the page she was looking for.

Her countenance went from soft to shrewd in the blink of an eye. "When Becks connected me with your father, the goals he expressed were for me to create additional revenue streams that utilize the resources at hand. He told me a little bit about the last few years. Between the drought, a disease outbreak in the herd, and the economy being trash, he wanted to expand beyond cattle as a failsafe if it happens again."

Guilt dropped into my stomach like an anvil.

I had done everything I could to keep the ranch afloat. I knew my dad was right, but that didn't mean it didn't suck balls.

No matter how much I tried to keep the bad stuff from happening—how much I tried to protect my family from it—dust storms happened.

"My goal is to bring ideas to the table that don't affect the day-to-day of the ranch."

I covered my discomfort with a laugh as I took a swig and stretched my arm across the back of the porch swing. "Just hit me with it, Cass."

"Working within the available budget, my recommendation is that the ranch builds an equine program. I'm thinking boarding, riding lessons, track-out camps and summer camps. An equine therapy program would be a great draw as well. There's a void in the community for programs that support kids with special needs. Copious amounts of evidence supports the idea that equine therapy greatly benefits children with autism spectrum disorders. You could coordinate with adult rehab programs for substance abuse or domestic abuse recovery. If Nathan is involved in any support groups for veterans, that would be a good connection. You could block out sessions to donate and use it as a tax write-off. Your biggest costs would be more horses, obviously. The barn could use an upgrade. Some cosmetic updates around the property—but just where customers would see. An indoor arena would be great, but it's not necessary for the first few years. You'd only need to bring on one staff member to run it. You or the ranch hands could pitch in if necessary."

I reached over and took the file from her, perusing the pages as she finished weighing the pros and cons of the equine program.

I had to admit, it was a good idea.

"No," I said as I closed the file and handed it back.

Cassandra paled. "What do you mean, no?"

"It's good, but it's not right."

Her face hardened, and her eyebrow twitched with frustration. "What is causing you concern the most? Let's start there." Her tone was unsettlingly frosty, like she wanted to rage and bitch me out, but she was holding it together for professionalism's sake.

"All of it."

Her fingers flexed, trembling before she balled them into a fist. "Be a problem solver, not a problem."

I chuckled. "I'm going to start using that with the girls."

Cassandra huffed and pressed her fingers into her temples. "Work with me here. I need to know what your concerns are so I can mitigate or eliminate them."

"It's not big enough."

She looked stunned. "You've gotta be fucking kidding me, Griffith," she muttered with manic disbelief as she pushed out of the swing and started pacing the porch.

"Listen, it's good. It's just—"

"Not enough." Cassandra looked gutted.

Shit. She thought this was about her.

My heart sank. "Cass, listen to me," I said as I hunched forward and rested my elbows on my knees. I tapped the folder. "This is good. It is. Any other client would probably give you a bonus for doing something reasonable and staying within the budget."

"Let me guess," she spouted off. "You're going to hit me with some vague cowboy fortune cookie saying that will give me an epiphany in the middle of the night, two months from now."

"Do you think I'm Mr. Miyagi or something?" I sifted my fingers through my hair. It had mostly dried and was starting to curl. "No, sweetheart. I just think if we're gonna do it, we've gotta make it worth our time."

Her long string of curses ended with "fucking cowboys."

I caught her hand when her pacing path came close enough. "Cass, listen to me. You did a good job. I want more because I want to see what happens when you don't hold yourself back."

Her jaw ticked, but she didn't pull away.

"The more you ask of me, the longer I'm here."

I leaned back on the swing seat and took another sip. "Do you have somewhere else to be?"

"Time is money."

"You're being paid well. I authorize the checks myself."

Her gaze darted away like she was avoiding the topic.

"Why'd you take this job?" I pressed.

"Becks—"

"I know Becks made the connection. But why did you say yes?"

Cassandra swallowed. "I either had to take my lumps and go on the assignment no one wanted, or be out of a job."

"What are you talking about?"

Her beer nearly slipped from her fingers. I caught the

bottle before it shattered on the porch and set it by my foot. "Hey—"

But Cassandra just waved me off as she blinked away the glossy coating that blurred her pretty eyes. "I'll circle back when I have a more concrete plan that aligns with your goals."

"Will you cut the corporate shit and just sit with me for two goddamn minutes?"

She looked stunned that I had snapped at her.

Frankly, so was I.

Not much fazed me. But she did.

I dropped the folder on the ground and patted the spot she had vacated. Cassandra's jaw flexed as she gritted her teeth, debating whether or not she would be compliant.

I waited her out and kept slowly rocking on the swing.

Finally, Cassandra plopped back down onto the swing. "Look, I've signed NDAs out the ass. So if I tell you this, you have to swear to me that you'll never say a word about it. Not to your brothers. Definitely not to your kids. Not even to the fucking cows."

I lifted my eyebrows, but didn't say anything.

Cassandra amused me. Her spunk was entertaining.

"Well?" she pressed.

"You told me not to say anything."

Cassandra huffed and rolled her eyes.

I took a swig of my beer and snickered. "I promise."

She took a deep breath. "Do you know who Lillian Monroe is?"

"Sounds vaguely familiar."

"She's an actress."

"Can't remember the last time I watched a movie."

Cassandra smirked as she leaned down and snagged her beer. "You're not missing much."

I reclined on the swing, kicking my feet out and resting my arm across the back of it. Her hair danced across my arm like a whisper. "Tell me."

Her spine stiffened when I grazed her shoulder with my fingers. "Lillian was my client. She had a very public meltdown at an awards show, threw me under the bus, and is now sunning herself in Spain while I got exiled to a cattle ranch that doesn't have WiFi."

"We have WiFi."

She shot me a glare, but there was a good-natured twinkle behind it. "It's basically dial-up without the obnoxious sound. Carrier pigeons would be faster."

"Isn't your 'betrothed' in Spain?" I asked as I finished off my beer.

Damn, I really wished I had another bottle. I hated thinking about that fetid sock puppet she was engaged to.

Cassandra muttered a handful of pointed profanities under her breath before taking a long drink. "Yeah," she said as she wiped her mouth with the back of her hand. "I became *persona non grata*, and he took over as her publicist."

"What happened?"

She leaned back, resting the back of her head against my arm. "She earned herself a second DUI. Her legal counsel and I worked some magic and got the judge to agree to inpatient rehab instead of jail time. She was admitted against her will by court order and did three months there while I did some serious damage control and cleaned up her reputation."

I gave a strand of cornsilk hair a gentle tug. "Still not seeing where you're the bad guy."

"I gave her a day after getting out of rehab to reintegrate into her life. Two days later, I had her presenting at an award show she was snubbed at last year. It was supposed to be a way for her to garner a little goodwill. You know—show how mature she had become. The whole 'clap for others even if you don't win' thing." Cassandra sighed. "I watched Lillian like a hawk. I swear I did. She only drank what I gave her and none of it was alcoholic. I wanted a second set of eyes on her in case I got pulled away, so Tripp worked the event with me. One of us was with her at all times. She was stone-cold sober when Tripp took her backstage to get ready to present, but when she went on stage she was swinging like a pendulum and slurring her words."

I saw the frustration in her eyes. Cassandra prided herself on how good she was at her job. For it to be taken away from her because she couldn't control a full-grown woman was unfair in every way.

I often spouted off the "life isn't fair" adage to the girls, but this wasn't fucking fair.

"She went off." Cassandra tipped her beer back and chugged. "And I mean *off*. Got up to the microphone, took one look at the teleprompter, then started ranting about how she should have won last year. How the girl who won didn't deserve it. She pulled a flask out from between her boobs, did a shot on live TV, then said I was the one who always got her drunk so I'd have a job. She said that I paid off the judge and sent her to a spa because she didn't need rehab. She accused me of starving her, hiding her keys, taking her phone away, and locking her out of her social media accounts so she couldn't communicate with anyone. She said a million other vile lies before they finally cut to commercial and Tripp swooped in to get her off the stage. The poor girl who was supposed to win the award was devastated that her moment was ruined, and I was ousted from the industry."

I scrubbed my hand down my beard. "Shit."

"You can say that again. None of it is true, by the way. I did my job. We honored the legal process. I tried to protect her from herself, but I wasn't a prison guard." She let out a quiet breath and looked out at the black sky full of stars. "I made my case to the higher-ups at the Carrington Group. I was relying on the fact that Tripp had been there with me and knew I did my job well, but he didn't back me up. Just said it would look bad if he was the only one defending me because we were engaged."

I looked down at her hand when she said "were" engaged.

But that fucking ring was still there.

"He should have been the first to defend you."

Cassandra didn't say anything as she traced the lip of the beer bottle with her finger. "He was the first to defend *her.*"

That raised my hackles.

"They said I was too much of a liability to pair with another high-profile client. Becks had been asking around about business consultants, so I got the ultimatum to either hide down here until the storm blew over and they could assign me to a new client or look for a new job."

"Look," I said, turning on the swing so I could face her. "Not that I'm not appreciative of the work you're doing here, but why the fuck did you take your lumps to stay with a company where you're not wanted?"

She tilted her head. Her ear grazed my arm as she quietly admitted, "I'm scared that if I leave my job, Tripp and I will grow apart."

"So you stayed, and yet you're still apart."

She swallowed and looked down, blinking back tears.

Just because I felt like she needed it, and it was something I'd do for my girls or Becks or my mom, I put my arm around her shoulders and pulled her to my side. "Let me tell you something, Cass."

I knew she wanted to argue with me for continuity's sake, but her lips quirked into a half-smile instead.

"We might have a whole lot of differences, but I see your value here and I appreciate your work. I'm not just putting up with you."

13

CASSANDRA

"Miss Cass!" Gracie shouted as she bolted in from school and threw her backpack across the living room.

I looked up from my laptop and observed the melee as Christian's children barreled in.

"Gracie, honey." Christian's mom, Claire, carted a cardboard diorama into the house and slid it onto the kitchen counter. "Miss Parker is still working."

"Okay, but I need to talk to Miss Cass," Bree announced when she strolled in.

Claire huffed. "Girls, head upstairs and do your homework." She checked her watch. "Your father should be back in an hour or so. I've gotta head up to my house and get started on supper."

"We're fine," they chirped.

Claire pointed a finger. "Give Miss Parker her space."

Were they just going to keep talking about me like I wasn't here?

"Yes ma'am," the girls mumbled together as they tromped up the stairs.

Her stern gaze turned to me. "You need anything, sweetheart?"

The moniker usually would have made my skin prickle. I still wasn't used to the homegrown workplace dynamic I had been thrust into, but it didn't make me want to crawl out of my skin as much as it had when I first arrived.

"I'm fine. Thanks," I said as I turned my attention back to the computer screen so Claire didn't feel like she had to linger.

But linger, she did.

"You coming up to the house for dinner with the rest of the motley crew?"

I glanced at the time. "Thank you for your hospitality, but no. I'll likely still be working."

"Hospitality?" She let out a blustering huff. "Cass, there ain't a shred of hospitality being doled out on this lot. I feed everyone because it's what I do." She planted her hands on her hips. "Now you can show up and eat a plate or you can ration whatever leftovers Chris has in his fridge. But this isn't hospitality. It's family. Learn the difference."

And with that, she stomped out the door with the grace of a bull.

I rubbed my eyes, trying to keep the numbers on the screen from blurring together. I had a migraine from looking at this damn budget.

If Christian wanted a revitalization project that was larger than his wallet, he was going to get one.

I settled back into the blissful quiet and had just finalized the list of investors I needed to reach out to when thunder erupted from upstairs.

Bree and Gracie tumbled past each other as they fought for first place in getting down the steps.

"Miss Cass!" Gracie shouted.

"No, I want to talk to her first!" Bree hollered.

"I got down here first," Gracie grunted as she elbowed her sister out of the way and rounded the corner into the living room.

"I'm older!"

"I don't care!"

"I want to—"

Without lifting my eyes from my screen, I raised my palm and stopped them in their tracks. The twin tornadoes ceased immediately.

I dropped my hands back onto the keyboard and typed the names of all the personal assistants that would still answer my calls. "What were the terms you all agreed to in exchange for information about my wedding dress?" I asked.

"Your lack of a wedding dress," Bree corrected.

"Two feet away at all times," Gracie recited.

"Gold star for you, Little Griffith," I clipped as I saved the spreadsheet.

Gracie beamed like I had just said she was a princess.

I sighed, lacing my hands together as I turned to them. "Yes?"

"Can you help me pick out an outfit for school tomorrow before my dad gets back?" Bree blurted out at the same time Gracie said, "I want big hair like the cheerleaders for Dallas. Can you do it?"

Instead of immediately shooting them down, I at least pretended to think it over.

I tapped my pen on the notebook in front of me. "No."

"Ugh," Bree groaned. "Why not?"

While the older Griffith turned on the teenage attitude, the younger one pulled out a set of killer puppy eyes.

"*Please*?" she begged. "We don't have a mom to help us with this stuff. Dad tries, but some things require a woman's touch."

What in Carrie Bradshaw's world was happening.

I pressed my fingers to my temples. "I'm sorry—what kind of eleven-year-old talks like that? I can't decide if you're trying to act like you're three or thirty. And second, did you just pull the dead mom card to try to guilt trip me?"

Gracie nodded with an ear-to-ear grin on her face. "Yep. It usually works too."

"Dear God, you two need to stop going to therapy. You skipped right over 'well adjusted' and headed straight for manipulative."

"Please," Bree begged.

Not my children, not my problem.

I hit them with a dismissive smile. "Well, with your dead mom, you're halfway to being fairytale princesses. It's statistically impossible to be a fantasy heroine without two dead parents or a dead parent and an evil stepmother. Find some mice and singing birds and figure it out, ladies."

Bree went on the offensive, surprising me when she planted both hands on the side of the roll-top desk that I had turned into my workspace. "I thought New York women loved makeovers."

"Ah, that's where you're correct. I love a good makeover. But like you said, New York *women* love makeovers. Come back when you're eighteen."

"Cass—"

"Excuse me?" I cut Gracie's whining off with a raised eyebrow. "That's Miss Parker or Cassandra to you. Now, if you'll excuse me, I have to get back to work."

I thought I was home free until the whispering started. Children whispering sounded like nails on a chalkboard. It made my skin crawl.

"What about Saturday?" Bree countered when they broke from the cone of near-silence.

"Excuse me?"

"You don't have to work on Saturday," Gracie said. "If Dad takes us into town, will you go shopping with us?"

"No."

"Why not?" Gracie griped.

"I am many things, but I am neither a babysitter nor a nanny. Ask your aunt or your grandma to take you."

"Grandma makes us shop in the kids section and Aunt Becks needs to stay off her feet," Bree chimed in.

I choked back a laugh. "I'm not sure if you've looked in the mirror lately, but you should be shopping in the kids' section because—spoiler alert—you are kids."

Bree rolled her eyes. "I'm a teenager, thank you very much."

That was evident.

"Doesn't your dad have a girlfriend or someone? Ask her. I have work to do."

"Dad doesn't date," Gracie said. "Well, not exactly. He

pretends like he doesn't go on dates, but we know he does. We just never meet them."

Interesting, but not surprising.

"Please," Bree begged in a whisper. "I need something cute to wear to school and my dad thinks Levis and a button-up are the answer to everything."

I turned back to the contact list I was working on. "Still no."

"Fine," Gracie said. "Will you be our evil stepmother?"

"Excuse me?" The rumbling voice came from the doorway. Christian stood with his hands on his hips and his eyebrows in his hairline.

Gracie shrugged. "I'm just saying. An evil stepmother is better than nothing. If we have an evil stepmother, it means we'll get to go to a ball or kiss a prince or get magical powers. Do you have any poisoned apples? Or a cloak? Those are usually required."

I arched an eyebrow. "You should be very concerned about the state of things if I'm the one feeding you." I dismissed them with a flick of my wrist. "Be gone, peasants."

They dashed through the living room and giggled all the way up the stairs.

Christian closed the door behind him. He looked filthy—covered in dirt and sweat. His hair was damp and dark. Loose strands framed his face and stuck to his skin.

"Your children are weird," I said with my back to him.

He chuckled as he hung his hat. "Yeah, I know. That's probably my fault."

I felt—no—I smelled his presence as he loomed behind me.

"I know you like to lean into the whole grizzled cowboy thing, but please go take a shower before the paint starts peeling off the walls. You smell like cows."

Christian laughed and gave my shoulder a gentle squeeze as he passed by. "You coming up to momma's house for dinner?"

"No. I'll be catching up on the twenty minutes your offspring stole from my workday, and then winding down with leftovers before Tripp calls."

"Ah, the ever-elusive fiancé," he teased as he did an uncanny imitation of a *National Geographic* narrator. "You gonna finally set a date or are you gonna spend a few more weeks staring at that ring like you want to throw it over a cliff?"

My stomach knotted as rage boiled up in my gut. *How dare he?*

"I'll bring you a plate back," Christian called as he disappeared into the bathroom.

As much as I tried to focus on the to-do list looming in front of me, I was distracted by the squeak of the shower and the ambient spray of water.

My thoughts drifted to the night I ran into him when he was coming out of the shower.

I could put up a good front. I could keep my face from cracking under the pressure of red carpets, press conferences, and crises. But Christian was a different story.

I wanted to hate being here. It wasn't my cup of tea.

But I didn't.

It dawned on me that I had never felt at peace around someone.

Tripp always put me on edge. I felt like I had to show up, keep up, and measure up.

My sex drive through my twenties was through the roof. I blamed its decline on turning thirty. *Along with the weird hairs on my chin and my inability to bounce back from more than two cocktails.*

But I was two years removed from the dirty thirty and had felt the rumblings of my libido coming back to life.

Maybe it wasn't me.

Maybe it was him.

Maybe it was both.

One man calling time of death, and the other resuscitating my craving for intimacy.

But that's not how this was going to go.

I wasn't a Hallmark heroine who was banished to a small town and was destined to learn the true meaning of Christmas and the evils of corporate life after being wooed by the local lumberjack.

Four things were for certain:

1. I loved my job.
2. I did not like flannel.
3. I would not apologize for climbing the corporate ladder and stepping on the occasional set of knuckles.
4. There was no mystical small-town magic when the air around the ranch smelled like livestock.

My phone rang as Christian was shuffling Bree and Gracie out the door.

Video Call from Tripp Meyers.

But instead of my heart skipping a beat the way it had

when I thought about Christian in the shower, a boulder of dread sank in my gut.

I waited to answer until the front door shut behind the Griffith clan, since I was bound to the confines of the house WiFi.

With a deep breath, I tapped the accept button and waited.

Tripp's grainy face filled the screen. I hadn't seen him since he abandoned me.

Dread was instantly replaced by rage.

"Cassandra," he said without so much as a hello. "I'm surprised you answered. I expected you to be working."

My eyebrows winged up. "Is that really the tone you're taking with me?"

"I'm still your boss. I have to make sure that everyone on my team is doing what's expected."

Oh, he was asking for it today.

"Mike is my boss now."

Tripp scoffed. "And here I was, thinking you'd be happy to talk to me."

I clawed the lacquered wood desk. "Why do you think I would be happy with you right now? You left me here because you couldn't be uncomfortable for a few hours."

He barely held back an eye roll. "It's not my fault you are where you are."

"No, it's hers."

As if on cue, Lillian Monroe—with the teased blonde hair she fried every month to hide her gray and brunette roots—appeared behind him like a bad omen.

"Ca-ssand-ra," Tripp hissed, enunciating every fucking syllable. "That is a client you're speaking about."

Lillian's pixelated smile was patronizing and malefic.

"Hello, Cassandra. You look... unwell. Been skipping the med spa, have you?"

I was a month overdue for a facial and it was all her fault.

I took a deep breath and tamped down my vitriol. "Lillian, if you could give Tripp and me a few minutes of privacy, that would be lovely."

But Lillian wasn't paying attention to me. She sat beside Tripp and snuggled up to him. "I thought you said she left the Carrington Group," she murmured as she fingered the point of his pressed collar. The corner of her mouth curved in a sickled smile. "You've got a little something—"

Red.

All I saw was red.

Red like the empty bottle of merlot between them.

Red like the scarlet lipstick on his collar.

Red like the crimson bite mark on his neck.

Red like the flames of rage that consumed me like a wildfire.

Red like the flags I should have seen.

Red like the blood I was out for.

14

CHRISTIAN

"Go up and get ready for bed," I said when I parked the truck in front of the house.

Gracie and Bree, with bellies full from a legendary meal at my momma's house, lumbered out of the backseat.

I followed them up, pausing when I heard an extra creak in the wood slats. The porch light was on, but that wasn't unusual.

The trail of melted ice cream was.

I told them I'd be up in a minute, then waited until the girls were out of earshot before rounding the corner.

Cassandra sat on the porch swing, staring out into the pasture. Mint chocolate chip ice cream had melted out of the bottom seam of the carton and ran in a rivulet down the wood planks.

I'd have to hose it off or we'd have a hoard of fire ants taking up residence on the porch.

Lucky for me, Mickey seemed to be taking care of it

just fine. He was lying against the house, lapping at the ice cream.

Cassandra didn't even seem to notice.

"Brought you a plate," I said as I lifted the Tupperware container full of meatloaf, mashed potatoes, and green beans.

She let out a caustic laugh and took another long drink from the nearly empty bottle of whiskey.

I set the leftovers on the porch rail. "I see you skipped dinner and went straight to dessert and drinks." I picked up the carton of soupy ice cream. "Didn't even make it a whiskey float?"

Her only response was to finish off the bottle.

"You gonna be okay on your own long enough for me to get the girls to bed?"

Cassandra's gaze was listless. "I'm fine."

"Sit tight."

I dipped inside, dumped the ice cream carton in the trash, and headed up the stairs, slipping into Gracie's room first.

"You ready for bed, pretty girl?"

She let out a yawn. "I'm not tired. I wanna hang out with Miss Cass."

"Too bad. You've got school in the morning."

"But—"

"No buts." The edge of her mattress sank as I sat down and rearranged the mountain of stuffed animals that lived on her bed.

I knew it was only a matter of time before she'd get too old for them. Bree had outgrown hers years before she was Gracie's age, but Gracie seemed to be holding on to childhood much more tightly.

Bree remembered her mother, which meant when we lost Gretchen, she was forced to grow up and face some harsh truths far earlier than any child should.

Gracie was too young to have any memories of Gretchen. To her, this was normal.

"Anything you wanna talk about tonight?" I asked.

She shook her head.

"You sure?"

"I'm sure."

I didn't push it anymore. "I love you."

"Love you, Daddy," she said when I kissed her head.

I closed her door and walked across the hall to Bree's room. "Ready for school in the morning?"

She just stared at the ceiling, so I sat on her bed and fixed the covers.

"Anything you want to talk about?"

Bree sighed. "Can we go shopping this weekend? I need some new stuff for school."

"What stuff? We got you new clothes at the beginning of the school year. You can't tell me you've already grown out of them."

"We got jeans and t-shirts," she huffed with a quintessential teenage attitude. "Can we *please* go? I need cute stuff."

I had shit I needed to get done on Saturday, but I didn't want the day to end on a bad note. "Your request is noted and is under further review."

She let out a dejected sigh and rolled onto her side.

"Hey," I said as I gently rubbed her back. "I know you're growing up. Just give me a chance to catch up, alright?"

I doled out another head kiss and an "I love you"

before turning out the light and slipping back down the stairs.

I snagged a glass of water on my way through the kitchen. Cassandra was right where I had left her.

Mickey had vacated the porch, leaving a path of sticky ice cream hoof prints.

"Drink this," I said as I took the empty fifth of whiskey from her and pushed the water into her hand.

"I'm fine."

"Obviously not if you think I'd believe that." I lowered down beside her on the swing. "Anything you want to talk about?"

"You were right."

I chuckled. "Of course I'm right. I'm always right."

Cassandra rolled her eyes.

I hesitated for a moment, then draped my arm around her shoulders. "Tell me why I'm right."

"Oh God, don't tell me you're one of those words of affirmation people."

"And you're not?"

"Nope."

"Drink your water."

To my surprise, she did. *Grumbling the entire time.*

When the glass was empty, I took it from her and set it by my foot.

"What's the matter?"

Cassandra stared blankly ahead, but it wasn't the kind of vacant gaze that meant nothing was going on in her head. It was the type of hollow, distant look when the person was emotionally checked out.

It was a look of brewing vengeance.

"He was cheating on me." Her delivery was loaded

and emotionless all at the same time. It was the tone of someone who had accepted the situation in a clinical way.

I swore under my breath. "Jesus—I'm sorry, Cass."

I'd had my suspicions when Tripp showed up with her on day one, then bolted. A man doesn't willingly leave a woman like Cassandra unless he doesn't have a fucking clue what he's got.

"When did you find out?"

"On the phone call. Lillian was there with him. It was pretty obvious."

"Shit." Gently, I pulled her into my side.

She stiffened, shrugging off my arm. "It's fine."

I eyed the ring on her finger. "You're fine with your fiancé cheating on you?"

Her temples pulled back and her mouth tightened. It was the practiced look of someone managing a situation rather than experiencing a heartbreak.

"It's not like it's a surprise. Things like this happen all the time."

"No, they don't, Cass."

The corner of her mouth trembled. "Maybe not in your world."

Since it was pretty damn obvious she wasn't going to let me comfort her, I hunched forward and rested my elbows on my thighs. "What are you gonna do?"

"I want him to hurt as badly as he hurt me." Malice and cruelly calculated anger hung on every word.

"Come on, Cass." I pulled my hair out of the bun it had been in all day long. "You know that's not the mature way to handle things."

She let out a beautifully wicked laugh. Her lips were

crimson like Cruella. If luck was a lady, revenge was a seductress named Cassandra.

"The wonderful thing about being newly single and unattached is that I don't have to set a good example for anyone. Why be mature, when you can be petty? And since I have plenty of time on my hands, I'm sure I'll be able to come up with a beautiful form of payback."

"I think being happy is the best form of revenge. Because that's something he could never give you or himself."

Cassandra pushed out of the swing and stood. Her bare feet kicked at one discarded stiletto. "Again with the mystical cowboy wisdom. Does being cryptic ever get old?"

I chuckled. "If moving on doesn't do it for you, I can dig a trench and bury him in a place where no one will find his body. Do you want him in the east pasture or the west?"

"That's more like it."

Cassandra chewed on her nail as she paced the porch. *Jesus, she was going to gnaw that thing down to nothing.*

"Hey—" I grabbed her hand on the pass that brought her closest to the swing. "That's a bad habit, you know."

She tried to jerk away, but I didn't let her. When I stood up, she tried to pull away again, but careened back toward me when I didn't let go. I planted my other hand on her hip, trapping her against the porch railing with my arms braced on either side of her.

"Give yourself a chance to feel upset and hurt, Cass."

She clawed at the wood railing. "You'd better let me go, Griffith."

"So that's it, huh? You'd rather chew off your fucking

finger while you plot your retaliation rather than taking a goddamn breath?"

"It's why I get acrylic nails. I don't have to wait for them to grow back."

I took a chance and closed my arms around her.

"Why do you care?" she said as she grunted and threw an elbow to get out of my grasp. "The sooner I'm out of here, the sooner you can get your life back."

"I'm looking out for you." I pressed my cheek to her temple. "I value what you bring to the table, and I'm trying to keep you from fucking imploding so you can show everyone else what I see in you."

She thrashed again, but I didn't budge.

"I've got at least a hundred and fifty pounds on you, Princess. Stop it."

"Christian." My name was a whispered tremble on her lips.

She didn't say my name often, but hearing her mutter it in that breathless tone had me picturing us this close in a different situation.

A very different situation.

Cassandra's knuckles turned white with pressure as she held on to the railing for dear life. Her shoulders were taut. The way she was grinding her teeth to maintain her composure made me think of sandpaper on rust.

"Please go."

"Cass—"

"I said, 'please,'" she snapped.

"You're angry," I began, but Cassandra cut me off before I could finish.

"Which is obviously something you've never felt in your entire fucking life!" She whirled around, blonde hair flying like a tornado. "You're a walking sedative! *Mr. Never-Raises-His-Voice*. I'm sure I look fucking crazy to you! Of course I'm angry, you serene fucking horse whisperer!"

Honest to God—I wanted to laugh, but it wasn't exactly the time for it. Cassandra was shaking with rage, and I didn't blame her.

I knew she had a lot to drink, but the woman could handle her liquor. She looked sober as a judge.

In a burst of fury, Cassandra balled up her fist and swung at one of the posts along the porch railing.

"Hey now," I grunted as I caught her fist in my palm. "You're gonna hurt those pretty hands, not him. Don't hurt yourself trying to take down someone else."

"I just—" One glimmering tear fell to her cheek, then another. Cassandra hiccuped.

Miraculously, she turned and rested her head on my chest. Oxygen rushed out of my lungs as I wrapped my arms around her, cradling her head in the palm of my hand.

"You loved him," I reasoned. "It's okay to be angry after someone betrays you like that."

"I didn't love him." Cassandra sniffed back tears, but they just kept streaming down her face, streaking her makeup. "I just wanted to be loved."

We stood there for what felt like an eternity, swaying together in the porch light as she cried.

Eventually I coaxed her inside. She fought me the entire way.

Sadie helped, nipping at Cassandra's ankles until she parked herself on the couch. Sadie kept watch while I heated up the leftovers.

"Eat," I said as I set the plate in her lap and handed her a fork. "If you're anything like me, drinking on an empty stomach will bite you in the ass in the morning."

She just poked around at the green beans.

I pitched a throw pillow across to the empty armchair and sat down beside her. "What does this mean for your job? He was your boss, right?"

"Boss adjacent," she clarified.

Good to see that her fire hadn't died. I liked her sass.

Cassandra stabbed a green bean with a little more force than necessary. "He liked to act like my boss, but after I got demoted back to business development, it took me out of his chain of command. At least I'm still employed."

"You really want to work near him?"

Her lips curled up. "Why should I be the one to leave? If he's uncomfortable with my presence, that's his problem."

"That's my girl."

Her attitude was strong, but her eyes were sad.

I settled in, stretching my arm around her shoulders and reaching for the remote. "You've got a place here as long as you want."

15

CASSANDRA

"Why isn't the damn horse moving!" I shouted from ten feet behind Christian and Libby.

Libby huffed, turning her giant head and glaring at me, annoyed that we had to stop yet again.

Christian's smile flashed brighter than the midday sun. The snicker he tried to hide beneath his beard pissed me off.

"Why are you laughing at me?" I shouted.

His eyes just crinkled beneath the brim of his cowboy hat as he turned Libby and trotted back to me.

If horses had resting bitch face, his did and it was aimed at me.

"This horse is broken," I said with a huff. Copping an attitude was better than admitting that I sucked at this and hated it. "Please take me back to the barn. I'll walk next time."

Christian sided up to me, facing the opposite direction like two cops sitting window-to-window in a parking lot. I jerked away when he reached out and touched my hand.

"Cass, you're white-knuckling the reins."

"I'm trying not to fall off!"

"You're not gonna fall off, but you're pulling on them so hard that Dottie here thinks she's supposed to stop."

"I don't know why you thought I was capable of riding a horse all the way out here. We're miles away and now I'm stuck on this animal for the foreseeable future."

He chuckled again and pointed behind me. "I can still see the barn."

I gritted my teeth for the millionth time, making my jaw ache.

I would have to see a dentist after this little sabbatical.

"Breathe, Princess," he said as Libby shifted close enough for him to squeeze my knee. "You're tense."

"I'm always tense. That's nothing new."

What was new was the fact that I was wearing blue jeans and the boots Christian gave me.

At least I hadn't chopped off my hair or given myself a bathroom sink dye job.

The ring I had worn for years was no longer on my finger. It was sitting on the nightstand in Christian's house until I figured out what to do with it.

If jeans and boots were rock bottom, I'd say I was handling the end of my relationship pretty damn well.

Then again, compartmentalization was my bread and butter.

I'd deal with the feelings later.

Or never.

It was fine.

I stared down at Christian's thumb as it stroked back

and forth over my knee. It was thick and rough with callouses. I saw him wash his hands often, but it seemed as though his cuticles were permanently dirty from doing tasks around the ranch.

"Look." His tongue darted out and wet his lip. "It's none of my business how you deal with your shit. Just don't blame the horse."

The man was delusional if he thought I'd be able to ride this monster without falling off and cracking my head open.

Christian must have telepathically told Libby to turn so we were facing the same direction because she slowly shuffled around and lined up with Dottie—the horse who had the misfortune of carting me around today.

Dottie. It sounded like a lunch lady with a hair net. Not a thousand pound mammal.

"Relax the reins. You can hold 'em tight if it makes you feel better, just don't yank on 'em."

Reluctantly, I wiggled my fingers and loosened my grip.

"You can rest your hands on the front of the saddle if you want something to hold on to, but you don't need it. You're not gonna fall off."

"Easy for you to say—fucking cocky cowboys," I muttered under my breath as I gripped the horn at the front of the saddle.

Christian let out an easy laugh. "What's the rule?"

I tapped a finger on my chin. "Rule number one: if you're going to kill someone, make it look like an accident, cry at the funeral, admit nothing, and deny everything."

"Jesus, you publicists are dark."

"Don't fuck with me, Griffith."

He reached over and pressed his palm against the small of my back. "Posture like a princess. Sit nice and tall."

"I am sitting tall," I snapped. "I'm not exactly a waif."

"You're sitting like a gargoyle," he countered, running his hand up the curve of my spine like a silent insult. "Shoulders back. Chest out. Back straight."

I let out a dramatic huff and slowly fixed my posture. "Better?"

"Push your ass out. You're caving in on yourself and sitting on your tailbone. It's why you feel wobbly."

Christian's eyes on my ass made goosebumps flood my neck. I knew he didn't mean it in any kind of way, but it had been a long time since a man looked at me without disdain.

He was warm and comforting. I was usually described as prickly, but I was beginning to understand why a cactus thrives in sunshine.

"There you go," he said, giving me a tip of his chin. "That's better." Christian's beard twitched around his mouth, and I knew he was trying not to smile. "You're too formidable to cower. Don't bow even if you want to."

I flinched when Dottie shifted, itching to get going. "Is that your way of saying, 'fake it 'til you make it?'"

He and Libby started off. Somehow Dottie knew to follow, and kept up with his slow pace. "Something like that."

We rode silently for a few minutes, heading out to one of the empty pastures I wanted to see.

I had been keeping my revitalization plans close to the vest until I had everything in order. If he said no to adding a single revenue stream, he was going to throw a fit about adding a handful of them.

Land was one thing I would need, and the one thing he probably wouldn't give up.

I was a fan of ripping the metaphorical Band-Aid off, but I was trying to make this as painless as possible.

"It'll clear, you know," Christian said out of nowhere.

"What will?"

He slowed up and looked over at me. "The dust storm."

I stared at the chestnut hairs of Dottie's mane. "What are you talking about?"

"All the shit that gets stirred up and clouds your mind. Eventually it'll settle. You'll be able to breathe easier." He looked ahead. "Doesn't make it better in the moment. Dust storms happen. It's okay to close your eyes and stumble through."

It was a nice little mantra I was certain he had coined when he was going through the loss of his wife.

But I didn't need niceties.

I lifted my chin, pushed my shoulders back, straightened my spine, and loosened my hips. "I'll be fine."

And maybe one day, I would believe it.

Christian took me out to the west side of the ranch to show me the land.

CJ and the ranch hands had rotated pastures, moving the herd south a few days ago, making this the perfect place to stake my claim for the development projects I had up my sleeve.

He waited patiently while I stared to the left for a while, then the right, imagining buildings springing up from the earth.

Christian would probably hate it.

But maybe we could do something natural—a log and stone exterior. Something with a view so the expanse of the ranch could be appreciated.

When I finally spoke up again, I nearly startled Christian.

"Which direction does the sun set?"

He pointed in front of me at the sprawling land that stretched as far as the eye could see. "The front gate is east. It's opposite where we are. Sun rises over there, and sets over that horizon."

"Perfect," I whispered. With the plan solidified in my mind, I had a mountain of work ahead of me.

"Ready to head back?"

"You can go if you have to get back to work."

Christian chuckled. "If I leave you, I'm afraid I might still find you out here in the morning." He winked. "But I like your confidence."

Taking his cues, Libby happily obliged. Her tail swished in front of me as we turned and headed back for the east side of the ranch.

"You gonna tell me what you've been working on?" he called to me.

I smirked. "When it's ready."

"Am I gonna ride out here and find you breaking ground on something that's gonna piss me off?"

That made me laugh. "I think it's physically impossible for you to get pissed off. I've never heard you raise your voice."

His chuckle was more of a growl. "Few things are worth raising my voice over."

Dottie picked up her pace, matching Libby so Christian and I were riding side by side. "Your daughters are lucky."

His beard twitched again. "Thanks, Cass. Means a lot." After a moment of silence, he asked, "Do you want kids?"

I cackled, tossing my head back and letting my hair spill down my spine. "Absolutely not. I do not have a single maternal bone in my body. Tripp didn't want kids either, so that was great. At least now that he's out of the picture, it's not like I'm losing out on something."

"So is this it?"

"Is what it?"

"This. Your job. Your life the way it is. You living the dream?"

"Something like that."

"What's the bigger dream, then?" When I didn't answer, he looked over at me, studying me from beneath the brim of his hat.

"Don't do that."

"Do what?" he countered, looking away.

"Don't do that thing where you stare at me until I crack. I hate that."

Christian laughed. "I'm not trying to make you crack."

I rolled my eyes. "Really."

"You fascinate me."

I let out a weighted breath, steeling myself for the impending heckling. "I want to be important."

But Christian didn't laugh. "What do you mean?"

The slow rock of my hips with each of Dottie's strides was soothing and hypnotic. There were no sounds except the soft grunts of the horses.

I wasn't religious, but this felt like church.

"I want to be the person that people go to when there's a problem. I want to be the one who gets the calls in the middle of the night to fix something that's going wrong. I want to be the one that holds everything together. I want to be irreplaceable."

Christian's brows were furrowed as he mulled on it. They softened after a while, but he still didn't make a comment about what I had said.

His silence was starting to irritate me.

He might be calm, cool, and collected, but I wasn't.

Vulnerability made me uneasy. Tripp didn't honor tenderness; he saw it as weakness.

The notion struck me like lightning.

I had never admitted the desires behind my career goals to Tripp. Deep down, I knew it was because I was afraid of him cutting them down.

"You're looking like a natural," Christian said, snapping me out of the stunned stupor.

I blinked the haze away. "What?"

"You're doing a lot better on Dottie. You've got an ease about you now. I'm proud of you."

"Really?" I scoffed. "I drop an emotional bomb and you follow up with how well I ride a horse?"

"Was that supposed to be an emotional bomb?"

"For me it was. I don't do feelings."

"Seems like that's working out pretty well for you." The unexpected sarcasm was cutting.

I yanked on the reins and Dottie came to an immediate halt. "What's that supposed to mean?" I shouted at his back.

Christian turned Libby around. "You wanna be irreplaceable? Let people love you." He said it as if it was the most obvious thing in the world. And with that emotional bomb, he tapped Libby with his boots and left me in the dust.

Fucking cowboys.

Somehow, I managed a less than graceful ride back to the barn.

"Ma'am," CJ said, acknowledging me as Dottie loped into the stables.

Libby glared at me from where she was tied off. *Because, of course, he made it back and then disappeared.*

I used the entire ride to crank up my indignation and fume over the man who decided to give me emotional whiplash.

"I don't know how to park a horse," I snapped.

CJ wasn't as easygoing as his brother, but he wasn't put off by my rancor. "Just hop down. I'll take care of her." He paused with a pitchfork in hand and gave me a quick assessment. "Did you take her out by yourself?"

"Nope," I said as I dropped the reins, grabbed the pommel, and wiggled my toe until it found the stirrup. "Your monk of a brother left me in the middle of a fucking field."

CJ grinned. "He was fuming when I saw him a little while ago. You must've really pissed him off."

"Right." My feet hit the ground. "And by fuming you mean in a near-catatonic state of pure, unbothered bliss."

"Something like that."

I turned to storm out of the barn, but CJ's sharp whistle caught me by surprise.

The hairs on the back of my neck stood up. "Excuse me?" I hissed as I slowly turned to face him.

He reached into his pocket and handed me a

peppermint. "Now, before you go and skin my brother alive, give Dottie a treat and tell her what a pretty girl she is."

I pressed my fingers to my temples. "I have work to do."

"We all have work to do." He pulled my wrist down and dropped the peppermint into my hand. "Now show her some appreciation for not bucking you off and leaving your city-girl ass in the middle of a goddamn field."

Dottie didn't seem fazed by the fact that I was wound tighter than a coiled spring. She snarfed down the peppermint when I offered it to her.

I shivered as her big hairy horse lips tickled my palm.

"Now what do you say?" he prodded.

I pressed my hand to her nose. "Dottie, you're a pretty girl."

"That'll do," CJ said, tipping his head toward the doors. "Get out of my barn."

Fine by me.

MY SPINE ITCHED.

It wasn't dry skin or an irritating shirt kind of itch.

It was agitation.

My skin was crawling with adrenaline. Focusing on the budget spreadsheet in front of me was impossible.

How dare he say that I didn't let people love me? He didn't even know me. We were opposites.

The clock ticked louder than a bomb. Each jolt of the minute hand fueled the fire I needed to burn off.

How dare he ride off like that, abandoning me in the middle of a fucking field?

I could have died.

If I had been back home, I would have cut out of the office and hit the treadmill to clear my mind.

But I wasn't home, and there was no treadmill here.

But I was working twenty feet from my bedroom...

I hadn't taken advantage of the lack of structure for my job here, but there was no time like the present.

One more glance at the clock told me it was the golden opportunity for a little *self-care.*

The girls would be at dance class until dinner time, which meant Christian wouldn't be around until his mom brought them back.

I pushed out of the chair and beelined for the guest room, yanking the door closed behind me as I shimmied out of the jeans I had put on this morning.

I hated jeans. They were stiff and restrictive. But they did make my ass look good, so at least there was an upside.

I tossed them on to the cowboy boots I discarded when I came back to the house to work. My underwear and blouse were quick to follow. I pawed around in my suitcase until I found the discreet velvet bag.

I pulled it out, pressed the button, and the vibrator buzzed to life. *Excellent.*

There was nothing worse than being horny and out of batteries.

I stretched out on top of the soft patchwork quilt and propped my head up on the pillow. My lungs relaxed as I slid the tip of the vibrator down my clit.

"God, yes," I whispered as my body relaxed.

I was so turned on that the vibrator slid right in. My breath caught as the silicone rabbit teased my clit.

My toes curled and I arched my back.

Blood rushed and roared in my ears like a tidal wave.

With all the chaos of Lillian Monroe torching my career with a metaphorical flamethrower, Tripp leaving me, cheating on me, and being exiled, I was seriously overdue for an orgasm.

... Or ten.

I bit into my lip to keep from moaning when I dragged the curved tip across my G-spot.

Who needs men when you have silicone?

I squeezed my eyes shut as my muscles clenched around the slick shaft. My skin was alive with pleasure as I pulled it out and circled my clit, edging out the orgasm just a little longer.

I sucked in a sharp breath as I plunged the vibrator into my pussy again. My back arched. Everything went white-hot as I—

Dead.

"No!" I shrieked as my eyes flew open. I tried the power button again.

Nothing.

"Fuck!"

In a fit of anger, I slammed the useless device onto the mattress.

Fucking batteries. I needed something with a cord and a three-pronged plug for maximum power.

It was fine. I had fingers.

Letting out a breath, I laid back and propped one knee up, trying to let go of the anger. I teased my clit, massaging it back and forth until the blissful tingles of arousal were back.

I let out a guttural groan of delight as I neared an orgasm again. Something thumped outside.

Probably the damn dog. Or the cow.

I shook it off and focused on the brewing pleasure in my core.

The door clicked open and I froze, paralyzed as Christian filled the doorway.

His eyes locked on my fingers.

My breath caught and my nipples tightened, aching immediately at the sight of him.

With an authoritative tone that could demand oceans to part, he said, “Don’t stop on my account.”

I didn’t move. I couldn’t move. I searched his eyes for something to clue me in on what was going through his head, but he was an enigma.

“Cass.”

“Yes,” I whispered.

The doorframe crackled and groaned as he gripped it with both hands. “Close your eyes.”

I hated taking orders, but for him I did.

“Index finger on your clit.” He didn’t make another sound until obeyed. “Two fingers from your other hand inside that pussy.”

“Christian—” I whispered.

“Curl those fingers inside of you.”

I did as he said and bucked my hips, arching off the mattress.

“Get to work on your clit, Princess. Make yourself get there.”

I didn't even care that my boss was watching me masturbate. This was the most alive I had felt in ages.

My breasts ached and strained against my bra. I wanted to rip it off. I wanted him to ravage me. I wanted his hands, his mouth, his cock.

"Make those pretty toes curl for me."

"Yes," I choked out as my spine electrified like a lightning rod. Sheer, unadulterated power ripped down my body as my pussy clenched around my fingers.

I arched off the bed, gasping as the adrenaline leached out of me in a rush.

I opened my eyes again, breathing like a marathon runner. Christian hadn't moved an inch in the doorway.

"Well?" I laid back on the pillow. "Make yourself useful."

Something powerful flashed in his eyes.

There it was. The storm he hid so well beneath his calm.

Christian's hands curled around the wood frame. *I wanted those hands.*

"Cassandra?"

My breath caught at hearing him use my full name. "Yes?"

"Get that goddamn ring out of my house."

16

CHRISTIAN

Her body was flushed the perfect shade of pink. Rounded breasts bounced as she lay back against the bed, gasping for breath as she came down from her high.

I knew she had been all worked up when we were out riding.

Honestly, if I went through all the shit she had in the last few weeks, I'd need more than an orgasm to deal with the stress. That was why I had left her alone.

I came back to the house to make sure she was alright. Walking in on her sprawled out across the bed while she played with herself was pure chance.

But damn, I wasn't complaining.

"Well?" she snapped as she flopped her head back on the pillow. "Make yourself useful."

Oh, so she wanted to be sassy with me.

Not fucking today.

I gripped the doorframe so hard I thought it would splinter in two. I gritted my teeth. "Cassandra?"

Her eyes went wide. "Yes?" It was barely a whisper.

I didn't look at that hideous diamond ring. I looked at her. "Get that goddamn ring out of my house."

And with that, I turned and stomped out the door.

I WAS A GODDAMN IDIOT.

Sweat beaded down my neck as I wedged the crowbar behind the cabinets and waited for the crack. Dust danced off every surface I touched. As the old, dry-rotted wood fell off the wall, I sneezed, stumbling back and nearly catching Mickey with the crowbar.

"Shit—"

I dropped the crowbar and grabbed onto the countertop, but it cracked and crumbled. I landed on my ass as a hailstorm of dust and debris rained down on me. I coughed, trying to get the asbestos out of my lungs.

I probably should have been wearing a respirator, but going without one was just another idiotic choice I had made today—right after walking away from Cassandra.

Make yourself useful.

She made it pretty damn clear I was welcome to join her. So why didn't I?

Well, I was filthy for one.

I had shit to get done before the kids got home.

I had just stopped by to make sure she made it back alright, though I already knew she had after watching the fit she pitched in the barn from a distance.

The way I saw it, Cass was a lot.

I didn't mind that. In fact, I liked it. But not everyone

could tolerate it. CJ hadn't been put off by her and responded to her just fine, so I didn't step in.

So why did I step in when she was playing with her body?

The devil inside me won this afternoon.

I rested my elbows on my knees as I resigned to sitting on the floor.

If Cassandra was going to be here any longer, things were going to be weird if we were under the same roof.

I had only meant to walk through the cabin to make a list of what needed to be taken care of to make it habitable.

Honestly, I would have bulldozed it, but the bones were good. It just needed work.

A lot of work that I didn't have the time or energy for.

The walk through turned into hauling all the old furniture out for the boys to pick up as I thought about the way her chin tipped up and the tendons of her neck stretched tight as she chased that orgasm.

That turned into me grabbing the crowbar to take a whack at the ramshackle cabinets while I pictured those long legs tipping open to give me a peek at her pretty pussy over and over again.

Blood trickled from the side of my thumb where I had hit the countertop. A shard of wood stuck out of my skin. I hissed as I pulled it out and used my shirt to wipe the blood off.

"Give up already?"

I looked over my shoulder and found Nate lingering in the doorway.

"Shouldn't you be on baby watch?" I asked as I pushed off the floor and wiped my dust-covered palms on my jeans.

He lifted a radio. "She kicked me out of the house."

I chuckled. "Yeah, Gretchen got like that when she was pregnant with Gracie."

Nate leaned on the doorframe, then quickly stood straight when it cracked. "What'd you do?"

"Took Bree to work with me and made sure there were peanut butter cups in the freezer at all times."

"You still miss her?"

I sighed and looked down at my hands. I had stopped wearing my ring somewhere around two years after Gretchen had passed. Bree told me it made her sad to see it, so I put it away in the box where I kept Gretchen's wedding band and engagement ring. Someday I'd pass them on to the girls.

I nodded. "She was my best friend. I think it'd hurt more if I didn't have the girls. I get to see all her goodness in them."

He nodded, looking around as he rubbed the scar tissue on his arm. "How has it been with Cassandra under your roof?"

I pitched the crowbar onto what was left of the countertop. "Fine."

Nathan scoffed. "Try again."

"It's fine," I said defensively. "She mostly keeps to herself."

"Right," he said as he eyed me suspiciously. "Keeps to herself until midnight when you two go on a casual horseback ride?"

I pinched the bridge of my nose. "It wasn't midnight."

"For you it was."

"Shouldn't you be getting sleep now while you can?"

He laughed. "You think a woman that's in her third trimester can sleep?"

He had a point.

"Becks just so happened to look out the kitchen window and saw you two out there. She wanted to cash in on the little bet we made, but I said you hadn't slept with her yet."

I swore under my breath. "I'm not hooking up with her."

Not that I didn't want to.

He held his hands up in surrender. "I'm not making accusations or saying you didn't love Gretch—"

"It's been a decade. I've... been with other women. It's fine."

"I know." He rubbed at the scar tissue again. "How do the girls like her?"

I chuckled. "The other night Gracie told me that Cass looks like a real-life Barbie doll. Bree looks at her like she's an angel. Pretty sure if you ask them what they want to be when they grow up, they'll say they wanted to be publicists."

"You trust her around them?"

"I don't think Becks would have recommended her if she wasn't someone I could trust."

Nate nodded.

I crossed my arms. "What are you trying to get at?"

"Just asking questions." His voice was as innocent as a baby lamb, but it was bullshit.

I laughed as I turned and left the mess of dilapidated wood for another day. "Just asking questions my ass."

"I'm just trying to catch up with my brother."

"Sorry. No time for a tea party. Not all of us can retire at forty."

Nate followed me out. "Retired from the Army, dipshit. Not life. Once Becks's maternity leave is over, we'll be traveling again."

"Good," I clipped with a smirk. "So when your baby is born I can start counting down the days until I can leave my house without you nosey Nellies watching my every move."

"Be straight with me," he said as he leaned against his truck. "Is something going on with Cassandra?"

I evaded the question. "Why would you ask that?"

"You keep her close. She hides out at your house. You're the only person she talks to."

I sighed as I stared out at the horizon. "She's having a time of it."

"What do you mean?"

"Her fiancé was cheating on her."

Nate swore under his breath. "Becks hates that guy. Always has."

"With the client that got her fired from her job," I added.

Nate laughed at the sky. "Where does Cass want him buried? In the east pasture or the west?"

For some reason, I liked that he was willing to commit a casual felony for Cassandra. I liked her being seen as one of ours.

As mine.

But I didn't say that out loud. "I think whatever she's got up her sleeve for the ranch will be good. She's just using the isolation as an excuse to lick her wounds."

He lifted an eyebrow. "That's very magnanimous of you. You hate change."

I shrugged. "Change is like the sunrise. It happens whether you want it to or not."

Nate combed his fingers through his growing beard. "Then maybe you should change your '*no bringing women home while your girls are there*' rule."

I laughed. "It will take an act of God for me to change my mind about that."

"YES, MY QUEEN!"

I yanked open the screen door to the sound of giggling girls. Dirt coated my palms, leaving a smear on the edge of the door handle.

Gracie was running back up the stairs while Bree was darting down to the living room.

My eyes widened as I looked around the wreckage that was pre-teen clothes, shoes, and accessories. "What in the—"

"Hi, Daddy!" Bree beamed as she did a twirl at the bottom of the steps.

I found Cassandra sitting prim and proper in my armchair, looking rather regal with a plastic tiara on top of pearl-blonde hair.

"I'm in hell," she said with a morose deadpan before picking up the matching plastic wand and pointing it at Bree. "No."

Bree huffed. "You said that about the last outfit too."

Cassandra tapped her on the head with the wand.

"Because you're wearing five of the loudest things in your closet."

"But Braxton likes girls who wear loud clothes."

Cassandra rolled her eyes. "First, any kid with an X in their name is a walking red flag. Just spell it the normal way." In a mutter she added, "Same goes for men named after accidents. Like Tripp." Refocusing, Cassandra waved the wand in the general direction of the bright pink shirt Bree had layered with a lime-green tank top. "And second, boys don't notice clothes. You dress up for yourself first and your girls second. Boys notice how you feel in your clothes. It probably seems like he likes girls who wear loud clothes when he really just likes girls who are confident in who they are." She flicked the wand, dismissing Bree. "Go do better."

"Yes, my queen," Bree blurted out, then dashed past me to go back up the stairs.

Part of me wanted to walk into the kitchen and start dinner like this Twilight Zone nightmare wasn't happening. The other part of me was curious.

Instead of pulling out the ingredients for barbecue chicken, I sauntered over and fixed the tiara that was sliding off her head. "Wanna explain to me why my children are calling you 'my queen'?"

Cassandra smirked. "I'm not big on the 'ma'am' thing. It makes me sound old. So I told them to rebrand. "My queen" was their idea, and I don't hate it."

I hid my smile behind a clenched fist pressed to my mouth. "And the bit about dressing for boys?"

She flopped back in the armchair as feet thundered overhead. "Dressing for boys is a rite of passage. Eventually they'll realize that men of any age don't notice clothes and they'll start dressing to impress their girlfriends—which is far more expensive and time consuming." She huffed dramatically, popping out the footrest and flopping one leg over the other, crossing her ankles. "Eventually they'll come to the realization that everyone sucks equally and just start doing what they want. I'd tell you there's hope, but I don't care enough to lie to you. It's a cycle that's happened for thousands of years and cannot be avoided. The sooner you accept it and get used to handing over your credit card, the easier your life will be."

I glanced over my shoulder to make sure the girls were still upstairs. "You're wrong about one thing."

Her frown was fierce. "I'm never wrong."

"You're wrong about men never noticing." The silk blouse she was in gave it away. My hands were filthy, so I trailed a knuckle down the exposed red bra strap peeking out on top of her shoulder. "I notice everything, Cass."

Her breath hitched. Long lashes shielded her eyes as they lowered to watch my finger.

"So I guess the question is, who are you wearing this for?"

Crimson lips curled in a victorious smile. "The last part of the equation."

"What was that?"

Her grin was feline. "Me."

I shoved my hand in my pocket. "Keep telling yourself that, Princess."

Cassandra relaxed. "It's 'my queen.'"

I laughed. "Sweetheart, there's only one situation where I'll call you that and, I promise you, this ain't it."

A devilish look sparkled in her eye. "Is that so?"

"Okay, what about this?" Bree blurted out as she rushed down the stairs in a skirt and a Cowboys football t-shirt that was at least two sizes too small and kept riding up her stomach. She had gotten the shirt when she was Gracie's age.

"Absolutely not," Cassandra and I said together.

Cass punctuated it with a wave of the wand. "Go do better."

"Yes, my queen!" Bree said as she bolted back up the stairs.

The charade lasted until I called the girls down for dinner. I was fairly certain they had emptied every garment out of their closets and were wading through clothes by the end.

I was half-tempted to make them pick it all up before they went to bed, then decided it could wait until the weekend.

We didn't live in a state of melancholy. I worked hard to get my head right after Gretchen passed. All three of us went to therapy—together and separately—and found healthy coping mechanisms that helped us live relatively normal lives.

But there was an energy about the girls that I hadn't seen in a long time.

Ever, if I was being honest.

Cassandra maintained her majestic composure and decorum throughout the meal, but entertained the onslaught of questions.

Gracie's inquisition mostly centered around life in New York, which she called the happiest place on earth.

Bree's curiosity massed around navigating friendships, an awful teacher, and a boy she had a crush on.

Cassandra's opinion was that everyone sucked and it wouldn't get better even when she got out of school, so she should just stop worrying about what other people are doing.

The jabbering didn't stop until the girls were brushing their teeth.

When I came back down the stairs after kissing the girls goodnight, I found Cassandra at the sink, drying dishes. I was surprised to say the least.

Her ass swayed with each swipe of the dish towel.

"I know you're watching me," she said without taking her eyes off the plate in her hand.

"What gave me away?"

She laughed softly. "You smell like the outdoors. A little bit like gasoline and exhaust."

"I was working on one of the tractors before I called it a day."

Cassandra turned, resting her ass on the edge of the counter as she dried her hands. She had put her high heels back on, even though she had been working from the living room after our ... run-in.

"What?" she said as she tossed the towel onto the countertop.

I just shook my head. "Don't know how you walk around in those things all day. Can't be comfortable."

She looked down at the stilettos. "They're more comfortable than the boots you gave me."

"Boots have to be broken in. Just takes time."

She wiggled a pointed toe at me. "These are already broken in."

The silence between us was heavy. I braced my hands

on the back of a chair and she kept to her spot by the sink.

I really didn't want to have this conversation.

I shouldn't be having this conversation.

I should have shut the fucking door this afternoon and walked away.

But I didn't.

I stood there, staring at her, like I had found the Holy Grail.

Maybe I had. But I wasn't worthy enough to touch it.

"Look, Cass... About earlier..." I glanced up, hoping to find her looking as uncomfortable as I felt.

But the devil was smirking.

"Yeah..." Her eyes trailed south. "I hope you found some time to take care of that boner." She pushed off the counter and walked to me, pausing when we were shoulder to shoulder. "Pretty sure if it lasts for more than four hours you're supposed to seek medical attention."

I caught her wrist as she reached to give me a placating pat on my arm. "I wasn't rejecting you. Just to be clear."

"Hmm. You have a funny way of showing it, Griffith."

"It won't happen again, is what I'm trying to say."

Her eyebrows lifted. "Why not?" She let out a light-hearted laugh. "Because if it's the whole workplace romance thing, I can assure you that I have no intentions of doing that again. Sex and romance are two different things."

My grip softened around her wrist.

Cassandra's eyes flicked down to where our skin met.

"I agree," I said, taking her by surprise.

"You do?"

I nodded. "But it doesn't matter. I don't bring women back to the house."

"I already live here," she whispered.

And damn if I wasn't tempted to break my rule...

"I don't bring temporary hook-ups into this house. Not while the girls live here. I've worked hard to give them stability and security. I don't jeopardize that—"

Her lips called to me. I wanted to see that lipstick smeared. I wanted to hear those breathy moans. I wanted to hear her beg. I wanted my hands all over the body I had commanded to come.

"—no matter how much I want to."

A soft, amusing exhale whispered from between her lips. "Then it's a good thing that I haven't gotten rid of the ring yet."

I growled, listening to her laugh as she disappeared into her room.

Great. Another fucking boner.

17

CASSANDRA

"You're up early," Christian said with a raised eyebrow as he zipped up a lunchbox that was speckled with daisies.

I stole the coffee pot out from the machine and dumped the remnants into a mug. "I need to go into town."

Christian was taking his girls to school this morning because he had to go do something farm-y, and I was going to hitch a ride.

He paused, trapping me between his chest and the corner of the kitchen counters when I replaced the coffee pot. "Don't take this the wrong way—"

I smirked over the lip of my mug. "Famous last words."

"But you're going into town like that?"

I knew exactly what he was getting at. My hair was tied in a low chignon, and I didn't have a speck of makeup on.

"I'm going to the hair salon." The coffee was warm and fortifying. "When you're going behind enemy lines, it's best to wear a disguise."

"Ah. That reconnaissance you were talking about. What are the silver beehives saying these days?"

I laughed under my breath. "That's for me to know and for you to accept when I give you my ranch revitalization plan."

He reached out, looped a loose tendril of hair around his finger, and grazed my cheek. "You're gonna let a legally blind seventy-year-old with a pair of scissors touch this?"

I studied the way his beard hid most of his mouth. The way silver streaked the strands of hair by his temples.

"I'm going to let her wash it, style it, and talk my ear off. Then I'll go next door to the cosmetics store and sit still while an employee makes me look like a 90s country music star."

His laugh was low and full of amusement. "You know, I always had a thing for Faith Hill." He reached over and zipped up the second lunchbox, never taking his eyes off me. "But just for the record—" he paused with his mouth beside my ear. "I like your freckles."

I pressed a hand to my cheek when he disappeared to make sure the girls were getting ready. I had been out in the sun a little more than usual and it had made my freckles come out.

Usually I kept them hidden beneath a full face of makeup, but I had been toning it down.

No one saw me around here. I was basically in

witness protection. What was the point in wearing makeup?

But Christian liked my freckles...

I tried to ignore the butterflies in my stomach. I didn't want butterflies. I didn't need butterflies.

Christian Griffith was a lot of things, but he wasn't my type.

"You're coming with us?" Gracie blurted out the moment her sneakers hit the landing. "Best. Morning. Ever."

Bree came down shortly after, grabbed one of the breakfast tacos Christian had wrapped up in aluminum foil, and took a hearty bite.

Her breezy white skirt stopped at her knees. The turquoise shirt she was in brought out her eyes and made her skin warm. The old Chuck Taylors with permanent marker scribbles on the toes were timeless.

"Is that what you're wearing to school?" I asked over the last sip of coffee.

Bree looked down. "Is it okay?"

I recognized each of the pieces from the fashion show I was forced to endure the night before, but she had paired them with other garments. This was a more curated version of Bree and it made her glow.

"You look like a great version of yourself." I tapped my thumb against the coffee mug. "Hold on."

I disappeared into the guest room and rummaged around until I found what I was looking for.

Bree was watching curiously as she finished her breakfast.

I let the gold necklace dangle from my fingertips. The

charm was a looping gold bow. It was dainty and feminine and perfect for her.

"Pull your hair back," I said as I unclasped it and looped it around her neck.

"This is probably really expensive," she said softly. "I don't want to break it or lose it or something."

"I wouldn't let you wear it if I thought you wouldn't take care of it." I fastened the necklace and smoothed her hair down. "Square necklines need a little something extra. And it'll make you hold your head high."

Bree threw her arms around me and squeezed.

"Okay, okay—" I shooed her away as my throat prickled. "That's unnecessary. It's just jewelry."

A male throat cleared behind me. "Everything okay here?" Christian asked.

"Daddy, look!" Bree beamed as she looked up and held out the charm.

Christian looked a little sad as he smiled back at her. "You look great, baby girl."

We piled into the truck and set off on the bumpy drive off the ranch. When we got to the girls' school, I avoided eye contact with the teachers who were overseeing the drop-off line, but they didn't avoid eye contact with me.

"They're just mad you're here because all the teachers and moms want to date dad," Gracie informed me, to Christian's utter dismay.

He tried his best to regain his composure. "Love you, Gracie. Love you, Bree. Have a good day."

I kept my laughter in until we were safely away from prying eyes. "I had no idea I was in the company of such a hot commodity."

Christian grunted. "I'm not a commodity. It's just slim pickings around here."

"Is that why you haven't remarried?" I asked, seizing the opportunity.

But he decided to avoid the question altogether. "Let's just get you to the beauty parlor so you can look like Dolly. I've got shit to do."

We rode silently to the little downtown strip. Christian pulled into a space and gave me the speech I imagine he had prepared for when he dropped his kids off on their own.

Call me if you need anything. Let me know if you go anywhere else. I'll be back in a few hours. Do you have your phone? Your wallet?

I wasn't certain he could turn off the "dad mode."

I slid out of the passenger's seat as he opened the door and ushered me onto the sidewalk. "Sure you'll be alright?"

I laughed. "What's the worst that could happen here? Barney Fife will arrest me for jaywalking?"

He cracked a smile. "Alright, smart ass. See you in a bit."

I pretended to walk down to the beauty parlor while Christian drove off, then scurried over to the standalone mail collection box. I pulled a thick, white envelope out of my purse, double-checked the address, and dropped it in the slot without so much as a breath of reflection.

It was over.

And I wasn't sad.

I was relieved.

Why wasn't I sad again?

I mused on it as I pushed open the door to the hair

salon and was assaulted by the smell of perm solution and hairspray.

I chewed on my nail as my hair was shampooed and conditioned. I worked it over and over in my mind as I sat under the dryer, half-eavesdropping on the two moms in the chairs beside me.

The writing had been on the wall for a long time. *So why had I stayed with him?*

I put my *ex*-fiancé out of my mind and focused on the conversation that was going on between the stylists.

When I worked for Hollywood's annoying elite, I'd take the temperature of the public by—well—snooping.

Go to the places where people simply talk for the sake of talking.

My nails were always done, my hair was always flawless, and I always lingered a little longer than necessary when picking up my morning coffee.

Small towns were no different.

Want the good gossip? Find a hair stylist.

"Alright, fancy," Amanda said as she whisked away the cape. She was a peppy thirty-something hairdresser who stepped in and saved me from a beehive done by the elderly owner.

"You're all done."

I waved away the fog of Aqua Net and studied my reflection in the mirror. To my surprise, it wasn't giving *entertainer of the year.* My brassy blonde hair had been toned in the shampoo bowl. She had given me smooth, old Hollywood waves. It was vintage and soft, but still savage.

"Now," Amanda said as she looped her arm in mine and waltzed toward the front desk to check me out. "Go next door and get gussied up. Dab on some perfume samples if you don't have any in your pocketbook."

I lifted an eyebrow as she ran my card. "How did you know I was going over there?"

She snickered and nudged her glasses up with her knuckle. "Honey, you don't honestly believe Christian Griffith can drop a woman off at my salon without an audience, do you?"

I added a tip to the receipt and handed it over. "Is this a regular occurrence?"

She gasped. "Heavens, no. That's why we've gotta get this one right. Now hurry on. You don't want him to catch you with half of a face on. Also, you need a trim. Next time he lets you off that ranch, give me a ring."

Amanda practically shoved me out onto the sidewalk, where someone else grabbed my arm and dragged me into Blush & Bashful.

The entire store was a nauseating shade of pink that made me think of diarrhea medicine.

I was nearly body-slammed by a woman in her sixties. She had bangs bigger than Mount Rushmore, eyeshadow that was the color of the blue liquid they use in pad commercials instead of just showing blood, and coral lipstick that was all over her teeth.

"Absolutely not, Nadine. Hands off the blonde."

Nadine stumbled back as a girl no older than eighteen or nineteen wedged in front of her.

She blew a pink bubble of chewing gum and let it pop before snapping it and chomping down again. "Don't worry. I won't let her give you the realtor special. Your bone structure is too good to make you look like you sell houses and pyramid scheme crap between PTA meetings and lunch with the ladies."

I blinked, taking her in. "Uh, thanks?" Looking around, I realized that no one else was coming to my rescue.

I gave the girl another assessment, starting with her black combat boots and moving up the ripped fishnets to the black miniskirt adorned with chains. She was wearing a Michael Jackson glove, a button-up shirt and vest duo complete with a necktie, charcoal black lipstick, and the heaviest smokey eye I had ever seen. She tucked her jet black shag behind her ears, showing off a row of piercings.

"I think I'll be just fine on my own," I said magnanimously.

The girl snapped her gum. "You touch my makeup samples and I'll kick you to the curb."

Now that was something. "*Your* makeup samples?" I looked around at all the pink, then at the goth princess in front of me.

She tapped her name tag. Beneath her printed name, *Roxy,* read, "owner."

"Don't be fooled by the pink. It's just marketing. Same with the name. Get an old lady to quote *Steel Magnolias* and she'll hand over her life savings."

She snapped her gum again, and the sound made my spine itch.

Roxy cocked her head to the over-teased lady she had hip-checked five seconds ago. "So's Nadine. The old bats around town love her, and she's in good with the mayor—if you know what I mean. She'll talk your ear off and stuff your basket."

Little Miss Ray of Death was savvy. I liked it.

"Now you're my kind of woman." I sat my ass down in the chair and grinned. "Alright, Doom Cookie. I'll let you work your magic on me in exchange for a little insider information."

Half an hour later, my face was perfection. Morticia flexed some serious skills. I had a new—unexpected—best friend, and the final details of my devious plot to make Christian Griffith shit a brick over what I wanted to do to his beloved ranch.

Roxy had gone simple, but her technique was flawless. She leaned into the vintage hair Amanda had given me and went with a creamy face, a light dusting of blush, winged liner with devastating mascara, and a savage lip that matched the red bottoms of my stilettos.

Roxy had just finished bagging up my reinforcements and handing over my receipt when I spotted the reflection of Christian's truck in the store windows.

"I'll expect a full report next time you're in town in exchange for the info I gave you," Roxy said as she unwrapped a new piece of bubble gum.

"A full report on what?"

"About whatever you've got cooking for the ranch. Keep me in the loop. But that thing about the mayor stays between us." She snickered. "And I'll need the scoop on whatever's about to happen with that cowboy who's looking at you like a coyote looks at a little baby bunny."

I didn't deign her last comment worth the time of a response. But deep inside, I felt it.

I craved it.

I wanted him to look.

So I made him.

Christian stood by the truck as I strutted out of the shop with a little extra swing in my hips. His boots were crossed at the ankle in an attempt to look casual, but I could feel the tension radiating off of him.

Slowly, he peeled away his sunglasses and peered at me, unencumbered, from beneath his cowboy hat.

Christian let out a low whistle. "Look at you, Princess." His eyes raked up and down the black sheath dress I had thrown on this morning, and he licked his lips.

I was about to say something sassy—maybe about how I was going for more Cruella and less Cinderella—but my phone rang.

I looked at the caller ID. It was a Texas number, but I didn't have the contact saved.

Maybe it was one of the investors calling me back from a local office.

"Cassandra Parker," I said, answering the call and giving Christian the "one moment" finger.

"Miss Cass?"

The sound of Bree's voice made my heart stop. *Why was she calling me? I didn't even know she had my number.*

"Bree?"

Christian went stiff and reached for the phone, but I swatted him away.

"I'm sorry, I tried calling my dad, and grandma, and Aunt Becks, but no one's answering their phones."

"Hold on, I'm with your father right now. Here he is."

Christian nearly took my hand off when he grabbed the phone. "Baby, what's the matter? Are you hurt? Sick?"

He paused, the look of concern instantly marring to frustration.

Or at least his watered down version of frustration. It was barely a twitch of his eye, but I caught it this time.

He sighed. "It'll probably be two hours before I can get home to get you a change of clothes and then drive back to the school. Are you sure they won't let you just go back to class? You'll miss most of the day waiting for me."

"What happened?" I hissed.

Christian covered the speaker with his hand. "She got dress-coded by the principal, who apparently has it out for her."

"Did she actually break the dress code?"

"Not technically. It's just how they're interpreting it."

I grabbed the phone back. "Sit tight. Do not say anything until we get there."

"What?"

"Why did you speak?" I snapped as I yanked open the truck door. "Did I not just tell you to shut the fuck up?"

"*Cassandra*," Christian hissed.

I paid him no mind. "Sit there. Think about something boring. Don't smile. Don't frown. Don't let them smell your fear. Admit nothing and shut your mouth. We'll be there in—"

"Ten minutes," Christian said as he hopped in and cranked the engine.

"Ten minutes. Don't speak."

Silence.

"Excellent." And with that, I hung up.

"For the hundredth time, you *cannot* talk to my children that way," he clipped as he strangled the steering wheel.

"I'm handling the situation, Christian. It's what I do." I

pulled down the visor and checked my lipstick in the mirror. “You don’t like it? Well, too damn bad. Fire me.”

“She’s a child,” he said. “You can’t treat her like she’s… Like she’s one of the upper-crust socialites you have to ‘contain.’”

I turned on him. “Your daughter is getting bullied by an *adult*. Celebrity or not, assholes are assholes.”

He pinched the bridge of his nose. “Do I even want to know what you’re about to do?”

I smirked. “I’m about to be the bigger asshole.”

18

CHRISTIAN

Cassandra didn't look up from her phone during the drive to the school. Every so often, I'd glance over and find her looking at the school website, deep-diving into the administration, and scouring the dress code that was digitized thanks to the district.

"I'm probably just gonna have to sign her out for the day," I said, instead of telling Cassandra that having it out with an administrator in front of my thirteen-year-old was a bad idea.

Cassandra laughed. "Nice try. I'm going in with you."

I pulled into a visitor's space and threw the truck into park. "Cass—"

"Listen to me." Blonde hair swished across her back as she turned in the seat to face me. "You want to be a good dad? Stand up for your kid instead of being amicable. Don't teach her to play dead just because you don't want to be confrontational."

I ran my tongue over my teeth to keep from admitting how much that stung.

She yanked on the door handle and pushed it open, but I was faster. I rounded the front of the truck and caught the edge of the door in my palm. "You know better than to open your own door."

Her lips turned up in a victorious smile. "I got your ass out of the seat, didn't I?"

I slammed the door shut as soon as her high heels hit the asphalt. "You'd better use your powers for good in there, Parker."

"Just because I don't sugarcoat things doesn't mean I'm a heartless bitch. I'm only a bitch for good causes," she said, her words on tempo with the tip tap of her shoes. "I'm a vigilante bitch."

I paused in front of the glass double doors. "Just... Give me a minute to see what's going on before you rip this old woman to shreds."

Her lips curled up in a wicked smirk. "I am feeling a little peckish. A little aged meat might tide me over until dinner."

"Jesus Christ," I muttered as I pulled my cowboy hat off and handed it to Cassandra. "Mind holding that for a second?"

I quickly yanked my hair out of the elastic and tied it back in a neater bun.

Her painted fingertips were hanging onto the hat by the brim.

"Like this," I said as I took it back by the crown. "Don't wanna bend the brim. Always hold it by the top."

She was unamused. "It's a hat."

"Yes, it is. There's etiquette around them. Respect it."

Cassandra looked taken aback.

I sighed and scrubbed my hand down my beard. "Sorry. Didn't mean to yell at you."

She laughed. "If you think that's yelling, then I hope you never have to see me order from a deli. I'll scare the shit out of you." Her eyes darkened, but amusement glinted in them like stars in a twilight sky. "But for the record—I wouldn't be opposed to you bossing me around, cowboy."

I yanked open the door to the school office. "Are you flirting with me?"

"Yes. That should be obvious. Now shut up and let me do the talking."

I put my hand on the small of her back and led her through the next set of doors. "You have to stop telling people to shut up."

Bree was sitting in a chair along the interior wall of the school office. Tears streaked her cheeks as her feet bounced nervously on the carpeted floor.

Fuck.

She looked up at me with red-rimmed eyes and whispered, "I'm sorry, Daddy."

"Mr. Griffith," Tanya, the receptionist, said as I scrawled my name and Cassandra's across the visitor's clipboard. "Principal Beeker will be with you shortly. Please have a seat."

Cassandra positioned herself as a sentry beside Bree. "Sit up straight and stop fidgeting," she clipped under her breath. "You look guilty."

I knelt in front of Bree, pulled a handkerchief out of my pocket, and handed it to her. "What happened, baby?"

She sniffed and wiped her eyes. "Principal Beeker was the sub for my English class today and said my shirt was too low and it was distracting."

"Well, that's bullshit," Cassandra scoffed, making every head in the office snap to attention.

I had a feeling that scene I was trying hard to avoid was going to happen whether I wanted it to or not.

Keys jingled down the hall—the foreboding sound of the principal approaching.

"I hate schools," Cassandra muttered as she looked around. "It's like a prison. No wonder the adults act like wardens."

"That's her," Bree whispered to Cassandra as Principal Beeker strolled through the office like she owned the place.

"Don't say a word," Cassandra hissed. "Make her talk first. Nine times out of ten people will dig their own graves. Let them."

"Is this really the time to be teaching my daughter how to manipulate people?" I whispered as we were led into the principal's office.

"Yes," Cassandra whispered back. "And I prefer to call it 'controlling the narrative.' Manipulation has such a negative connotation."

"Cass—"

She paused in the doorway, anger flaring in her eyes as she whispered, "This isn't about her clothes."

"It's unfortunate that we're interrupting our day to have this meeting," Principal Beeker said as she lifted her chained bifocals to the tip of her nose. "Bree was told that she could return to class when she changed into something more appropriate, so I'm not sure why we're all here." She eyed Cassandra. "Or who you are."

I was fully expecting Cassandra to take the bait, but she didn't make a peep. Her face was passive. Her body was relaxed. The only tell that she was nervous was the way she trailed her finger along the edge of her phone.

This was the part of parenting I hated.

I cleared my throat. "I teach my girls to follow the rules, and we make sure their clothes abide by the dress code."

"Well," Principal Beeker said with a gleeful smile. "Children can be deceptive. Perhaps Bree left home wearing something else this morning, then changed into—" she wagged her finger in Bree's direction "—this."

"I didn't—"

Before Bree could argue, Cassandra cupped a hand over her mouth. "What did I tell you on the phone?" she hissed

Bree looked up at her and nodded, and Cassandra removed her hand.

"Don't take the bait," Cassandra whispered.

"No," I said to the principal. "This is what Bree was wearing when I dropped her off this morning, so please think twice before you call my daughter a liar again."

Bree looked up at me with wide eyes.

Principal Beeker huffed. "The fact of the matter is that she's out of dress code."

"How?" Cassandra pressed. "Because according to the dress code, blouse necklines are to be no lower than three inches below the lowest point of the clavicle. Now, I'm more familiar with things that are bigger than three inches, but I can see how you may be more in tune to things of that size."

I choked on an impulsive laugh.

"Would you like to get a ruler?" Cassandra looked around. "This is a place of learning, after all. I'm sure there's one around."

Principal Beeker settled behind her desk and folded her hands together. "While her blouse may fit the *technical* dress code guidelines," she began pragmatically. "It's my job to interpret those guidelines to make sure that students aren't a distraction to their peers." She looked at me with a snide smile. "You know how boys can be at this age."

I glanced at Cassandra, expecting to see her about to go nuclear, but she was smiling.

That was *way* worse.

"Why don't you save us all some time and say why you thought the situation was so dire that Bree's learning had to be interrupted to protect a small segment of her class from being 'distracted?'" Cassandra said, backing the principal into a metaphorical corner.

Principal Beeker huffed. "Bree has developed womanly features sooner than most of her female peers. The blouses that smaller girls may be able to wear within the dress code are simply inappropriate on her body."

Bree's face turned beet red.

Before I could speak up, Cassandra did. "Let's cut the crap. This isn't about the dress code, which—for the record—is *not* up for interpretation. Bree hasn't violated the rules, which you just admitted yourself. But I think the school board would be *very* interested to hear about how the administration has been sexualizing the minors under their care. Underage students show up to this school, intending to have a safe place to learn. But instead, they're judged by adults in positions of power based on how quickly their bodies are developing, and pulled from class because of it."

My throat went dry.

Principal Beeker looked like she was about to explode.

Bree crossed her arms over her stomach and hunched over, trying to hide herself.

Cassandra gave her a nudge, and Bree sat up straight.

"I'm looking out for the reputation of the school and the good of the students," Principal Beeker said.

Cassandra smiled. "You and I both know that's not the case. Either you're a principal on a power trip—" her voice turned lethal "—or you're an adult in a position of power over a minor, and chose to cause a scene in her classroom, making her a distraction to her peers after you assessed her genitals."

Tears flooded Bree's eyes, and rage boiled up in my gut. I wanted to grab her and run, leaving Cassandra to have her cage match with the principal.

Then, Cassandra took Bree's hand and squeezed.

My heart lurched.

The flight instincts slammed to a halt, and I saw Cassandra passing some of her fight to Bree.

"Just who do you think you are, coming into my office and making these outlandish accusations?" Principal Beeker gasped.

"I'm the Griffith family's publicist," Cassandra snapped as she tapped the screen of her phone with her thumb and turned it to show the principal. "And while this little repartee has been fun, I'm getting rather bored of dealing with you. Frankly, you disgust me. I think the best course of action would be for Bree to go back to class and for you not to try me, don't you?"

A recording icon ticked away steadily on Cassandra's phone. She had the principal dead to rights, and she had evidence.

Principal Beeker's nails clawed at the heavy wooden desk. "You can't come in here and record a private conversation! That's illegal!"

"That's where you're wrong," Cassandra said with a rather bored tone in her voice as her phone continued to record. "You see, Texas is a one-party consent state, and *I* consented to recording this conversation. And before you bring up the reasonable expectation of privacy, there's no reasonable expectation of privacy in a school office with the door open after you humiliated my girl in front of her entire class."

I was starting to wonder if bringing Cass was a great idea or if it was about to bankrupt me. I didn't have the kind of petty cash on hand to pay her bail when she murdered this woman.

But the way Bree radiated with energy when Cassandra said "my girl" was worth every penny I had to my name.

Principal Beeker scoffed. "You think you're going to—what? Run a smear campaign against me?"

"I have no hobbies and, frankly, hate the outdoors. Living on a ranch is my version of hell." Cassandra grinned like a dragon about to breathe fire. "So trust me when I say that a smear campaign is child's play for me. I have all the time in the world to do it. I'll run for the school board and my first order of business will be to have your head served on a silver platter. I'll personally use your resignation letter as my napkin. You wanna look up my track record? The last political campaign I worked on was a senate race and the man ended up in the president's cabinet after three months. I dare you to try me."

The silence was dangerous. The room buzzed with the kind of electricity that pulses before a storm. The office outside was deadly quiet. Every ear was turned in our direction.

Principal Beeker's eyes turned to Bree, and it took everything in me to keep from throttling the judgmental old bat for looking at my kid.

"Bree, get a hall pass from Miss Tanya and go to your fourth period class. We're done here," she said as she stood.

Bree hurried out with a quiet, "yes, ma'am."

I took Cassandra's hand—mostly to keep her from launching herself at the principal—and laced our fingers together.

"Don't make me come back here, Bonna," Cassandra stated with a pointed finger, leaving the old lady fuming.

Principal Beeker's first name was Bonna?

As much as I wanted to see them fight it out to the death, I dragged Cassandra out and caught Bree as she was leaving the office.

"I'm sorry, daddy," she said as she wrapped her arms around me, clutching her hall pass.

"You didn't do anything wrong," I said as I let go of Cassandra's hand and held her tight. "That was hard, and I'm proud of you for sitting through it."

She sniffed. "Thanks for coming." Before I could say

another word, she leaped to Cassandra and hugged her. "Thank you."

Cassandra hugged her back, then cupped her cheeks, wiping away Bree's tears. "Head up high. People will whisper. Those people might be teachers. That doesn't give you a right to talk back. They can only get you in trouble if you break the rules. Don't give them that opportunity."

Bree nodded and touched the necklace Cassandra had given her this morning.

"We'll debrief when you get home," Cassandra said.

"I love you," I said as I kissed Bree's head.

She seemed a little brighter as she said, "Love you too, daddy." She gave Cassandra a little wave. "Thanks for coming, Miss Cass."

"Anytime."

We walked out to the truck in silence. Neither of us said a peep as I headed back to the ranch. The truck bumped and bobbed as the pavement turned to gravel, then to dirt.

I had a lot of shit to do, but my head wasn't in it. Not when I was stuck on the woman in the passenger's seat.

"If you're expecting me to apologize, don't hold your breath," Cassandra said as she unbuckled her seatbelt.

I slammed my door with a little more force than necessary. I had been replaying the showdown at the school in my head on the drive back.

To my surprise, Cassandra waited for me to open her door. I curled my fingers around the metal edge to keep from reaching for her as she slid down and adjusted the hem of her dress.

I wanted it off.

"From the looks of it, no one has ever put that bitch in her place. It was overdue. I was performing a public service." Her shoes clicked as she scaled each step. The swing of her ass was hypnotizing.

The front door to my house was unlocked—because it always was—and Cassandra strolled inside like she owned the damn place.

"I swear, if Bree tells me that one fucking comment was made about her after today, I'll burn the place down."

And then my self-control snapped.

19

CASSANDRA

"Take your dress off."

I froze in place. My spine stiffened at the growl echoing from the door frame, but I didn't turn around. "Excuse me?"

His wide hands spanned my waist, sliding up and down before he found the zipper tucked away on the side. "Do you still want this?"

"What?" I played dumb to force his hand.

Fingers threaded up my neck, tangling in the back of my hair. They curled against my scalp, tugging firmly. The bite of pain was delicious.

"I don't do mind games, Princess." His beard scratched my ear as he whispered against my skin. "If you want me to finish what you started the other day, then take off your dress."

"And if I don't?"

My eyes fluttered closed as he pulled my hips backward until my ass nestled against the front of his jeans.

"If you don't, I'm going to walk back out that door. We'll both go on with our days like this never happened."

My body still hummed with electricity after the public dressing down I had the pleasure of giving back at the school. As much as I wanted to egg him on a little longer, I just wanted him. I needed to release all that pent-up energy.

Our fingers brushed as I reached for the zipper and pulled it down.

"So, you *do* know how to follow directions," Christian said as he took off his hat and hung it on the rack. His voice was warm and strong like a shot of whiskey.

"Don't sound so fucking smug," I grumbled as I wiggled out of the sleeves and pushed the top half of the dress down to my waist.

Rough fingertips grazed my bare skin, sending a torrent of goosebumps skittering across my stomach.

"You're wasting time."

"You could help me get undressed," I sassed.

Christian chuckled. "You're doing just fine on your own. Besides—" he brushed my hair aside and dotted the crook of my neck with the whisper of a kiss "—I like watching you."

I shoved the dress off my hips, letting it fall in a pool of black fabric. "If you're just watching, I'll need some fresh batteries."

His knuckle trailed down my cheek. "One day that smart mouth is gonna get you in trouble."

Christian made my ankles weak. I wobbled on the heels of my stilettos and tipped backward into him. For the shortest second in human history, I let myself lean into him, trusting that he'd catch me.

And he did.

"Is today that day?" I asked.

Hands slid around my waist, across my stomach, then up my ribs—exploring and mapping my body. He took his time, but never once grazed my bra or panties. Warm lips dotted the back of my neck with a line of kisses.

I ached to turn and fall into his chest. To be held. To feel safe.

"Not today." Christian dug his fingers into my hips and spun me to face him. I matched each of his steps forward with a step back. My back hit the wall, but he kept pressing forward. "I like it when you use your powers for good."

I tipped my chin up and grazed his lips. "Then just imagine the damage I can do when I'm feeling naughty. Don't test me."

"We'll see about that," he growled the moment before his lips met mine.

I gasped into the kiss as his hands skated up my abdomen. Fingers curled around my bra strap, yanking it down my shoulder. Christian caressed the swell of my breast with the back of his knuckles as he traced my lips with his tongue. I couldn't help the desperate moan that slipped out of my mouth when he scraped his fingers over the place where my bra hid my nipple.

"Make that sound for me again." He slid one hand into my bra, gently squeezing my breast before smoothing a calloused finger over my nipple.

Heat and wanton desire flashed like lightning, striking my pussy in an instant. I bit my lip, stifling it as I tried to clench my thighs together to ease the emptiness.

Christian stopped me. He wedged his knee between

my legs, eyes darkening as he cupped my jaw in his palm. "Don't hold back on my account."

I pressed my palms squarely on his chest, feeling his heart racing through me like an electrical current. "I have a feeling you're the one holding back. Do you think I want you to be nice and make love to me or something?"

Christian's face split in a grin as he grabbed the back of my thighs and threw me over his shoulder.

I grunted as the wind was knocked out of my lungs. "What is the matter with you?" I wheezed and muttered, "Caveman."

He palmed my ass as he took heavy strides across the kitchen. His boots clomped and echoed through the empty house. Christian yanked open the door to the guest room and, without warning, threw me onto the bed.

I screeched as I plummeted, trying to spot the landing, but I bounced. My shoulder smacked the wall and I collapsed into the space between the bed and the wall in a crumpled heap of tangled limbs.

"Burning daylight," he said, unbothered, as he toed off his boots and unbuttoned his shirt.

I sat up and dropped my chin onto the mattress as strands of hair fell in front of my face. "Oh, I'm sorry. I'd already be on the bed if you hadn't *thrown* me across the room."

"Right," Christian said with a smirk. He stopped taking his clothes off to scoop me up and drop me gently onto the mattress. "I forgot. You're not used to being with someone who can manhandle you."

I rolled my eyes and scooted back against the pillows. "Let me be clear. I do not like being dominated. *I'm* in charge."

His chuckle was dark. "It's cute that you think that. But let *me* be clear." He grabbed a condom from his pocket, tossed it on the bed, and dropped his jeans. "This is the only place I want to dominate you. And I think you're going to like it."

I pressed my finger to his lips as he prowled up the bed. "The princess thing is cute because you think it gets under my skin, but if you expect me to kneel—"

Christian took my wrists in his hands, turned them up, and kissed my palms. "The only time you'll kneel will be over my face so I can pleasure my queen the way she deserves."

I wasn't sure if the gasp that escaped my mouth was shock or arousal. Probably a little of both.

"Men don't talk like that anymore," I rasped as he pulled my hips beneath his and braced himself over me.

Christian cupped my cheek and kissed me. "I do."

I was a tall woman, topping out at six feet—more when I was in heels. Men were always steering clear of me because they didn't want to feel insecure. But not Christian.

He sat back on his haunches and curled his fingers into the edge of my thong. I watched through heavy lids as he tugged my panties down and cupped my pussy in his palm.

"Let me guess," I said between labored breaths. "You prefer your women *au naturel* or something."

He studied my eyes with an unbreakable gaze as he pressed his thumb to my clit.

"You know, since you're ... like ..." I bit my lip, whimpering when he pinched my clit between two fingers and slowly massaged it. "All rugged and—"

"And what?" he asked as he slid a finger through my slick entrance.

"You're like a human bear."

He chuckled. "You need to stop assuming that you know what I like, Cass."

With the lightest touches, Christian was making me feel more turned on and vulnerable than I had in years.

There was something to be said about bad sex where the other person is selfish or doesn't know what the hell they're doing. It never made me feel exposed or fragile. Especially when I was in control.

But Christian made me feel like a window pane with spider web cracks racing through the glass.

My toes curled as he kept steady pressure on my clit.

I was on the verge of shattering.

He reached around and unclasped my bra, pulling the cups away and uncovering my breasts.

"You want to know what I like?" Christian leaned down and pulled my nipple into his mouth, forcing me to arch off the bed as my body sought his touch. He released it with a *pop* and kissed down my sternum while skating his hand up and down my thigh. "I like seeing you in those high heels you love. Your legs are a fucking dream in them. I like the way you always take the time to put on perfume even if you're working from the house. I don't want you rough and rugged, Cass." He slid a thick finger into my pussy and slowly curled it, dragging the tip along my sensitive walls. "I like your softness."

He moved down and slowly lapped at my clit with the flat of his tongue.

Fireworks sizzled across my hips as he eased me close

to an orgasm. I clenched my thigh around his ears, desperate not to let it fade.

Christian teased me as he drew his finger from my core and grabbed my thighs. "You're more than welcome to ride my beard as much as you want, but right now I want these legs open wide."

I groaned as he slid two fingers inside me. "Least sexy position of all time. I look like a spatchcocked turkey."

He growled and grazed my clit with his teeth as he shoved my legs apart with his shoulders. "Is that what that little bitch boy told you?"

"Something like that," I gasped when he found my G-spot.

"Well." He leaned up and pressed his palm to my pussy, stroking inside of me as he stimulated my clit with the heel of his hand. "Allow me to make it up to you."

"Christian—" I groaned as he edged me again, closer to the precipice this time.

"That's right. *My* fingers in your cunt. *My* name on your lips. He doesn't get this body anymore. Not his ring on your finger, not a fucking inkling of him in your mind. I'm going to replace every thought of him. Mark my words, princess."

"The ring's gone," I whispered when he let off the pressure again, dragging my climax out.

Christian paused. "What?"

I swallowed. "I put it in the mail this morning. I sent it to his assistant. She'll open it in the office and get the rumor mill going because of the note I added about him cheating with a client and framing me for her public outburst."

He looked up with a wicked smile. "Why didn't you go to human resources?"

"So he can get a slap on the wrist?" I let out a caustic laugh. "I want revenge, not red tape."

His fingers moved inside of me. "I think revenge turns you on," he said as he showed me the wetness that hung like dew-covered webs between his fingers.

My cheeks burned with embarrassment, but a larger part of me was turned on by the note of praise in his voice.

"What can I say? I like being bad."

Christian grabbed the condom he had tossed on top of the sheets and handed it to me. "Then enjoy what it feels like to be my good girl."

He shucked off his boxers and straddled my hips. His cock was thick and heavy, bobbing in front of me as he plucked my nipple. "You know what to do. Put that on me."

"Prepared. I like it." I tore the packet open and fitted the condom on the head of his cock, then rolled it down his shaft. I salivated over the groan that ripped from his hair-covered chest when I cupped his balls in my palm.

"*Fuck.*" His whisper slipped as I gently rolled them in my hand and gave them a tug. His eyes squeezed shut and he exhaled a heady breath. "Do you know how many times I fucked my hand thinking about you?"

"Ah. So you don't have the supernatural self-control I thought you did. Good to know you're human."

His laugh turned into a kiss. "Kings, tyrants, and gods couldn't resist you, darling. How could I?"

Blunt pressure nudged against my pussy as he notched

himself in my entrance. I vaulted back, my spine bending as he pushed inside. Christian wrapped me up in his arms, keeping me safe against his chest as he sank into my pussy.

"Breathe," he soothed as he caressed my breast, kneading and teasing it as a distraction.

But it wasn't the fullness that made my lungs ache. It was him.

"Sorry. It's been a while," I lied, tucking my forehead into the crook of his neck as he eased out and thrust in again.

"I've got you."

"Christian," I cried out as he held deep inside of me and ground the base of his shaft against my clit. I squeezed my legs around his hips, desperate to keep him close.

"You feel so fucking good," he whispered into my neck, punctuating it with a kiss. "I want to feel you come around me."

I nodded, desperately craving the orgasm. "Make me come."

"Yes, ma'am," he grunted as he kept a steady rhythm, always pausing to give my clit some attention.

"I hate being called 'ma'am.'"

Warm brown eyes locked on mine as he thrust inside of me. He cupped the back of my neck and tangled his fingers in my hair.

His whisper against my neck was reverent. "Yes, my queen."

Sparks danced across my body. Every part of me craved him. My nipples ached for his touch, and my breasts felt heavy. I wanted his mouth on mine. I wanted his eyes on my body. I wanted his hands everywhere—touching and teasing me.

I exploded and collapsed like a supernova, glowing with white-hot energy as my release racked my body. Christian froze, swearing under his breath as he jerked, filling the condom.

We lay there, chest to chest, catching our breath as sweat-slicked skin stuck to each other. I flopped my head to the side and peered at the clock on the nightstand. "You probably need to get back to work."

Christian chuckled as he pecked my lips, then eased out of me. "Are you kicking me out of my own house?"

I trailed my fingertips down his chest. "I'm giving you an easy out."

"I don't need an out, Cass. Hang tight."

I laid there as he slipped out to the bathroom to deal with the condom. He came back a minute later with two washcloths—one warm and damp, and the other dry.

His posture was humble as he knelt between my thighs and gently wiped them clean, then dry.

"Admirable, but unnecessary," I said as I rolled over to my side. "You have a weirdly 'nice' style of domination."

Christian shook with laughter as he pulled on his boxers, then slid into bed behind me. "You think it's just being tied up and spanked?"

"Something like that. I don't mind a little spanky panky."

He brushed my hair aside and kissed up the back of my neck. "Well, to me it means that a partner is trusting me to be in control of their pleasure."

I shivered as he ghosted his fingers up and down my waist.

"There's a lot of gray area in that. You wanna be tied up and teased? I've got rope. You want me to pull your hair and turn your ass red? It would be my pleasure, Princess." He wrapped his arms around me and pulled my body against his chest. "But if you just want me to put you first and make you feel good, you can trust me to do that because making you feel good turns me on."

"I'm not a cuddler," I huffed as I turned in his arms and rested my temple against his soft chest.

Christian was ridiculously sexy. His body was comforting. It was a safe place I could get lost in.

He buried his nose in my hair and inhaled deeply. "You have a funny way of showing it."

"I don't hate it quite as much as I usually do," I hedged. "This is like snuggling with a teddy bear." I wrapped my arms around his neck and tugged his hair out of the mussed bun. "I like it."

He groaned as I scratched his scalp, easing the tension from having his hair up all the time.

"Do you get those sore spots on your head when you make your bun too tight?" I asked.

Christian closed his eyes as he soaked it in. "Yeah. That feels good."

"Why do you have long hair? It seems like it gets in the way."

He lifted an eyebrow. "Do you not like it?"

"I didn't say that. I was asking why you have it. In all the photos on your mantle, your hair is short."

"It wasn't practical to keep asking my mom to help me with the girls' hair. I grew mine out so I could practice on myself and learn how to take care of it so I could teach them. I've gone to work with braids, curls, rollers—you name it."

My heart seized.

Christian looked at the clock and sighed. "I have to get back to work." He tipped my chin up and pressed a kiss to my lips. "Are you okay?"

"I'm fine."

"Wanna come out with me? Ride out to where the boys are?"

I laughed. "If you plan on fucking me again, I highly recommend that you don't make me sore from riding a horse."

He laughed. "That's fair."

"Go to work," I said, playfully shoving him off of me. I shimmied up the bed and sat against the pillows as he tugged his jeans back on.

He worked down the line of buttons on his shirt. "You sure there's not something you wanna talk about?"

Fucking mind-reading cowboys...

"What changed your mind?" I asked.

"About what?" he asked as he buckled his belt. "Fucking?"

"Yes."

His smile was bashful. "Cass, I've been fantasizing about you since I saw you get out of that car the day you arrived. Not fucking you the day I walked in here and saw you touching yourself had nothing to do with you."

"Because you have kids."

"I do." He stomped into his boots. "And today you stood up for them and protected them." He leaned over the bed and kissed me. "Nothing is more attractive to me than that."

20

CHRISTIAN

"You've been avoiding me."

"Jesus! Fuck!" Coffee sloshed across the countertop as the ceramic mug fell out of Cassandra's hand. She slumped against the kitchen cabinets and pressed her hand to her chest like she was trying to stave off a heart attack. "I thought you were gone."

"So, you admit that you were avoiding me," I said as I closed the front door behind me, stealing a moment to take her in.

She was still in her pajamas—a pair of long, silky pants and a tight, long-sleeved shirt that clung to every delicious inch of her chest.

"No," she said defensively. "I've been busy."

"You live in my house."

"I wasn't avoiding you. I just thought you had left early this morning and were out somewhere doing cow things."

"Cass."

Her eyes drifted to the paper bag and coffee cup in my hand.

"I took the girls to school this morning." I dropped the lump wrapped in wax paper on the table and approached her with cool tactfulness. "Walked Bree to her homeroom to make sure no one gave her any shit."

"A show of force is never a bad idea," she said cooly as she peered curiously at the coffee.

"Stopped by the fancy coffee place and picked up your concoction."

Cassandra lifted an eyebrow and popped the lid on the paper cup to peer inside before giving it a sniff. "Okay, be serious. I know I give you shit about being a mind reader, but how do you know the kind of latte I drink?"

I leaned in and let my beard tickle her ear as I whispered, "All I had to do was walk inside and ask if a loud New Yorker had been in lately. And then I asked them to give me whatever she ordered."

She snorted as she raised the coffee to her lips. "Impressive."

I grabbed the breakfast sandwich off of the table. "Bacon, egg, and cheese on a roll."

Cassandra looked genuinely surprised. "It's not on a biscuit?"

"Not on a biscuit."

She set the coffee aside and started ripping into the wax paper. "I could kiss you right now."

"Fine by me." Before she could get her hands on the sandwich, I grabbed her hips and pinned her against the counter, kissing her until we were both breathless. I tangled her hair around my fingers and gave it a gentle tug down, forcing her to look up at me. "Will you stop avoiding me now?"

She licked her lips. "Are you bribing me?"

"Is it working?"

"We'll see."

"Then I'll keep bribing you."

"So, you admit to bribing me," she said with a hint of smug victory in her voice.

I dropped her mug into the sink, ripped a paper towel off the roll, and wiped up the coffee spill. "And you just admitted to avoiding me. I think we can call it even."

A mischievous smirk worked up her lips as she took a bite. "You keep bringing me breakfast, and I might keep avoiding you. It's working out pretty well for me."

She was trying to put up a good front, but I could see the mistrust and hurt lingering in the steel blades of her eyes.

I had a laundry list of things to do today. Usually I would have been three or four hours into my workday by now. But for some reason my boots were rooted to the kitchen floor and that to-do list didn't seem so important.

"How'd you sleep?" I asked, resting my ass on the counter's edge and crossing one ankle over the other like I had all the time in the world.

"Fine," she mumbled around the roll.

"I suppose so." I stretched my arm out behind her back, and she hunched forward. "Especially since you went to bed at what—seven? You know, after you ate dinner over at Becks and Nate's house."

"She wanted to catch up, then I was tired," Cassandra objected.

"Cut the shit, princess."

She balled up the wax paper, tossed it in the trash, and started to pace. "What do you want me to say?"

I stayed right where I was, not wanting to add to her nervous energy. "I want you to be honest with me. Are you okay?"

"No." She threw her hands in the air. "I'm not. Is that what you want to hear?"

Shit.

"Cass..."

She ran a hand back through her hair. "I felt like I was going to start climbing the walls. Okay? It was quiet after you left, I just kept watching the clock for the girls to get home, and then I panicked. I didn't know what would happen after the situation at the school with Bree, then after what we ... you know... did. I needed time to think it over. So yeah—" she threw her hands in the air "—I walked down to see if Becks was home. The repairs on their house are done, so I helped her fold baby clothes and put things away in the nursery. And, yes. I came back after I knew you'd have the girls getting ready for bed so I could slip in undetected. I didn't have the capacity to deal with feelings or not swearing around them or whatever you obviously have the patience to deal with every fucking day."

"Cass."

"If avoiding a situation I didn't have a plan for makes me the bad guy then—"

"Cassandra." I caught her around the waist. "Stop."

Tears filled her eyes and it broke something inside of me.

I cupped her cheeks. "What's the matter?"

"I just told you—"

"No. You told me why you were scarce last night, and that's fair. I don't blame you." I wiped beneath her eyes. "Why are you crying, sweetheart?"

She looked at her right hand as it lay against my chest. "I think it finally hit me last night."

I knew that feeling all too well. Realizing that the person I thought I would spend the rest of my life with was gone without warning.

Grief doesn't come in stages. Frankly, it would be easier if it did. It ebbs and flows like waves. Bad days always follow good days, but better days are never far behind.

Unfortunately, coping with grief is easier said than lived.

"Come here," I said as I wrapped her up in my arms.

Cassandra folded against my chest without an ounce of fight.

"Don't run away from me, princess. Not without leaving a glass slipper." I kissed the top of her head as she laughed softly. "And if you need a healthy coping mechanism other than avoiding me, you know where to find me."

Cassandra wiped her eyes. "I don't think hooking up is a healthy coping mechanism."

"I wasn't talking about sex."

"I have a hard time believing that," she countered.

"I have firearms, hatchets, and throwing knives. Pick your poison."

She looked up with curiosity in her eyes. "Do you have Tripp-shaped targets?"

I chuckled. "We'll have to get a better printer in the office."

To my surprise, Cassandra rested her head on my chest and closed her eyes as she sank into me. "How was Bree this morning?"

I raked my fingers through her hair. "A little skittish going back to class. She wanted to wear a turtleneck."

Cassandra swore under her breath.

"She wore the necklace you gave her again. I hope that was okay."

"It's fine."

I debated bringing it up when Cass was already feeling down, but Bree had been torn up when Cassandra wasn't around to talk when she got home from school. "Bree missed you last night."

Cassandra pushed away from me.

"Cass."

"What?" she clipped as she reached for her overpriced coffee.

"You promised her that you'd be there to debrief when she got home from school."

"So? She has you and a therapist. Sometimes I think you should have been a therapist instead of a cowboy."

"That's not the point. Don't make a promise to my girls if you're not going to keep it."

"If you haven't noticed, I'm not a kid person. I guarantee you, it's a good thing I didn't talk to her yesterday. I was a mess."

"See, you keep saying shit like that, and yet I don't believe you."

Her eyes turned down to the coffee.

"As much as I try to turn back the clock, they're not babies anymore." I slipped my finger beneath the hem of her shirt and traced the skin along the waistband of her silk pants. "So, you can keep saying you're not a kid person, but you know what I see?"

"I have a feeling you'll tell me," she mumbled.

I hooked my fingers around the elastic waist and tugged her hips against mine. "You're a protector."

Cassandra's cheek pressed against mine as she whispered, "You think I'm a better person than I am. I'm just a bitch and I know how to monetize that."

I tilted my head and kissed the corner of her mouth. "I think you're a better person than you let yourself believe you are."

Her whisper was a ghost floating against my skin. "All I wanted was some good dick."

"Pretty sure I delivered on that, princess. But if you need me to help jog your memory, it'd be my pleasure."

The radio on my hip crackled with CJ's voice. "Chris—you around?"

Cassandra broke away, using the interruption to disappear into her room.

"Go ahead," I said into the radio.

"Grab the vet bag and get out here. I need an extra set of hands."

I watched Cassandra sashay around, pulling clothes out of her suitcase to get dressed for the day. *She hadn't even unpacked...*

What was I thinking?

I shook it off. "Yeah, I'll be out. Hang tight."

"Everything okay?" Cassandra asked from the guest room.

"Uh, I'm not sure. Sounds like one of the animals is in trouble or something. I'll be back up after a while."

Her breasts bounced in a black bra as she pulled on a

blouse. "I'm going to need an hour of your workday today," she said, shedding the vulnerable woman who had admitted she was heartbroken, and donning the armor of Cassandra the publicist.

"Do I finally get to see what I've been paying you to do all this time?" I asked as I filled up a thermos with coffee from the pot.

"More like you'll get to see what you're going to fork out an exorbitant amount of money for over the next few years."

"I'm sorry—*years*?"

She popped her head back into the bedroom doorway. "You told me to go big."

"STOP RIGHT THERE."

I froze in the doorway of the office. Cassandra sat behind my desk, looking a little green around the gills.

She held out a hand to keep me at a distance. "Dear God, you smell atrocious. *What is that*?"

"It's hot out today," I said, taking a step inside. "Probably got a little sweaty."

She pinched her nose. "No. Out. You smell like death."

"I thought you needed an hour of my time."

She flicked her manicured hand toward the door. "I can condense it. Spend thirty minutes of that with some soap and hot water. Do I even want to know why you smell like the bottom of a garbage truck in July?"

"There was a situation."

Cassandra blinked. "A situation."

I dropped the heavy vet bag on the threshold. "CJ had a momma casting her withers after she birthed a calf. Doc was out in Maren, a little town east, and couldn't get out here to help."

Her eyebrows lifted. "So you did?"

I shrugged. "Prolapsed uterus. Stitched her up and got her stable. Doc'll be out here in a few hours to check her over."

Cassandra's eyes fell back on her computer screen. "I'll pretend like you didn't just tell me you had your whole arm up a cow's—"

"Two arms, actually," I said, just to clarify.

"Shower," she said.

"I'll hose off outside if it'll help you untwist those panties. I don't wanna waste time going up to the house."

Her fingers flew over the keys. "Unless you've got industrial grade soap and are okay with stripping down and flashing this entire ranch, you will go take a proper shower."

I was planning on it, but verbal ping-pong with Cassandra was quickly becoming my favorite hobby. "You'd like that, wouldn't you?"

A reckless little smile flirted with her lips. "Stop wasting my time and go shower."

"You could join me."

Cassandra's eyes flicked upward in surprise. "I'm on the clock."

"That's not a no," I said with a smirk.

"Your children will be home soon."

That was a no.

Cassandra pursed her lips, trying to stave off her amusement and keep that hardened shell on, but a laugh slipped. "I'll meet you up at the house in twenty. Get your checkbook ready."

I hustled up to the house and hopped in the shower to rinse off the day. As much as I tried to make it quick, I couldn't get Cassandra out of my mind.

The blouse she was in wasn't all that low-cut, but she had been leaning over the desk and it gave me an immaculate view of her breasts as they swelled against her lace bra.

I pressed my palm against the side of the shower, bracing myself against the wall as I wrapped my hand around my dick. Tension flooded away from my shoulder, rushing to my cock as I pumped it. I imagined Cassandra trussed up beneath me, squirming as I worshiped her body until she begged me to stop.

I wanted to fuck her again.

I groaned as my cum slapped the wall in harsh lines.

Well, that was short-lived. I needed to get my stamina back.

I sprayed the shower down and hopped out, wrapping a towel around my waist. My phone was buzzing across the bathroom countertop.

"Hello?"

"Surprised you picked up," Ray said.

I chuckled. "Then why'd you call?"

"Figured I'd just leave a voicemail."

I slipped out of the bathroom and caught Cassandra sitting at the kitchen table. I pointed to the phone and then dipped into my bedroom.

"So, what are you calling about? Shouldn't you be getting chased by buckle bunnies right about now?"

Ray, the brother between CJ and me, was a champion bull rider who was living it up on the rodeo circuit.

"Nah, we're moving. Rode Cinch in North Carolina. Heading to Florida for the weekend."

I looked over my shoulder as I shimmied on a clean pair of jeans. "You gonna be coming to Houston?"

"Looks like it. You gonna bring my favorite girls to come see me?"

Bree and Gracie adored their Uncle Ray. From birth, he had been wrapped around their fingers.

"Dunno. You gonna win? I'd hate for them to watch you suck."

"Fuck off. Look, I gotta go. But I'll be out your way soon. You cool with me crashing at your place for the night before we go to Houston?"

"Actually—"

I didn't even get my thought out before Ray cut me off. "Wait. Don't say it. You got someone there with you, don't you?"

"She works for the ranch," I said under my breath. "On the—uh—business side. Becks brought her in."

"Uh-huh. And she's living in your house?"

"The cabins are shit."

"Damn. I'll have to get CJ and Nate to pay up. Nate thought it'd be at least two years before you brought someone around the girls. CJ had six months left on his bet."

"Fuck off. It's not like that," I groused.

"Sure. You keep telling yourself that. I gotta call Mom anyway. I'll get her to tell me."

"Mom doesn't know shit. Don't go putting ideas in her head. I have enough problems on my plate. I don't need her pestering me about getting serious about someone that I'm not seeing to begin with."

Ray laughed. "That's a big defense for someone who supposedly doesn't have anything to be defensive about."

"I gotta get back to work. Anything else you need before you start churning that rumor mill?"

"Nah," he snickered. "I'll see you soon. Don't worry about getting that guest room ready. I'll just bunk with CJ and the boys."

"Drive careful. Don't get trampled."

I shoved my phone in my pocket and threw on a shirt before heading out to Cassandra.

"What was that about?" she asked, looking up from the stack of papers in her hands as she lounged in my armchair like it was her throne.

She looked damn good on it.

"My brother," I said as I sat on the couch and patted the spot beside me.

To my surprise, Cassandra was amenable and sunk down next to me. "Considering CJ and Nate are less than a mile away, I'll assume it was the other one."

"Yeah." I draped my arm around her shoulders and tried to steal a peek at the documents she had on her lap. "Ray called to say he's gonna be in town in a few weeks for the Houston Rodeo. He's gonna come visit."

"Hmm." She tapped her lips. "That works for me."

"Should I be scared of what you've concocted in here?" I said as I pressed my luck and kissed the crown of her head.

"Probably," she said as she flipped to a typed rundown. "You wanted me to go big? Well, welcome to the Griffith Brothers Ranch Revitalization Project. And before you start whining about the budget, I have investors on board."

I hated the idea of investors. I didn't like being in debt to anyone, much less faceless suits who didn't give a damn about the heritage of the ranch or the care we took to be an integral part of the food cycle.

"Stop growling," she clipped.

I cleared my throat and resigned to hearing her out, hating it, and figuring out a way to let her down easy. "Continue."

"Phase one will be short-term projects that are in-budget. The equine program I pitched to you originally will be the cornerstone of that. You'd be crazy not to take advantage of the resources and infrastructure you already have in place. And I don't think you Griffiths are crazy. Just stubborn."

She flipped to the next page.

"Renewable energy leasing options will bring in immediate income as the herd is rotated from pasture to pasture. I've got written offers for solar and wind, and cell tower leasing. If I may add a personal preference, put a damn cell tower out here so you can stop living in the Stone Age. The benefits are stable income and it can take up as little or as much land as you're willing to give up. We can find spots to put them that won't be an eyesore for the next phase."

I opened my mouth to argue, but she cut me off.

"I looked into some studies and talked to CJ about it. The cows will adjust. They'll be fine." Her eyes flicked up to mine. "If that's what you were about to bring up."

I huffed. "Continue."

"Where we should use the immediate available

budget is the equine program and land acquisition. There are two properties north of the ranch that are willing to sell off a parcel of their land, and they'd rather it go to you all than to some developer."

"And you're not a developer?" I asked, tapping on the exposed edge of a set of architectural mock-ups and floor plans.

"Better the devil you know than the devil you don't," she clipped.

"Fair."

"The additional land will give the herd more space, with the ability to expand it if you want. The land closer to the existing infrastructure—water, electric, etcetera—can be developed."

I groaned. "You're losing me."

"Just hear me out. You paid big money for this conversation."

I traced my fingers over her shoulders, soothing the tension that balled up by her neck.

"A restaurant. Farm to table. Everything made in-house. Dry-aged steaks, local produce, world-class chefs. People won't drive out here for a chain-restaurant meal. It has to be a destination. If things go well, some kind of artisanal or specialty foods shop could be added on. We could start bee keeping and sell honey or make sauces and baked goods. Maybe a mail-order steak service. The options are endless."

She turned to the next page.

"And because getting out here isn't exactly a quick trip from Austin, Houston, or Dallas, we'd need to build lodging. An inn of some sort. The cabins could be renovated and rented out separately. Lodging and a restaurant also opens you up to more than one-night stays. You'd have a destination for luxury weddings. Corporations would book it out for the 'ranch experience.' Team building and all that bullshit. Build an extension from the lodge and have a day spa. Given the boots-on-the-ground research I've done, there are plenty of locals itching for somewhere to get away to relax or celebrate a special occasion."

She flipped to the last page. It was a fax from some real estate firm based in New York.

"Lawson International is willing to back the project."

I let out a low whistle as I looked at the numbers. "Ten million dollars. This... company will give us ten million dollars?"

Cassandra lifted her chin. "I know powerful people, Christian. We're not building a roadside motel. This will be a luxury destination. The investment reflects that, as will the prices when guests come to dine and stay."

I couldn't help but laugh. "Who do you know with ten million dollars?"

She didn't even blink. "Isaac Lawson is worth far more than ten million dollars. He probably keeps that in cash by his bedside." She tapped the page. "The terms of the partnership are spelled out, and they already have a preference for the restaurateur that's brought in on the deal."

I pinched the bridge of my nose. "How do you know that we can trust these people?" I still couldn't believe my eyes. "How do you know them to begin with?"

"You're forgetting that I was a publicist before I landed on your ranch. I know Mr. Lawson's publicist, and his personal assistant. I know all his dirty laundry, and

I've assisted in a cover-up or two. Making the phone call was easy. The deal was not. I'd recommend reviewing it in detail with your legal counsel before making any decisions. The development and terms of the contract will likely outlive you. Think of the girls and the next generation when you're discussing the terms and making your decision."

Cassandra shuffled the papers together and tapped them on her lap to straighten the pages.

I rested my elbows on my knees and ran my hands through my hair. "I hate this."

"I know you do," she said without a care in the world.

"CJ is gonna hate it even more."

Cassandra handed over the revitalization plans. "Probably."

I sighed. "You went big."

Her eyes softened. "You told me to."

"Fuck," I huffed as I sat back against the couch and stared at the ceiling. "Let's do it."

21

CASSANDRA

"So, this is weird." Becks closed her front door and let out a heavy breath.

I watched warily as she rested her hands on top of her belly. "Are you sure you should be leaving the property without your designated driver?"

She scooped her red hair into a bun and tied it up on top of her head. "You can drive if I go into labor."

I laughed. "You trust *me* to drive?"

Becks laughed as she lumbered down the porch steps. "Let me guess. At least six months since you've driven a car?"

"Eighteen months," I said as I followed her to Nate's truck. "Tripp had a driver, and if I was traveling with a client, I just rode with them and their driver."

"Ah, the city life," she said as she heaved herself up into the driver's seat.

It felt strange opening my own door. Christian always picked at me for trying, but I shook it off and climbed in.

Nathan Griffith's truck had the same sort of smell that

Christian's did. It was a comforting cocktail of motor oil, hay, and cologne.

"Do you ever miss it?" I asked as she pulled away from the house.

I stared in the side mirror as Christian's house grew to a faint speck. It was Saturday, so Bree and Gracie were out of school and running circles around the front yard. Sadie deemed it fit to sit on the top step of the porch and keep a watchful eye on them from the shade, ready to herd them if necessary.

I had questioned Christian when he said he and his brothers were going to spend their Saturday working on the cabins. Bree and Gracie were just left there? Alone?

With an annoyingly smug look on his face, Christian promised me they were fine.

"What? Do I miss living in Manhattan?" Becks shook her head. "Not in the least. I kind of dread going back to work and flying up there. Missing it was only a problem during my first trimester. I craved hotdogs, but I wanted the ones from the cart outside the studio. Nothing else sounded good."

I peeled my eyes away from the girls and focused on the drive out of the ranch. "How much longer until you're due?"

Becks huffed as she adjusted the seatbelt over her belly. "Any day now. I'm technically due next week, but my OB said I might have to be induced. We'll see what happens at my next appointment." She looked over and smiled as she checked to make sure the road was clear before turning out of the ranch's driveway. "I'm glad you suggested this. It's been ages since I've gone out with a girlfriend. You know—since that damn ranch is flooded with cowboys. Momma Griff is great, but she helps with Chris's girls so much that I don't want to take up her time getting our nails done, you know?"

I faked a smile to ease my discomfort. I didn't know how to go out with friends. I didn't do that. I worked. I attended events. Pampering was done on my own time when I needed to decompress or do research.

But I wanted to leave the ranch. Getting Becks in on it was the easiest way for Christian to let me leave without an inquisition.

"Why don't you come up to the house when Claire cooks? Everyone does."

I artfully avoided those big family dinners, always conjuring some excuse as to why I'd just stay back at Christian's house and eat a sandwich or whatever left-overs he brought.

I have a headache.

I told my parents I'd call and they're at that age—I need to make sure they're okay.

I'm expecting a call from the investment team about the revitalization project.

I'm not used to your early mornings. I'm going to bed early.

I talked to a lot of people today. I just need a quiet night to myself.

"I'm not family," I said as if it was as simple as that. "I don't want to intrude."

Becks laughed. "You're living with Chris. The line between personal and professional has already been crossed." I stiffened, and Becks slammed on the brakes. "Wait—" she gasped.

I pressed my fingers to my temples. "Don't go there."

She threw her head back. "Oh my god! How did I not see it before? I blame the hormones. They've made me insane. But *oh my god*!"

"Rebecca Davis—"

"Griffith," she corrected.

"Please, just go to the nail salon."

"No, no, no," she said with a laugh as she pulled over into a vacant gas station parking lot and stopped the truck. "Too many busybodies. You won't tell me a thing. *What happened*?"

I drummed my fingers on the center console, debating how much to say.

I didn't know how to go out with girlfriends. But more than that, I didn't have girlfriends. It had never seemed important.

I had Tripp. I had my career. I had my clients. I was working and socializing *for them* all the time.

Why did I need my own life?

But weekends on the ranch were lonely.

Christian spent as much time as he could with Bree and Gracie. They rode horses together. They cleaned the house and did laundry together. Nights were spent in the living room watching movies.

And there I was. The creepy lady hiding in the guest room.

One of them always invited me to join them, but that wasn't a line I would cross.

Not that I was opposed to taking him up on round two, but sleeping with Christian was different than playing house.

Going out with Becks—even if it was a little awkward —was the reprieve I needed.

"Nothing happened," I lied with the practiced efficacy of a seasoned red carpet wrangler.

"You do realize that I know how to lie on camera too, right?" Becks rolled her eyes. "Look. I know we aren't sister wives or anything like that, but we're not strangers. You can tell me. It has to be lonely being out here."

"Nothing happened. It's just been a tense few days. CJ's not happy about the revitalization project, and Christian's trying to get everyone on board before things move forward."

She smirked. "Don't change the subject."

"I'm so out of practice." I groaned and slumped into the truck seat. "I should've known better. Rule number one: never get stuck sitting with a journalist."

Becks laughed. "And you're stuck with me for the next few hours. But at least you know I can keep my mouth shut. And unless your situation with Chris is classified as 'foreign affairs,' I can't use it for work."

I glared at her. "Off the record?"

She zipped her lips. "I won't say a word."

"Not even to your husband?"

"I promise."

I pointed at her. "No spousal privilege. I'm serious."

Becks breathed heavily and readjusted her posture. "Do you want me to slice my finger open and write an NDA on the dashboard in blood? Just tell me already. It stays between us."

I sat back and cringed. "Christian and I hooked up." I peered out of the corner of my eye, waiting for her reaction.

"And?" she pressed.

"And nothing. We slept together once. That's it."

Satisfied, she pulled out of the lot and headed toward town. "And do you want to do it again?"

I picked at my nail beds. "Are you really asking for details? He's your brother-in-law."

Becks smirked. "He's not your usual type, and that's not a bad thing."

She was right about that.

I shrugged. "My type hasn't been working for me lately. Or ever. I think a short fling was just what I needed."

"And what? You're going to stay here for the next few years to oversee the revitalization project, but you're not going to touch each other again? What if he starts dating?"

"First of all," I said as she pulled into a space in front of the nail salon. "I don't care if he starts dating. That's his business, not mine." *But the pang in my chest told me I was a dirty liar.* "Second, I'm here until the contracts are signed and things are rolling on their own. I'll find local contacts to see the plans through. I won't be here much longer."

"So you can get back to what? Working for the Carrington Group with your cheater ex-fiancé? Being tied to your phone twenty-four seven? Spending your days off in airport lounges and hotel rooms?"

I hopped out and stepped up onto the sidewalk, breathing in clean, small town air. "I miss the smell of jet fuel and terminal coffee."

"Keep telling yourself that," Becks said as she locked the truck and hooked her arm around mine. "The girls will miss you."

The tightness in my chest returned as she yanked

open the door and I was hit with the comforting smell of acetone and polish.

But this time, Becks was none the wiser. "Come on. I want my toes pretty for when a million doctors and nurses are watching me push out a baby."

IT WAS late afternoon by the time Becks and I returned to the ranch. Nail appointments turned into lunch and a stop by a store for some nursery items that Becks couldn't remember if she had already gotten or not.

I said my goodbyes, made a tentative promise to do an outing next weekend if she hadn't gone into labor yet, then made the long walk down the dirt path that led from Becks and Nate's house to Christian's.

The lights were on, but the house was oddly quiet.

They were probably out for a ride or something.

I loped up the steps, pausing at the top to pull my heels off. I wiggled my freshly painted toes on the weathered wood and slumped against the post.

Tired. I was damn tired. Not after today—though it had been a while since I socialized, and I was a little rusty.

I was just tired. Period.

My mind always felt loud and hurried. If I was being honest, the quiet around the ranch was nice. I understood why Becks felt safe here after a year and a half in a war zone with Nate.

It was probably a nice break from flying all over the world to cover global conflicts.

Instead of immediately heading inside, I pivoted to

the porch swing. The breeze was gentle as I used one foot to rock back and forth. The back of the swing pressed against my neck as I draped my head backward and let out a heavy breath.

Maybe Becks had a book I could borrow. Did Christian have wine in the house?

I wanted to stay out here until the skies turned to cotton candy, sipping something full-bodied, and reading something salacious.

The dog popped out of nowhere and darted up onto the porch, plopping down beneath the swing.

"You're back already?" Christian surprised me when he stepped out the front door.

I sat up quickly. "I thought you were out with the girls."

A dish towel was draped over his shoulder. He pulled it down and wiped his hands. "They're up at my mom's house for the night. She has them sleep over once a month so I can have a night to myself."

"Oh." I glanced toward Claire and Silas's house. "I'll make myself scarce so I don't intrude on your night."

"I'd rather you didn't." And with that, he left the front door wide open, and disappeared inside.

When I finally left the swing, I found him at the sink, scrubbing plastic containers.

"You're really living it up on your day off."

Christian chuckled as he rinsed the last one off and unplugged the drain. "I put off cleaning out the fridge as long as I could. Things were starting to walk around in there." He glanced down at my bare feet. "Did you have a good time out with Becks?"

"Surprisingly, yes."

He sprayed the sink down, then dried his hands. "Why is that surprising?"

I followed him to the living room and curled up on one end of the couch while he took the other. "We were professional acquaintances, not friends. I never spent time with her outside of work or events."

Christian stretched his arm across the back of the couch, letting his fingertips play with my hair, but he never closed the space between us. "I have a feeling you have a lot of 'professional acquaintances, but not friends.'"

"You can stick that judgmental tone up your—"

He laughed. "I'm not judging you, Cass. Just making an observation. Besides, I'm not one to talk. Not like I have a social life."

His fingers grazed my scalp, and I melted. *Maybe if I sat a little closer, he'd massage my head.* I disguised moving six inches closer by readjusting the throw pillow behind my back.

"So, what do you do when you're kid-free?" I asked as he dug his fingers into my hair and scratched up and down. *Oh my god, that was better than an orgasm.*

Christian kept scratching my head. "I'll catch up on housework. Sometimes Nate or CJ will come down and we'll have beers."

"That sounds dreadful," I said, letting my head rest more heavily against his hand as my eyes fluttered closed. "You need to learn how to go out."

Christian didn't immediately answer.

I tilted my head backward. "Tell me what you really do."

"I just told you."

"I believe you. But I doubt all you do is wash dishes and drink beer."

His hand moved from my head, squeezing all the way down my neck, working at the knots in my muscles.

I scooted a little closer.

"Sometimes I'll get out of town for the night."

I smirked. "Now that, I believe." I looked back at him again. "Where do you go?"

"Little town east. There's a bar called The Silver Spur. It's a good time. I'll go out there and get a motel room after. Let off a little steam."

A soft hum escaped my mouth. "I respect not shitting where you sleep."

"I didn't say I—"

"I know what getting a room in another town means. In my previous life, I was the one booking those rooms for people. I even booked a few of my own."

He was silent.

"Were you planning on leaving the ranch tonight?" I asked.

"No."

And for some reason, I believed him.

22

CHRISTIAN

Cassandra was four inches away from finally sitting beside me of her own free will.

Four fucking inches, and she had to go and ask about what I do with my nights alone.

I didn't give a shit about what I used to do, or who I did it with.

"So, what were you planning to do tonight?" she pressed.

I squeezed her biceps and she practically liquefied. I brushed her hair away and kissed the side of her neck. "I was hoping you wouldn't be tired of me yet."

"Hopes and wishes do not a plan make," she mumbled as she tipped her head back onto my shoulder.

I cupped her jaw. "I was hoping and wishing that you'd stay with me tonight."

Cassandra relaxed into me as I kissed up and down her jaw. "Then tell me what the plan is."

Not *here's my plan.*

Not *let's make a plan.*

Tell me.

"I thought you liked being in charge," I mumbled against her warm skin.

She craned her neck, giving me a little more room to pepper her throat with kisses. "I suppose it wasn't completely abysmal last time."

I shifted, pulling her down with me as I stretched out on the couch. She was stiff, but quickly settled on top of me.

"I'm gonna wear you down, princess."

Cassandra unbuttoned the top of my flannel and traced abstract shapes in my chest hair. "Or we could just enjoy the moment and not think about what happens later."

I dismissed the absurdity with a kiss. I wasn't going to waste time arguing with her. Not now.

She tasted like coffee and cinnamon.

I thought Cassandra was wrapping her arms around my neck, then I felt her hands in my hair, pulling the elastic out.

"What do you want?" I murmured against her lips.

Heavy eyes lifted to mine as she ran her hands through my hair. "Princes are overrated. I always liked the beast better."

I growled into her neck, making her laugh as I flipped us, pinning her down to the couch.

Her blouse was silken and smooth, spilling over her breasts like liquid satin. I devoured her, kissing my way down her throat, across her chest, and over her cleavage. I stole a moment, burying my face between her breasts and savoring the warm notes of her perfume.

Her soft hum of satisfaction turned to shameless

moans and desperate gasps as I pulled her neckline down and bared her breasts.

"Look at you." I scraped my teeth across her nipple. "Goddamn, you take my breath away."

Cassandra's fingers tightened in my hair, sending shockwaves of shivers down my spine. I groaned, pressing my hard-on into her as I pulled her nipple between my teeth. She whined, thrashing beneath me, but I kept her trapped under my weight. I cupped her breasts and pushed them together, taking time to lavish each one with kisses. Her thighs clenched in a futile attempt to ease the ache.

But we were just getting started.

"We doing this again?" I asked into her tits before taking one into my mouth.

"Pretty sure the 'yes' was implied when I let you put your hands on me," she sassed.

"It's never implied. Yes or no."

"Yes—okay? Just fuck me already," she retorted.

"Watch your mouth, princess. I'm just getting started."

Cassandra reached down between our bodies and—

"*Fuck*," I grunted when she wrapped her hand around the bulge in my jeans and squeezed.

She did it again, jerking my junk just to get a rise out of me. It worked.

My cock ached and throbbed in her hand. "Don't tease me," I rasped.

It had been a long week. With the development plans approved and lawyers pestering me to close the deals, CJ at my throat over the changes, and Cassandra being a daily cocktease, I was at my limit with stress. It's why my Mom had taken the girls for the night.

Cassandra unzipped my fly and slid her hand beneath the waistband of my boxers, grazing the head of my cock. It twitched and jerked from the lightest touch of her fingertips.

"Cass, don't fucking tease me. Not today."

She looked like sin incarnate as she smirked and eased up, sliding her hand further around my shaft. "I think I want to tease you." She skimmed my balls with her fingertips.

I grunted, pounding my fist into the arm of the couch as pleasure threatened to rip out of me without warning. "Cassandra," I snapped.

She licked her lips. "I think I want to see what happens when you lose control." She left feather-light kisses on the edge of my ear, making me shudder as she kept a firm grip on my cock.

I snapped. Grabbing Cassandra's wrist, I yanked her hands away from my body and twisted them behind her back as I hooked my leg around hers, flipping her onto her stomach.

"Christian!" Her squeal was muffled by the throw pillow as her face was squished into the couch.

"I told you not to fucking test me."

She thrashed and squirmed, but there was no way she could get out of the hold I had her trapped in. Not that she wanted to. That shit-eating grin on her face made it clear that she was enjoying herself.

I kept her wrists shackled in my hand as I swung my leg off the couch, dragging her down to the floor with me. Her knees hit the soft rug on the floor as I forced her to bend over the couch seat.

"I told you, Cass." I pulled a condom out of my pocket

before dropping my jeans down just enough to pull my cock all the way out and get the rubber on. "I told you not to test me, and you didn't listen."

Cassandra turned her head to the side, resting her cheek on the couch. "Listening is overrated. I prefer calling the shots."

I scraped my fingers up her scalp and fisted her hair by the roots. She gasped and groaned as I yanked her head backward and pressed my mouth to her ear. "Well, congratulations, Princess. You're not doing either tonight." I bit her earlobe, leaving red teeth marks on her porcelain skin. "Now be obedient and drop those pants to your knees before I tear them off your body."

She glared at me with lightning bolts in her storm-cloud eyes. "Don't you dare leave a fucking hickey on me like an amateur."

I yanked her head backward again, latching onto her throat. "I will do what I goddamn please. If I want to mark your perfect body, I will fucking do so because it belongs to me."

Cassandra cried out in desperation as I sucked and nipped at her throat until her skin bloomed like a rose.

I tightened my grip on her hair. "You will not cover that up tomorrow. Do you understand me?"

"Yes," she said, breathless and panting.

I reached around and pinched her nipple, holding it between two fingers. "Yes, *what?*"

She licked her lips and gasped like she was dying in a desert. "Yes, Sir."

"Hold on to the cushion," I ordered as I untied the bow at the waist of her pants. They were my favorite pair of hers—long, loose, and flowy. They cupped her ass in obscene ways and tied around her waist in a thick looping bow."

The fabric billowed around her knees.

"What? You're not even going to undress me all the way?"

I palmed her ass before tugging her thong down around her thighs. "I like seeing you like this. Such a dirty girl, dropping these panties and bending over to get fucked. You can't even look me in the eye."

She arched her back, teasing me with that ass again. "I fully intend to finish the job with my battery operated boyfriend."

I chuckled. "So much sass for someone who's going to avoid walking tomorrow."

"You talk a big game for someone who—"

But her words were cut off with my fingers pushing into her cunt.

"Greedy girl," I groaned. "Already soaked and desperate for me." I steadily worked her clit. "This pussy must be dying since you finally found someone who can make you come better than a toy."

"You made me come. I never said it was better than a toy," she choked out between breaths.

"You didn't say it." I edged my cock inside of her, then thrust home. "Your body did."

Her cry of desperation gutted me as I grabbed her hips and drove into her soaked pussy.

"I've got you, princess. Let me make you feel good."

"Christian—"

"You can take it. Just trust me and let go."

"Easier said than done," she rasped.

I pushed the back of her shirt up and pressed my

mouth to her spine, kissing her gently. "I'm not going to take it easy on you, so if you need me to stop, say it."

"I'm good. I'm fine—I just need a second."

I kissed her spine again, leeching some of the tension from her bones. Cassandra let out a breath, relaxing into the couch cushion. Her hips loosened as she rested her head and closed her eyes.

"That's my girl," I soothed as I ran my hand up and down her spine. "You ready?"

Cassandra nodded and pushed back against me.

I dug my fingers into her hips as I pulled out, then slammed in again, guided by her wetness.

"Goddamn, you're so tight," I grunted, trying to catch my breath as I set a punishing pace. "Jesus, Cass."

She let out a soft, breathy laugh.

I smoothed my hand over her ass again and again, savoring how soft it felt in my palm. All of her was.

She didn't want to admit it, but I saw the writing on the wall. Cassandra was tough because she had to be. It was a survival instinct. But when she put her claws away and purred, I was so far gone for her.

"You're coming first, Princess."

Cassandra nodded as I pushed deep inside of her and played with her clit.

"Take what's yours."

She stilled, focusing on the brewing fever pitch inside of her. I studied her, watching as her fingers curled into the cushion. The way her breath turned ragged and still. The way her eyes clenched in concentration.

Then, one hitch in her lungs and she detonated.

I drove into her again and again as heavy shudders racked her body. My dick grew impossibly harder as blood roared at the base of my spine. I jerked, slamming my hips into her ass as I held her there. My orgasm sapped my remaining stores of energy. I collapsed around her, bracing my arms beside hers as I caught my breath.

My stomach stuck to her exposed lower back, sweat fusing us together.

"You okay?" I murmured, pressing my lips to her temple.

Her nose wrinkled when my beard tickled it. "Yeah." She kissed me. "You made me feel good."

I carried her into the bathroom and stripped her all the way down before squeezing into the shower with her for a quick rinse. A towel was the extent of what I let her wear when we got out. I heated up leftovers with a towel around my waist while she curled back up on the couch.

We reconvened over yesterday's baked chicken and vegetables, eating side by side. I listened to her talk about the progress she had made with the surveyors and the groundbreaking celebration plans she had pulled out of her ass.

"Let me get that for you," I said, getting up to take my dishes to the sink. I piled hers on top.

"I can do that, you know. You didn't fuck my legs off."

I chuckled as I walked over and dropped them in the sink. "I didn't know that was the standard. I'll try harder next time."

Cassandra laughed softly. "Thank you, though."

She was curled up naked, covered by a blanket. I dropped my towel, picked up one end, and eased under the blanket with her.

She tensed when I pulled her into my lap.

"You don't do well with intimacy, do you?" I mused as

I got her situated on top of me. It was like trying to cuddle a two-by-four. She was stiff and unyielding.

Her nose wrinkled. "This is intimacy to you?"

I buried my nose in her hair, searching beneath the blanket for her hand. "Yes." I laced our fingers together. "You haven't just laid with someone before?"

"Not naked on a couch."

"I love lying naked together," I murmured as my hand left hers and explored her body. "It's relaxing." I caressed the soft curve of her breast. "When else do I get to do this? No pretense. No expectations. No endgame."

Her sharp eyes blurred. Cassandra shifted to her side, lying between my legs. She tucked herself around my belly and rested her head on my chest.

"Cass?" I said softly as I brushed her hair away from her face.

"Hm?"

"Tell me something."

"What?"

"Anything. We've spent all this time together... We've hooked up—twice. You've gone to bat for my kid. You're about to turn my life upside down—" I cupped her cheek "—and I don't know you."

She rested her head against my chest and closed her eyes to avoid engaging with me. "You know what you need to know about me."

"Where are you from?"

"New York."

"Did you grow up there, or move there?"

She hesitated. "I moved to the city after college."

"Hmm." I pressed my lips to her temple. "I didn't know that about you."

"Smart ass," she grumbled, tracing shapes across my chest with her finger.

I waited her out.

After a stretch of silence, she finally piped up again. "I grew up in Vermont."

And I waited some more, combing my fingers through her hair.

"I went to Syracuse. I liked their communications program."

Still, I didn't say anything.

"I did a college internship with the network Becks was with when she went overseas, and then got my job with the Carrington Group. That's when I met Tripp."

"What's your family like?"

"I have an older sister," she said calmly. "My parents are retired now."

"Are you all close??"

"No," she said simply. It was odd, though. There was no animosity. She was simply stating a fact. Still, I held her a little closer.

"Do you talk to them?"

"I usually call my parents every weekend and make sure they're alright. My sister lives nearby, so she keeps an eye on them." She huffed. "Are you just going to keep playing twenty questions or are you going to ask what you really want to know?"

I cupped her chin, forcing her to look up at me. "If I asked, I don't think you'd tell me."

"Try me."

I laughed. "I just want to know why you are the way you are."

She didn't even hesitate. "Not all of us grew up in this

idyllic little commune. You basically raised your children on the set of a sitcom."

"You think me losing my wife, and my daughters losing their mom was idyllic?" The accusation slipped out before I could hold it back. I knew Cassandra didn't mean it like that.

"Shit," she muttered under her breath before rolling away from me. "I just—"

"Cass, I know what you meant." Before she could wiggle out of the blanket, I had her back against my chest.

She felt so fucking good there.

"It wasn't easy," I said softly, not wanting to make her feel bad for what she said.

In fact, revealed more about her than she realized.

"It was really fucking hard. I felt like a ghost. But I had the girls to think about. I had to put them first, so that meant dealing with it and going to fucking therapy to make sure my head was right, and taking them too. Do you know how many weird looks I still get? It meant sitting through the 'mommy and me' days when they were in elementary school instead of asking my mom to do it. It means keeping pictures of Gretchen around the house even though it still hurts to see them because it means a lot to the girls. "

"That's what I meant," Cassandra said, quiet as a cricket in the winter. "You don't just tell them that you love them. You show them." She swallowed. "My family isn't like yours. There's no room for that. Everyone's so ... analytical. There's no feelings. Growing up always felt like a job interview. How was I in school? What were my goals? Did I have a plan to get into college on a scholarship? What was my plan for after college? We never just spent time together..." Her hand came to a stop against my skin. "Not like you Griffiths."

I wasn't the kind of man who held back. If I had something to say, I'd say it.

But now wasn't the time.

"There's room." I kissed her, drinking her in deep as she melted around me. Cassandra gave as much in that kiss as I did. For once, she wasn't just using me to take what she needed; though I didn't mind when she did that.

She was giving.

I pulled back and pressed a kiss to her forehead. "There's room, Princess."

23

CASSANDRA

"Cass, you in the office?"

I rolled my eyes. The desk chair squeaked as a wheel caught on a loose piece of hay.

"Cass?"

I was alone, so I let a giddy smile slip at the sound of Christian's voice. I grabbed the radio. "Right here, cowboy. Where else would I be?"

Static crackled. "Didn't know if you decided to go get some fresh air or go on a ride or something."

I laughed. "As if I'd get on a wild animal voluntarily."

He snickered. "You did alright the other night."

Was he talking about the family trail ride he forced me to join in on, or the clandestine hookup we had in the office after the girls were in bed? I certainly did alright riding him.

The radio clicked. "Stop flirting on the line," CJ groused.

Christian came back on. "You've got a suit poking around at the front gates. Might wanna go see what he wants before one of the ranch hands sees fit to hogtie him and smoke him low and slow."

I groaned. "There's no one closer?"

"We're out on the far side of the property. Trail cameras picked up the car. Take Dottie. She's tacked up."

My stomach dropped. "Can't I take your truck?"

"Can you drive stick?"

Grumbling, I kicked off my heels and yanked open the desk drawer for a pair of socks. "Don't be mad when I wreck your horse."

I had stolen a thick pair of Christian's socks to keep on hand for when he made me do outdoorsy activities against my will. The boots he got me lived under the desk for moments like this.

I stared at the target on the far wall as I pulled the boots on. Christian had mounted a piece of plywood on the wall so I could practice with his throwing knives.

The photos I found online of Tripp and Principal Beeker were sliced to ribbons.

I looked absolutely ridiculous in a blazer, high-waisted trousers, and cowboy boots, but it was better than ruining my beloved heels.

I trudged out to the barn and found Dottie hanging out in her stall.

She looked at me with those big horse eyes as if to say, "Oh. You again."

For a brief moment, I contemplated walking, then decided better of it. I didn't have time to trek up there or take my blouse to the dry cleaner to deal with the sweat stains.

"Alright, work with me," I said as I hesitantly took the rope, leading her out of her stall.

She came willingly, but that didn't make me feel any better. I was certain I could mount her, make it out of the barn, and then I would fall to my death.

Dottie stood still as I held on to the saddle and let out a breath. Placing my foot in the stirrup, I pushed up and swung my leg over her back.

Okay, I could do this.

Dottie shifted, but I kept my hips loose.

"Posture like a princess, hips like a whore," I whispered to myself as I gave her a little squeeze with my legs.

I felt ridiculous as Dottie loped past the office building, barns, and equipment shops. Sadie spotted us as we passed the house and bolted off the porch to follow.

When had I started calling it "the house?" I had always called it Christian's house. I liked the distance of that language.

And when had Sadie stopped trying to herd me?

Mickey was hanging out in the shade of the tree in front of Becks and Nate's porch. She was in town at yet another doctor's appointment.

Becks had made it another week without spontaneously combusting or being induced, which meant we had spent another Saturday in town together.

At least it had been less awkward the second time around. We spent the afternoon spitballing ideas for a groundbreaking party, then switched to talking shit about people we used to know over chips and salsa for her and a margarita for me.

I adjusted my grip on the reins, keeping my arms relaxed. A gentle breeze caressed my skin, picking up my hair and making the strands dance across my back.

Sure enough, I spotted a car bobbing down the long drive. Dottie parked herself at the post while Sadie took off like a bullet out of a gun, running after the car to herd it.

"Please don't move, please don't move," I whispered to Dottie as I braced my toe in the stirrup and slid off rather ungracefully. She blew out a sharp breath from her massive nostrils, obviously annoyed but tolerant.

The car stopped and a gray-haired man in a suit got out. "Cassandra Griffith?"

"Parker," I said, extending my hand. "I'm not a Griffith. I just work for them. And considering you know who I am, but I don't know who you are, I'll let you go first."

He chuckled. "My apologies, Ms. Parker. Mayor Charles Getty."

I shook his hand. "To what do I owe the pleasure, Mr. Mayor?"

Rule number one: if someone introduces themselves using their job title, they think they're more important than they are.

"Well," he said, hitching his thumbs in his belt loops. "Rumor has it y'all are planning on making some big changes around here."

Nothing had been made public about the revitalization project, but Christian and I had applied for a few permits and asked around about local ordinances to grease the wheels when the money started flowing. The rumor mill must have been churning fast today.

While the mayor rambled on, prattling about the beauties of the town and the service we would be doing by bringing tax dollars to the local economy, a jacked-up truck emblazoned with brand logos blew down the drive, kicking up a tornado of dust before speeding off toward the barns.

Christian would pick up the truck on one of the

cameras and send a ranch hand to deal with whoever was driving like a daredevil.

"Anyway, the Chamber of Commerce meets every Tuesday. You're welcome to join us for a time or two to get your feet wet." He made himself laugh. "After that you'll have to be a paying member."

I peered out the corner of my eye and saw the truck gunning it toward Christian's house.

No one was coming up from the pastures.

"I appreciate the invitation, but I'll have to discuss joining the Chamber with Mr. Griffith."

Just saying "Mr. Griffith" instead of Christian made a strange, acrid taste coat my tongue.

The mayor hitched his pants up. "Rumor has it, Silas's son is running things now."

"That's correct. Christian oversees the operations."

A strange smile worked across his mouth. "Ain't that something. And now he's got a pretty thing like you working for him. I suppose those cowboys know a thing or two about picking a heifer. Nothing wrong with wanting something nice to look at."

I should have brought one of those throwing knives with me.

I was half tempted to give him a business card with my name under the Carrington Group logo, but that didn't mean much around here.

Instead, I steeled my face, ridding any evidence of a smile from my expression. "Well, you're probably a busy man, so I won't bore you with who I am or what my job entails. But if you're curious—which you are, given the way you're leering at me—you should stop by the middle school and have a chat with Principal Beeker. Rumor has it, she announced that she's retiring early, but I'm sure you knew that."

He immediately looked toward the house and cleared his throat. "I may have heard something about that."

I lifted my chin. "And I may have had something to do with that. I imagine unseating a mayor would be just as easy. Tell me, how's your mistress? Nadine, the lady who works at Blush & Bashful. That's her lipstick on your collar, isn't it?"

He paled in the midday sun, tugging at his collar like it was strangling him.

I stepped in close. "Word of advice, Mr. Mayor. If you're going to have a side piece, don't give her expensive perfume as a gift. It lingers."

I wasn't psychic. I got lucky with the lipstick print on his crisp dress shirt. The real information was thanks to Wednesday Addams's lookalike, who was more than willing to spill a few small-town secrets while she did my makeup.

"Well," he rasped, eyes darting to his overpriced car. "I'll let you get on with your day."

"I think that's best for both of us."

I waited until he was easing back into the driver's seat before I spoke up again. "One more thing, Mr. Mayor—" I grabbed the top of his door. "When the invitations go out for the groundbreaking, you will receive one. You will RSVP. You will tell every important person in town to come. You'll arrive on time, have exactly one drink, sing this family's praises and be a loud supporter of our projects, and then leave early."

He swallowed. "Don't tell my wife."

"That's your business." I narrowed my eyes. "Don't make it mine." And with that, I slammed the door.

It was already my business, but I'd find a more discreet way to speed up karma's swift and steady hand.

Dottie matched my energy on the way back, taking off at a canter. I matched my breathing to the pounding of her hooves. The fury kept me grounded.

I kept an eye out for the truck as Dottie raced back to the barn, but it was nowhere in sight.

Maybe the driver had gone out to where Christian and the boys were.

Dottie tossed her head back as we neared the barn, and I ran a hand down her mane. She slowed and loped inside like an old pro, standing still so I could hop down.

I fished around in my pocket and found a spare peppermint. Miraculously, I managed not to cringe when she nibbled it off my palm.

The office was just as I had left it—an absolute disaster. Development timelines, grant proposals, contracts, and contractor quotes littered my desk.

Christian's desk. I self-corrected the intrusive thought. It wasn't mine.

I changed my shoes again, sifted through the pages to find the keyboard, and did a quick internet search. I waited while the printer spat out a photo, then tacked it to the wall and dove back into the mess.

Organizing the documents Christian needed to sign was the easy part. Getting him inside long enough to sign them was the hard part. The stack he needed to address was growing by the minute.

If I kept them in the office, he would keep finding something more important to do...

Deciding better of it, I scooped up the stack and carried them over to the house. I could flash my tits and coax him into taking ten minutes to go over everything.

When I rounded the narrow corridor between the barn and office, I stopped.

That truck was parked in front of Christian's house.

I clicked the pen on top of the stack. If he was in there, I'd get these done even sooner.

But I didn't hear male voices when I jogged up the porch. Not Christian's, at least.

"No!" Gracie's giggle was clear.

A deep laugh joined in and I paused to listen.

"Pass the purple," Bree said.

What time was it? I had just eaten lunch before the mayor showed up. It couldn't have been much past one in the afternoon.

"I think we need glitter," Gracie said.

"Nah, you know your dad's rule. No glitter in the house."

Bree and Gracie were supposed to be at school. Christian's mom was in town. The girls had dance tonight. Why were they home?

Fear and adrenaline crept up the back of my neck like snaking vines as I hurried up the steps and let myself inside.

I froze mid-stride and blinked.

"Miss Cass!" Gracie shrieked as she dropped a handful of markers on the rug. She scrambled away from the tattooed man that was pinned to the floor, and bolted toward me.

"Ah-ah-ah—" I stopped her with a single finger.

"What are you girls doing home? You're supposed to be in school."

"We were kidnapped," Bree said casually as she capped a pink marker, then grabbed a blue one and continued to use the shirtless man as a human coloring book.

The Parent Trap played on the TV in the background, and everyone seemed to be acting like this was a normal afternoon activity.

Deciding that no one was in imminent danger, I decided it was best not to ask questions. I dropped the papers on the kitchen table. "Right. Have a nice abduction."

"C'mere, Miss Cass," Gracie said, grabbing my hand. "You gotta meet our funcle."

"I don't think your father lets you use that kind of language yet."

"Not—" her voice dropped to a whisper "—*that* F-word." She yanked my arm until I relented and let her lead me to the living room. "This is Funcle Ray."

The shirtless man, who was sprawled out prone on the living room floor, lifted his head and looked up at me. "Yep. Totally get it now."

"Get what?" Bree asked.

"Nothing, squirt," the man said without taking his eyes off me.

I had the distinct feeling I knew what he "got."

I twisted my ankle, showing off the sharp stiletto. "It's not as fine as a tattoo needle, but I can poke some holes in you if need be."

He grinned from ear to ear.

I raised an eyebrow. "Does need be?"

He chuckled. "No, ma'am."

"You're supposed to say, 'no, my queen,' Gracie whispered.

"Yeah, I'll leave that to your dad," he said with a twinkle of amusement in his eyes. He stretched an arm across the floor, as if he was going to shake hands with my foot. "Funcle Ray at your service. Pleasure to meet you."

"It means 'fun uncle,'" Gracie said, filling me in as she grabbed a marker. "Wanna color with us?"

"Ah." I nodded. "The other Griffith brother."

"So you have heard of me," he said, dropping his head and returning to the prone position so as not to disturb the girls.

"Aren't you a little old to be coloring?" I said to the girls.

"It's tradition. We always color in Uncle Ray's tattoos."

"He got them for us," Gracie said with a grin.

Most of Ray's back and arms had been filled in with washable markers, turning his black and white outlines into full color.

"Stay in the lines, Picasso," he said when Gracie got a little marker-happy. "At least you wildebeests are better at coloring now than you were when you were three." He stretched his left arm out. "You missed a spot on my shoulder."

This family just kept getting weirder and weirder.

I pinched the bridge of my nose. "Does your father know you're not in school right now?"

Bree clammed up.

I stared her down. "Bree?"

Her eyes shifted.

I tapped my foot. "Want to tell me why you're skipping school and risking getting in trouble after I went to bat for you?"

"You told me to shut up when I'm being asked questions that could get me in trouble," she whispered.

Ray cackled.

I bent at the waist and crooked my finger, beckoning her closer. "You're already there," I whispered back.

"Don't worry. I'm not actually a kidnapper," Ray said. "I signed them out at the school office before I put the hoods over their heads and tossed them in the backseat of my truck."

"Oh my god," I muttered under my breath, shaking my head as I walked out.

It was the voices that started up after I slipped out the front door that made me pause.

"So, that's her, huh?" Ray said.

"Isn't she so pretty?" Gracie gushed.

"She's a badass," Bree said.

"You're not supposed to say that!" Gracie shrieked.

"Hey, what'd I teach you, kid?" Ray said.

"Snitches get stitches," Gracie chirped.

"She lives here with y'all?" he asked.

"Yeah," Bree said. "I keep asking dad to ask her how she does her hair so she can teach him so he can do it for me, but he won't."

"Or you could just ask her yourself," Ray said. "I don't think she breathes fire. But maybe have a fire extinguisher just in case."

The girls giggled, and I couldn't help but smile.

"She doesn't like kids, but we're working on that," Bree said.

Ray sounded truly appalled. "Doesn't like kids? Who doesn't like kids? Especially you two wombats."

"We're wearing her down," Gracie said.

"What does your dad think?" he asked.

The girls giggled again, and I found myself leaning a little closer to the crack in the door to hear.

I couldn't catch what they said because a deep voice echoed from behind me. "Wanna tell me why there's a picture of the mayor on the dartboard?"

24

CHRISTIAN

I pressed my fist to my mouth to keep from smiling. Cassandra looked so fucking guilty when I caught her with her ear to the door.

She pressed her hand to her chest, letting out a sharp breath. "You scared the shit out of me. How the hell did you sneak up those stairs?"

Trying to play it off all casual, I stroked my beard. "I know all the creaky spots. Stick around long enough and you'll learn them."

"Your brother's here," she hissed.

"I know," I said in a hushed voice that matched hers. "I saw him come in on the cameras."

"He kidnapped your children," she whisper-yelled.

"He does that."

Her eyes widened. "And you're okay with that?"

Dammit. I liked when she was worried about the girls.

"Why are we whispering?" I said.

"Because I don't want them to know I'm still out here!"

A slow grin spread across my face. "If I didn't know better, I'd say either you care or you're curious. Maybe both."

"I don't. I'm just a professional. Letting a client get kidnapped is typically bad for business."

"My daughters aren't your clients."

"They're client-adjacent." She swatted my stomach. "Stop with the semantics."

I snickered under my breath. "I'm just messing with you." Since she was blocking the door, I used it to my advantage and trapped her against it, pinning her down with my hips. "You never explained why there's a photo of the mayor with a knife in it."

The soft silver clouds in her eyes turned to razor blades. "He pissed me off. Apparently, anger helps with throwing accuracy."

I lifted my eyebrows. "Do I want to know what happened?"

Cassandra patted my chest. "I handled it."

No one was around to see us, so I cupped her cheek and kissed her. "That's my girl."

She pulled away. "What are you doing? Someone might see."

The edge in her voice stung.

"No one's going to see. They're inside and we're out here."

Her hand pressing against my chest stopped me. "So? I'm not risking it."

"Risking what?"

I was the one with the rule about my kids not being exposed to the casual nature of my romantic life. I was the one who had to keep this house from crumbling. I was the one with everything on the line.

If she was worried about someone seeing, then she needed to admit that there was something to hide.

"I should get back to work," she said, trying to squeeze by.

I stopped her with a hand on her waist. "Why were you eavesdropping?"

"I was just leaving."

"Bullshit." I fisted the back of her hair, bringing her mouth to mine again.

Her eyes grew heavy and her lips dropped open, grazing mine. It was like I had accessed the master controls to her submission.

"See?" I murmured against the corner of her mouth. "I told you that you'd like it when I'm in control." I tightened my grip at the base of her scalp.

Cassandra didn't bother arguing. She knew I'd call bullshit.

"You're going to walk inside with me," I whispered.

"No, I'm not."

"Then I'll carry you inside over my shoulder. Your choice."

I was testing her and she knew it. I wanted her to acknowledge that she felt something between us.

We had been playing for fun, but I wanted to play for money. We were in a game of chicken, but she wasn't flinching.

I crooked a finger beneath her chin and tipped it up. "Don't stand outside pressing your ear to the door when there's a seat for you at the table."

"I told you to stop speaking like a cowboy fortune cookie," she said softly.

I kissed her again. "And I told you there was room."

"Christian, we shouldn't—"

The door handle clicked as I pushed it open.

"Daddy!" Gracie shrieked from inside the house.

Cassandra broke away and I let her, but I kept her hand in mine.

"What are you doing?" she spat.

"I'm telling you it's okay to care," I snapped as I whipped around. "Alright? It doesn't make you weak or less in control."

Her eyes widened as a small body careened into my hip.

"Hey, baby girl." I refused to let Cassandra's hand go as I hugged Gracie. "How was school?"

Cassandra dug her nails into my palm. I squeezed harder.

"It was great! Uncle Ray surprised us. He picked us up and took us out to lunch and brought us back and now we're coloring and watching a movie!"

"*Kidnapper*," Cassandra sang under her breath.

Gracie's smile grew when she peeked around me and saw that Cassandra was still here. She gasped. "You didn't leave!"

Knife, meet heart.

"Can you be done working today?" she begged.

I flicked my wrist and looked at the time. Usually, I had a strict policy against cutting out of work early. And, in all honesty, I had just come back to the house to tell Cassandra that Ray was here. I had more things I needed to do today.

But damn that look.

"Yeah, baby. I'm done for today. Let me get my shoes off and I'll come in."

"Yay!" she squealed, jumping up and down. "Miss Cass, are you done working too?"

"I'm not finish—"

"She's done," I said. "Pretty sure Uncle CJ will be up here in a minute. Do you have homework?"

Gracie shook her head.

"Alright, go finish coloring Uncle Ray's tattoos before supper."

"I'm still working," Cassandra snapped when Gracie ran back inside.

"The ranch is closed. You're off the clock."

"The ranch is never closed."

"I'll put a padlock on the office."

Her eyes narrowed. "You wouldn't."

"You wanna try me, princess? There's more to life than clocking forty hours a week."

She guffawed. "Like you're one to talk. You work twice that."

"My job makes me happy and it puts food on the table. Your job only does one of those things. I hope your full fridge is worth it."

"I'm happy." She had the words, but she didn't have the music.

"Maybe someday I'll believe you."

And with that, I dragged her inside.

I was right. CJ came up from the fields before the workday was done. Soon, my living room was packed as ranch hands filtered in to see Ray.

To my surprise, Cassandra didn't hide away in her

room. She made my armchair her throne, staying accessible but silent.

I wasn't sure what had crawled up her ass, but I was done with it. This standoff would end one way or another, just as soon as I could get her alone.

When Momma called everyone up to the main house for dinner, Bree and Gracie talked Cassandra's ear off.

She tolerated it a little more than usual.

When we shuffled through the buffet line that was spread out across the kitchen counters, Becks waddled beside Cassandra so they could catch up on some piece of gossip she had heard while in town.

When we sat down at the long row of folding tables that had been pushed against the dining room table, I made sure to take the seat beside Cassandra.

And to my surprise, she held my hand and let me lace our fingers together when my father stood and said grace.

"You and I are gonna have a conversation later," I murmured as food was shoveled into mouths and Ray was peppered with questions about his last competition.

Cassandra, sitting prim and proper with her back straight and her napkin across her lap, cut her eyes at me. "That's unnecessary."

"Fine. A business meeting then."

I was ready to haul her out like a caveman, but Becks let out a gasp that made the table go silent.

"Oh—"

Nate put his hand on her back as she hunched over. "Talk to me, Red," he said quietly.

It had been eleven years since I'd seen a woman with that look on her face, but I remembered it like it was yesterday.

After thirty seconds of holding her breath in tense silence, Becks dropped her fork and nodded. "Time to go."

Momma dabbed her mouth with her napkin. "Already?"

Becks's eyes were glassy. "I've been having contractions since lunch."

"Well, why didn't you say anything?" she exclaimed.

"I didn't know how long it would be and I didn't want to get everyone into a tizzy," Becks said as Nate helped her up, bracing her elbow and back.

Gracie gasped. "You mean you're gonna have the baby, Aunt Becks?"

Becks nodded with a watery smile. "Seems like it."

Nate was older than me, but I had been a father for thirteen years. I felt a sense of pride watching him dote on Becks and help her out of the kitchen.

Ray lifted his beer. "Mazel tov."

CJ and the ranch hands joined in, toasting them.

Becks made it to the door before she had to pause and breathe through a contraction. My throat tightened as Nate knelt in front of her, letting her rest her forearms on his shoulders. He kept a protective hand on her belly.

Nate looked up and his eyes met mine.

I gave him a nod, not needing to say anything else.

Momma hurried after them with a grocery bag full of food so they wouldn't be hungry.

"Is Aunt Becks gonna have a boy or girl?" Bree asked as dinner resumed.

"We'll just have to wait and see," I said. "They decided not to find out until the baby's born."

"Did you find out if we were girls or boys before we were born?" Gracie asked.

I nodded. "Yeah. Your mom wanted to know right away." A wistful smile forced itself onto my face. "She was so excited to have girls."

"Do you want children?" My dad asked Cassandra.

She choked on a sip of water and laughed. "No. I can't think of anything worse than pushing out a baby."

"Kidney stones," CJ said.

I chuckled. "Not even close."

Ray piped up. "Getting kicked by a bull."

I thought it over. "Once or for thirteen hours straight?"

He glowered. "Fine. Babies are worse."

"Do you want more babies?" Gracie asked me around a massive bite of mashed potatoes.

"Don't talk with your mouth full," I reminded her, hoping that would derail that conversation.

Every once in a while, Bree and Gracie got on a streak of begging for another sister.

They were very clear that it had to be a girl, though. No boys allowed.

Gracie swallowed. "Will we ever have another sibling?"

Just fucking great.

My brothers snickered behind their beers. Even Cassandra cracked a smile.

"You're about to have a baby cousin. And Uncle Nate and Aunt Becks live here on the ranch so it'll be like having a sibling."

"You're avoiding the question," Bree said with a smirk that was way too grown up for her.

"I'd have to have a wife for that," I said. "Which means you'd have a step-mom. And if we've learned anything from those princess movies you force me to watch, step-moms are evil. I'm doing you a favor."

"That's a non-answer," Bree pressed. "You don't have to have a wife to have a baby."

I stared at my daughter across the table. "Excuse me, Miss *Thirteen going on Thirty*. Who taught you to debate?"

"Miss Cass," she said with a grin.

Cassandra laughed. "I told you, I'm a bad influence on children. You should have known better than to leave them unsupervised around me."

And just like that, I was back to caveman mode.

I looked up and found my dad and brothers wearing ear-to-ear grins.

"Someone needs to check the fence out by Nate's house," Momma said as she walked back in. "Looks like there's a break in it."

That was my cue.

I wiped my mouth and stood. "I want clean plates," I said to Bree and Gracie. "Help Grandma with the dishes." I tapped Cassandra on her shoulder. "Get up, trouble. You're coming with me."

"Why?" she said with her fork halfway to her mouth.

"You just told me I can't leave you unsupervised. You wanna change my ranch, you gotta fix it first."

"Fence-mending is not my forte. I'm more of a bridge burner."

"I'll go with you," CJ said, finishing off his beer.

"Nah." I hit Cassandra with a fiery look. "We'll handle it. Let's go."

Luckily, I was able to march her out of the house without a single argument.

That was, until we got off the porch.

"I'm in heels. I don't know what crawled up your ass in there, but I'm not walking all the way to their house in heels to watch you fix a fucking fence—"

Her words turned to a screech as I threw her over my shoulder and marched across the grass.

My boots sunk into the dirt with each step.

Cassandra kicked, nearly stabbing me in the cheek with her shoe. "Put me down, Colossus! What is with this family and kidnapping people?"

I wrapped an arm around her legs to keep her still. "Do you need to be tied up, or will you stop trying to puncture me with a stiletto?"

"I'll stop when you stop kidnapping me."

"I asked nicely, and you didn't come. So, let me be frank. You're going to come, and I'm not going to ask."

"Why do I have the feeling you're not talking about fixing the fence?" she wheezed.

I cut through the grove of trees that shrouded Nate's house from the rest of the property. The backside of their house edged the fence line on the front side of the ranch.

Sure enough, two of the posts were leaning.

I'd fix it later.

Cassandra was still yammering when I dropped her back on her feet. "What is the fucking matter with you, you giant, impossible, motherfuc—"

I pushed her up against the fence post and slammed my mouth to hers. Cassandra never saw it coming. I devoured her gasp, kissing her until she was a whimpering, frantic mess. My tongue slid against hers, sealing our desperation. I didn't want to let her go.

Her breasts flattened against my chest and she arched closer, whimpering as her body begged for more. My cock ached as she rocked back and forth, pressing and teasing me with each shift of her feet.

I wanted her deeper. Longer. I wanted her in every way imaginable.

I wanted her under me and on top of me. But more than that, I wanted her beside me in every way. In every situation. Good or bad.

Maybe I shouldn't have, but I trusted her.

That was something I couldn't resist. Rules be damned.

"I thought we were going to have a conversation," she gasped when we broke apart."

"You wanna talk?" I rasped as I fisted her hair and yanked her head back.

"I'd like to know why I'm being mauled," she said as she grappled at my belt, nearly tearing my pants off.

I kissed up her throat. "And I'd like to know why you're being so fucking hot and cold with me." I felt her pulse racing beneath my mouth, and sucked on the spot. "Get your shit together, princess. Do you want this or not?"

"Fuck me."

"With pleasure." I bit harder, leaving another bright mark. "But you have to decide if you want more than a quick fuck. Because if that's all you want, this will be the last time."

She stiffened. "Why?"

I pinned her to the fence post. "Because I like who

you are when you're not in denial. You give me this soft side of you. The human side of you. And then you turn it off and push me away when you're done. That doesn't work for me. I will break my rules for you, but not if you're going to keep playing these games." My mouth brushed hers. "So, if you're going to keep ignoring me, avoiding me, and antagonizing me to get a rise out of me, then this will be your last orgasm. Make your choice."

"A choice entails an alternative," she said softly.

"You know what the alternative is, Cass. But if you want me to spell it out for you, I will. I want you to stay here with us. Period. My 'us' is not an option. My kids think you're the greatest thing to walk the fucking earth. Frankly, so do I. I want to see what you're like when you're willing to accept that you have feelings for *us*. I know you got your heart broken, but I'm not sorry about that. I'm glad that shit stain is gone. And as fucked up as the situation is that brought you to me, I'm fucking glad it happened because I like seeing you here every day. I like walking into the office and seeing you there. I like watching you try to ride a horse. You suck at it, by the way. I like finding you with a bowl of ice cream and whiskey after a bad day, and I will always keep it on hand as long as you're here. But you have to choose to be here. You want to finish your job and pack up? I don't want that, but I'll respect it." My forehead rested against hers. "There's your choice, princess. It's us or nothing."

Her jaw clenched, setting angrily as her voice trembled. "That's not fair."

"I didn't say it was fair. I said you had to make a choice."

For a moment, tears glimmered in her eyes. They

shone like brilliant stars in the night sky. She blinked, staring into the expanse of the universe. "So, this is what you're like when you're angry."

"I'm not angry." I started at her blouse, unfastening the three buttons that held the silky neckline closed. I pushed the sides of fabric apart until the tops of her breasts were exposed.

"You're angry that I'm not giving you what you want," she whispered.

Her trousers were next. It was another pair of those soft, flowy pants that tied at the waist. "I'm not angry at you, Cass. I'm disappointed." I yanked on the sash, ripping the bow out of the loops. "Pretending like you don't care doesn't keep you from getting hurt." I gritted my teeth. "Hands behind you."

Her eyes darted left toward the house.

"I didn't tell you to see if someone was coming. I told you to put your hands behind that goddamn fence post."

She lifted her chin as she clasped her hands behind the post. I grabbed her wrists and quickly tied them together with the sash. She jerked, her eyes flashing with surprise when it wasn't loose enough for her to escape.

I pulled the hat off of my head and dropped it on top of her pretty hair.

"I thought I wasn't supposed to mess with your hat. Pretty sure that means I shouldn't wear it," she sassed.

I gripped her jaw in my palm. "You wanna be mine? You put that hat on."

And with that, I pushed her trousers off of her hips and dropped to my knees.

Cassandra fought against the fence post as I worked

the pants off of her ankles, tore her panties off of her hips, and threw her leg over my shoulder.

"Christian—" she gasped as I parted her dripping sex with my fingers. It was the softest shade of pink. Her sex was warm and swollen with arousal as I lapped at her clit.

A bite of cool air made us both stop and shiver.

"All you get is this orgasm, Cassandra." I slid two fingers inside of her, crooking them and slowly stroking.

The fence creaked as she went weak in the knees.

"That's all you want anyway, right?" I circled her clit with my tongue. "You use all that bravado with everyone else. Ripping them a new one and putting them in their place. You're not willing to use it to fight for yourself. For what you want."

"Christian, please—"

I cupped her ass in my hand as I devoured her. She swore at the sky. She pleaded to me, to deities, to anything with ears. She pulled and pulled against that damn fence post.

I didn't let up.

Maybe I was out of my goddamn mind. She wasn't looking for a relationship. She hated this ranch. She didn't like kids. She despised nearly everything about my way of life.

And yet she was perfect for it.

I saw it every time I looked at her.

Cassandra had an unmatched strength. She was confident in ways I had never seen. She had a stubborn streak that supported that confidence. She was protective. She never took "no" for an answer when she wanted a "yes." She was wildly arrogant, brash, and abrasive.

And every bit of me loved her for it.

Her breasts nearly spilled out of her bra as she thrashed against the post. Blonde tresses flung recklessly in every direction.

"Make me come," she whispered as she pushed her hips out, desperately seeking my mouth and hands.

My hair was spilling out of the bun I tied it in. My beard was damp with her arousal. The taste of her coated my tongue.

Still, it wasn't enough.

Her breathing turned frantic.

Silence.

A gasp.

Then the explosion.

She whimpered, her thighs quivering as she shattered. Cassandra threw her head back, letting out a string of muttered profanities so loud it was probably heard at the bunkhouse. I didn't let up, lapping at her cunt until she was begging me to stop and pushing me away with her foot.

Without a word, I dried her thighs and pussy with her torn panties, then helped her back into her pants. She stood still as I silently untied her wrists and threaded the sash back through her belt loops.

Cassandra rubbed the red marks circling her skin as I buttoned her blouse.

My hat teetered backward on her head when she looked up at me regretfully.

I plucked my hat off of her head and put it back on. "Why do you look sad?" I cupped her cheek. "You got what you wanted."

I was waiting for her to say it.

To say it wasn't *everything* she wanted.

I was waiting for her to admit to being stubborn because it was safe.

But she didn't.

The corner of her mouth trembled. "I don't know what to tell you. I'm not the kind of person you should be involved with." She swallowed, strengthening her resolve. "I won't change."

"I'm not asking you to." I ran my hand down my beard. "I just want you to be honest with yourself. With me."

"I am," she shot back.

"No," I barked, cutting her off. "If you were honest, you wouldn't be so fucking wishy-washy—wanting me and then pushing me away. I'm done with that. If you were honest, you'd admit you're miserable doing what you're doing. But that's on you. If you want to be miserable, then be my guest. You want so badly to be right that you can't even tolerate the thought that *maybe*, just fucking maybe you and I could have something good. So yeah. I'm asking for it, Cass. Because I'm not a coward."

The last sentence hit her like a shot.

The fence post creaked and let out a groan as it tipped, cracked, and fell into the grass.

Neither of us flinched.

So much for playing for money. I was leaving the table with empty pockets.

We walked back to the house in silence and found the rest of my family cleaning up from dinner.

CJ smirked when he saw us. "How's that fence?"

Cassandra flipped him off.

I trudged in behind her, angrier than when I had left. "I'll fix it in the morning."

25

CASSANDRA

"He tied me to a fence and fucked me." I stabbed my spoon into my bowl of ice cream.

Mickey blinked at me from across the office, letting out a deep bovine grunt.

The pool noodles on his horns had been replaced yesterday. He now sported a lime-green one on the left and purple on the right.

I stared at the bottle of bourbon that had been on my —Christian's—desk since, presumably, the wee hours of the morning. The note that had been stuck to the front taunted me.

Bourbon pairs better with mint chocolate chip.

No signature. No initials. *Not that I needed it to know who had left the liquor.*

It had been two days since Christian demanded I make a choice that I wasn't ready for. And two days of me avoiding him.

"After giving me an ultimatum," I grumbled over a mouthful of ice cream.

I had just gotten off a call with Mike—my boss at the Carrington Group—who let me know that, while the Griffiths had given raving feedback about my job performance, I would still have to meet with HR due to the aftermath of my relationship with Tripp.

Just fucking great.

I had gone through an entire fling after ending things with Tripp, and yet he was still haunting me.

But after a quick call to Spenser Crenshaw, an old contact who owed me a favor, I'd be haunting Tripp soon enough.

Anger made me revenge-y. And since I couldn't take that anger out on Christian, Tripp was the next best target.

The knife in his face on the dartboard wasn't enough to satisfy my blood lust.

"I mean, how dare he? We hooked up a handful of times. It's not like we were in a relationship and I put my foot down that it wasn't going any further. I'm not the one at fault here. *He's* the one who nuked it." I pointed my spoon at the cow who had let himself into the office and laid on top of Sadie's dog bed, flattening it.

Mickey huffed in annoyance.

The cow peered out of one eye, glaring at me as I turned back and forth in the desk chair.

"*He's* the one who blindsided me. You can't ambush someone when they have their pants off, and demand a relationship. That's highway robbery."

Mickey groaned and closed his eyes.

Bourbon and mint burned my throat as I scooped the remnants out of the bottom of the bowl.

"So. He blows it up, makes *me* the bad guy because I don't want to dive headfirst into a family unit where I'll always be the fourth wheel, then puts ice cream and fucking bourbon in here—assuming I'd be torn up about it!"

The cow groaned in annoyance, lumbered up to his hooves, and sauntered out to get some peace elsewhere. The pool noodles smacked the doorway as he squeezed out.

"Great." I dropped the bowl onto the desk and tossed the spoon in. "Even the cows hate me."

Not even five seconds later, Christian waltzed in. "You kicked Mickey out?" he asked without making eye contact with me as he shuffled through the stack of paperwork piled on the corner of the desk.

"Apparently, I talk too much."

He chuckled. "You know you're settled in when you start talking to the cows."

I gritted my teeth.

How dare he pretend like nothing was wrong?

Christian's brows knitted together as he started through the stack again.

I huffed. "What are you looking for?"

"The records for—"

I grabbed a manila folder from the top of the printer and handed it to him.

"Oh. Thanks. Do you know where the—"

"Invoice for feed from George Thompson is already paid." I handed him the printed sheet, confirming the payment. "I authorized the check."

He stroked his beard. "You didn't have to do that."

"It's fine. I was waiting for a phone call from a tent guy for the groundbreaking party. I didn't know when you'd be back up here, so I took care of it."

"Thanks. I've gotta do payroll, and then I'll get out of your hair."

"It's done," I clipped. "Checks are signed. I'll tape them up on the door when the boys call it a day."

Christian stared at me. "That's not in your job description."

I hit him with a frosty glare. "You authorized me to write checks, did you not?"

He frowned. "I did."

"It doesn't take a brain surgeon to do payroll."

"So, why'd you do it?"

I turned my back to him and scrolled through my email inbox, looking for the rental confirmation for tables and chairs. "So you wouldn't have a reason to be in here."

A heavy hand landed on my shoulder with a feather-light touch. "Cass..."

"Cassandra," I clipped.

Christian froze with his hand on my shoulder. But before he could come up with something to say—because this was all his fault—the radio chirped.

"Cass, honey, it's Claire. A courier just delivered a big stack of papers from Lawson International to the house. Want me to bring it to the office or your house?"

I grabbed the radio. "No need. I'll come get it."

"Princess—" Christian said as I shoved away from the desk.

"I'm not the one throwing up mixed signals," I

snapped. "I never pretended like I wanted anything other than a fling, and you're the one who said you could separate sex and romance."

His eyes darkened. "You're selling yourself short if you think that was a fling."

"I sold myself short for years because I attached myself to someone who didn't love me. Trust me, I know when I'm selling myself short. And I won't be doing that again."

I skipped the barn, and decided I'd rather have blisters on my feet from walking up to Claire and Silas's house rather than be around Christian any longer.

I regretted it as I passed Becks and Nate's house. An extra car—Becks's mom—was parked in front of the fence that had been repaired after Christian tied me to it.

Becks, Nate, and their brand new baby girl, Charlotte, had just gotten home from the hospital. Everyone had been filtering over to see them as much as work and school schedules allowed, but I held back.

She was my friend, but they weren't my family. It would just be weird. That, and I had never held a baby.

"Cassie, I told you I'd bring it to ya," Claire said as she tipped back and forth on the old rocking chair that lived on the front porch. "If I'da known you were walking, I would'a saved you the trip."

My heart was racing and my feet burned. "I needed the fresh air."

"I'll say," Claire said with a chuckle. "You've been holed up in Chris's office for days."

"I have a lot to do before the groundbreaking." I reached for the yellow mailer sitting in her lap. "I should be getting back to work."

"Well, hold on now." She patted the rocking chair beside her. "You walked all the way up here. Take a rest and sit a spell before you hike back."

"I shouldn't. I'm on the clock."

"And if my son gives you shit about it, I'll deal with him." Claire pointed to the rocking chair. "Sit."

She wasn't asking this time. It was an order.

My feet screamed as I lowered into the rocking chair. Red blisters streaked the edges of my heels.

"You want somethin'ta drink? I've got tea, lemonade—"

"I'm fine, thanks."

"I've got vodka, too."

"I assumed this was a whiskey family," I said as I eased my feet halfway out of my shoes and rocked back and forth.

Claire laughed. "Maybe for the boys, but I'm a vodka girl myself. Belvedere, neat. Nothing fancy."

I'd have to remember that and make sure the bar was stocked with Belvedere for the party. Maybe I could get a signature cocktail on the menu. One for Claire and one for Silas.

"You have good taste," I said, working my nail into a groove in the chair's wooden arm.

She smirked, fluffing her plume of silver hair as she surveyed the property from her throne on the porch. "How is event planning for the groundbreaking going? Chris isn't giving you a hard time, is he?"

My throat tightened. "No, he's deferring to me for most things. It's made it quite easy, actually."

Her lips pursed into a pleased smile. "He trusts you.

Christian is usually hands-on with everything that happens within the fence. He doesn't delegate well."

I would have called it avoidance, but delegation was fine.

"I'm not sure if Christian told you, but the date for the groundbreaking celebration is locked in. It'll be the night before the rodeo championship. I'm hoping Ray will be our guest of honor. It'll be a great draw for the community—him being the hometown boy and all that."

Claire sat in thoughtful silence for a moment. "That'll be a tough call. If he makes it through to the wild card rounds, he usually goes radio silent. Won't leave his hotel room. Won't party. None of that stuff. As much as it scares the bejeezus out of me, he's serious about what he does and is very, very good at it."

"I looked up his record. He's made quite a name for himself."

Claire nodded proudly. "I wonder when he'll hang it up, but bull riding is his first love. It'll have to be something monumental for him to decide his body's been through enough. Those championship payouts and sponsorships keep him coming back. That, and the love of the sport."

"It took me longer than I'd like to admit to realize that the boots Christian gave me were from Ray's line. He's a celebrity. I never knew how big bull riding was."

"I suppose not," Claire said with a smile. "Has the culture shock worn off yet?"

"I don't think it ever will. Sometimes I can't sleep because of how quiet it is at night."

She nodded knowingly. "I remember Becks saying the same thing when she moved in with Nathan. She'd sleep with the TV on for background noise. City girls falling for cowboys has become a common occurrence around here."

I was about to argue that I hadn't fallen for Christian when she cut me off.

"I was a Chicago girl." Her smile was wistful. "Moved down here for college back in the sixties. Swore up and down that I wouldn't fall in love with a cowboy. I had my eyes set on California after I got my degree."

"What did you study?"

"I got a degree in accounting at Methodist. Made it all four years without dating a cowboy. I was working an internship with the Department of Agriculture when in walks this tall drink of water. I remember it like it was yesterday."

I could feel a slow smile forcing my melancholy away as Claire rambled on.

"I was tucked away in an office, going over the books, and was annoyed because his boots were so damn loud. Apparently, no one was at the front desk, because he just let himself back and poked around until he found someone."

"He found you, didn't he?"

Claire smiled. "He had on a white Stetson. Took it off and tipped his head like the most polite troublemaker to ever walk the planet, and asked me if I knew where the boss was."

"What did you say?"

She snorted. "I looked him dead in the eye and said, "Why are you assuming I'm not the boss?""

I snickered. "What did he say?"

Claire grinned. "He said, "Well if you're the boss, then

I owe you money. And it'll be real awkward for both of us if it looks like I'm trying to get out of a debt by taking you on a date.'"

Tears of laughter leaked from the corners of my eyes, and I dabbed them away. "How presumptuous."

"Tell me about it. I told him he had a snowball's chance in hell of taking me out if that was his pickup line."

"What did he do?"

Claire beamed. "He came back every week with a different pickup line. I was willing to let it go on longer, but the old bat who usually guarded the front desk got tired of him showing up to see the intern every Friday. It went on through the rest of my senior year. Finally, she took pity on him and told him that I refused to date cowboys."

"I'm going to assume he didn't stop."

"Oh—he did," Claire said. "I think it was two or three weeks later when I got a letter in the mail with a job offer. A ranch down in Temple needed an accountant and they wanted little ol' me. I thought I had it made. I figured I'd work a little and save up some money before I moved to California for bigger and better. I showed up for my first day of work and—what do you know—guess who was waiting for me at the front gate?" She pointed to the dirt drive.

"Your cowboy."

Claire nodded. "I lit into him. Told him that if this was some kind of joke, then I'd kill him. But he promised there was a job and it was mine." She let out a low huff. "My first day, Silas asked me to dinner after work. I said no, and he asked why I wouldn't date a cowboy." She hunched over. "I told him I didn't want to be with someone who was out in a field from sun up to sun down and never had time for me. I didn't want to be some little wife at home, barefoot and pregnant. I had dreams of my own and I didn't want someone who was tied to a piece of land."

"How did he take that?"

Claire smiled. "He just nodded and said, 'Yes, ma'am.' And that was that. Or so I thought. The next day I showed up to work and he had a tablecloth over my desk. You know—the one you and Christian use now. It's the same one. There were candles and flowers. He said we'd have a business meeting instead, then grilled me a steak." She cut her eyes to me. "Steak is the way to my heart, and I was a broke college graduate. I didn't say no. Slowly but surely, he wore me down. Popping with flowers he picked in the fields. Teaching me how to ride. Taking me on horseback rides when the day was done. Leaving me little notes on my desk."

"That's sweet."

"I thought so too. We kept things professional. Never crossed any lines. That was, until I had been here a year and it was time for a performance review. I was gonna ask for a raise. So, I sat down with Silas's daddy—the Griffith brother in charge at the time—and made my case."

I was hanging on her every word. "Did you get it?"

"Well, not exactly." Claire clasped her hands together. "He told me I'd have to talk to Silas, since my paycheck was coming out of his."

I gasped. "No..."

"You can imagine how angry I was. I thought I had a legitimate job. I was putting away money so I could move away. But I had been here a whole year and fell in love with this land and a goddamn cowboy, whether I liked it or not."

My throat tightened. "He convinced you to stay."

"No, his momma did," she said. "There weren't other women around here, so she and I got to know each other real well. One day I asked her how she put up with the boys being gone all day long, barely coming in to eat dinner and sleep. You know—being the good wife when she didn't get much out of it."

Claire's eyes locked on mine and I could feel the shift. We weren't talking about her and Silas anymore.

"This life isn't for weak women, Cassandra. When Silas was running things, I carried half the load. I raised the boys, took care of the house, kept the books and tried to keep us out of bankruptcy, while he was building onto the legacy of the Griffiths that came before him. I found that I liked the solace of living away from the city. The quiet was exactly what I needed after long days. It takes a strong woman to carry that load, and Silas knew that. It's why he smiled at me when I told him off the first day he showed up in my office."

I swallowed the rock that lodged in my throat.

She reached over the rocking chair arms and squeezed my hand. "It's not for everyone. That's for damn sure. But I see the women that my boys set their sights on, and know they learned from their daddy." She patted my hand before letting go. "It takes a strong cowboy to put up with a bull, and a strong woman to put up with a cowboy."

26

CHRISTIAN

Two weeks.

She ignored me for two goddamn weeks.

I was about to lose my fucking mind if I walked into that office one more time to find she had already done whatever I needed to do, just so I didn't have a reason to be around her.

I wasn't sure when she had learned how to handle all the administrative tasks I was in charge of, but I sure as hell didn't like it.

Two weeks of her disappearing between five o' clock and nine o'clock, then slipping into her room like a thief, taking little pieces of me with each burglary.

I wiped the grease off my hands with a stained shop towel and let out a breath as I laid on my back and stared up at the conglomerate of metal tractor parts.

I shouldn't have pushed her like that.

I shouldn't have let my temper get the best of me.

I lost my shit, and I lost her.

But did I really have her to begin with?

It didn't matter now.

I eased out from under the tractor and sat up, resting my forearms on my knees. It had been quiet around the front of the property today. Ray had gone back to Houston and had made it through three rounds of the bull riding competition. The girls were at school. Cassandra was avoiding me. CJ and the boys were working to move the herd to the far side of the land so they were out of range of the groundbreaking ceremony.

Of course, construction on the lodge and restaurant wouldn't start for half a year. But Cassandra insisted that, for it to be a success with the locals, we needed a celebration that brought them in from the start, not just when they had to battle tourists for a table.

So, we were throwing a damn party. The quiet wouldn't last for long.

I cleaned up my shit and put it away, taking the time to sort the tools back onto the wall hooks, rather than leaving it for tomorrow. Glancing at the time, I realized it was almost five.

Thursdays were always hectic. Mom would pick the girls up from school when the bell rang. She'd take Gracie to dance class and Bree to therapy. Then, they'd swap. She'd pick up Bree from therapy and take her to the studio, where she would get Gracie and take her to the therapist's office.

I didn't know what I'd do without my family. Without this ranch.

Heritage meant stability. I had people around me that I knew I could rely on. I had almost lost Nate, then I had actually lost Gretchen. This land was my haven. It was where I could keep the people I loved safe. One day I'd pass it on to my girls, or Nate's little one, or hell—CJ or Ray's kids, if they ever found partners.

It was selfish to expect Cassandra to give up her life and take on mine. I knew that as soon as I asked her to make a choice.

But I couldn't leave, and she was already here.

I pitched the rag into a pile that needed to be washed. Why was this shit so fucking hard?

I tried to date. I'd go out on the off chance that my mom let the girls sleep over at her house. Over the years there had been a few women I went out with more than once, testing the waters to see if it would last.

It never did.

Now, the one woman I actually wanted to stick around was ready to go.

The writing was on the wall.

More like on my desk.

Yesterday she had addressed a letter to the ranch—to me specifically—detailing that groundbreaking celebration would be her last day. After that, she would pack up and return to her life in New York, and be available remotely if needed.

And I couldn't even get her in a room long enough to talk to me.

I cut the light off and pulled the door behind me.

Everything was silent.

It wasn't uncommon, but it was unnerving.

Momma's mini van was parked in front of her house, which meant she was back with the girls.

Mom would have Bree and Gracie taking showers, which left me itching to see what Cassandra was doing.

I trudged past the office, but the lights were off and the door was shut. I headed to my house and slipped in.

Huh. It was empty.

Momma must've had them showering up at her place.

But Cassandra wasn't there either.

I checked the time.

5:30 on the dot—right when she always performed her disappearing act.

It wasn't until I was nearly done making my rounds—checking the animals, refilling water, and making sure nothing glaring was out of sorts—that I realized Dottie was gone.

Curiosity got the best of me. I lingered in the barn, tinkering around in one of the empty stalls for over an hour. Just when I was about to give up and go home for the night, hooves approached.

But it wasn't just Dottie.

I peered through a wood slat and watched as CJ rode in on his jet black horse, Anny. *Short for Anarchy.* He hopped down and, not a second later, Cassandra trotted into the barn on Dottie.

Jealousy bubbled up my veins like acid as I watched her dismount with the ease of a seasoned rider.

"Unsaddle and check her over," Carson said. "Hang your shit up. Don't leave it lying around."

Cassandra came into view through the wood crevice. Blue jeans molded around her ass and thighs like a goddamn painting. She eased up on her toes and boots peeked out.

The pair I had gotten her.

She was wearing one of the heavy jackets I kept in the

office. It was speckled with dried grass and hay from when I'd worn it this morning to do chores.

CJ supervised Cassandra while she took off the saddle and bridle. Without a word, she picked up the brush and started working Dottie over, cleaning her up and making sure she wasn't injured or uncomfortable.

When she was done, CJ stood beside her and talked her through safely checking Dottie's hooves and helped her give them a quick clean.

Cassandra seemed more confident with Dottie. She didn't shy away from grooming her or rubbing her down.

Their rapport was odd. It was ... familiar. Like this wasn't the first time they had gone riding.

My throat burned and I gritted my teeth as possibilities raced through my head.

"That's enough," CJ said. "Go on and turn her out."

There was some shuffling, and Cassandra disappeared out of view.

"You gonna shower at the bunkhouse again?" he called after her.

"Do you mind?" she asked.

The fuck?

"Nah, just don't use all the hot water or you'll cause a riot."

Cassandra laughed as she disappeared from the barn.

CJ was right behind her, leading Anny out to the fenced paddock for a little free-roaming.

What the ever-loving fuck was going on?

I stewed as I plodded around, doing a whole lot of nothing while looking busy. I couldn't focus on jack shit.

So, that's where she disappeared to every day. Riding with my brother, showering off in the bunkhouse, and then waiting for the right moment to slip in my front door and go to her room. I bet she fucking ate over there too.

CJ's guys were decent, but she was a pretty thing and they lacked general manners, civility, and hygiene.

It wasn't a fox in a hen house. It was a hen walking into the fox den.

Well... Maybe not so much.

Cassandra could hold her own.

Maybe that's why I hated it. She didn't need me.

The house was empty when I went back. I was just going to heat up leftovers for dinner, so there was no prep that needed to happen.

I paced the kitchen long enough to know that if I didn't do something, I'd start climbing the walls.

So fucking quiet.

Surely someone needed something.

But no one was around.

I hopped in the shower and took my time scrubbing the day away. Thoughts of her filled my mind as I shampooed my hair. I couldn't help myself. While the conditioner sat in my hair, I fisted my dick and rubbed one out to the thought of Cassandra touching herself on her bed.

By the time I finished and dressed, I was certain the girls would be back.

But they weren't.

I grabbed the radio and changed the channel, calling up to my parents' house to make sure Bree and Gracie weren't getting into trouble. It was a school night after all. They'd need to do homework and get in bed soon.

No answer.

Fine. I'd just go up to the house myself.

But before I set foot over the threshold, the radio chirped. Jackon's voice crackled over the line. "Hey, boss. Looks like it's gonna rain and there's shit outside the cabins."

"I'll take care of it," I said, knowing if I sent Jackson out there, all my tools would get rained on.

We had made progress on the cabins. They were mostly livable now, with four sturdy walls, plumbing and electric, new counters and cabinets.

Appliances would be installed the next week, and Cassandra had been hoping to get at least one of them furnished and decorated so it could be toured as part of the groundbreaking. I didn't tell her the furniture had already come in. I had intercepted the delivery, hoping to corner her in the cabin so she would have to talk to me.

Gray clouds loomed overhead, threatening to pour as I hopped in my truck and rode out to the cabins. I didn't mind the rain. Whatever made the grass grow, paid the bills, and kept food on the table was fine by me.

"Huh." I threw the truck in park when I pulled up between the two buildings.

The tools and equipment that had been in the grass earlier today were gone.

I sat back for a moment, wondering why the hell Jackson would call me all the way out here to pick the shit up if someone got to it first.

I knew it wasn't CJ. Supposedly, he was back in the bunkhouse.

Nate was in full daddy mode as he settled into newborn life with Becks and baby Charlie.

Maybe my dad had been piddling around and picked everything up?

The light was on in the cabin, so I hopped out to go turn it off.

When I slammed the truck door and turned, Cassandra was standing there, looking pretty as a summer day in a long, flowing dress that had flowers stitched all over it. Her hair was damp and tied back in a braid. She looked fresh-faced from the shower.

"What are *you* doing here?" she snapped.

I scoffed. "I'm supposed to be picking up tools, and this is my ranch. I can go wherever I please. What are you doing here?"

She sneered. "I was told an inspector was coming to approve the work, and I needed to be down here to sign some papers."

I narrowed my eyes. "Who told you that?"

"Jackson. Who told you there were tools to be picked up?"

"Jackson," I said.

Cassandra eyed the cabin warily, and I saw her riding the same train of thought I was on.

There were no tools, and there was no inspector.

Feet pitter-pattered from inside the cabin. *Now, those footsteps I would recognize in my sleep.*

"We're being set up," Cassandra said without a hint of amusement.

I sighed and headed up to the little porch. "Just... be nice."

Reluctantly, Cassandra followed.

Warm light bathed the inside of the cabin as I poked my head in the door. "Girls?"

Giggles echoed from the kitchen.

The whole place had been cleaned top to bottom.

The smell of grilled steak mingled with the fresh lumber, wood stain, and paint.

"You didn't tell me the furniture came in," Cassandra hissed under her breath.

I stopped and spun. Her chest bounced off of mine, but I caught her before she teetered backward. "I would have if you hadn't been ignoring me."

"Now I can't return it if they're not the right pieces."

"They're the right pieces, I double-checked the order invoice," I countered.

She huffed like I was daft. "Just because they're the right pieces doesn't mean they're right for the space."

I rested my forehead on hers. "Now who's speaking in cowboy proverbs?"

"Let's get this over with," she said as she brushed by me. "Girls," she said as she entered the kitchen and looked around. "What's going on?"

Bree and Gracie stood beside the two-seater kitchen table with their hands clasped behind their backs, looking rather smug.

"Welcome, Dad. Miss Cass," Bree said. Cassandra's necklace gleamed around her neck.

I stood behind Cassandra, close enough to feel her body heat against my chest. "Would one of my mischievous daughters care to explain what you're doing all the way out here by yourselves?" I glanced at the table. "And why there's steak."

"Grandma's here!" Gracie blurted out, pointing to the corner where my mother stood, tucked away with an apron around her waist.

I raised an eyebrow. "Fine. Co-conspirators, please tell me why you're not doing homework under my roof."

Bree and Gracie looked at each other without the slightest bit of guilt. Apparently, Gracie was the brave one now. "Dad, we want Miss Cass to stay and we want you to date her."

Cassandra stiffened.

I raised my eyebrows, glancing over at my mother, who gave me a little nod.

"We made dinner," Bree said. "Well, Grandma helped and so did Uncle CJ. But this was all our idea."

"Right." I groaned as I pressed my fingertips into my eye sockets. "Girls, maybe this is something we should talk about back at the house. Dating... that's a grown-up decision that people have to make on their own. You can't trick people into it."

Gracie looked crushed. Her eyes welled up instantly and her lip quivered.

"But..." Bree's eyebrows drew in. "You like each other. And you look at her like you used to look at Mom."

Fuck. Me.

Gracie sniffed. "We thought maybe you never had a chance to take Miss Cass out on a date because you're always working." She ramped up the waterworks. "We love you, Daddy, and—"

"Fine! Dinner! We'll eat it!" Cassandra blurted out, spinning around and putting her back to the girls.

I leaned down and whispered, "You gotta build up an immunity to the puppy face or you'll go broke."

She rubbed her temples. "Make it stop. I can't take that look."

I sighed. "We will... appreciate... all your hard work. Thank you for being thoughtful and putting together this nice dinner."

Gracie's face changed instantly. "So, you'll date her?"

"Jesus, do you know how long it takes me to coach clients into crying during interviews? That child needs to teach acting classes," Cassandra whispered.

"Girls, we can talk about this at home, but it's getting late and—"

"Come along," Momma said as she eased out of the corner she had been hiding in. "Let's leave your dad and Cass to eat in peace, knowing that homework is already done. And since you've got some dishes to help me with back at my house, we'll make it a sleepover and I'll get you to school in the morning." She gave me a passing wink.

Bree and Gracie scurried out of the kitchen and threw their arms around me, then hugged Cassandra.

"Please talk to her, Daddy," Bree said, letting go of Cass and grabbing my hand the way she used to when she was little. "Please?"

I kissed her head. "I love you, baby girl. Thank you for doing this. It was very thoughtful of you."

One by one, they filed out and headed back.

Cassandra let out a weighted breath and slumped against the brand new cabinets. "I don't know how parents put up with the emotional manipulation. That was exhausting."

"It starts early," I said, taking a peek at the plates that were packed full. "You build up an immunity."

Cassandra looked around. "So, what do we do now? Wait until they're far enough away and then leave?"

I pulled out one of the kitchen chairs. "We eat."

27

CASSANDRA

I huffed, slumping against the countertops. "Christian, I can't do this."

The cabin was decorated in flickering candles and string lights. An old school record player played softly in the background as Nat King Cole spelled out L-O-V-E.

It was all too much.

"Cass." His voice was soft. "It's just dinner."

As much as I wanted to fight it, I was tired. I had been working non-stop, getting all the pieces in place for the groundbreaking celebration. When it was all said and done, so was I.

The investment deal with Lawson International had been signed. I connected Christian with one of their representatives, and then made sure that she had Momma Griffith's and Becks's contact information just in case.

Christian had a penchant for escaping to the pastures

when he got stressed. It gave me a contingency plan to make sure things ran smoothly and they wouldn't have to call me.

But part of me—a larger part than I wanted to admit—wanted that phone call.

I wanted to be needed.

But was being needed worth getting hurt again?

"How about this?" Christian said. "If I promise not to say a word, will you eat with me?" He glanced down at the plated meal set out on the table. "Looks like the girls put a lot of work into it... Probably the least we can do before I go back and have a talk with them."

Relenting, I sat and let him push my seat in because I knew better than to argue with him about it.

Christian's silence was unnerving as we cut into our steaks.

They were perfectly cooked to medium rare with flawless cross-hatched grill marks. I paused with my knife over the middle of the steak. "Is that..." I cocked my head. "Is that a brand?" I asked, looking up at him.

Sure enough, there was a circle around the middle of the steak with the outline of a longhorn cow and the ranch's initials.

Christian's lips twitched in a smile, but he didn't make a peep.

"Right." I stabbed a small bite and popped it into my mouth. "Not talking."

His eyes turned down to his plate and he kept eating.

I made it halfway through my roasted potatoes before I couldn't take it anymore. "Fine. Let's talk," I blurted out, dropping my fork onto the plate with a clatter.

His beard fluttered, and I knew that jackass was smiling underneath it.

Christian slowly set his fork and knife down and looked me dead in the eye. "Would you like some wine?"

"Really? That's what you wanted to ask? I can pour my own fucking wine."

Apparently, Christian took that as a "yes." He reached into the ice bucket perched on the edge of the table and pulled the cork out of a bottle of Salado Diamond Back. I watched as the red blend splashed into the crystal glass, and contemplated what the hell I was doing with my life.

I was tired.

Christian set the bottle down and slid a glass to my side of the table.

"How was your ride?" he asked, and I froze. "Yeah, I know about it," Christian said as he resumed eating.

"It was fine," I hedged, pushing an asparagus spear across the plate. "It's a good way to clear my head."

To my surprise, he nodded as he took a sip of wine. Ruby droplets clung to his mustache. "It is."

I gritted my teeth, grinding the steak to a paste. *Why was he being so amicable?*

Fine. If he was going to play nice, then I'd ask what I really wanted to know. At least I didn't have to tiptoe around him the way I used to do around Tripp.

"What are you going to tell Bree and Gracie?"

Christian sighed. His warm eyes looked like soft flames in the candlelight. "That I tried."

Ice flooded my veins. "You tried."

"That's right."

"You didn't try, cowboy. You tied me to a pole and gave me an ultimatum."

"Fence post."

"Same thing."

Christian picked up his glass by the stem and swirled the wine around. "I tried my best, Cass. Did I do it right? No. But that's what I'm going to tell them. Because they learn by watching me. They deserve to know that I put myself out there. Success isn't guaranteed. Happily ever after isn't guaranteed. Happily ever eternity sure as fuck isn't guaranteed, but they learned that one a long time ago. The only thing I expect of them is that they try in life because that's what I expect of myself." His gaze was heavy and stern. "What do you expect of yourself?"

I jabbed my fork into the potatoes. "Excellence."

Christian sat back, looking a little surprised. "And you think that excludes you from a relationship because you can't do it… excellently?"

It wasn't that. Not exactly, anyway. I was fine in relationships. Frankly, I was a fucking saint in relationships.

I put up with Tripp and his bullshit for years.

It was the other aspect of Christian's life I wasn't totally comfortable with. And, if I was honest with myself, it's because I didn't like being bad at things.

I wasn't a kid person. So what? Not everyone was. I wasn't a fairytale villain who wanted to lure children to a giant gingerbread house and cook them alive. I just wasn't good at leveling with kids.

I was too blunt.

Too abrasive.

I wasn't nurturing or maternal.

Christian needed someone who could fill those sensible shoes. My high heels didn't fit the mold.

I swallowed. "It excludes me from this one."

"Because I have kids."

"Yes."

Christian did the one thing I never expected. He laughed. "Cass—" he reached across the table and laid his hand over mine "—I'm not looking for someone to be a mom. I'm looking for someone to be *my* partner." He sipped his wine and took pause. "A prerequisite for that is that they're trustworthy around my kids, but the girls aren't babies anymore. In a few years, Bree will be driving even though that makes me physically ill. Gracie's not far behind. And if you'll let me pat myself on the back, I think I'm doing okay raising them. I'm not perfect, but I try. And they know that. I'm not looking for someone to take that over."

I looked down at my plate, not really feeling all that hungry anymore.

"You expected me to move here. To live here," I said, holding tight to those last threads of my arguments. "What if I expected you to move to New York?"

"I would do that if it was in everyone's best interest," he said without a moment of hesitation. "But it's not, and I think you know that. Whether or not you want to admit it, you're at peace here."

I scoffed. "Voluntarily riding Dottie does not make me at peace."

"No, but asking for CJ's help does. And my momma's. You're not hiding anymore." He tipped his head to the side, debating it. "Well. Except from me."

I knew he was prodding me to tell him more, but I wanted to know just how much he was privy to.

"You know how I am when you force me to play

Russian roulette with a shotgun. I'll shoot, and I won't even blink."

Christian licked his lips and his voice turned to a growl. "Something going on with CJ?"

"No," I clipped. "He caught me sneaking out of the office to hide in the barn until the coast was clear to get back to your house, and told me to tack up Dottie. I didn't know how, so he taught me. I figured a general knowledge of horse care would be good if I'm going to talk up the equine program during the groundbreaking. We've been going on a ride every afternoon. He's not as nice as you are."

Christian chuckled. "You and Carson are two of the most blunt people I know. You're peas in a pod."

"He keeps the rest of the guys busy for a half hour so I can shower in the bunkhouse and not be bothered."

"You think I'd bother you if you showered at home?"

That wasn't it. Not entirely, anyway.

I trailed my finger along the rim of my wine glass. "I think I would have bothered you."

"I want you to," he admitted. "Cass..." Christian sat back, took his hat off, and ran a hand through his hair. "I want you to stay."

Tears welled up in my eyes. For years, that was all I wanted to hear.

Stay.

Be here with me.

Don't go.

But all Tripp ever told me was to go. To leave.

"You have a place here."

"I already put my notice in. Mike knows I'm coming back to New York."

Christian shook his head. "I don't accept."

I reared back. "Excuse me?"

Christian chuckled. "You think you're stubborn? Princess, I deal with bulls, mules, and my kids. Two can play that game. I'll call New York and tell them you're not done here." He drained his wine and dropped the glass back on the table. "And if that doesn't work, I believe you know how adept Griffiths are at kidnapping."

I pressed my fingertips to the edge of the table. "I am not a rancher. I'm not a stay-at-home wife—er—a stay-at-ranch wife."

"No, you're a workhorse. You're incredibly resourceful. You adapt to whatever is asked of you. Your skill set should be used for more than being some celebrity's filter."

"Like what."

"Like being the property manager."

I froze. "What?"

He shrugged. "Someone has to do it. It's not going to be me. I'll never sleep again. Nate and Becks could help sometimes, but they've got their hands full and she'll be going back to work when her leave is over. Someone needs to be the liaison between the ranching operation and the development projects while they're being built. Someone is going to have to connect and manage all the people running the restaurant and the programs and lodging—all that shit. Did you really think you could just leave?"

"You should hire someone with management or hospitality experience. I can compile a shortlist of candidates who—"

"You're it."

"Christian, stop. I can't—"

"What do you expect of yourself, Cass? Because I expect you to try, and you expect excellence. Where's the hang-up?"

"You. I can't work for you."

"I'll have you report to my momma. She keeps the books, it'll be fine."

"Chris..."

"Tell me where the problem is. You don't want me? I will deal with it. But I want you to stay, regardless. You want your own space?" He motioned around. "The cabin's done. We'll go back to the way things were supposed to be."

"What if I disappoint myself?" I whispered.

The lines wrinkling his forehead softened as tears welled up in my eyes.

"What if I disappoint you? What if I disappoint the girls? I don't want to hurt them. I told you—I'm not warm and fuzzy."

Christian eased out of his seat and rounded the table until he was cupping my cheeks. "You know what we do when there's a dust storm?" His lips were soft as he pressed them to my forehead. "We stand at the windows and watch, because being near something that powerful and uncontainable is worth the risk."

"Morning, beautiful." Christian's beard tickled my neck as he kissed his way down my throat and across my shoulder.

I shivered as goosebumps skittered across my skin.

Groaning, I rolled into him and nuzzled into his chest. "Too early."

"I'm sorry I kept you up late," he mumbled unapologetically as he slid his hand up and down my waist.

It was still dark outside, though the light behind the windows was turning from black to royal blue as it crept closer and closer to dawn.

I smirked and stretched my legs, curling my toes like a cat. I could still feel the ache from being absolutely railed last night. "I wanna go back to sleep."

His chuckle was soft and deep as he pulled me closer. "Fine by me."

"But I should go," I yawned.

"Stay a few more minutes," he asked quietly, rolling onto his back and pulling me on top of him. "Just a little longer."

I settled into the soft bulk of his chest and stomach and felt my heart rate slow.

Christian smiled as he lifted an arm and pushed his hair out of his face. "I used to have abs," he said sheepishly. "It's been a long ten years. Sorry you missed 'em."

"I'm not sorry at all," I said with a happy sigh against his chest as I smoothed my hand up and down the gentle mountains and valleys of his torso. "If I didn't make it clear before, I'm quite attracted to you."

His beard twitched. "Yeah?"

"Mhmm." I closed my eyes and decided a few more minutes in his bed wouldn't hurt. "You make me feel safe. I love when you hug me because it feels like nothing in the world can touch me. You're like a cave where I can hide when I've had a bad day and I know nothing can hurt me. And if memory serves, this body

—" I tapped his sternum "—made me come three times last night."

Christian's cock thickened beneath me. "More where that came from." He kissed my head. "Go back to sleep."

"I need to get up before—"

Like I had conjured it, feet thundered overhead.

I groaned. "Before the girls get up. Why do they wake up so fucking early? I thought teenagers were supposed to want to sleep all day."

"Something you should know about kids..." He tucked his arm behind his head, making his bicep bulge. "Whenever you *don't* want them to catch you, they will."

"Then I should go back to my room before they come downstairs."

"Cass, we're both dressed. It's fine."

"I'm not wearing a bra."

His hand found my boob and squeezed. "I'm not complaining."

"You're insatiable."

"Yes, ma'am."

I tipped my chin up. "I still hate that."

Christian grinned, rolling us both over until he was on top of me, bracketing my arms with his. He pulled down the neckline of my tank top and buried his face in my chest. "Always insatiable for you, my queen."

I rolled my eyes and shooed him away. "Off. I have morning breath and your children will be down here any second. I need to get back to my room."

Christian rolled to his side and yanked me into him until we were spooning. "I told you it's fine. We're not naked. We're not partaking in adult activities."

I pulled his arms a little tighter around my waist. "I'm not ready for it."

Four days ago, Christian and I hashed it out in the cabin. He cleared up his wants and needs, and listened as I talked through what scared me about getting involved with him.

I promised to think about staying on staff after the groundbreaking, and he promised to prove to me that I could handle being in a relationship with a single father.

Hence, why I was in his bed, struggling to motivate myself to get out of his arms.

Every night, I'd sneak into his room after we were certain the girls were asleep. And every morning I'd sneak back to my room before they were awake.

There had only been one or two near-misses, but so far no one was the wiser.

Except Claire. She *definitely* knew, which meant most of the over-eighteen population of the ranch knew as well.

CJ gave me shit for it the next time I met up with him to go riding.

I gave him shit for being a miserable son of a bitch.

Even Ray called to give Christian his two cents.

But, at my request, no one said a word to the girls about Christian and me. It made the 'figuring it out' part a little easier.

Christian had worked so hard to give Bree and Gracie stability. I didn't want to mess that up by letting them get their hopes up about a precarious relationship.

"Dad!" Bree shouted as she stomped down the stairs.

"Shit," I muttered as I rubbed the sleep from my eyes.

Christian had lulled me back into a warm slumber and I forgot I needed to get out.

Christian tipped his head away from my ear and yelled. "Yeah, baby. What do you need?"

"Can Miss Cass do my hair for school today? I want curls and you hate the curling iron."

"I can use a fucking curling iron," he grumbled under his breath.

I clapped my hand over my mouth to hide my laughter.

"Uh, maybe if she wakes up in time, but you'll have to ask her," he yelled back.

"Can you ask her?" Bree countered.

I rolled my eyes. "I'm not the Wicked Witch of the West."

Christian leaned close to my ear. "You have some reputation damage control to do, then. I've been telling everyone your broom is in the shop and that's why you have to hitch rides everywhere."

I swatted his stomach.

A lazy smile graced him. It was a good look.

"I'll ask her when she comes out of her room," he hollered, spinning a little white lie.

Silently, I mouthed, "Thank you."

Christian nodded.

Bree groaned. "Ugh. Dad, I know she's in your room. I need extra time getting ready today, so I got up early. Y'all are usually up by now anyway. I hear you walking around every morning."

I dropped my hand onto my face.

"Busted," he whispered before burying his face into my hair. "She's got an attitude like her momma had."

"Thirteen going on thirty. The sass is strong with that one." With a huff, I yelled, "Give me ten minutes and go start the coffee pot."

"Thank you!" Bree squealed, scurrying away from the door and running into the kitchen.

I glared at Christian. "You said they'd never know."

He shrugged. "They do now. But you know what?"

"Hmm?"

Christian tightened his arms around me. "The world didn't end."

28

CHRISTIAN

The ranch was alive. Cars and trucks were parked in neat lines along the front pasture. String lights and lanterns marked the path that started at the front gate and looped around the property.

Cassandra had convinced a local company to donate a fleet of golf carts to ferry guests down the freshly grated dirt lane.

Ranch hands were mounted on horses, keeping curious guests from peeking behind the metaphorical curtain.

Cassandra and Ray had worked with his sponsors to have them pony up for the bar and catering. *With adequate signage and company representatives on sight to rub elbows with the who's who of groundbreaking attendees.*

The billowing white tent had been donated, thanks to a local rental company that Cassandra promised would be an exclusively recommended vendor when the event space was up and running.

She fucking pulled it off.

I could barely believe it. The ranch looked *good*. It had been a push to get the place cleaned up and ready, but she had whipped everyone into shape.

Using her newfound friendship with CJ, Cassandra managed to get the ranch hands to work a little overtime and get the barns looking nearly new. Fresh landscaping had been put down and the siding had been power washed and painted.

Even the mayor was here.

That was a surprise. I thought Cassandra hated him.

Which begged the question, where was the woman of the hour?

Spenser Crenshaw, a representative from Lawson International, was poking around outside the tent. He looked harmless enough, but I was certain Cassandra wanted him to stay within the parameters she set for the party.

Giant blueprints and architectural renderings had been printed and displayed, showing off what was to come over the next—well— the next decade.

It would be a long project. That was for damn sure.

But little by little, we were solidifying the future of the Griffith Brothers Ranch.

She did that.

So where was she?

"Mr. Griffith," a feminine voice said from behind me as I walked away from the tent.

I turned to find a blonde, but it wasn't *my* blonde. "Yes, ma'am. Can I help you?"

She smiled from ear to ear as she extended her hand. A massive engagement ring that should have required a forklift glinted on her finger. "Elena Callaway. Allegiant Holding Group. Pleasure to meet you."

"Likewise, ma'am."

"We partnered with Lawson International at the last minute to invest in the hotel. We're excited about the venture."

"As are we." I looked around, searching for Cassandra.

"I was hoping to speak with Ms. Parker." She smiled warmly. "It's always good to put a face to a name, especially now that I hear she will continue to be the project liaison."

I nodded. "Yes ma'am. We're incredibly lucky to have her leading the ranch revitalization projects. She's irreplaceable."

Elena smiled knowingly. "Better hold on to her. If she's everything I've seen through long-distance communication, someone might come along and poach her."

Didn't I know it.

The band beneath the tent transitioned into an old country tune, and partygoers filled the dance floor.

"Great party, Griffith," Mayor Getty said as he came up and shook my hand.

Elena excused herself and disappeared into the crowd.

"Thank you, Mr. Mayor. We appreciate you coming out here. Did you have a chance to get a drink and take a look around?"

He stammered. "Just one drink for me. Time to call it a night." He patted me on the back. "Very good. Gonna be great for the community."

I watched as he hurried away like someone power

walking through a haunted house. It was like he was trying to not seem scared, but inside he was terrified.

I'd have to ask Cass about that.

Speaking of. I needed to find her.

Partitions disguised as a photo backdrop shrouded the office from public view, but I saw a faint light glowing between the panels.

"Pretty sure the guest of honor isn't supposed to be hiding in the office, answering emails," I said as I slipped inside and shut the door behind me.

Mickey and Sadie were both seeking respite from the chaos in the quiet building.

Cassandra's old Hollywood waves swished across her back as she looked over her shoulder. "What? Sorry. I was checking the status of a permit we need for—"

I knelt down beside her and fished around in my pocket. I wasn't much of a suit guy, but I had pulled out my Sunday best for the occasion.

Her eyes widened. "What are you doing? Why are you on your knee? You're not doing what I think you're doing. Because if you're doing what I think you're doing, then I'm going to say 'no,' and it's going to be very awkward for the next few days."

I chuckled as I opened my palm.

"Christian, I can't—" she froze and looked at my hand. "What's that?"

I chuckled under my breath. "They—uh—they go on your heels. You know, so it's easier to walk in dirt and not sink in."

I held one of the little wooden blocks between my fingers. It wasn't very wide, but it had a deep notch in the top that fit the spike of her stiletto, and a flat, flared base for more surface area on the ground.

"I stained them so they'd match your shoes and not stand out so much," I said as I lifted her ankle to rest on my knee and wedged the little piece onto the tip of the heel.

Cassandra sat still as I gently put her foot down and lifted the other one to do the same.

She looked completely dumbfounded. "That's... the sweetest thing someone's ever done for me."

I shrugged it off. "Just something I fiddled with while I helped the girls with their homework. If they work I can make some more. You know, so you have them to match all your shoes." I took her hand and kissed it. "Maybe someday we'll have sidewalks around here for you."

"I can always go to New York when I need my fix," she said, draping her arms around my neck.

I pecked her lips. "Just as long as you come back to me."

I closed my eyes as she combed her fingers through my hair. I'd left it down today at the girls' request. "Feels good," I murmured listlessly.

"Bree was actually asking me about New York this morning."

I leaned into her touch. "Yeah?"

"Mhmm. She wants to go. Apparently between me and Becks she's convinced that New York is the most magical place on earth."

"You told her about the crime rate?"

She laughed. "No, I told her about Broadway and Times Square and this little hole-in-the-wall place in the Village that has the best pastries."

"And about the crime rate."

"I told her about the Met, and what it's like during Fashion Week, and—"

"And the crime rate, *right*?"

She stopped massaging my scalp. "Has anyone told you that you worry too much?"

I pecked her lips. "Yeah, I pay a therapist to tell me that once a month. What's your point?"

"I'm not going to tell you to stop worrying," she said softly. "It's attractive."

"Then between the ranch, the building projects, and raising teenagers I'm going to be irresistible these next few years."

She shut down the computer. "How's the party going?"

I stole another kiss and took her hand. "It needs its hostess before Ray makes it all about him."

Cassandra laughed, standing as the black dress she was in cascaded down her body. "While that's fair, considering he's at the top of the leaderboard going into the finals tomorrow, we might need to make sure his ego can still fit inside the tent."

The party was still in full swing. My folks were cutting it up on the dance floor. Ray had not one, but two women on his arms. He was wearing a button-up emblazoned with his team and sponsor logos, but sleeves were cuffed, showing off the tattoos on his arms that the girls had colored in earlier today.

CJ was posted up on the edge of the tent, having no fun at all as he watched the guests with an eagle eye, making sure no one wandered off.

Becks was seated, chatting up a journalist who was

looking at her like she was a fictional hero. Nate stood close by with their baby wrapped up in a swaddle, tucked safely against his chest.

Bree and Gracie were dancing with each other, taking turns leading.

Cassandra lifted her chin, surveying the chaos. All around, chatter about the restaurant, lodge, and community programs floated to the heavens.

I rested my hands on her shoulders. "You did it."

I felt her ease back into me, resting against my chest. Her fingers brushed mine, and she squeezed. "Thank you."

"For what?"

"For not sending me packing the first day."

"It was mostly pity." I laughed when she swatted my leg. "Fine. That, and your ass."

Cassandra huffed. "I'm trying to be serious here."

"Go on."

She turned her back to the party. "Thank you."

Instead of responding, I kissed her, letting the party spin around us in a blur.

Somewhere in the mirage, I heard my girls squealing and guests clapping.

Cassandra's mouth was soft and pliant, deferring to my lead as I fused my lips to hers. Gone was whiskey and mint. She tasted like champagne.

Like happiness.

"Tell me you decided to stay," I said softly against her mouth. She had already given a tentative yes on the job offer, but hadn't quit her job with the Carrington Group. But more than that, I wanted her to stay. With me.

Her eyes were misty. "We can talk tonight."

I bumped my nose against hers. "Do I need to get the girls involved?"

"Absolutely not," she clipped. "If Gracie does those damn puppy eyes and makes herself cry—"

Like she knew people were talking about her, Gracie bolted over and rammed into my leg. "Did you ask her?" she whispered in the loudest whisper known to man.

Cassandra pursed her lips to tuck away her amusement.

"She said we'd talk later," I shout-whispered back.

"Did you tell her she can still have the guest room if she doesn't wanna share your room?"

Cassandra clapped her hand over her mouth and walked away, laughing.

I pulled Gracie into a hug, wrapping her up in my arms. "She knows, baby."

"Good, 'cause I want her to stay."

"Hi, Daddy," Bree said as she wrapped her arms around my waist and tucked her head under my arm.

"Having fun?"

"Mhmm. But there's no one here my age."

"Sorry about it. Maybe when we start having grand openings you can invite some friends."

"What about a boy?" she asked.

My answer was immediate and definite. "No."

"But what if—"

"No."

"I'm gonna ask Miss Cass."

"Still no."

As the band faded out, Cassandra stepped up on stage and thanked everyone for coming. I felt Bree squeeze a little closer as she listened to Cassandra's speech about the project and the good it would do in the community.

"I like her," she said thoughtfully.

My heart tightened. "Yeah?"

Bree nodded. "I mean, I know we have Grandma and Aunt Becks, but Miss Cass is—like—*ours*."

I fixed my eyes on Cassandra as she called up each member of the Griffith family to take one of the ornate gold shovels while she spoke animatedly about the future of the ranch.

And as I stood shoulder-to-shoulder with her, my parents, brothers, Becks, and the next generation as we dug into the soil, all I could think was *yes*.

"THOUGHT YOU MIGHT LIKE THESE," I said as I came up behind Cassandra and offered the slippers I had snagged from her things when I took Bree and Gracie back up to the house to go to bed.

She was supervising the flurry of activity as the last of the rentals were packed, loaded, and hauled off.

Cassandra groaned as she slipped out of her heels and wiggled her toes in the grass. "Thank you. You're a godsend."

I knelt in front of her and slipped them on her feet. "Least I could do after you made us look civilized and successful."

Her laugh was tired. "I think it went well. Only time will tell, but I have high expectations."

"Not high hopes?"

She shook her head. "Hope is simply hanging onto

threads of abstract desire. Expectations are the application of hope. I expect excellence, and I will work for it. "

I pressed a kiss to her forehead. "Poetic."

"I learned from you."

I waited until the tent was down, the vendors were tipped, and the last box truck disappeared down the lane before I spoke up again. "You make it sound like you'll stay."

Cassandra slipped her hand in mine. "What if I did?"

Our steps were quiet as we walked back to the house. Although no one was out to hear us, it still felt a little like sneaking around. My parents had retired shortly after the party ended. Ray left early to head back to Houston before the championship tomorrow. Nate and Becks pulled the baby card and went back to their house—not that I blamed them in the least.

"You know what I want," I said.

She let out a breath. "Then maybe you should know I called Mike earlier today."

I stroked my beard for dramatic effect. "Really."

"We caught up on the project a little bit. I sent in my final projections so he could add it to the never-ending metric of success. He told me Tripp had been put on administrative leave because of yet another Lillian Monroe headline that should have never made the news."

"Those two fuckers really deserve each other," I muttered.

Cassandra laughed. "He doesn't even know what's coming. Looking back, I have no idea what I saw in him."

"You're not sad?"

She thought for a moment. "I'm sad that I wasted my time, but I learned my lesson. The people you should be around will make it very clear that you're wanted and valued."

I chuckled. "And how about the people you're around now?"

"They smell. They wake up far too early. They're bull-headed and stubborn and infuriating."

"And?" I pressed as we made our way up the porch steps.

Cassandra paused at the top. "And I've never felt more at home."

"Is that all you talked about with Mike?"

Slowly, she shook her head. "Not quite."

I slid my hands around her waist and gently stroked her hip. "What else?"

"I emailed my resignation before we got on the call. He told me that he'd pass it along and get the paperwork started." Pearly teeth sank into a crimson lip. "So, I hope that job offer still stands. And maybe the housing stipend. A commute from my apartment to the ranch is a little out of the question."

I grinned like the luckiest son of a gun to ever live as I backed her up against the porch column and kissed her. "It stands."

We weren't frantically trying to get in the house, but our lazy kisses under the porch light grew needy as moths flitted overhead. Cassandra whimpered into my mouth when I dragged my hand up her thigh, hitching it around my waist.

"Tell me you're gonna stay," I whispered into her mouth as I cradled the back of her neck.

Cassandra nodded. "Yes."

I grabbed the back of her thighs and picked her up as

she wrapped her legs around me. "We need to set some ground rules," I said as I carried her in and kicked the door closed behind me.

Her arms snaked around my neck. "Rules already?" She stuck her tongue out. "You're such a dad."

I wove through the house on silent feet before tossing her on the bed and closing—and locking—the door behind me. "I think you'll like these."

Cassandra shimmied up the bed.

"What's mine is yours. My house, my—"

"Truck?" she guessed.

"You still can't drive stick."

"I'm a quick learner."

"We'll work on it," I promised as I undressed and climbed up with her. "I trust you. Even as we are now—no rings, no long-term vows—you're part of this ranch. You're part of this family. You're part of this legacy. You want something done? You have the weight of my name in your own."

"I already knew that," she said with a coy little look. When I paused curiously, she said, "I overheard you telling CJ's boys that when I first arrived."

I cupped her jaw. "I meant every word."

Silver eyes grew heavy as I hovered over her mouth. She nodded slowly, solemnly, and soberly. "I know."

Piece by piece, I undressed her until we were skin-to-skin. Her breath was hot and staccato against my neck as I squeezed her breast, working it in my palm.

"Christian," she begged, trying her best to keep quiet. Her lungs hitched and strained as a whine escaped when I thumbed her nipple. Cassandra squeezed her thighs together, trying to ease the ache I was causing.

Good. I wanted her to know how much it pained me when she wasn't near.

She twisted and thrashed, but I kept her pinned beneath me, teasing her rosy nipples until they were flushed bright pink and pebbled.

I drove my knee between her legs and pressed it against her hot cunt. "There you go, Princess. Make yourself come. Show me how much you want my cock." I sucked on the paper-thin skin behind her ear and made her gasp. "Do a good job for me and I'll fill your little pussy up."

"Just fuck me already," she gasped as she rolled her hips, rubbing herself against me like an animal in heat.

"Keep going," I said as I cupped one heavy breast and sucked her nipple between my teeth.

She pressed harder against me, jolting with each thrust as she edged closer and closer to an orgasm.

"Don't stop now, Princess. Show me how pretty you look when you come with my name on your lips." I pinched her nipple and relished the shock that morphed into a moan. "That's what you wanted that day I walked in on you touching yourself. You wanted me to be the one making you come."

Cassandra nodded desperately. "Yes."

"Then make yourself finish like the dirty girl you are, and I'll make that fantasy come true."

I hissed as her teeth sunk into my shoulder as she came. Before she had even finished orgasming, I rolled on a condom and sank deep inside her soaked pussy.

"Goddamn, you feel incredible."

Lingering flutters of her release teased my cock as I pushed inside.

"Yes," she said, releasing a weighted breath. "That's what I needed."

I stole a kiss. "I'll always give you what you need. Tell me how good it feels, princess."

Cassandra hissed as I thrust into her again. Her words were strained and tense. "Full. So tight," she whimpered, resting her forehead on my shoulder.

I slammed my hips into hers. "I know it is, but you're a tough little thing. You can take it."

"Christian," she keened as I scraped my fingers up and down her tits, teasing her peaks with each pass.

Her pussy clenched around my dick, desperate and wanton. "I feel you, Princess. Come when you want. There's more where that came from."

Cassandra gasped, her back arching off the bed when I reached between us and slowly, steadily massaged her clit.

"I'll always give you what you need," I promised over and over again as she begged and pleaded for another release.

I breathed through waves of arousal that threatened to push me over the edge until she broke apart beneath me. We collapsed, chest-to-chest as my cock jerked, pouring into the condom.

Her cunt still strangled me, even as we lay together, slowly catching our breath.

"Christian?" she said quietly as she tipped her head back on the pillow and closed her eyes.

I peppered her chest with dotted kisses. "Hmm?"

"Thank you for being patient with me."

My hair hung around us as I pressed a kiss to her lips. "I love you too."

29

CASSANDRA

"This looks weird." I turned in the mirror and stared at my butt. "I hate wearing jeans."

"You should wear them more," Christian said with a near-giddy smile as he squeezed my ass. "You look damn good."

"I'm changing into my clothes."

"You'll get filthy."

"We're just watching Ray. I'm not riding a bull."

Going to the rodeo had been the last thing on my mind. I had been so caught up with planning and executing the groundbreaking ceremony and running away from Christian that I had nothing to wear.

I made it work like I always did.

Blue jeans, the boots Christian had given me, and a silk button-up paired nicely for the occasion.

"Can't wait to take this off later," Christian murmured as he hooked a finger in the neckline of my blouse. Heavy clouds of lust lingered in his eyes.

I mirrored him, trailing my finger around his obnoxiously large belt buckle, then dragging him against me. "Likewise." I smoothed my hands up his stomach and chest, savoring the softness.

I loved his body. Those broad shoulders. His thick biceps and thighs. The way I pressed into him when he hugged me like he was trying to make a mold of the feeling and hold on to it for eternity. I loved the way I could tuck in right around his hip and rest in the curve of his belly. He was sturdy and steadfast, but gentle. He handled me with care.

"I've got something for you," he said as he reached over my shoulder.

Gracie darted in and shoved a gift bag into his hand, then dashed away, giggling.

"Presents and compliments," I mused as I pulled the tissue paper out. "I might stick around."

I reached in and touched rough, heavy fabric. Curious, I pulled it out.

"You didn't have to get me anything." I studied the canvas jacket. It was a warm tan color that matched his jacket.

"Actually, I did," Christian said, taking the jacket and turning it around to show me the embroidered Griffith Brothers Ranch logo. "You're part of the ranch. The team. The family. You get a jacket."

I laughed as I stretched my arms out and let him put it on me. "If I had known I would get clothes, you might have convinced me to stay sooner."

"I'll remember that," he said as he smoothed his palms over my shoulders.

It took us nearly three hours for our caravan to drive to Houston. Christian, the girls, and I were in his truck, while CJ, Becks, Nate, and baby Charlie followed in their new SUV. Claire and Silas had driven to the arena earlier in the day.

Christian gave my hand a squeeze as we trekked through the parking lot.

"This is…" I looked around. "Chaos."

"Best. Day. Ever!" Bree squealed.

"Do you think Uncle Ray will let us near the chute?" Gracie asked.

"Can I get a snack?" Bree asked.

"What concerts are happening again?"

"I wanna go see the—"

"That's enough," I clipped. "You'll make me dizzy if you keep that up."

Christian gave me a nudge of approval and a wink.

It wasn't a big deal.

"How about we go scope everything out and see how much time we have?" he said as he kept a hand on Gracie's shoulder, but still laced our fingers together.

"Our boots match," Bree said, beaming as she looked down at our feet and matched her stride to mine. The boots were a gift from Christian from Ray's line of western wear.

Usually, I would have said something sassy like, "I know," or, "You have good taste if you're dressing like me."

But Bree's confidence was about more than shoes. I knew it in my bones, because I felt it too. Funny how a pair of shoes made me feel like I belonged.

"We look good, don't we?" I said, tossing my arm around Bree.

Bree put her arm around my waist. “Daddy, do you think Uncle Ray will get more sponsorships? Because he should do ads for clothes so I can get free stuff.”

Christian laughed. “I don’t think kids clothing brands sponsor many bull riders. Usually just boots and jeans.”

“But he’s done—like—those underwear ads.”

I lifted an eyebrow at Christian and mouthed, “Which ones?”

He shot me a look so sharp I nearly tripped.

The arena was deafening. Instinctively, I held on tight to Bree and followed Christian and Gracie through the throngs of people milling about. He kept a tight grip on my hand, weaving through the masses as we made our way to an area that had been cordoned off with metal gates and rope.

“Uncle Ray!” Gracie screamed in excitement.

I honestly had no idea how Gracie picked him out of the mass of men dressed like clones of each other. But Ray looked up and grinned as he elbowed his way through the bodies.

“There’s my Gracie Girl!” he said, snatching her up and putting her on his shoulders.

If I had been treated like that at eleven, I would have insisted I was too big to sit on someone’s shoulders. But not Gracie.

Bree hugged Ray. “Daddy showed me the video of your ride last night!”

“Yeah?” He squeezed her tight. “What’d you think?”

Bree tapped her chin. “Underscored, but I’ll let it slide since you’re still on top.”

“That’s my girl,” he said, fist bumping her.

The rest of the Griffith crew condensed, saying hello to Ray and wishing him luck.

Gracie hopped off his shoulders and scurried over to me so Ray could hold his newest niece, who was sporting a pair of baby-sized noise canceling headphones.

"Good thing she looks like Becks and not your ugly mug," Ray said, carefully elbowing Nate in the ribs.

Nate pressed a kiss to the side of his wife's head. Becks slipped her hand in Nate's. His rough, scarred skin wrapped around hers like a protective shield.

I knew the basics of what they had been through—meeting in Afghanistan and falling in love—but in that moment, I realized that I had only heard about it from Becks.

Christian never mentioned it.

Ray's sharp eyes landed on me. "You ever watched bull riding before?"

"This will be a first."

He grinned. "You're gonna hate it."

Ray brought over his manager, Marty, who hooked us up with passes to be in the staging area.

"I'm glad you're here," Becks said as she bounced from foot to foot as she tried to soothe the baby. Nate and Christian were taking Bree and Gracie around, leaving us on the small deck under the sponsor tent. "I've been wondering when one of the boys would bring a woman around long-term."

I curled my fingers around the metal gate. "I don't know about long-term."

I saw the age in her eyes as she studied me. "You're good for him. For all of them. Christian needed someone like you."

"What do you mean?"

She shifted Charlotte to her shoulder and rubbed her tiny little back. "Someone who doesn't kiss his ass. Someone who doesn't want to take over his role as the girls' parent. When Nathan and I got stateside and I moved down here, I offered to help Christian all the time. He never took me up on it. At first I thought it was because he didn't like me, but Nathan said it was because Christian thought he had to prove to himself that he could do it. That he could do their hair, fix the lunches, have the puberty talks, show up to mommy-and-me activities in all his burly cowboy glory without a hint of remorse. That he was capable of doing all the things Gretchen did. A few years ago he started asking for a hand, but only because he needed it or because schedules were crazy, not because he couldn't do it." She turned her back to the arena. "But I think he realized that he needs you. He doesn't need you to be their mom. He needs your tenacity."

"It's weird thinking about leaving New York for good. Packing up my apartment. Leaving the dream behind."

She smoothed her hand over the tufts of ginger hair that coated Charlie's head. "Trust me, I know what that feels like. People look at you like you're insane when you pivot and chase what makes you happy instead of what makes you look good."

Hands slipped around my hips. I didn't even have to turn around to know it was Christian pulling me against his chest.

"Hey," I said as I looked up.

His beard brushed the side of my head as I tilted and stole a chaste kiss. "Where are the girls?"

"Nate and CJ are bringing 'em up. They wanted to go look at livestock."

"They have a pet cow that lives in my office and eats my ice cream, and they want to see *more* cows?"

Christian buried his nose in the back of my hair. "I like that you just called it 'your' office."

"Slip of the tongue."

He chuckled. "I know where I'd like to slip my tongue."

"We are around your family," I hissed.

"Don't mind me," Becks said with a snicker. "Just pretend I'm not here."

Chaos in the arena caught my attention as the announcer introduced the first competitor riding for the championship.

"Oh my god," I whispered as I clapped my hands over my mouth.

"It looks brutal," Becks said. "But they're usually fine after."

"*Usually*?" I squeaked.

The animal that the rider had mounted bucked and thrashed against the corral, nearly pinning him to the wall.

"Ray's going to ride *that*?"

Christian's hold on me tightened. "No, that's Ball Buster. Ray drew Homewrecker."

"That sounds way worse."

"It is, but it's a good thing," Christian said. "He's one of the meanest ones. Homewrecker and Ray have a history. Homewrecker tries to kill him, and Ray wins a shit ton of money. Apparently, it's worth it to him."

"You Griffiths are psychotic. Why—pray tell—is

riding the meanest bull a good thing? Get one that's nice and tuckered out."

Christian pointed to the scoreboard. "Each rider has the possibility of getting a hundred points. Fifty points come from the rider's performance. Fifty points come from how hard the bull bucks."

It was starting to make more sense. "So, the meaner the bull, the more points you get."

"That's right."

The gate released and the bull jumped—*jumped*—out. A thousand pounds of ornery muscle flew through the air and landed with an earth-shaking rumble. The rider was whipped left and right, looking unnaturally fluid as he held on to the rope.

"How is his spine not in four pieces?" I shouted over the melee.

I shrieked and jumped back into Christian when the rider was flung off and landed in a tumble of limbs.

Christian didn't even wobble. He just wrapped me up in his brawny arms and held me close.

My whole body was electric. It was like watching a horror movie—terrifying, but I couldn't bear to look away.

The staging area filled up as it got closer and closer to Ray's turn. Bree and Gracie sported evidence of funnel cake as they wiggled through to the front to watch.

Ray was the second to last rider of the night. With each change in the leaderboard, Bree did the calculation and updated us on what he needed to win.

"What's my number, squirt?" Ray asked Bree over the partition as he smoothed down the medical tape on his wrist, slid on a glove, then taped it down again.

"Ninety-one point one."

"How hard is that?" I whispered to Christian.

He grimaced, but tried not to show it. "Most scores land between eighty-five and ninety."

Ray had been in the lead after the wildcard rounds, but the riders before him showed up to win.

I could hear Homewrecker stamping and kicking against the corral. He was already pissed. Ray zipped up the padded vest that protected his abdomen.

"Where's your helmet, daredevil?" Nate shouted.

Ray grinned and adjusted his cowboy hat. "Helmets just mean you can have an open casket." And with that, he put his mouthguard in and climbed down onto the back of the bull.

His team and the chute boss were clustered around him.

"Oh my god," I whispered, clutching my hands to my chest.

Christian let out a sharp whistle and clapped over my head. "Let's go, brother!"

Bree and Gracie were jumping up and down, screaming, "Go Uncle Ray!"

"He's good, Cass," Christian whispered, squeezing my shoulders. "Top of the circuit. He's good."

I wasn't sure if he was trying to convince me or himself.

The gate swung wide and Homewrecker paused. *Was that supposed to happen?*

Realizing there was a way out, the bull jolted and nearly threw Ray off on his way out into the arena. The animal spun like a tornado, slamming forward and back with each buck. The platform under our feet shook with the intensity of it all.

Ray fought to hold on. He whipped around, sometimes going with the direction of the bull, and sometimes countering it to keep his balance. Homewrecker jolted left, then stopped hard and whipped right.

My heart leaped into my throat.

The crowd went ballistic, and I looked at the timer.

Seven and a half seconds.

Screams and shouts grew deafening as it ticked closer to eight seconds.

A sudden change of direction caught Ray by surprise. Homewrecker stamped his hooves, soaring from front to back. Ray tilted the opposite direction to counter it, but the bull thrashed right again, flinging him off. Ray fell, but the bull was still going. A hoof collided with his stomach, mid-air.

Claire screamed as his head slammed into the dirt.

Men jumped into the ring to distract the bull and get him away.

My fingers trembled as I grabbed Christian's hand. "Why isn't he moving?"

All the other riders were quick to get up and jump the barrier to get out of the arena.

I squeezed his hand. "Christian—"

Ray laid in the dirt. Lifeless.

Bodies flooded the arena. Marty, a team of medics, and support staff leaped to action.

I felt Christian jolt behind me.

My heart was racing. Blood rushed in my ears like a tidal wave. "Baby—"

Realization slammed into Christian like a freight train, and he roared. "*Ray*!"

"Go," I said, letting go of him. "I've got the girls."

Christian threw himself over the barrier. Nate and CJ were right on his tail as they ran across the dirt.

Bree and Gracie turned in a panic. Claire broke away from Becks to tend to them, but they were already clinging to me.

30

CHRISTIAN

Sirens screamed as we floored it to the hospital. The back of the ambulance jostled, shaking the containers of supplies.

I tried to sit still and stay out of the way, but it was an impossible feat. We were crammed in like sardines. Two medics worked on Ray, monitoring his vitals, checking and double-checking the breathing tube down his throat. His vest was back at the arena, and his shirt had been cut up the front.

His black and blue abdomen was streaked by patches of skin colored in by washable markers. I held his hand, careful of the pulse oximeter on his finger, but it felt like holding a corpse.

Patches with wire leads were placed on his chest and hooked into a monitor.

The neck brace and straps held him still as we came to a skidding halt at the emergency room doors.

I followed the paramedics in, keeping a hand on Ray as he was rushed in and evaluated.

Then all I could do was wait.

The entrance to the waiting room flew open as my family piled in.

"Where is he?" My mom was shaking, hanging on to my dad like her life depended on it.

I took my hat off and dug my fingers into my hair. "He's in surgery. I don't know anything yet. They were talking about broken ribs. Possible internal bleeding."

Her weathered hands trembled as she cupped them over her mouth. "H-He wasn't m-moving."

There was no use sugarcoating it. She knew the reality of the situation as well as I did. "He landed on his head. Even if..." I choked up and couldn't get the words out quite right. "Even if he wakes up..."

"Christian—" Becks ran in with Nate behind her, carrying a car seat.

CJ was next, arriving with Marty, Ray's manager.

Where was Cassandra?

I repeated the spiel I gave my mom to the rest of the crew. Marty stepped away and started making calls. Becks and momma hugged. CJ took a seat in the corner with my dad, saying nothing at all.

Which left Nate.

"This isn't on you."

"I know it's not," I clipped, just a little irritated that he would make that comment. I started to pace. "I didn't tell him to get in the ring. I didn't tell him to be a fucking bull rider. In fact, I told him the opposite quite a few times. I didn't—"

"You didn't tell Gretchen to go through that intersection. You didn't tell the clouds to stop raining for two years. You didn't tell the herd to get sick. You didn't tell me to join the Army," Nate said. His mottled, scarred hand curled and stretched. "You didn't tell me to walk up to a suicide bomber, and yet you still blame yourself for not stopping it."

I froze mid-stride.

"Where's Cass?" I snapped. "And the girls."

Nate shrugged. "I dunno. They were out of the arena before we got out." He put a hand on my arm. "You gotta chill out. This is not your fault. You can't control everything. Don't make it about you."

With that, he went over to Becks and sat down.

Irritation sprang up my back, eating at me from the inside. I checked my phone. *No calls.*

I punched in her number, walked over to the empty half of the waiting room, and waited.

"Hey, Daddy." But it wasn't my kids answering the phone. It was Cass.

The sound of her steady voice was a balm. I let out a sharp breath. My blood pressure lowered at the sound of her voice. "What are you doing answering the phone like that? Where are you?"

Cassandra laughed softly. "It's your fault. You put yourself in my phone as 'Cowboy Daddy.'"

I slumped against the Coke machine and squeezed my forehead. That day felt like forever ago. "I forgot."

She was never one to beat around the bush, and got right to it. "How's Ray? How are you?"

"He—uh... Are the girls around?"

"They're out of earshot," she clipped.

"He's in surgery. Between us, I don't know if..." *Shit.*

My eyes burned as heat and salt clouded my vision. I sucked in a sharp breath and tried to let it out, but I couldn't. "I don't know if he's gonna wake up, Cass," I choked out. "He might not make it."

Tears streamed down my face and soaked my beard as I cried.

Cassandra was quiet. All that passed between us was the reassuring sound of her breathing.

I hunched over and braced my hands on my knees, letting out a long exhale. "Where are you at? Are the girls okay?"

"They're fine. Don't worry about us," she said. "I'm at the burger place across the street from the hospital. I figured it would give you a chance to get settled before I bring them into the chaos."

The burn in my lungs fizzled away. "How... How'd you get the truck out of the lot?"

Her laugh was music to my ears. "Bree helped me."

"I'm sorry. It sounded like you just said my thirteen-year-old helped you drive."

"Not like that." Her words were soft and reassuring. "She sat up front with me and explained how to use a clutch and shift gears. I only ran over one or two cars."

I chuckled at her sarcasm. "Are the girls okay?"

"They're worried about Ray," she said honestly. "But like I told you, I've got it. I don't want you to worry about us."

"Come on over when the girls are ready. We're in the waiting room. It could be a while."

We said our goodbyes and I hung up.

Half an hour later, Cassandra, Bree, and Gracie walked through the doors, carrying grease-soaked bags of burgers and fries for the family. Bree and Gracie curled up in the chairs beside my parents, looking only a little worse for the wear.

"Hey, cowboy. I brought you a—"

I grabbed the front of her shirt and slammed her mouth to mine, kissing her hard and deep. It was wholly inappropriate for a hospital waiting room, but I needed her. I needed to feel her. I needed to know that she was safe.

"You've been pacing," Cassandra said when she pulled back, lips full and swollen from the pressure of the moment.

I frowned. "How do you know I've been pacing?"

"Because there's nowhere for you to escape. There's no horse to ride to clear your head. There's no machinery for you to tinker with." She wrapped her arms around my neck and raked her fingers through my hair. "Sit down."

"I'll just get antsy and start pacing again," I admitted.

"Sit, Christian." She pushed the burger bag into my hand. "Eat."

"Cass—"

"I'm not asking."

And for some reason, I was okay with not being in charge for once.

Cassandra sat beside me as I unwrapped the burger and took a few bites. I knew I needed to eat, but my appetite had vanished.

My leg started bouncing as all those "what ifs" came rushing back. I started picking at a spot on my jeans. Every time the doors opened, I whipped around to see if it was someone coming to give us an update about Ray.

Hours passed with no news. With each loop of the clock, my legs jittered harder and harder.

"Come on," Cassandra said, taking my hand.

I pulled my gaze away from the doors. "Where?"

"If you're going to pace, then I'm going to pace with you."

Cassandra linked our fingers together, not caring that my family was watching as she led me away and started a loop around a section of chairs.

"Talk to me, cowboy."

I gave her hand a squeeze, but I didn't know where to start.

"When I first started going to a therapist, I couldn't sit down," I admitted.

"After Gretchen died?" she asked.

I shook my head. "Before that. I, uh... I started going after Nate got hurt overseas."

She bumped my arm with her head. "Wanna tell me about it?"

I swallowed, reliving the moment we found out what had happened. "Nate... He, uh—he was deployed in Iraq and was caught in an attack by a suicide bomber. One of his guys was killed. He was injured and airlifted out to an Army hospital in Germany. At the time, he was married to this woman named Vanessa. She got the notification that he had been injured and came out of the house screaming. Terrified. I was coming up from the pasture with my dad. I saw her from a distance and caught up to her. You know what it's like living that close to each other. You hear everything. Gretchen was pregnant with Gracie, and Bree was a toddler. Gretchen came out of the house to see what the ruckus was about, and Vanessa lost it. She was hysterical. It took me, Gretchen, and my parents to calm her down, all while we were wondering if he was alive or not."

Cassandra squeezed my hand. "I can't imagine coping with that."

"I wasn't sleeping. I'd work all day, then work some more. But after Nate was brought home, it didn't get better. Gretchen passed away. Nate and Vanessa separated. He got deployed again. They divorced. And I..."

She looked up, waiting for me to bring myself to say it.

"I blamed myself." I stroked my hand down my beard. "I blamed myself for all of it. I would lie awake at night, wondering if I could have done something that would have made him stay and work on the ranch rather than joining the Army."

"But it's also where he met Becks, right?"

I nodded. "Gretchen's accident happened not long after Nate came home. I was finally starting to let go of some of that guilt. Gracie was born. Then Gretchen was taken away from me. I blamed myself for that too. I'd pace the house, in the middle of the night, trying to get Gracie to stop crying, and wonder why I hadn't gone to get the groceries for her. And now—"

Cassandra stopped me in the middle of our loop and pressed her hands to my cheeks. "I need you to hear me. It's not your fault."

I held on to her wrists, keeping her hands there. Cassandra's touch felt good. "That's easier to say than to live with."

"I know that." Her gray eyes were boulders, steady and strong. "What matters most is that you keep showing up and stepping up for your family, no matter what the circumstance is. You're strong and reliable. You're steady. You're loyal and resilient." She stepped onto the steel toes of my boots and pressed her lips to mine. "But one thing you are not, is guilty. You're the one everyone runs to for safety."

I pressed my forehead against hers. "Thank you, Cass."

Her breath hitched. "And..."

I waited.

Her fingers flexed against my cheeks. "And it's why I love you."

"Mr. Griffith?" A nurse stood in the doorway, and looked surprised when four of us snapped to attention. She stammered. "Uh, the one that came in on the ambulance."

"Go," Cassandra whispered as she rubbed my back, easing me toward the woman. "I'll handle the room."

I was ushered through a set of double doors, following the short woman as she led me through to the ICU.

I always forgot how tall Cassandra was. I wasn't around many women apart from my kids and my mom, so towering over a grown woman as she wove through the emergency department, leading me deeper into the hospital, felt strange.

The nurse paused outside a patient room and snapped her fingers to get my attention. "The doctor will be in shortly to talk you through what's going on with your brother. After that, I can let your family back two at a time."

She opened the door and my knees buckled.

It was my brother, but there was no life. Monitors beeped and chirped in steady rhythms. He was covered from head to toe in tubes, wires, gauze, and a neck and back brace.

The nurse disappeared, leaving me alone with Ray.

I took the vinyl-covered chair beside him and waited.

And waited.

And waited.

Hospital time and standard time were two different things, I realized. "Shortly" must have meant anywhere from two hours to eternity.

Somewhere at the two hour and forty-five minute mark, a woman with dark skin and short hair, wearing green surgical scrubs, knocked on the door. "Mr. Griffith?"

"That's both of us," I said as I looked at Ray.

"And you are—"

"Christian Griffith. Ray's brother."

"Right." She flipped open her chart. "Nice to meet you. I'm Dr. Oladokun. I was on the surgical team that tended to your brother when he was brought in. I know this is not a good day for either of you, so I'll get right to it." She walked around to the opposite side of Ray's bed and used a pen to point without touching him. "Ray broke his C2 and C3 vertebrae. That's toward the top of the spine at the base of his skull. After imaging, we determined there were fracture fragments that needed to be removed. We did a posterior fusion and placed a rod and screws to stabilize his vertebra. He has three broken ribs, a punctured lung, and internal bleeding."

I laced my fingers behind my neck and swore at the floor.

"Is he ... is he awake?"

"He's sedated," she said with an unnerving calm in her voice. "I'll level with you, Mr. Griffith. His vitals are strong, and his brain activity is shockingly high. But I've been at this hospital for a long time. I've seen many bull riders come through my doors. Most who suffer that type of spinal injury are paralyzed for the rest of their lives. I don't want you to get your hopes up. There's a difference between numbers on a monitor and quality of life."

I let out a sharp breath as I fixed my eyes on Ray's swollen hands. "What... Um. What's next?"

"More surgeries," she said definitively. "I'm not going to give you a promise of when I think he'll be out of the woods. But once we have a better idea of the damage done, we can put together a long-term care plan."

"Thank you, ma'am," I rasped.

"And Mr. Griffith—" she said as she adjusted one of the monitors, then walked to the door.

"Ma'am?"

"Medically speaking, I can't be completely sure, but I believe he can hear you. Talk to him."

I hung my head low. "Yes ma'am. Thank you."

"Any family you'd like for me to bring back for you, Mr. Griffith?"

I thought over who to call first, but one name came to mind. "Cassandra Griffith," I said, the white lie coming off easy. "And Claire Griffith. They're in the waiting room."

A few minutes later, a nurse escorted Cassandra and Mom to the room. I gave the run-down of the surgeries and diagnosis to them, then stepped out with Cassandra so my mom could have some time alone with Ray.

"You should have let Nate or CJ or your dad come back first," Cassandra said. "I'm not family. Why'd you say I was a Griffith?"

"I needed you." The knot in my chest eased when I pulled her into my arms. "I'm certain of a few things. I know the sun's gonna rise tomorrow. I know that my brother's gonna wake up. And I know that you're gonna have my last name. I'm just letting you try it on for size."

"Christian," she whispered. "This—today—it's not about me. Or us."

"I know." I pressed my lips to her forehead. "Thank you for being here."

Cassandra wrapped her arms around me. "I wouldn't be anywhere else."

We stood like that, holding each other, and simply resting.

"I gotta figure out what we're gonna do. I don't want to leave my folks out here alone. It could be weeks before he comes home… If…"

"Don't think like that," she said quickly. "*When*. Not if."

"I don't want people trying to go around Marty to pester my folks for statements, but I need to be back at the ranch. CJ's gonna want to be up here too. Nate's got the baby to think about." I sighed and scrubbed my hands down my face. I was *exhausted.*

Cassandra rested her palms squarely on my chest. "I've got it."

I shook my head. "What do you mean you—"

"I mean it. I've got it handled." She gripped my collar and kissed me. "You don't have to work through this. Stay with Ray and your parents."

"Cass, I can't ask you to—"

"You're not asking."

"But the girls have school, and—"

Cassandra lifted her chin and leveled with me. "I love you, and I've got it."

31

CASSANDRA

There are certain soft skills that are universally imperative no matter what the job is. Organization. Discipline. Time management. Information literacy and research skills. Self-starting and problem solving.

I could handle washed-up starlets on benders. How hard could cows and a half-dozen ranch hands be?

Famous last words.

But there's another quality that is imperative to success: being a stubborn asshole who refuses to fail.

That was my favorite thing about myself. I simply refused to quit.

Christian's alarm clock blared at the wicked hour of four-thirty on the dot. I slapped the decrepit machine and shoved my head, face first, into the pillow.

It had been a week and a half since Ray's accident.

Claire, Silas, Nate, CJ, and Christian had established a rotating schedule of forty-eight hours at the hospital in Houston, and forty-eight hours at home. Two people were always with Ray, waiting. Hoping. Praying for him to wake up.

Christian and Nate had left to go back to Houston yesterday, trading off with Claire and Silas so they could rest and recuperate.

I had arranged the extra pillows on his side of the bed so it didn't feel like I was completely alone, but I still found myself waking in the middle of the night, seeking his body.

The alarm clock went off again.

I hated that dreadful sound.

Just once, I wanted to go to bed and wake up whenever my body felt like it.

Christian swore up and down I'd get used to the ranch schedule, but I was months into it and I still hated every wake-up call.

But I refused to quit.

Swearing up and down, I rolled out of bed, tugged on a pair of jeans, and shouldered Christian's thick jacket. It was the closest I could get to hugging him.

I slipped out the door, not bothering to fix my hair, and trudged to the stables.

Dottie, Libby, Anny, and the rest of the horses had the audacity to look at me like I was running late. The sun wasn't even up.

I went through the routine of feeding and watering the divas, scooping food into Sadie's bowl, then turned them out so I could muck the stalls.

By the time I kicked off the rubber boots that lived in the barn and plodded back to the house, the girls were rumbling around upstairs.

The smell of coffee hit me when I yanked open the door.

"I love you," I declared to Becks.

Like most mornings when Christian and Nate were gone, she woke up to feed Charlotte, put her in a baby carrier, then walked down to Christian's house.

She handed me a mug. "Don't say that too loudly or Christian might change the locks so I can't get in."

I snickered as I downed half of the coffee in one gulp. "That would be true if he actually locked the door."

Bree thundered down the steps first. "Morning, Miss Cass! Morning Aunt Becks."

"Morning," we said in tandem.

"What kind of cereal do you want today?" Becks asked while I pulled out the tackle box of hair supplies.

Bree grabbed the milk from the fridge. "Lucky Charms."

"Girl after my own heart," Becks said as she reached into the top of the pantry and pulled the box down.

"We're almost out of milk," Bree said as she filled her bowl with cereal, and topped it with milk. She brought it to the table and sat in front of me.

I went to work on the tumbleweed on top of her head.

Truthfully, I always thought it was a little strange that Christian still did his children's hair every morning. They were both big enough to do it themselves.

But ten mornings in, I realized that this was his intentional time with them each day. I knew it was eating at him to be away from them. But, for once, I wanted him to be able to sit with his family in crisis, rather than having to truck through to keep things running.

"I'll pick some up after I drop you guys off at school. I've gotta get lunch stuff." I parted her hair and started a neat Dutch braid. "Do you need anything for your house, Becks?"

She looked a little sheepish. "Toilet paper, if you don't mind. That's really why I was down here so early today."

Bree and I laughed.

"What are we doing for dinner tonight?" I asked as Gracie loped down the stairs, dressed but still rubbing the sleep from her eyes.

"Claire's cooking," Becks said.

Thank goodness for that.

Gracie got her cereal, then sat down for her hair to be done. "Can I just leave it down today?"

"You can do whatever you want," I said, giving her blonde hair a quick brush. "It's your hair. Your body."

She dropped her chin into her hand and swirled her spoon in the cereal.

My instincts were telling me to leave her alone and not bring up the obvious mood when we had to leave in a few minutes, which is why I did the opposite.

"What's the matter?"

Her eyes were sad, locked on the floating pieces of cereal. "I miss Daddy."

My heart sank. "Me too."

She looked up at me. "Really?"

"Yeah." I nudged her shoulder with mine. "I miss him a lot, but he'll be back tomorrow."

She managed a measly bite. "Do you think Uncle Ray's gonna wake up?"

"I don't know," I said honestly. There was no use in lying. "I wish I did know. What I can tell you is that the surgeries he needed are over, which means the doctors will start trying to help him come back."

"So they've been keeping him asleep?"

"Kind of. He hit his head really hard and they needed to give him plenty of time to rest so it didn't get worse. When I talked to your dad last night, he said that they're hoping to run some tests today to see when he might wake up."

I glanced at the clock. *We really needed to get going.*

"Can we go see Uncle Ray this weekend?"

"I don't know," I said honestly. "But I will ask your dad."

"Promise?"

I arched an eyebrow. "Do I lie to you?"

She smiled down at the cereal that was quickly turning to mush. "No."

"Good. Eat or you'll be a cranky, miserable child for your teachers."

"Yes, ma'am."

"Excuse me?"

Gracie snickered. "Yes, my queen."

"That's better. Be ready to go in ten minutes."

"Miss Cass—"

I turned to find Gracie spinning in her chair to catch me before I went to change clothes.

"What do you need?"

She worked her lip with her teeth for a moment. "If Daddy ever gets married again and we get an evil stepmother, I hope it's you."

Well, shit. "I promise to limit poisoning attempts with apples to twice a day," I said as I hustled back to my room, blinking back tears.

Becks was sitting on my bed, nursing the baby again. "Well, that was the cutest thing I've ever heard in my entire life."

"Say nothing," I clipped as I shirked off the chore clothes and wiggled into a pair of flowing trousers and a tailored blouse.

Becks rolled her lips between her teeth. "Come on. You can admit that you like kids."

"I don't like kids," I said as I ran a brush over my hair and twisted it into a low bun. "I like *those* kids. There's a difference."

We made it out the door and into Becks's SUV in record time. She had offered it to me since it was easier to drive than Christian's truck.

Bree and Gracie talked the entire way to school and didn't stop as the doors flung open in the drop-off line.

"Bye Miss Cass. Love you," Bree said as she shouldered her bag.

"Thanks, Miss Cass," Gracie chirped, grabbing her lunch box. "I love you."

"Love you too. Have a good day," I called after them, then froze.

The minivan behind me honked and I didn't even feel the urge to flip them the bird.

Gracie and Bree stared back at me, blinking.

Slowly, smiles grew until they were ear to ear, first aimed at me, then each other.

Christian called as soon as I pulled out of the school parking lot.

"Hey," I said as I took a left and headed to the grocery store. "How was your night?"

"Doctors and nurses coming in every hour," he said

with a sigh. "But I don't want to talk about me. You doing okay?"

My throat was still tight from saying 'I love you' to Bree and Gracie. Why was it easier to say it to Christian than to the girls?

I didn't regret it in the slightest, but it left me reeling.

I could expect things from Christian. As much as people liked to say that relationships were unconditional, that was the furthest thing from the truth. I expected his love and support, and he expected the same of me.

But kids were one-sided. They had expectations of the caregivers and protectors in their lives, but that love didn't have to be reciprocated.

They didn't owe me anything.

But they said they loved me anyway.

"I told you not to worry. I've got it handled."

"Cass..." He sounded more tired than I had ever heard.

"I don't want you to worry." I pulled into the grocery store lot and threw the car into park. "Focus on Ray. Things are fine."

"Did the girls get to school okay? How'd it go this morning?"

I yawned, feeling the coffee wearing off already. "Got up at the ass crack of evil and fed the animals. Becks was over by the time I got back up to the house. Got the girls fed and I just dropped them off. I'm gonna run into the store and get a few things for us and Becks, and head back to start work. Your mom's picking them up from school and taking care of dinner tonight."

It sounded like he let out a sigh of relief. "You have the company credit card, right? I don't want you paying out of pocket for my groceries. Use that one and I'll sort it out."

"Christian, it's fine. I'm not charging it to the ranch."

"Cass, please," he begged.

"No."

He was arguing, but I could hear the tightness in his voice easing. "Have I told you how much I love you?"

"Not since last night, so feel free to tell me again."

"I love you."

I closed my eyes and reveled in the comfortable silence that lingered between us. "You know, I actually believe you when you say it."

"Yeah?"

"Mhm." I chewed on my lip. "Your—um..." I took a deep breath. "Your girls said 'I love you' this morning... to me."

There was a slight note of surprise in his voice. "Really?"

"Yes. And I said it back. But it was just kind of a spur of the moment thing. And if you're not cool with that, then you might need to have that conversation with them," I blurted out.

"Cass?"

"Dear God, yes. Please say something. I hate rambling."

Christian chuckled. "I know."

"Wait..." I blinked. "What do you mean you know? You know that they said it or you know that I hate rambling?"

"Bree has been standing in front of her mirror, practicing saying it for about two weeks. They finally brought it up, and we talked about it when I called to say goodnight yesterday."

Oxygen leeched from my lungs. "Oh."

"Gracie wasn't a surprise," he admitted. "She's adored you since the moment you met. But Bree..."

"Bree remembers Gretchen," I said.

"She and I had a long talk about it," Christian said.

I didn't realize that his reassurance was exactly what I needed.

"Are you sure this is okay?" I pressed. "I'm not trying to put myself in the middle of your—"

"I want you in the middle of it, Cass. So do the girls. We've just been waiting on you."

Before I could come up with something to say, he butted in.

"Hey, a doc's coming in. I'll call you back."

"Okay, I love you," I said. Goosebumps tickled my cheeks when he said it back.

The grocery store was nearly empty, so I ran in and out as fast as humanly possible.

When I made it back to the ranch, Becks was on Christian's couch with the TV on.

"I got your toilet paper," I said, hauling the bags in and dropping them on the kitchen counter.

"Get over here," she said, her eyes locked on the TV.

I pulled the milk out and slid it into the fridge. "I gotta go check in with CJ to make sure he's good, and then get to the office to do payroll."

"Shut your beautiful face and look at the TV," she demanded.

"I really have to go—"

"Cass! *Look*!"

I was a little antsy because Christian hadn't called back. *Was that good or had something happened and Ray took a turn for the worst?* I huffed and craned around to look at the TV.

"Oh my god." I crammed onto the couch with Becks and baby Charlie as I watched Tripp be led away from his apartment building in handcuffs in a flurry of flashing blue lights.

"Disgraced A-lister publicist arrested after client pressed charges for embezzlement." Becks cackled. "He cheated on you with Lillian Monroe and then stole her money?"

"Spenser Crenshaw must have taken the tip I gave him and worked his magic. This is even better than I had hoped." I was laughing too hard to even be the slightest bit mad. "Now *that* is poetic justice."

Becks lifted her coffee and toasted me. "Karma's a bitch. What goes around comes around, motherfucker!" she shouted at footage of Tripp being shoved into the back of an NYPD cruiser.

I thought about my apartment that had been sitting untouched for months. I couldn't wait to go back to New York, but only to pack it up and come back here.

To community.

To sisterhood.

To family.

To home.

To him.

32

CHRISTIAN

I paced in the corner of Ray's room as doctors and nurses hovered over his bed, and prayed that his vitals would stay stable as they lowered the drugs that were keeping him sedated.

I pressed my back into the corner and cupped my hands over my mouth, wishing Cassandra was here.

I could have used her grit right now.

She would have had her chin up, striking everyone with that exacting gaze, demanding excellence without even saying a word.

I closed my eyes and listened, keeping a close ear on the steady rhythm of the monitors, listening for any changes that might be cause for alarm.

The sun had risen this morning, just like it had for the last three weeks of constant rotations in and out of the hospital.

I still believed the other two things would happen.

I needed him to fucking wake up.

The doctors were talking in hushed tones to the respiratory therapist, discussing the breathing tube.

I needed room to pace, but I didn't want to get in the way.

My mom was here today, but she had stepped out to get food from the cafeteria since the doctors said that lowering the sedative would take hours to kick in.

I watched with a grotesque sort of fascination as the breathing tube was slowly removed.

And then all I could do was wait some more.

I sat beside Ray and watched the shallow rise and fall of his chest. The breathing tube had been replaced with an oxygen mask. IV lines and electrical leads still covered seemingly every inch of his body.

The Jordan Loft novel I had grabbed from the house two days ago was open on my lap, but I didn't have the focus to read.

Every time I tried to look at a page, I would jolt up, certain that I heard Ray move or make a noise.

But he never did.

Sitting beside an unresponsive body for three weeks had my mind playing constant tricks on me.

I looked down at the book, scanning a few lines before turning the page. My eyes snapped up when I thought the blanket moved, but Ray was still as a statue.

Twice, I thought I heard my name, but it was just the nurses talking at the station outside the door.

I needed to get some sleep.

Chris.

I turned another page, glossing over letters and punctuation. Why was I even attempting to read? I should have just turned on the TV to watch the replay of Cassandra's ex-fiancé getting arrested for the thousandth time.

Chris.

Maybe I should call Cassandra. It was about lunch time. She'd be taking a break and heading up to the house.

Then again, one of the renewable energy companies she courted was going to begin installing solar panels on top of all the barns and warehouses. It was the first stage before they broke ground on the south side of the property. My stipulation was that they used land the cattle never touched. Cassandra's demand was that it was out of sight of the future lodge and restaurant.

Guilt ate at me for not being there today. She and CJ were capable, but I should have been there to handle it.

Chris.

I sighed and looked up at Ray.

Heavy eyes blinked back at me.

My heart stopped.

Breath clouded the oxygen mask. I watched—not quite believing my eyes—as he licked his lips.

"Ray?" My voice was a hoarse whisper.

He tried to say something, but I couldn't quite make it out. The mix of adrenaline and relief was too much to bear.

I slammed my hand into the call button to get the nurses in here as tears welled up in my eyes.

His eyes flicked down to the oxygen mask, then back up at me. Carefully, I lifted it just enough to hear him.

"My score?" The whisper was dry and cracked, like someone crawling out of a grave and cheating death.

I handed over the championship buckle that had been sitting by his bedside for three weeks.

I placed it in his fingers, but they never moved to grip it.

"Ninety-one point nine."

NIGHT HAD FALLEN by the time I made it back to the ranch. The rest of the day had been filled with tears of grief and gratitude.

Quadriplegic.

I rolled the word around in my head as I parked the truck in front of the house.

He was paralyzed from the neck down, but he was alive.

Conversations surrounding step-down care and moving him home circulated throughout his room for hours.

Ray's throat was hoarse from the tube. He would break out into coughing fits that he couldn't control. The nurses did their best to keep him comfortable, but the road to recovery—whatever that looked like—would be far from it.

The lights were on downstairs, but I stayed quiet as I crept into the house. The kitchen table was littered with paperwork and, on top of it, was Cassandra.

Her blonde hair was sprayed across the files as she snored softly, resting her head on her folded arms.

Instead of waking her, I started shuffling the papers into neat piles to make it easier to go through them in the morning.

It was just after nine and the girls were probably asleep.

Cassandra stirred as I slid a budget sheet out from under her cheek. "Hmm—" she blinked "—Christian?"

"Hey beautiful," I said softly as I knelt beside her chair and smoothed her hair away from her face. "Wanna go to bed?"

Cassandra sat up and pressed her fingers to her eyes. "What time is it?"

"9:15."

She blinked. "I swear I just closed my eyes for a second. I didn't even hear you come in."

"Hey." I cupped her cheeks. "Don't apologize. You've..." I let out a sharp breath. "You've done more than I could have ever asked. More than I can ever repay you for."

"How's Ray?" she asked immediately, and I fell just a little more in love with her because of it. "I haven't said anything to the girls. I figured that was a conversation you should have with them."

"Angry," I admitted as I let my hair down and released the tension on my scalp. I sighed. "I've never seen him like that. He... he had this look in his eyes when the doctors were talking to him and explaining the prognosis."

"I can't imagine waking up and realizing that your life as you knew it is over." She cupped my cheek, stroking my beard with her thumb. "When will he get to come home?"

"Probably a week or so. He's gonna move back into my parents' house because he'll have to have round-the-clock care. Marty's gonna pack up his place in Colorado and ship his stuff down. It's… gonna be an adjustment for all of us."

Her eyes were tired, but stalwart. "I'm here for all of it. Whatever you need."

"Right now I need you in bed."

She pecked my lips. "I was hoping you'd say that."

I dropped my hat and wallet on the nightstand so I could find them in the morning, then joined her in the bathroom. We stood side by side at the sink, brushing our teeth and wiping off the day, before climbing into bed.

"Come here," I growled lowly as I pulled her into my arms. "I've missed this."

Cassandra let out a heavy breath as she snuggled into my side. Her elegant fingers traced shapes on my chest. "I need to make a request."

"Anything." I cradled her head against my chest, keeping her close.

After the day I'd had, I wanted to run upstairs and hold Bree and Gracie and revel in the realization that my beautiful daughters were loved, safe, and cared for, thanks to the woman in my arms. But I also didn't want to scare them.

"I need time off to go back to New York," she said.

I laced our hands together and brought her knuckles to my lips. "Promise me you'll come back."

"Promise me you'll have room for my shoes when I bring them all," she said with a sly smile.

"Promise me something else, Princess," I said as I rolled on top of her, straddling her hips. My stomach hung, pressing against her skin as I kissed across her collarbone.

"What's that?"

"Promise me that you're staying for good." I pushed her loose tank top over her bare breasts. "Please stay." I kissed her sternum, breathing in the warm, woodsy fragrance of her perfume. "I thought I could handle it all, but you made me realize that I don't have to." I brushed my lips across hers. "And that I don't want to. I want it to be you."

I pushed her cheeky little panties down and shucked off my boxers as I reached for a condom.

Cassandra caught my wrist and shook her head. "Maybe not this time. I'm on birth control and I went to the clinic in town last week and got checked out after I found out about Tripp. We hadn't been intimate in a long time, but I wanted to be sure. The results were negative."

"You sure? Birth control isn't foolproof."

She laughed softly. "I know. But if there's anyone I'd risk it with, it's you."

"Cass." I shook my head. "You don't have to do that just to make me happy. It doesn't matter to me."

"I want to feel you," she admitted.

I smoothed my knuckles down her cheek. "If you're sure. My last check was good, too."

Cassandra dug her fingers into my hair, curling them at the root to draw me closer. "The sun rose this morning." She smiled as I kissed down her neck. "And Ray woke up."

"I still believe all three things, Princess. Mark my words."

"Good," she whispered. "Because I do too."

"You know what else I believe?" I said as I slid my knuckles through her pussy and worked the wetness around her entrance. "I think we're gonna have a good life, no matter what the days bring."

She wrapped her mile-long legs around me, pressing her cunt against the head of my dick.

I laced our hands together and pinned them above her head, stretching her out so her breasts scraped my chest with each thrust as I shunted myself inside of her.

Cassandra bit down into my skin to keep from making a sound. The pierce of pain was unexpected, but arousing. My cock throbbed inside of her.

"There you go, princess." I thrust inside of her again, knocking the breath from her lungs. "You know how to take it. Now show me what a good girl you can be for me."

She was tight and hot around me, squeezing me like a vise.

"I needed this," she groaned.

"That's right. You did. Now take what you need."

Cassandra bucked against me, matching each of my thrusts with one of her own. We moved fluidly, taking and giving until we were panting and desperate.

"Come inside of me," she whispered, nipping my earlobe to punctuate her point.

I shook my head. "Cass, I don't have to come. I can take care of business in a minute. Let me make you feel good."

"I want you to," she said, wiggling her wrists out of my grasp and scraping her nails down my chest. She bit my lip and sucked it between her teeth.

"Goddamn, you play dirty," I admitted with a wicked grin.

"I know what I want, cowboy."

I wrapped an arm around her waist and flipped us, settling her on top of me. I shoved a stack of pillows behind my back. "Then ride me."

Cassandra straddled me and slid down onto my cock. I groaned as the tight pressure built around me again.

But instead of chasing an orgasm, she reached forward and grabbed my hat off the nightstand.

I skated my hands up her abdomen and cupped her breasts. "What are you doing, princess?"

She smiled as she worked her hips up and down, chasing ecstasy. "You told me to put that hat on when I wanted to be yours." She tossed her hair to the side and dropped it on her head, eyes sparkling in the darkness. "And I want to be yours."

EPILOGUE

CASSANDRA

August

Bree clung to the airplane armrest as we made the descent over DFW. "Gracie's gonna be so jealous," she said with a giggle as she pressed her nose to the window.

I smiled to myself as I raised the seat back tray and fastened it. "She'll get her turn for her birthday."

"Yeah, but I got to go first."

"You're the oldest. Your dad decided you were the test subject. That way if you got kidnapped, he still has a spare."

Bree laughed and dropped her head onto my shoulder. "You like us."

I huffed dramatically. "I suppose you're not awful." But she knew I was kidding.

I loved the girls.

"You're gonna miss us when school starts again."

I pressed my cheek to the top of her head. "Maybe

I'll have to make an appearance to scare the hell out of your teachers or come have lunch with you or something. "

"At least Principal Beeker is gone."

I stuck my tongue out and gagged. "Thank goodness for that."

Bree laughed. "You know, I'm glad you're with Dad."

"Yeah?"

I had officially become a Texas resident at the beginning of the summer and moved all my things out of my apartment and into Christian's house.

He severely underestimated my clothing collection and quickly realized that giving me half of his closet wouldn't cut it. The guest room became the ladies dressing room, and Bree and Gracie went nuts.

Christian just chalked it up to a future investment since his daughter's social lives were blooming and their wardrobes were exploding.

He would have a cow—*ha*—at the haul Bree and I were bringing back from the city.

We had spent four blissful days traipsing around Manhattan, posing like tourists, eating our way through the city, and going to show after show.

Bree and I were blissfully exhausted, and a little thankful to be going home.

I still couldn't believe a cattle ranch was home, but it was.

"You're the best evil stepmother," she said as she pressed into my arm.

I had joined Christian and Claire in the rotation of after-school activity pickup, which prompted Bree and Gracie to start introducing me by saying, "This is our evil stepmother, Cassandra. She's only given us two poison apples today."

I loved the terrified looks that the dance teachers, swim instructors, and summer camp counselors had.

A little fear was healthy.

When they had pulled that line the first time I picked them up from therapy, the therapist died laughing.

"I'm glad I'm with your dad, too," I said, nudging her back. "I think I got a pretty good three-for-one deal. I won't lock you in a tower ... today."

Bree went quiet for a moment. "Do you think Uncle Ray will let me see him when we get back?"

I didn't want to crush her spirit, but I had a feeling that Ray hadn't made much progress in the few days we had been gone.

He was home and had made some physical progress, thanks to an experimental therapy program. But he had closed himself off, refusing to see anyone.

It broke the girls.

Their favorite person in the entire world wouldn't even talk to them.

"I think your dad was going to see if he was feeling up to it, but he still needs a lot of rest." I pointed to the bag of bagels under the seat in front of me. "But Becks is going to love those."

"Yeah, she is," Bree said with a grin.

"Maybe we'll do a girls' trip when you turn sixteen. You, me, Gracie, Becks, and Charlotte."

"Really?"

That seemed to lift her spirits.

"Yeah. It'll be fun."

"Okay," she said, wiggling in her seat. "But I really did like this trip. You know, just you and me."

"I'm glad."

"I like hanging out with you."

I could tell she was hedging toward something.

"I like hanging out with you too."

She picked at her nail beds. "And I'm glad you're with my dad."

"You already said that a few minutes ago."

"I know," she said with a sigh. "I just want you to know that I mean it. And I'm glad you work for the ranch. And I know my dad likes you working for the ranch. You're really good at it."

The plane shuddered as we landed on the runway and came to a skidding halt.

"I like working at the ranch. Most of the time."

She smiled. "And I like that you're honest and you don't treat us like babies or keep things from us to protect our feelings. You treat us like adults."

"Where's this all coming from?" I asked as the plane taxied to the gate.

"Nothing," she said quickly. Guilt was painted all over her angelic little face.

I narrowed my eyes. "I already bought you all the clothes in Manhattan. What else are you trying to squeeze out of me?"

"I told you—nothing."

"And I don't believe you," I whispered.

Bree bit back a smile as we collected our bags and carry-ons and exited the plane.

"I'm so excited to see Dad," she said as we raced through the terminal.

Christian and Gracie were waiting on the other side to pick us up.

People held signs and bouquets of flowers. Passengers clumped together as they met their loved ones.

"I see his hat," Bree said as she pointed out the tall cowboy who stood head and shoulders over the rest.

"There's my girls," Christian said as he scooped up his teenager and spun her around. "I missed you."

I hugged Gracie. "You and me next time."

"I missed you," she said as she buried her head into me.

"I swear you grew ten inches in four days."

She laughed.

"Come here, you," Christian murmured as he slid his hands around my waist and tilted his head, leaning in for a kiss. "I missed you."

The girls squealed as I wrapped my arms around his neck and kissed him. Christian's lips were warm and tasted like mint.

"Promise me you won't leave again," he said quietly.

"That much work for you, huh?" I gave him one last kiss.

He chuckled. "No, I just don't like sleeping alone."

"Fair."

Christian moved in for another kiss, but I pressed my hands to his chest. "Sir, we are in an airport."

"Like I care," he clipped, then dipped me all the way back, sliding his tongue along mine.

"Dad!" Gracie shrieked.

His soft grunt as he stole my breath made fire explode inside of me.

"I love you," he said quietly as he helped me back to my feet.

"I love you too."

"Dad! Look at my hair!" Bree spun around and gave it a fluff. "Miss Cass took me to her favorite salon and I got *highlights*!"

Christian's eyes welled up at the sight of Bree's hair. It was just a little trim and a few foils, but she did look more grown-up.

"You look beautiful, baby," he said, running his hand down the back of her head. "You look just like your mom."

I squeezed his hand.

Christian pressed a kiss to my temple. "Thank you."

"It was fun," I said honestly. "I think we bonded."

"Miss Cass, do you wanna watch a movie tonight?" Gracie asked. "I missed you."

"We can do that," I said. "And—you know—you can just call me Cassandra. Or Cass. You don't have to call me *Miss* Cass."

Christian's arms tightened around me as Bree and Gracie nodded.

We waited around the luggage carousel as suitcases came out one-by-one. Bree rambled non-stop about the trip while Christian held me against his chest.

The drive to the ranch was filled with comfortable silence. Bree, tired from our early wake-up call to get to LaGuardia, crashed the moment Christian pulled onto the highway.

I sat in the front with my hand twined around his, resting my head on his thick arm.

The sun was setting by the time we arrived at the house. Christian carried the bags in, grumbling about how much heavier they were than when we had left for New York.

Claire was in Christian's kitchen, stirring something on the stove that smelled wonderful.

"How was the trip, Cass?" she asked with a gleam in her eye.

I kicked my heels off. "It was good. I think Bree had a good time."

"Hey, throw your boots on real quick," Christian said as he appeared in the kitchen.

"Why?"

"Builders came out and marked the foundation for the lodge today."

My eyebrows lifted. "Really?"

"Come on. We'll ride out there before it gets dark."

I changed into shorts and tugged on a pair of socks and my boots.

They were starting to show wear with how much I wore them, but it just made me love them even more.

Christian and I rode Dottie and Libby out to the lodge sight. Little flags and spray paint etched out an enormous footprint in the west pasture.

"Wow," I said, hopping off of Dottie to walk around, careful of the stakes jutting out of the grass.

The sunset was glorious.

I propped my hands on my hips and let out a breath. "This is going to be incredible."

"You know," Christian said as he took my hand and walked to the back side of the future building that would look over the sprawling vista. "I think you might be right. We should hold weddings here."

"People will pay big money for a view like this. Add in the amenities of having a restaurant and lodging on-site, and couples will be fighting each other to get married here."

"Do you think we should have an outdoor wedding spot? You know, add some landscaping and make it intentional?"

"I can see what's in the budget. It might not be a year one thing, but we can plan for it."

"Right here," Christian said, stopping suddenly.

"What?" I looked around. The grass was lit up like a fire. Golden rays of sunshine reflected off the pond. It was serene and heavenly.

Christian turned to me. "Right here. This is where it should be."

I tapped my chin. "I'll run the numbers and get some quotes."

"We can call it a personal expense. Because this is where I want to marry you." He reached into his pocket and pulled out a small box as he lowered to one knee. "Right here where it all began. The land where we came together. The place where the sun rises and sets. I want the first wedding here to be ours."

I gasped as the diamond flashed, reflecting the sunset. "Christian..."

"Will you marry me, Cass?"

All I could do was nod as he slid the ring on my finger. It was beautifully minimal. Sleek and sophisticated.

"There are three things I know for certain," he said as he stood and sifted his fingers through my hair. "The sun is gonna rise tomorrow. My girls love you. And you were meant to be ours."

And I believed them too.

BONUS EPILOGUE

CHRISTIAN

Eleven Years Later

I tucked the bouquet of flowers behind my back as I snuck up to Cassandra's office. An oil diffuser in the foyer made the place smell like cedar. It was nice. Soft music played as I climbed the stairs.

A few years ago, we broke down and renovated the warehouse office. With the lodge, restaurant, event space, and equine program going full steam, we needed a proper headquarters.

Gone was the corrugated metal siding and cement floor.

The office building was two stories and built in the same style as the lodge. Beautiful hardwood and cool stone mixed in an earthy blend. The main floor sported offices for the equine program staff, print rooms, and supply storage. The top floor housed a conference room, the office that was mine, but I never used, and Cassandra's lair.

A few staffers spotted the flowers behind my back and tittered among themselves as I plodded up the steps.

I pushed open the French doors to Cassandra's office and waited patiently as she glanced up from a phone call with a coy smile.

She tucked her hair behind her ear, looking me up and down as she wrapped up the conversation.

The phone clicked into the receiver cradle, and she rested her elbows on the desk. "Five o' clock on the dot and you're in my office?" She turned in her chair and pushed away from her desk. Her high heels clicked against the wood floors. "To what do I owe the pleasure?"

I pulled the flowers from behind my back. "I made dinner reservations."

Her lips turned up as she slinked closer and closer. "Do you have to make reservations when you co-own the restaurant?"

I chuckled. "Yes. That's what happens when the property manager is a marketing genius and makes it a popular spot." I cradled the back of her neck as I kissed her deep and slow. "Can't even get dinner at our own place."

Truthfully, most nights we ate dinner curled up on the couch. With the girls out of the house, we leaned into the empty-nester life.

Cassandra snaked her arms around my neck, smiling against my mouth. "Mmm. I'll stop doing my job so well."

I shook my head, brushing our noses. "No, ma'am. I like watching you kick ass."

Her eyes grew heavy again as she looked down at my mouth. "Excuse me?"

I cupped her chin and drew her in for another kiss. "No, my queen."

Finally, we broke apart, grinning like teenagers.

"Flattery, flowers, and dinner reservations." She took the bouquet from me and brought the blooms to her nose. "Do you have something to apologize for?"

I laughed. "No. I just thought we were due for a date night."

I stared at her ass as she strutted back to her desk to close her computer. "No arguments there."

I waited on the couch that faced a wide picture window while she wrapped up. At the slide of her desk drawer, I looked over my shoulder and watched her dab perfume on her wrists and neck. She traded it for lipstick, swiping a coat of ruby on.

"You ready, cowboy?"

We took my truck down the two-lane road that led to the restaurant.

The hostess, Molly, greeted us with a smile and led us right to a table on the rooftop that had an immaculate view of the land.

The cattle were close today, dotting the horizon as they grazed.

"This is perfect," Cassandra said as she perused the wine list. "The weather's just beautiful."

The open-air dining space was one of my favorite features of the restaurant. An iron railing left the space open and airy. Candles dotted the white linen tables, the flames flickering in the breeze.

"You look beautiful, Cass," I said as the waiter left with our drink orders.

She laughed. "I'm in my work clothes."

"Still beautiful, princess. Always beautiful."

Cassandra reached across the table and traced circles around my palm with her ring finger. "Our wedding anniversary is coming up."

"Can't believe it's been ten years."

"A lot's happened," she said. "Gracie said she was planning to come up for the weekend if she could get time off work."

I still couldn't believe my youngest baby was a grown woman. A college graduate, living on her own.

Though, I suppose at twenty-two, she would probably object to me calling her my baby.

She never did, though.

"Bree texted me a little bit ago and wanted to know if we wanted to spend our anniversary at her place."

I laughed. "There's not enough oxygen in that closet for the three of us. We'd have to get a hotel."

Bree, now twenty-four, was living in New York City. *Much to my dismay.* But considering I had been the one to drive her up there and help her move in for college at NYU, I couldn't whine about it too much.

Her studio apartment left much to be desired, but the city life suited her just fine.

Out of the corner of my eye, a young couple was seated a few tables away. The man looked vaguely familiar, and the exchange between him and the server confirmed it.

"That's George Thompson's young'un," I said to Cassandra, tipping my head toward the man."

Cassandra rolled her eyes. "He has to be what—mid-thirties? Late thirties? I don't think you can call him a young'un."

"Do you mind? I'll just be a minute."

Cassandra laughed softly, her eyes crinkling with deep lines around the corners. *My god, she just got prettier every day.* Her soft blonde hair was now silver and gold. It suited her.

"Go on," she said. "I'll order for you."

I kissed her cheek, then eased back and headed over to the table against the railing.

"Pardon me," I said as I eased up to them.

The woman looked at me curiously.

"I apologize for interrupting your evening. I couldn't help but overhear—are you a Thompson?"

The man nodded. "Yes."

"Any chance you're kin to the Thompson Farm? Thompson Grain and Feed?"

"One and the same." He extended his hand and shook mine. "Vaughan Thompson. This my date, Joelle Reed. She owns and operates the agricultural aviation business that cares for the land."

I couldn't help but grin. "No shit. Christian Griffith. I believe we spoke on the phone a few weeks back." I nodded at Joelle. "Pleasure to meet you, ma'am." Turning back to Vaughan, I asked, "How's your growing season looking this year? I'll tell you what—I need to remember to give you another call. We're expecting a big calving season, but you know how dry it's been, save for the storm a few days ago. You'll probably be hearing from us when winter rolls around. Hell, we might just clean out your silos. We try to source local feed, but sometimes the herd has an appetite bigger than the little farms around us can grow, and our main supplier's been actin' a little squirrely lately."

He reached into his pocket and found a business card. "Give me a call anytime."

I took it and tucked it into my shirt pocket. "I'll let y'all enjoy your dinner."

"You've never met a stranger, have you?" Cassandra said with a soft laugh when I sat back down.

"Neither have you." I picked up the whiskey that had been put down at my place setting. "Difference between us is that I'm just making connections for business. You gather intelligence."

"I do whatever it takes to protect this family."

"That's why I love you."

We gorged ourselves on a phenomenal dinner, taking our time with dessert so we could enjoy the sunset.

There was nothing like it.

While Cassandra popped down into the kitchen to tell the staff what a great job they were doing, I brought the truck around.

Ten years together hadn't been easy, but there wasn't anyone else I would have chosen to do it with.

Cassandra was the piece to our family that I didn't know was missing.

She was a workhorse with a steel backbone who loved harder than she fought.

And that woman would fight to the death for any one of us.

I had two beautiful daughters that looked just like their mother. But thanks to Cassandra, they became women that Gretchen would have been proud of.

When we pulled up to the house, Cassandra sat still and waited for me to come around and open her door.

The high heels she was in were fitted with the little

stoppers I made to keep them from sinking into the ground.

At the moment, I was caught up, having made a set to match each pair of her shoes.

I carried the flowers while Cassandra held on to my arm as we made our way up the steps and slipped inside.

"Thanks for thinking of that," she said as she kicked her shoes off. "It's been a while since we've gone out."

My torso pressed against her back as I hung my hat up and let down my hair.

Although the girls were grown, I kept it long. Maybe I'd cut it someday, but Cassandra seemed to like it the way it was.

Well. Except when I used the last of her shampoo.

"Stop right there, love." I pressed my hand between her shoulder blades.

Cassandra laughed softly. "What are you doing?"

I kicked the door closed and reached around her shoulders, unbuttoning her blouse.

I watched over her shoulder as her lace bra came into sight with each button unfastened.

"Beautiful," I murmured against her skin, pressing a kiss to the side of her neck. "Arms up."

Cassandra didn't even argue, which was rare for her. She raised her arms and let me undress her, piece by piece.

I tugged on the fabric sash that was tied to hold her flowing trousers up. That was one thing I loved about her. She looked classic, always. Her style hadn't changed a bit. She was still high heels, full makeup, and city sass.

It was a good look on her.

I pushed her trousers down and took her hand to

help her step out of them. "I like this," I mumbled as I trailed a knuckle down her side, grazing the matching bra and panties.

Cassandra tipped her head back. Soft curls of pearl-colored hair spilled down her spine. "I thought you would."

"What are you talking about?"

Cassandra turned, smoothing her hands down the front of my shirt. "You should know by now that if my underwear is matching, I was thinking three moves head of you."

I laughed as I backed her against the fridge. "So that's why you had perfume and lipstick in your desk drawer."

Her eyes creased with delight and mischief. "I had a feeling."

I tucked her hair behind her ear and cupped her cheek. "Did someone tell you I made reservations?"

She shook her head. "You should know by now that I'm aware of *everything* that goes on around this ranch." She pecked my lips. "Charlotte may have stopped by my office and told me that she and Becks ran into you in town when you were buying the flowers."

I just shook my head. "Damn this family."

She combed her fingers through my hair, eyes twinkling as they locked on mine. "Well? Are you going to let this go to waste?"

"Absolutely not."

I carried her into the bedroom and laid her out on the bed before kicking my boots off and shirking off my clothes. "Open your legs for me, Princess. Let me see how wet you are for me."

Her panties strained against her soft mound. A quarter-sized damp spot soaked the gusset.

"That's my girl. That's what I like to see." I climbed up the bed and wiggled them down her legs. "No, no, no," I chided when she clenched her thighs. "Nice and wide for me. Let me see what's mine.

Cassandra just smiled as she shook her head.

I pressed a sloppy, open-mouthed kiss to her cunt. She let out a soft sigh that turned into a deep moan when I used the flat of my tongue to tease her clit.

I gripped her thighs, holding them wide open as I devoured her like I hadn't just eaten a five star dinner and dessert. She was better than both.

I kissed the inside of her thighs, softly nipping and teasing as I slid my fingers into her pussy until she was a sobbing, trembling mess. I liked to draw out the foreplay. I wanted to serve her until she was begging—*begging*—me to put my cock inside of her.

Cassandra whimpered, tangling her hands into my hair to hold me against her cunt when I went down on her again. She bucked her hips, desperate for more pressure. For more sensation. For more everything.

"Christian," she whispered.

"Say my name again, beautiful."

"Christian, *please*," she gasped when I slid two fingers back inside of her and crooked them, stroking her walls.

Her thighs were quivering, and her fingers curled into the sheets.

"Get inside of me right now," she whimpered.

I added a third finger and clicked my tongue. "Ahh—I don't know if you're there yet, Princess."

"Christian!"

She was nearly at her peak. Her pussy tightened around my fingers. I withdrew them and played with her clit again.

She groaned in a mix of agony and ecstasy. “Fuck me already.”

“Maybe a little longer and then you’ll be ready,” I teased. “Get that bra off and play with your pretty little nipples. Maybe that’ll take your mind off how much you want my dick.”

Her toes curled as I sucked on her clit.

“Come on, Princess. Play with your tits and I’ll let you come.”

“We’re gonna need flood insurance at this rate,” she muttered as she shimmied out of her bra.

I hitched her thigh around my hip and slid into her without the slightest bit of resistance.

“How’s that, love?”

Cassandra groaned in relief. “God, yes. That’s so much better.”

I worshipped her skin with soft, warm kisses as I slowly pumped inside of her, keeping her teetering on the edge.

“That’s my beautiful wife,” I said as I took a moment to brush her hair away from her face. I shifted onto my forearm and cupped her breast.

She let out a soft gasp and pushed her hips closer. “Please,” she begged. “Please let me come.”

“Alright, Princess.” I drove into her harder, then paused to grind against her clit. “Only because you asked so nicely.”

Her back arched as I pushed her over the edge.

I loved when she came. Cassandra always leaned

forward enough to tuck her head into the crook of my neck. Her warm breath on my collarbone was a caress as my release filled her up.

"So pretty when you come," I said, then kissed her.

When Cassandra finally caught her breath, she laughed.

"What?" I said, wiping a joy-filled tear from the corner of her eye.

She just shook her head. "I changed my mind."

"About what?"

"Spending our anniversary in New York with Bree." She tipped her head up just far enough to kiss me. "I want you all to myself."

AUTHOR'S NOTE TO THE READER

This is my fifteenth book, and I'm realizing that I have increasingly little to say back here. Still, my acknowledgments page gets longer and longer. Christian and Cassandra's love story has been a long time coming. In fact, they've been waiting since the very beginning.

My debut novel was Nathan and Becks's story. At the end, I wrote a short scene where he hangs out with his brother.

Christian and his two adorable daughters have lived in my mind since that first book.

Fifteen books later, the three of them finally found "their person." I want to give a special thank you to the readers who have stuck around since book one. Thank you for allowing me to pursue this crazy passion and make it a career. Thank you for trusting me with your hearts and your bookshelves.

With Love and Happily Ever Afters,

- Mags -

PS. Because you're super cool, let's be friends!

ACKNOWLEDGMENTS

To Landon: For listening to me complain about how much my hands hurt. For telling me my book doesn't suck. For leaving unhinged commentary (I fixed the scene where he would need a 24-inch, boomerang-shaped dick, okay?). I love you more. Go Bobcats!

To Mikayla and Mandy: For being there through the sweet, salty, and the hella spicy. I never really feel like whatever I write back here means enough or sums up how thankful I am for you two, but dammit, I'm glad we found each other. Here's to friendships that make it out of the DMs.

To Kayla: For your social media prowess and reliability! I'm so damn thankful for you!

To My Street Team: Thank you for your enthusiasm and encouragement! You all are an essential part of my book team, and I'm so grateful for every recommendation, video, and post!

To Mel: for coming up with the most BADASS cover from my weird ideas!

To Jen, Josette, Erica, Megan, and the Entire Team at Grey's Promotions: Thank you SO much for all your hard work and hyping up this book!

To The HEA Babes: For laughs, arm-licking, inexplicable microtropes, and an excellent place to overshare.

To The Good Vibe Tribe: For creating a safe community and offering support and encouragement.

To My ARC Team: You guys are the greatest! Your excitement and support astound me daily. You make me feel like the coolest human being alive. I'm so grateful for each one of you. Thank you for volunteering your time and platforms to boost my books!

To My Readers: because naming all of you one by one would double the length of this book: You all are the reason I keep writing books. I'm convinced there's no greater group of people than my real-life poker club. Y'all are amazing human beings! Thank you for loving these characters and getting as excited as I am about their stories! Thank you for your hype, encouragement, and excitement!

To The Starbucks Baristas: You don't talk to me and never question why I sit in the corner 40+ hours a week. Please bring back the almond croissant. I'm begging you.

ALSO BY MAGGIE GATES

Standalone Novels

The Stars Above Us: A Steamy Military Romance

Nothing Less Than Everything: A Sports Romance

Cry About It: An Enemies to Lovers Romance

100 Lifetimes of Us: A Hot Bodyguard Romance

Pretty Things on Shelves: A Second Chance Romance

The Beaufort Poker Club Series

Poker Face: A Small Town Romance

Wild Card: A Second Chance Romance

Square Deal: A Playboy Romance

In Spades: A Small Town Billionaire Romance

Not in the Cards: A Best Friend's Brother Romance

Betting Man: A Friends to Lovers Romance

The Falls Creek Series

What Hurts Us: A Small Town Fake Engagement Romance

What Heals Us: An Age Gap Romance

What Saves Us: A Small Town Single Mom Romance

The Griffith Brothers Series

Dust Storm: A Single Dad Romance

Downpour (Coming 2024)

Fire Line (Coming 2024)

ABOUT THE AUTHOR

MAGGIE GATES

Maggie Gates writes raw, relatable romance novels full of heat and humor. She calls North Carolina home. In her spare time, she enjoys daydreaming about her characters, jamming to country music, and eating all the BBQ and tacos she can find! Her Kindle is always within reach due to a love of small-town romances that borders on obsession.

For future book updates, follow Maggie on social media.

facebook.com/AuthorMaggieGates

instagram.com/authormaggiegates

tiktok.com/@authormaggiegates

Made in United States
Troutdale, OR
05/19/2025